Anthony Price was born in Hertfordshire in 1928, was educated at King's School, Canterbury, and studied history at Merton College, Oxford. Apart from some temporary peace-time soldiering he has been a journalist all his life, beginning as a reviewer of historical books, going on to become crime reviewer on the *Oxford Mail*, then Deputy Editor and finally Editor of the *Oxford Times*.

He won the Crime Writers' Association's Silver Dagger for his first novel *The Labyrinth Makers* and later their Gold Dagger for *Other Paths to Glory*. All his novels reflect his intense interest in history and archaeology and in particular in military history.

D1333692

By the same author

ANTHONY PRICE

Sion Crossing

GRAFTON BOOKS
A Division of the Collins Publishing Group

LONDON GLASGOW
TORONTO SYDNEY AUCKLAND

Grafton Books
A Division of the Collins Publishing Group
8 Grafton Street, London W1X 3LA

Published by Grafton Books 1985

First published in Great Britain by
Victor Gollancz Ltd 1984

Copyright © Anthony Price 1984

ISBN 0-586-06524-5

Printed and bound in Great Britain by
Collins, Glasgow

Set in Times

For Katherine

1

Latimer in London: Temptation

Latimer was trapped between the devil and the deep blue sea.

Coming to the Oxbridge Club had been a mistake, for he almost always met people he disliked there. But some wayward impulse, generated by the minor annoyances and petty defeats of the day, had turned him into it off Piccadilly, and now he was justly served: the bar had been bad enough, and he had retreated from it; so he was caught between the CIA man and a colleague he detested, and he must face one of them – Howard Morris up the stairs or David Audley on the other side of the entrance doors.

Nevertheless, once identified, the dilemma was not too hard to resolve. The swarthy CIA man would merely nod, looking through him with blank unfriendliness, but Audley might well be amused enough to give him a Judas smile. And after the day's tribulations that was not to be risked.

He relinquished the brass handle of the door and turned towards the stairs again, for all the world as though just arriving.

'Oliver, my dear fellow!' The American's face lit up, and he took the first marble step down towards Latimer.

But that was all wrong – Latimer's own foot, directed upwards, tried to change direction and only just cleared the rising tread. Not the voice . . . Howard Morris might look like one of Zapata's lieutenants, but long years on the right side of the Atlantic had anglicized his diction and his vocabulary with monstrous deception . . . not the voice, but the friendliness was unnerving.

'Just the man!' The American took another step down,

and then another, until further retreat would have been impossibly discourteous, even for Latimer.

For the first time in his life Latimer looked for Audley's arrival with relief, waiting for the *swish* of the heavy doors to rescue him. For Audley and Morris were – almost notoriously were – thick as thieves, exchanging favours and feeding each other with classified tit-bits to their mutual benefit. They would surely be glad to see one another, to his happy exclusion.

But no *swish* delivered him, and there came no change in the muted hum of the Piccadilly traffic-jam behind him.

'Just the very man!' Morris took another step, and then stopped. 'Come on up, my dear fellow – come on up!'

Still no merciful *swish*. Latimer looked quickly over his shoulder, and was galled to see that there was nobody there now. But he couldn't have imagined Audley. He had been there, on the outer step beyond the doors. He had been there, but now he wasn't.

'Come on up, Oliver!'

What the devil could the CIA man want? Latimer felt himself drawn upwards inexorably, and now the CIA man was gesturing him up, instead of beckoning.

'Let's not go to the bar.' The American cocked his head at Latimer. 'There are some dreadful guys there . . . This time of day, with only a bit of luck, they may serve us a crafty drink in the library, if there's no one about.'

Such exact knowledge clearly indicated that the CIA man was an Oxbridge member, and not just a lurking guest. And though he was not, so far as Latimer's suddenly-fevered recollection of his dossier could recall, either an Oxford or a Cambridge product . . . yet that still left Trinity College, Dublin . . . Could he be a TCD man?

He knew where the library was, anyway. Also, the nod he gave to the white-coated servant hovering at the intersection was born of recognition and experience. But, in any case, no American (let alone a CIA friend of Audley's) could be taken for granted.

'Ah!' The CIA man surveyed the empty library with satisfaction. The Oxbridge club library was reputed to be more than adequate on sport and good enough on globe-trotting, but useless on everything else, so that it was usually empty during opening hours, 'Over there, I think.'

Latimer followed the line of the pointing finger, to the most shaded and obscure corner, full of doubt. If nothing could be taken for granted where Howard Morris was concerned, what indeed could be taken by *Oliver, my dear fellow*?

Something less than nothing. But it would be rude, when for some reason his instinct was towards politeness, to inquire about Trinity College, Dublin . . . Besides which, it would be to admit that he didn't know any better.

'Let's do something about that drink – eh?' The CIA man knew where the bell was. 'I don't know about you, but . . . for me, it's been one of those days, Oliver.'

Oliver further cooled Latimer. They had met, and he had raised his eyebrows and moved obediently to commands, but he hadn't said anything yet . . . not even *Hullo* – but Morris didn't seem to mind.

And now there wasn't time for that. On the wink, the white-coated servant had followed them, radar-directed to the biggest tip of the evening.

'What'll it be?' Howard Morris gave the man a nod for his usual, whatever it was in the library at this usefully dead hour. He had done this before, that nod indicated.

'I'll have – ' He didn't want anything, but he couldn't say *nothing* ' – the bar red – the French, not the Spanish.' He looked at the American candidly, absurdly strengthened by that trivial decision. 'You know, Colonel, I was tempted to say "That's very civil of you, Howard". But that would be to insult us both, I think.'

White teeth showed in the brown face. 'Yes?'

'Yes.' Strength, however irrationally, fed on strength: it was a quality which pulled itself up by its own bootstraps,

9

for the most inadequate reasons. 'Let's put it at its lowest level: you're buying me a drink – and that arouses my curiosity more than my gratitude, I suppose.'

The CIA man looked at him, but the friendly – almost amused – expression in his eyes didn't change. 'Yes, I can go along with that. But it's quite simple really. I was looking for David Audley – I heard he might be dropping in here.' He shrugged. 'He hasn't turned up. I thought you might know where he is.'

Latimer hoped his face didn't betray his thoughts: it was quite simple – all too bloody simple for words. If the man was in some hole, who but Audley would he want to see? Not Oliver St John Latimer, for sure!

But that hardly justified a drink in private.

'Audley?' He echoed the detested name casually to give himself time to think the thought through. It had been on the tip of his tongue to deny all knowledge of, and interest in, the bloody man, and end matters there. But that would hardly deceive the American, who could be relied on to know all about the old rivalries and their recent ironic and humiliating outcome – he might even know of that from Audley's own lips, for it was a tale Audley would enjoy telling.

'You haven't seen him, by any chance?'

'Yes.' Truth. 'Not far from here.' More truth. 'But I rather think you've missed him.' It would have been easy for the American to ask that simple question on the stairs, without the necessity of this prolonged encounter. That was no less true – perhaps even more true.

Morris looked at his watch. 'So . . . he'll most likely be on his way home by now?'

'Very likely.' The thought was running smoothly now towards its destination. The American's information had been correct: Audley *had* been coming to the Oxbridge. And as Latimer himself had prevented the encounter purely by chance – by arriving himself in the club on impulse – the American couldn't have known *that*.

'Yes. And he likes his family weekends.' Morris was thinking aloud, and Latimer could follow his train of thought. 'Otherwise . . . he's pretty busy at the moment, isn't he?'

It was Latimer's turn to shrug. 'I don't doubt it.' Morris was undoubtedly in some hole, and with very little time to climb out of it, if he was reduced to clutching at Oliver St John Latimer.

'Still Cheltenham?'

Latimer said nothing. Cheltenham was highly classified, and it rankled with him that he wasn't there instead of Audley (and he would not have miked off home every weekend, either). But the possibility that he was about to get some interesting information because of that soothed his rancour somewhat.

Morris nodded, eyeing him with transparent casualness. 'And I take it that Jack Butler's working you to the bone as well?'

'Oh . . . I've one or two things on the go.' Now it was certain. And the pure healing joy of it was that what he was about to receive had been intended for Audley. Indeed, it was so just and appropriate that he changed his mind on that instant and reached out into the pit to meet Morris halfway. 'Nothing madly urgent.'

The servant materialized beside him, setting down their drinks on the table.

'Cheers, Latimer.' The CIA man drank deeply and gratefully from a pewter tankard, then touched away the froth from his moustache with a brown finger. There was some intriguing ancestry there somewhere, thought Latimer. Possibly red indian? Hadn't even Winston Churchill some of that fierce blood in him, from his American connection?

He raised his glass, and, although it was the same stuff as he had drunk at the bar earlier, it tasted very much better. For the first time in a long while he felt better too.

Morris set his tankard down. 'You know Senator Cookridge is in town?'

Senator Cookridge. From somewhere in the Mid-West, or the further West . . . it didn't matter. Americans were not his business, thank God!

'You ever met him?' Morris took his silence as an affirmative.

'No.' He recalled that the Senator headed some American Defence and Security committee – again not his business.

'No, I guess not. American affairs are not exactly your scene, at that.' The white teeth flashed. 'Hell! I've only met him once – across a crowded room. Not my scene either. Until now.'

Latimer felt he had to make some contribution by way of encouragement. 'Defence and security . . . ?' He took another sip of wine to cover the vagueness of his knowledge. He felt more at home in the Politburo and the Supreme Soviet than the American Senate.

'Now, he is. Agriculture was his . . . speciality.' Morris pronounced the word in the British way. 'The ultimate weapon – you've been out there, Latimer?'

The man knew perfectly well. 'I've never been to the New World, Colonel.'

'For God's sake – anything but "Colonel".' The American's eyes clouded momentarily. 'The last thing I flew was a P-51 – as a captain. I was in sole command of one man, and he was scared shitless that last time.' The eyes unclouded, and the teeth showed again. 'Where Cookridge comes from . . . you could feed half the world. And heat the other half with the fossil fuel underneath.'

He was talking about power in more senses than one, decided Latimer. 'But now he's in defence and security.'

'And political muscle.' Morris paused. 'He came to it late, but he's in it now – he whispers, and it deafens me, you'd better believe it.'

The ex-P-51 captain was flying scared again, it seemed

12

to Latimer. But, since he himself was still grounded firmly on British soil, with nothing promised or owed, that only made matters more interesting.

On the other hand, in his helpful *vice*-Audley role, he could afford to be sympathetic, with all his options still open. 'I do believe it.' He couldn't say 'Colonel', but he couldn't bring himself to say 'Howard' even now. 'We have something of the same problem . . . if less acutely, I suppose.'

'Yeah, I guess you have.' Under stress Morris became less anglicized. 'But . . . the hell of it is, Latimer . . . I want a favour of you.'

'A favour?' That was spelling it out with almost indecent clarity – so much so that Latimer was momentarily surprised. For there was not one single reason why Oliver St John Latimer should do Colonel Howard Morris a favour. Morris had never done him any good – Morris was David Audley's friend and ally, not his.

'And there isn't a single goddam' reason why you should do it – I know.' It was as though the American had eavesdropped on his thoughts. 'Not now, of all times. I know that too.'

He knew that too, thought Latimer a little wearily. And the plain burden of that was . . . the American knew the still-classified result of the promotion contest – knew that Butler, who hadn't looked to compete, had been forced to win when Audley had scorned to do so . . . and that Oliver St John Latimer, who had run the best race, had been fobbed off with second place.

For Christ's sake . . . who wanted to be deputy-director?

'No, I suppose there isn't.' He freed himself from further contemplation of the recent and disastrous past quite easily: it had been crowding his thoughts too much over the last few days, with no result itself except to diminish his customary efficiency in the discharge of routine matters. But pure chance might now be offering something which might be of real significance, and he knew he was not going to reject the opportunity. Rather, it concentrated his understanding of the pointlessness of any further analysis of the setback. Because he had *not* resigned, then he *was* deputy-director – or would be so in just one week's time. That was the situation exactly: he would have more money, which he didn't need, and more power, but not enough of it, and not the power he wanted. But he must make the best of it, and he would start doing that now – right here and now.

Senator Cookridge.

Senator Thomas Cookridge, from somewhere in the limitless Mid-West, the world's granary, who was now chairman of the President's new Atlantic Defence Committee – in London for a flying visit to meet British defence chiefs: that, together with a blurred photograph of the Senator in *The Times*, was what he remembered.

He took another sip of wine, saw that his glass was almost empty, and reached towards the bell. And then looked at the CIA man. 'However . . . be that as it may –' This was the deputy-director speaking, by God! ' – just what is the Senator's problem?'

Morris met the look, and then relaxed perceptibly in his armchair as the white-coated servant appeared again.

'The same?' Latimer inquired politely. It warmed him to know that he had moved out of debit and far into credit at a stroke. Perhaps the Americans hadn't influenced the promotion decision directly. For, flawed though Colonel Butler's decision might have been – flawed though it *had* been – he was not the man to let a foreign power's influence play any significant part in it. Butler's greatest strength and greatest weakness was that he was an honest man.

The American nodded, and the nod accepted more than another drink. 'Thanks, Latimer.'

Rather than American influence, direct or indirect, it might very well have been his own lack of American experience and contacts such as this, thought Latimer self-critically. And, to be unmercifully honest with himself, that had been not simply due to his ambitious calculation that treason and danger came out of the East, not the West, but also a matter of personal preference and prejudice. As always, failure and defeat began at home, no matter what external reasons presented themselves at the end.

But that was in the past now – for now he was in the present and the future. He still had a few precious years over Butler and Audley both, and chance was giving him a promising beginning.

'It isn't exactly a problem he's gotten himself – no.' Morris's mouth twisted. 'It's . . . *he* wants a favour – that would be more accurate. I'm just the middle-man . . . the messenger boy, to sound you out.'

On one level that was disappointing. The degree of difficulty and challenge lessened, and the urgency and possible profit with them. But at least, if Morris had effectively lowered the stakes, he had thereby almost certainly eliminated the grosser and more egregious ingredients of scandal too. Sex and violence and corruption, alike the British tabloid newspapers' preoccupation and the KGB's opportunity, happily receded: Latimer had been forced to deal with all three all too often, albeit safely at second or third hand; but he had never enjoyed the dealing, or been able to resign himself to them as facts of life.

'What does he want?' A third level, tantalizingly nebulous, brightened Latimer. Even if it was none of those, it was something which Howard Morris couldn't' handle easily by himself, without this humiliation. And, since Morris was a man of great experience, considerable seniority, and undoubted ingenuity, the lost difficulty and challenge of the first level were reinstated: whatever it was the Senator wanted, it wasn't going to be easy to give it to him.

The servant returned, with another glass and another

frothing tankard, and a chit to sign. Expansively, Latimer dropped one of the pound coins which had been weighing down his trouser-pocket on to the silver tray; from which it disappeared like lightning, with not the slightest acknowledgement of the excess. If that was the going price of service in the library it was no wonder the man had been hovering for the second round, he concluded.

'You,' said Morris.

'What?' Latimer's hand, closing round his new glass, slopped its contents on the table.

'He'll be here in about half-an-hour – ' Morris looked at his watch again ' – or nearer forty minutes if he's running to schedule. By the back entrance – there's a room booked on the third floor, if I give the word. And as he's due to speak at the North Atlantic Union dinner, you better believe he'll be on time, Latimer . . . By which time I'll be safe on the other side of London, with an unbreakable alibi – and you can surely rely on that, because that's the way he wants it.' He reached for his new tankard, and drank from it. But this time the line of froth remained on his moustache. 'And the way he wants it is the way he gets it, old buddy.'

'Me?' That could not be true. Since his presence in the Oxbridge was an accident he was only an improvisation. 'You mean . . . Audley, not me.' He was not simply second-best – he was all Howard Morris could produce at such short notice, when Audley had failed to turn up.

'Yes, that's the goddam' truth.' Morris didn't attempt to dispute the indisputable. 'I was going for David – I can't deny that.'

'Because he's a friend of yours.' No question, that.

'Dam' right.' The American's chin went up. 'And I hardly know you, Mister Deputy-Director.'

That was laying it on the line: that was admitting everything, but at the same time it was mixing its challenge with an offer – it was throwing obligation and advantage and self-interest on to the scales: *as of now,*

16

Mister Deputy-Director, we both need each other, to do business!

'Which makes what you're doing now even more surprising.'

The American smiled. 'Hardly less surprising than what you're doing.'

'No.' Latimer shook his head. 'A colleague representing a friendly power . . . a close ally . . . wants a favour. Naturally, I have listened to him. The favour consists of doing a favour for one of his political masters. And I'll listen to him, by the same token. But I have promised nothing – equally naturally. That is not at all surprising, any of it.' He raised his glass to his lips, but only pretended to drink. Two glasses were enough for the time being.

'No one writes blank cheques.' Morris nodded. 'Fair enough.'

'Yes. But the difference is . . . that you know what is to be written on the cheque – and, on the basis of your friendship with Audley, you must have believed he'd sign. Whereas in my case, as you have said yourself, there is no such basis.'

'Uh-uh.' Latimer estimated the CIA man hadn't intended to tell him anything, he had been concerned only to set up the meeting. Whatever he got from him in advance was therefore all the more valuable.

'I don't know what the Senator wants. At least, not in any detail.' Morris considered him for a moment. 'And I wasn't at all sure David would buy it – though he was the right man for it.' He paused. 'Which is perhaps more than I can say for you, Latimer.'

'You just had to take what there was. Hobson's choice, it's called over here.'

'Yeah.' Morris frowned suddenly. 'Who the hell was Hobson?'

'I believe he was a Cambridge ostler who offered the next horse on the list or nothing.'

'Maybe he only had one horse.'

'Perhaps.' Latimer looked at his watch. 'It looks as though you have only one horse, anyway.'

'Or none. I could disappoint the Senator.'

'If it was Audley he wanted, you already have.' They were only playing with each other, Latimer realized. 'What does he want, exactly? Or . . . since you don't know in any detail . . . what does he want in general?'

The white teeth showed, but in a thin white line. 'Brains.'

'That is . . . rather general.' Then a thought struck Latimer. '*British* brains, obviously . . . since you ought to be able to supply some of the American sort, I would have thought.' With all his power, Senator Cookridge could have had any variety of American brain. So it must be a British one he wanted, whatever other attributes he required. 'Audley's sort, evidently. Rather than mine?'

Morris gave him another considering look. 'Would you say there's any difference?'

Under other circumstances Latimer would have said just that. Instead, he shrugged and sipped his wine.

Morris looked at the wine. 'Maybe you're right, at that. Different vintage year, but much the same vineyard. And the same goddam' wine merchant – that's for sure.'

'And yet you consider me less suitable than Audley?' In such a strong position Latimer felt inclined to push his luck in exchange for even indirect information.

'You haven't got his special knowledge.'

'His . . . special knowledge?' Self-knowledge only just curbed Latimer's instinctive reaction. In most areas he would back himself against Audley, but in all things American he had to admit that he lacked expertise. 'And what sort of . . . special knowledge would that be?'

The American laughed. 'Don't let it upset you – '

'It doesn't upset me.' He must have betrayed himself somehow. 'I'm merely curious, that's all.'

'Of course. Don't get me wrong – I didn't mean . . .

professional knowledge.' The brown hand waved away any temporary misunderstanding. 'I meant . . . knowledge from way back, Latimer.'

What the devil did that mean? Audley had the edge on him in years too, but that was hardly an advantage now; indeed, it was more of a disadvantage – even the fact that Audley could boast war-experience, brief though it was and in his extreme youth, only served to associate him with a generation which had had its day and was pensionable. And Colonel Butler with him, by God!

'I meant history,' said Morris.

'History?' Latimer echoed him stupidly, but couldn't help himself. 'The war, you mean?'

'Huh! The war – dam' right!' Morris only half-smiled, almost winced. 'I mean . . . David's a historian. He studied history at Cambridge – he writes history books.'

Latimer frowned at him. The conversation had been verging on the opaque, but now it had become incoherent. 'Medieval history books.'

'History.' The American triumphantly lumped medieval and modern history together, the Normans in England in 1066, and the English in Normandy in 1944. 'But you studied . . . English, was it?'

'I read English,' Latimer knew that Morris was only pretending to guess. He would know where and when as well as what. And, most particularly, he would know under whom – that above all. 'And then economics.'

'So you wouldn't be an authority on American history, exactly?'

That displayed a target which was irresistible. 'Is there such a thing?'

Morris winced. 'But American literature? Say . . . Stephen Crane – William Faulkner?'

Latimer frowned, Stephen Crane was a most obscure novelist, who had written one allegedly good book, about the American Civil War, in which he had not taken part but which was reputed to be accurate nevertheless; and

19

Faulkner's prose was decidedly eccentric – very possibly because he had been three sheets in the wind when his fingers hit the typewriter keys.

'Faulkner? Crane?'

The last time he had seen a Faulkner novel had been on Colonel Butler's desk – the desk he had aspired to sit behind and control, which was now Butler's desk by appointment and promotion. So maybe there was more in both Faulkner and Butler than he had imagined.

Faulkner and Crane – they sounded like Solicitors and Commissioners for Oaths – what had they in common, apart from fiction?

'You know what I'm talking about?'

'I think I do, yes.' Faulkner had written quite a few books, but most of them had been set in the same territory. And Crane, whatever he had written, was remembered for just that one book: the ignorant farm boy caught up in a war he didn't understand – someone had made a film of it, long ago, in black-and-white, in which the fictional-heroic farm boy had been played by an actually-heroic farm boy from the recent war, Audley's war – that had been the gimmick. 'Audie Murphy?'

The CIA man regarded him curiously, frowning slightly. 'Audie – ?' His face cleared suddenly. 'Yes, that's right. He played the youth in *The Red Badge* – you're right.'

'The Youth' – that was right too: the farm boy hero had had no name. And . . . 'the war' – when Morris had said '*The war – damn right*' he had worn an odd, almost apologetic, expression. And he was wearing the same expression now.

'That is to say . . . I believe I have identified your war, Morris.' In his turn, Latimer frowned as he recalled their starting point. Or Senator Cookridge's war. But I can't say I'm making any sense of it. I know more about cowboys and Indians, anyway.'

'But you do know something about the War between the States?'

20

The War between the States? It took Latimer a second to translate that presumably-alternative description of the Senator's war, with more than half his brain busy wrestling with a much more taxing conundrum: *what the devil did the chairman of the new Atlantic Defence Committee have to do with the American Civil War that needed a senior CIA trouble-shooter as middleman*?

'You do know about the war?' The American was staring at him, more doubtful than apologetic now, evidently misreading the emotions of surprise and incomprehension he was observing.

Or rather, *not* misreading, thought Latimer with a swirl of fear. Because, in all this laughable conjunction of accident and misunderstanding, there was one near-certainty and one absolute certainty.

The near-certainty was that Howard Morris would on balance prefer not to damage his credibility with the Senator by producing an ignorant Englishman, whose knowledge of the Senator's war was limited to Audie Murphy and a teenage reading of *Gone With the Wind* thirty years before. Better at such unreasonably short notice, to produce no Englishman at all.

And the certainty – the absolute certainty – was that his own knowledge was in fact limited to . . . Audie Murphy and . . . and, at this remove in time, more to a youthful fixation on Vivien Leigh as Scarlett O'Hara than to any detailed memory of the course of the 'War between the States'.

But . . . by God, there was also one more certainty –

'My dear Morris – ' If there was one more certainty, it was that this was an entirely absorbing conundrum in itself; which, the more so – most of all so – he wasn't going to pass up, because he had stolen it from Audley, right under the man's nose, too! Because . . . to get in with the Americans would be damned useful. And whatever Audley could do, Oliver St John Latimer could do – and do better, by God! 'My dear Morris – I'm actually something of an expert on it . . . in a small way, you know. It's an interesting war.'

All wars were interesting if that sort of thing turned you on, so that was a safe thing to say. And, although he mustn't look at his watch to check the time, he had maybe a quarter of an hour to make himself an expert on it. And that was by no means beyond the bounds of possibility.

'You are?' Morris sounded wisely uncertain about an accidental occurrence which was too good to be true and not in the Latimer file.

'Yes.' The man mustn't ask him a question to establish that claim, because the odds were hugely that he wouldn't be able to answer it. It had occurred in the mid-19th century, but he couldn't even date it accurately. So he needed to head off that possibility –

Time was on his side: he *could* reasonably look at his watch – there was hardly time for questions now –

Fourteen minutes. And time wasn't really on his side –

He looked around, vaguely. Time was running out.

Books everywhere. Dry-smelling, dust-smelling . . . mostly books on sport and travel, rather than the American Civil War.

Dry-smelling, dust-smelling – the dry dust-motes swimming in the still air of that faded room in the sunshine, viewed from the canyon between the high-backed chair and the bookshelves, all those years ago –

Colonel Marmaduke St John's *Diary of the War in America*, with its spine sun-bleached from blue to an indeterminate off-white, and the mottled-brown page-edges uncut, every other one –

'Yes.' The memory of his Uncle's library, in which he had spent so many childhood hours, came back to Latimer with crystal clarity now. 'As a matter of fact, one of my St John ancestors fought in your civil war, Morris – Colonel Marmaduke St John. He even wrote a book about his adventures.'

The American stared at him in surprise. 'He wrote a book?'

'*Diary of the War in America.*' Latimer nodded, but as he did so his confidence weakened. For the crystal memory of the library did not actually include that particular volume, he remembered: one glance at it had been enough, in fact.

'I'll be damned!' exclaimed Morris.

Latimer nodded again. 'Fascinating book.' It had certainly not been fascinating: with a mighty effort he conjured up the faded picture of Marmaduke himself from the frontispiece . . . the mutton-chop whiskers, bald head and fixed blank stare into the Victorian camera. 'He was a fine soldier, was Colonel St John.'

Had he been? Another effort produced old Mutton-Chop's framed commission, on the library wall to the right of the door –

The Supreme Government of India.

To Marmaduke Henry Arthur St John, Greeting.

We, reposing especial Trust and Confidence in your Loyalty, Courage and Good Conduct, Do by these Presents constitute you to be and appoint you, Marmaduke Henry Arthur St John Esquire, to be a Lieutenant of Artillery in the Service of the East India Company, in the Bengal Establishment –

'Indian Army,' Latimer grasped the recollection like a drowning man. 'A gunner . . . He fought on the Delhi Ridge during the Mutiny.' That was right: Aunt Muriel had included that fact in her own memories of India's dreadful climate.

'Which side did he fight on?' inquired Morris.

Latimer frowned at him. 'Ours, of course. He wasn't an Indian Mutineer, Morris.'

Morris waved an Indian-brown hand. 'I mean, in *our* war? Was he for the Johnny Rebs . . . or for the Yankees?'

'Ah . . . I see!' It was a question he could hardly fluff,

as an expert . . . for no doubt there was a copy of Mutton-Chop's book in the British Museum which Morris could easily check on, so he had to pick the right answer. 'Which side . . . ?'

Morris grinned. 'Which side would an Englishman fight for?'

Latimer looked at his watch. 'What time did you say the Senator was coming here?'

'I didn't exactly.' Morris looked at his own watch for a moment, then at Latimer. 'Yeah . . . okay, Latimer . . . I'll give him his call, then.' He stood up, but then looked down at Latimer again. 'Which side *did* he fight for?'

Whose side would an English gentleman have fought for? wondered Latimer desperately – Scarlett O'Hara's or Abraham Lincoln's?

Inspiration came like a flash of light – 'Colonel Morris!' He mocked the CIA man with false courage. 'Which side would you *expect* an English gentleman to support? It is not a question which requires an answer!'

2

Latimer in London: Temptation (continued)

Far away in the porter's lodge at Oxford the phone was ringing.

Latimer drew a piece of club notepaper from one of the Secretary's pigeon-holes and began to rough out his letter.

Dear Butler,

   Further to my acceptance of your offer –

That, at least, would put Butler's mind at rest, that he wasn't going to renege on his decision. Poor old Butler hadn't wanted the top job, for which he knew he was ill-suited. But duty was everything to him, and his own wishes and convenience and private life came nowhere in the reckoning.

The phone answered him, and it was an under-porter on it.

'Is Mr Bates there?'

Butler was really rather admirable. However much they disliked each other, Latimer had to concede that. To have turned him down – as he had half-expected Latimer to do, since he always expected the worst – would have been rather like kicking the old dog that brought one's slippers and newspaper all tattered and covered with revolting saliva, but nonetheless faithfully.

   – I think I'd like to take a few days' leave, from the months owed to me, which I shall never get round to taking –

'Bates? Oliver Latimer here. Is Dr Burge in college this evening?'

It was a long shot. It was about as likely that Philip would be in Oxford in August, rather than in some more congenial foreign watering-hole, than that their common St John ancestors in the Indian Civil Service had remained

in the sweltering plains during the hot season in preference for Simla. But there was just an outside chance that
he might be putting the finishing touches to his book on
Anglo-American relations in the twentieth century.

'Dr Burge, Sir?' Bates thought for a moment. 'I'm
afraid he's not in college today.'

'Or in Oxford?' Loyalty would animate anything Bates
said, but he might allow for the blood-relationship.

'I don't believe he is up at the moment, sir,' admitted
Bates cautiously.

'No – of course.' The long shot lengthened towards
infinity. 'Is anyone else dining this evening? Dr Franklin?
Mr . . . er . . . Mr Smith? Or Dr Horam?'

Silence descended as Bates consulted his records.

– which I shall never get round to taking. Butler would
not object to him taking a few days at this juncture; he had
plainly thought the better of Latimer for taking the No. 2
job – the job which they both knew was dust and ashes in
his mouth – without protest; he might even have assumed
that Latimer also was bowing to the dictates of duty, as
blind as the cruel pronouncements of justice. But he
would expect an explanation, nevertheless. *I need to take
stock of the job –*

'No, sir.' Bates knew exactly who was dining on High
Table, but he had allowed time for an unnecessary study
of the absentees.

Latimer crossed out *I need to take stock of the job*. It
was a lie which belittled them both, and he might as well
start with the truth.

'There's no one dining in tonight, sir.' Some ancient
memory of the young Mr Oliver St John Latimer impelled
Bates to honesty. No historians remained in the sweltering
plains of Oxford in the hot season. And no chemists, or
physicists, or biologists, or classicists, or anyone else. It
was August, and Oxford was empty.

'Thank you, Bates.' Perhaps it was surprising that Bates
himself was there. But they probably didn't pay him

enough to be anywhere else – and there probably wasn't anywhere else that he wanted to be, with the access he had to the cellars. Some things didn't change.

It was no good ringing anywhere else, it would be the same everywhere, even if he could think of other names. Time was running out – had almost run out, to the minute . . . and he was stuck with The Youth and Scarlett O'Hara. And, in a better and more forgiving world, he would have had time to check up on Senator Cookridge with the Duty Officer in the section.

He stared at the crossed out line on the sheet of club notepaper. Things done too quickly, with inadequate thought, were rarely things done well.

I have a small private matter to resolve, he wrote. That, strictly speaking, was the truth, according to Howard Morris. And it was hard to imagine how the Senator's interest in the American Civil War would be anything but private.

All the same, he felt strangely guilty. This might be – damn it, it bloody well *was* – the sort of thing the man Audley did all the time. So he could well understand why Morris had thought of Audley first. But it was also the sort of thing that he himself had never done. But he was doing it now.

And doing it not very well, too. Because he had maybe another five minutes, and the second-hand ticked remorselessly to remind him that he had half-claimed to be an expert on that damned war; and although Old Muttonchops might be good enough for Howard Morris, he wouldn't be enough for the Senator. But who, in five minutes, could rectify that deficiency? Failing Philip . . . not the Duty Officer, certainly, even with the computer at his fingertips: the American Civil War did not figure in late twentieth century British security. So he had been foolish –

Suddenly he found himself staring at the Ackerman print on the wall of the Secretary's office, and remembering who the Duty Officer was this holiday weekend Friday. And remembering more than that.

His finger dialled the number. 'James Cable?' Lieutenant-Commander Cable was one of Colonel Butler's young service recruits. But no fool, for all that. 'This is Oliver St John Latimer, Cable.'

'Sir?' Blank surprise came back down the line.

'Do you know anything about the American Civil War, Cable?'

'Sir?' Surprise became incredulity. 'This is an open line, sir.'

'I know that, man. You were attached to the US navy a few years back – Norfolk, Virginia, was it?' It was a faint hope, but it was all he had: Rhett Butler had made his fortune out-smarting the US navy, so there had been a naval civil war. 'I'm having this argument about the American Civil War. What do you know about it? You must know something, Cable?'

There was a slight pause. 'Sod all, I'm afraid, sir.' Another pause. 'Except . . . I knew one of their underwater fellows who was always trying to locate pieces of the USS *Monitor* off Cape Hatteras or somewhere . . . where she went down – she was a damn Yankee boat from that time.'

'The USS *Monitor*?' Anything was better than nothing.

'The first ironclad. Or . . . technically, maybe the *second* . . . or, I suppose the *Gloire* and the *Warrior* were both ahead of it – and the Confederate *Merrimac* too. But it was the first turret-ship – and it was the first one into battle with another ironclad. Hampton Roads – eighteen-sixty-something.' Pause. 'Was it naval history you were arguing?'

What the hell might he be arguing about? Only Senator Cookridge could answer that –

'But hold on a moment, sir.' James Cable pressed on. 'I have got an expert here who's forgotten more about Gettysburg and all that than I shall ever know, I'll bet – hold on!'

Latimer stared at the instrument in his hand, frowning. For a disconcerted moment he feared that it might be Audley himself who was about to come on the line: the man had all sorts of esoteric historical knowledge, not all of it medieval and some of it military; and it had been Audley whom Howard Morris had wanted, so some of that military history might be American; and it was just possible that he had been on his way to the section via the club this evening, not on his way home. But, against that – James Cable was a very proper young man, with a very proper sense of rank and seniority, and unlikely to refer to Audley in such cavalier terms.

'Hullo, there.' The voice was not Audley's. 'Latimer?'

Mitchell? Damn it!

'Oliver?' Paul Mitchell was *not* a very proper young man, having been born without any sense of rank and seniority: he merely sounded somewhat surprised. And with that surprise there would inevitably be curiosity – *Damn it*!

'Mitchell? What are you doing there?'

'Doing?' Mitchell didn't pretend he was answering a sensible question. 'Working, oddly enough. But later on I'm going down the pub to play dominoes – at five pence a spot. I've got this theory . . . unlucky in love and war, lucky at dominoes.' He sniffed slightly. 'What's this about . . . the American Civil War, was it?' He sounded frankly disbelieving.

'You're an expert on it?' A denial would only make matters worse. So far as Latimer was aware, Mitchell was an expert in only two fields: the 1914–18 War and killing people. He had written several books on the former, but steadfastly maintained that his other reputation had been forced on him by a mixture of accidental but inescapable circumstances and undeserved bad luck. For his own part, Latimer suspected that Mitchell, had he been born a century earlier, would have been a happy machine-gunner in the trenches.

'Indirectly – yes.'

'Indirectly?' But, born killer or not, the man was a trained historian, with a doctoral thesis on his favourite bloodbath to prove it. 'What does that mean?'

'It means . . . George Francis Robert Henderson.'

'Who?' He was going to be late for the senator, but he had sacrificed too much to withdraw now.

'G. F. R. Henderson. York and Lancaster Regiment. Oxford, Sandhurst, the Staff College. Born 1854, or thereabouts. Died 1903.'

'Get to the point, Mitchell.'

'I'm there, Oliver. Henderson was the brains in our Staff College in the 1890s. Somebody asked him in '97 who, among the latest batch of hopefuls, was going to make it to the top. He fingered Douglas Haig. He taught most of the top '14–'18 men.'

To Latimer, that didn't sound like a recommendation. 'So what?'

'So what do you want? The American Civil War?'

Latimer winced. 'Yes.'

'That was Henderson's speciality. He made his name with it – he *rescued* it. Fredericksburg. Grant in Northern Virginia . . . the big biography for Stonewall Jackson. They were studying the Franco-Prussian War before he came on the scene, because that was the most modern war – *and*, of course, the Prussian army was the top army. The fashions proved that; spikes on the top of helmets were the "in" thing. We wore them . . . so did the Americans for that matter, with their dress uniforms, when both sides in their Civil War had worn little French képis a few years before –' Mitchell stopped abruptly. 'But Henderson – he realized that it was the American war that pointed to the shape of things to come; citizen armies and entrenchments – he caught a whiff of the Somme in Northern Virginia in '64 and '65.'

Latimer looked at his watch again. But this was the pure gold of enthusiasm, not to be discouraged. 'He did?'

'Close enough. Of course, he didn't get everything right. He couldn't quite believe his own evidence about small-arms fire . . . and the end of cavalry – that died harder in theory than in practice . . . and he'd only an inkling of what artillery was going to do.' Mitchell sniffed. 'You know they had machine-guns in the American Civil War, Latimer – at the very end?'

Latimer cleared his throat non-committally. 'Yes?'

'And barbed-wire. And aerial observation. And – ' Mitchell stopped again. 'Just what is it that you want, Latimer?'

Caution had replaced enthusiasm: perhaps the fellow was remembering belatedly how much they disliked one another, thought Latimer. But however true that might be, it wouldn't do this evening. 'This . . . Henderson. He sounds a remarkable man.' He offered Mitchell the thought with unaccustomed diffidence, like an olive branch.

'He was. History scholar at Oxford before he took the Queen's shilling. But he died tragically young. Caught a bug, or something, just when he was taking over as Roberts' Director of Intelligence in South Africa.' Mitchell couldn't fight his own enthusiasm for the subject. 'But it was his teaching that counted. And that was where the American Civil War came in, you see. The way people think now, he maybe didn't rate Sherman's operations in the West as important as they really were – it was Grant's war of attrition in the East that counted for him. But I'm not so sure that he wasn't right, at that . . . Bruce Catton – he described Sherman's March to the Sea as the nineteeth century version of the World War Two bombing offensive . . . If it was, then he only had soft civilian targets to take out, and no Confederate Luftwaffe to contend with after Atlanta. So he was lucky. It was Grant who had Lee's Panzer divisions to fight.'

Latimer could make little sense of that mixture of wars and warriors. And who was Bruce Catton?

But time had run out.

'Well – '

'But either way, you can maybe relate what Henderson taught to what happened: Grant in the Wilderness – Haig on the Western front . . . and maybe Montgomery and Eisenhower too . . . with Patton as Sherman, and Rommel as Robert E. Lee – '

'Yes.' Latimer cut him off decisively. 'Well . . . that's interesting, Mitchell.'

'Is it?' Curiosity underlined the bantering tone. 'What is this . . . argument . . . ?'

'I'll tell you some other time. I'm most grateful to you. But I must go now – good night to you, Mitchell.'

Latimer replaced the receiver and snatched up his unfinished letter, knowing that he was late for his appointment.

The club steward was hovering just outside his purloined office, with a slightly pained look on his face.

'I'm sorry to have been so long, Mr Wilberforce.' Latimer stuffed the letter into his pocket. There would be time enough for that later, if he was not too late. And it was galling to think that he had promised Mitchell some sort of explanation, whether it was too late or not.

'That's all right, Mr Latimer, sir.' There was also curiosity in the steward's face. But then he probably had a pretty shrewd idea, however vague and uninformed, of how *Mr Latimer, sir* was employed. Club stewards always knew too much. 'Your . . . ah . . . guests have arrived sir. They are waiting for you in Room 12, on the second floor, to the left of the staircase.'

Guests? Plural?

'Thank you, Mr Wilberforce.'

Plural – of course. Senator Cookridge would not be abroad in a foreign city unescorted: he would be discreetly surrounded by Special Branch men, armed to the teeth, as well as his own people. That was to be expected in these dark times.

32

He took the stairs at a run, aware that he was already sweating slightly. But that, he realized, was not so much because of the excess weight he carried as because of the unaccustomed excess excitement at the prospect ahead. He was not used to the sharp end of the business, that was a fact: he was used to calling tunes for other men to play. Yet, more than that, he was going in unbriefed and uninformed, and he was even less accustomed to doing that.

Senator Cookridge: the sad truth was that he knew little more about the Senator than what Howard Morris had told him.

Must slow down. Late or not, it would never do to arrive out of breath, with a sweaty palm for the Senator to shake.

Bruce Catton – who was he? An historian, presumably.

He had over-estimated his ability to become an instant expert on the American Civil War, that was plain.

Generals Sherman and Grant and Lee . . . and Haig and Montgomery . . . and Patton and Rommel – and Henderson –

He rounded the turn of the staircase. On the landing at the head of the stairs above him was a man in a dinner jacket.

Mustn't pause – just take it easy, like in the old forgotten days of long ago.

Henderson – would he have been another general? Probably not, if he had just come from a Staff College lectureship to that last appointment – what was it?

He exchanged a blank glance of unrecognition with the dinner-jacketed man. The man was youngish and broad-shouldered and short-haired, and he wasn't doing anything rather obviously. Or rather, with that curiously characteristic see-through expression, he was trying to follow his profession as unobstrusively as possible, simply keyed-up to react to the slightest hint of any hostile action on Latimer's part – to react so quickly that he could overtake such an action in spite of the disadvantage of having to react to it.

Latimer smiled inwardly as he turned towards the left, at once cooled and slightly exhilarated by his conclusion. He had never had to act or react himself, except intellectually to the stimulus of information or orders received, requiring him in turn to make decisions and give orders. But the old knowledge hadn't quite deserted him – hadn't damn-well deserted him at all!

There was another man down the passage ahead of him, also dinner-jacketed, but standing with his back to a door – the door to Room 12, for sure – and not pretending to be anything other than what he was.

Henderson would have been a colonel. Probably a full colonel, like Colonel Butler . . . Or, since Butler had refused further promotion in the army, because of that prim conscience of his, just possibly a brigadier.

Not that it mattered. Because all that mattered was that this was rather fun, really: to act out of character and out of his accustomed rôle, which had somehow deepened from a groove into a canyon into which his career and his ambitions had both descended to his disadvantage. Because, here and now, for once he had nothing to lose that he hadn't lost, and everything to gain, which – in a year or two – he might still gain, if he played his cards right in the next ten minutes. And it was having so few cards to play that made it such fun, really.

He stopped in front of the second man, who was built . . . like a London double-decker bus, was his first thought. But Audley, who liked to shock his listeners with occasional obscenity, used for effect, would have said *like a brick shit-house*. And this was (which was another happy thought) an opportunity which Audley should have enjoyed –

'Excuse me.' He gestured with a finger to shift the brick shit-house out of his way.

The brick shit-house made the grave mistake of looking down the corridor, while not moving an inch.

Latimer allowed himself to follow the look, and was

rewarded by a view of the first man turned towards them with his dinner jacket unbuttoned, ready to leap into the two-handed firing position which the distance down the corridor required.

Amateurs, thought Latimer derisively. They could have hired actors to play these rôles, and managed just as well. Perhaps that was something he could tighten up in his own rôle as Deputy-Director.

'My name's Latimer. Oliver St John Latimer – ' It occurred to Latimer suddenly that this whole charade might be occurring because they had expected Audley ' – I'm here instead of Dr Audley.'

'Yes, sir.' The brick shit-house was Special Branch, the voice betrayed. 'Could I see your identification, sir?'

'Yes . . . of course.' Latimer remembered to extract his credentials gingerly, with thumb and forefinger, because the man down the corridor would undoubtedly be a good marksman, however unobtrusive he might be.

The Special Branch man scanned the face before him, and then its likeness, and then returned it. 'If you don't mind, sir – ?'

Latimer raised his arms. They really were shutting the stable-door to check the horse after it had very obviously not tried to escape. But they were right, of course.

'Thank you, sir.' The Special Branch man stood aside, and then tapped his pre-arranged safe signal – *tap* . . . *tap-tap* – to *Open Sesame*.

It was an ordinary club bedroom, decidedly spartan, even a little threadbare, in keeping with the admirably low annual subscription required of members.

'*Mister Lat*imer – ' The room blanked out as the Senator advanced towards him ' – or should it be *Doctor* Latimer – ?' The Senator thrust out a welcoming hand even as he left his greeting in the air.

'Mister will do.' Latimer just had time to wipe his palm before he grasped the hand. Oddly, the hand was as sweaty as his own had been, although bigger and stronger.

'But . . . Doctor of Philosophy, is it?'

'English literature, actually.' At this moment Oxford was a far cry. '"D. Phil." is a rather generalized signal for post-graduate work, Senator.' Latimer took the room in quickly. The Senator was weather-beaten but well-groomed, and impressive in full evening-dress, with a wedge of miniature decorations on his breast. And there was another dinner-jacketed young man, bespectacled and not quite so big as the man on the landing, but out of the same general mould, away on the right, and prudently out-of-range in a single glance.

'Uh-huh?' The Senator nodded. 'But philosophy is the name of the game, I guess – your game and mine: *the love and pursuit of wisdom, or of knowledge of things and their causes, theoretical or practical* – that's what the book says, and if it isn't the Good Book, it's the next best thing . . . Right?'

Another actor, thought Latimer. More like than unlike the American on the landing – only unlike in that he was a better performer, with his lines at his fingertips.

'You could say that, sir, I suppose.' Self-interest, rather than mere politeness, prompted the answer. He must cultivate this skill with foreigners, as he had not done before.

'I could – and I will.' Senator Cookridge looked quickly towards the young man. 'Okay, Bob – just you give us some time, then – okay?'

'Yes, sir. The young man drew a breath. 'Though it's time we're running short of, sir.'

The Senator waved a big hand. 'You let me worry about that, son. There's all that London traffic out there to delay us. The North Atlantic-goddam'-Fellowship can wait a few minutes for the United States of America.'

'Yes, sir.' The young man jutted his chin. 'It can wait a few minutes because HRH will be five minutes late. But not more than that. Which gives us ten minutes at the outside . . . *sir*.'

'*Okay*. Then don't take any more of my minutes, goddam' it. You just join King-Kong out there – *right*?'

The Senator watched the young man depart, then turned to Latimer with a shake of the head. 'Protocol, he calls it! You suffer from that, Mister Latimer?'

'I suffer from a lot of things, Senator.'

'I'll bet you do!' The Senator tossed his head. 'And now from me, eh?'

'And now from you, Senator.' Truth, where it could be used as an ally, was always to be preferred. For truth carried the deceptive labels of honesty and sincerity on it. 'What do you want from me?'

The big American looked at him. 'Well, that's straight – I like that. So maybe we can do business after all, Mister Latimer.'

'You had your doubts, did you?' The way things were going, perhaps honesty and sincerity need not be false.

Another look. 'Straight both ways, then. Yes – I had my doubts. And I still have them.'

Straight both ways then. 'You were expecting someone else?'

'I was. A man named Audley. A history man – right?'

This sudden onrush of truth and honesty was positively disconcerting. 'A history man . . . originally. And just about the best man we've got, in terms of pure intellect.' But there were limits. 'He has his . . . disadvantages, of course.' He shrugged.

'And you should know – because you're his new boss – eh?' The shrug came back to him, as one top man to another, below the line of official recommendation. 'And that's another problem. Because I think you're going to be too busy for me, is what I think.'

That wouldn't do. 'You could be wrong there. I don't take over for another week. At the moment . . . I've got a little time in hand.' Latimer looked at his watch ostentatiously. 'Which I'm thinking you haven't got – ' Another 24 hours would work wonders for the American Civil War

' – and, apart from HRH and the North Atlantic Fellowship, I could meet you here tomorrow just as easily, Senator.'

'Screw that?' The Senator grimaced. 'And screw HRH and the North Atlantic Fellowship! This time tomorrow I've got to be nice to the goddam' Frogs – *Mon*sieur Mitterand – who talks left and acts right . . . And after that Rome . . . So you can screw that! This is personal – and this is now or never . . . You'd better understand that.'

'At the moment, I can't say that I do.'

'No.' Senator Cookridge was on a knife-edge.

'And I'm not David Audley.' But the Senator must slide down on the right side of the knife, no matter what the risk. 'But that doesn't mean I don't know anything about . . . history.'

'No.' The Senator estimated him, second-running against his own risk – his personal risk. 'So I've been told.' The estimation became more shrewd. 'You had someone – your great-grandpa . . . great grandfather, would that be . . . someone who fought in the Civil War?'

'That's right.' Latimer almost wished he hadn't remembered old Mutton-Chops – except that the historic connection appeared to cheer the Senator somewhat.

'And he fought for the South, Colonel Morris tells me? For the Johnny Rebs? Is that so? And wrote a book?' The Senator nodded. 'So that makes you something of an expert, does it?'

There was the slightest hint of challenge in that last question, and it had to be met just right.

He shook his head. 'In itself . . . no.' Another shake. It was Mitchell, not Mutton-Chops, whom he must call to his aid. 'But it makes for a personal interest. And, of course, my ancestor overlapped with Henderson.' He toyed with the possibility of claiming a close relationship between Mutton-Chops and Mitchell's expert, but decided against it; if Henderson was so well-known, then the Senator might have heard of him. 'G. F. R. Henderson.'

'Henderson?' Blissfully, Senator Cookridge didn't sound as though he knew Henderson from any other name in Queen Victoria's Army List.

'Oxford and the Staff College. And the Yorkshire Light Infantry . . . He was a younger contemporary of my ancestor – a military academic who wrote books about the war – Sherman and Grant and . . . Stonewall Jackson.' He pronounced the last name with false confidence. He had heard it somewhere, but it had an unlikely ring to it, the christian name element: in that long-lost America the christian names would more likely be actually Christian, out of the Bible. Yet that, surely, had been what Mitchell had said over the telephone – and there was an echo in his memory which confirmed it.

'Stonewall Jackson?' The Senator recognized the name, and Latimer's own half-certainty firmed up.

'That's right.' But it would be advisable to steer away from the man Jackson, who sounded more like a tail-end cricketer than a general, towards someone he could invest with more proof of his expertise. 'And Sherman, of course.'

'Sherman?' Senator Cookridge visibly perked up at the repetition of this name, as though encouraged by it.

'Yes.' Desperation once again elongated Latimer's memory. Not only had Mitchell mentioned Sherman, but there was also a recollection of prep school music lessons for the unmusical, which had been glorified sing-songs of catchy tunes from the tattered song-books of the music department, some of which had been quite dreadfully wet –

Nymphs and shepherds, come away –

– but some of which had at least been honestly patriotic –

Heart of oak are our ships,
Heart of oak are our men –

– and a few of which had been honestly jolly, if quite incomprehensible at the time –

> Allons, enfants de la patrie,
> Le jour de gloire est arrivé –

– and

> Hurrah! hurrah! we bring the Jubilee!
> Hurrah! hurrah! the flag that makes you free!
> So we sang the chorus from Atlanta to the sea,
> As we were marching through Georgia.

And that, murmured prep school memory in a loud stage-whisper, was what Mitchell and 'Bruce Catton' both had meant by *Sherman's 'March to the Sea'*, of course.

'Actually, opinions differ about Sherman, Senator.' He cocked his head knowingly. Mitchell had said something quite incomprehensible, quoting Bruce Catton, comparing what Sherman had done with what Bomber Command had done in the Second World War. But he wasn't about to chance his luck with that.

'You know about Sherman, then?'

Like the man at the top of the stairs, Latimer was just one fraction of a second ahead of the possibility of that question, reaction out-guessing action. 'I've only got a British opinion of him. It wasn't our war . . . so I'm open to argument.'

'You'll do.' Cookridge moved from one phase of estimation to the next. 'I guess you've got the background. And – I'll be frank – that's a lot more than I expected, even if it isn't the most important thing.' He paused there.

The pause lengthened. 'And what is the important thing, Senator?'

A sharp *tap-tap* punctuated the question.

'*Okay*!' Cookridge lifted his voice to the sound. 'First, you've got the time – a couple of days – three-four days, maybe . . . you sound like you've got that?'

'Possibly.'

'Possibly.' Cookridge acknowledged the qualification. 'Colonel Morris indicated as much. Second, you have the general inclination to help me – the willingness, shall we put it like that? The time and the willingness, they are really what counts. Being an expert on this old war of ours –' Cookridge held up his hand quickly ' – I know! You don't want to admit that – that's not the British way . . . But I guess you are one, and that's a bonus. But it's just a bonus, no more than that. Because it wasn't the real qualification – it wasn't what I was looking for. You've already got what I need, you see, Mister Latimer.'

He was being complimentary, if it was Howard Morris's 'brains' to which he was referring. But he was also making Latimer uneasy. 'But it was Dr Audley you were after in the first place, Senator.'

'Same thing.' Cookridge smiled. '"Not a historian", Morris said. "But the same type of man". And he was right.'

In ordinary circumstances Latimer might have taken that as derogatory, if not grossly insulting. But these were not ordinary circumstances.

'I know what you're thinking.' The Senator raised a finger.

Latimer swallowed. 'You do?'

'I surely do. You're thinking what I'd be thinking.' The smile twisted wryly. 'But we'll come back to that . . . We're talking about *types* now. The man for the job – that isn't *half* the battle. The battle's just the footnote to your decision, telling you whether you got it right or wrong. You chose the wrong general – you already lost the battle. You chose the right man – start working on the peace treaty, don't worry about the battle, that's his business.'

Latimer thought for a moment. 'Senator . . . tell me about your peace treaty.'

Cookridge stared at him for a moment, then chuckled.

41

'I like that, goddam' it! You don't even want to know what I want you to do – I like that! Morris was right, the son-of-a-bitch!'

Latimer's unease increased. 'I'd quite like to know that too.' Beneath the homespun Mid-West frankness, this old American was sharp as a needle: he had manoeuvred his victim into a position from which he could hardly withdraw now without loss of face, no matter what he wanted.

'I'll bet you do – ' Another *tap-tap* interrupted the Senator's enjoyment. '*Okay, Bob – just two minutes!*' The Senator winked at Latimer. '*Protocol* – what Bob doesn't know – I know how to keep the President of the United States waiting – I guess I'm just dam' good at apologizing, and that's the truth . . . We've got men back home who are real smart and know their business – give them a rifle and a scent, and some good ol' dogs, and they'll chase any varmint on earth, two legs or four, until it's done running. But they're the *hunters*, do you see? And hunting is what comes naturally to most men – it's in their blood from way back, when it was all that made the difference between having a full belly or an empty one . . . and some men are better at it than others, but it's something they all understand well enough. So there's no shortage of hunters.' He studied Latimer. 'But a hunter you're not, Mister Latimer.'

'No?' The Senator knew exactly what he was. But a question seemed to be required. 'And what am I then, Senator?'

'Huh! I heard it called a lot of fancy names. In the old times you were the guys who threw the bones to see how they fell, and sang the songs and made the pictures . . . to see what was true and what was false.' The Senator nodded. 'You don't look for needles in haystacks – you look at the haystack, and you know whether there's a needle in it. Right?'

It was a curious description of the work of Research

and Development. But it was not altogether wide of the mark in its homespun way, thought Latimer.

'Son, I'm going to tell you a story – ' Senator Cookridge didn't wait for confirmation of his statement ' – but it's going to have to be a short one . . . Fortunately, you already know about General Sherman – okay?'

Not okay. 'I know that he . . . marched through Georegia. To the sea, I believe?'

The Senator grinned at what he took to be scholarly modesty. 'Spreading fire and the sword sixty miles wide – "bringing the jubilee". They still remember him in those parts.' He paused. 'Ever heard of a place called Sion Crossing?'

Now the trouble was starting. '"Sion" is biblical – the Holy City, is it? The Promised Land?' He shrugged slightly. 'I can't say I have, Senator.'

Mercifully, the Senator did not seem surprised. 'Billy Sherman's boys came through there in '64. It was right on the edge of their march. But they burnt it all the same.'

Latimer nodded. This was pure *Gone With the Wind* history. Sherman seemed to have burnt practically everything.

'Sion Crossing was a great plantation, Mister Latimer. It was the home of the Alexander family – the Alexanders of Sion Crossing. The first Alexander was a Scotsman who fought the Indians and carved his fields out of the forest – had a son killed crossing the river, and built a church on the spot. And his grandson married an heiress from the coast – Marie-Louise de Brissac. And *her* grandfather was reputedly a pirate, who'd robbed the Spaniards and the English up and down the Spanish Main in his time – '

Knock knock-knock!

'I hear you!' Cookridge scowled at the door, and drew a deep breath. 'I guess I'll skip the rest until the war – James Alexander inherited in '59, after the fever took his parents. There were to younger brothers and a sister, Marie-Louise. The boys were all killed in the war – one died in a prison camp . . . James died in the trenches in '65. And Marie-Louise died of small-pox in Savannah in '66. That was the end of the Alexanders. And Sion Crossing went back to the woods.' He paused.

'Very tragic.' The pause called for some reaction. 'Authentic *Gone With the Wind* stuff, Senator. But – '

'But that's not the full story, son. Colonel James Alexander – James the Third – he was a Republican and a Scotsman at heart, even though he did fight for the Sovereign State of Georgia when it came to the war. So he kept a sizeable part of his fortune in gold, in a bank in Atlanta, and didn't give it all to "The Cause". And in '64, when Sherman got close to Atlanta, he had it moved to Sion Crossing for safety.'

Latimer nodded, remembering from both the book and the film what had happened to Atlanta in 1864. 'Very prudent.'

'Marie-Louise was running the plantation.' Cookridge looked at his watch. 'She had the strong-box buried in the garden. She reckoned, if Sherman's men came, they'd plunder the house from top to bottom – she didn't reckon on them burning it.'

'But they did – ?' Latimer couldn't see where the story was going.

'When it came to burning, she couldn't bear the thought, Mister Latimer. So she offered to buy them off – the gold in exchange for the house.'

Latimer frowned. 'They chose the house?'

Cookridge shook his head. 'They chose the gold. But she'd also sent off one of the house-slaves – one of the few who hadn't run away . . . Because there was a company of Confederate militia camped just down the road. And they turned up just as the Yankees were digging up the strong-box. So then there was a fight – a skirmish through the woods more like, as the Yankees tried to get back across the river, where their regiment was.' He shook his head. 'Maybe they thought she'd delayed them deliberately . . .

44

maybe they fired the house to delay pursuit – maybe it was just an accident . . . Nobody knows for sure.'

'But the gold?' It had to be the gold.

'They couldn't carry the strong-box and fight the Johnny Rebs – it was too heavy. So they shot open the lock and divided up what was inside – each man took what he thought he could carry, apparently. And then they fought their way through the woods, and the survivors swam the creek.'

'The survivors?'

'The Rebs killed some of them.' Cookridge nodded. 'That's how the whole story of the gold came out . . . And . . . and they reckon some of 'em drowned – the ones who'd taken the most gold, maybe . . .'

'So it's mostly at the bottom of the river?' It was odd how gold fired the imagination.

'Some of it is, sure. But with what they recovered – and Marie-Louise gave that to the Confederacy, mostly – and what the Yankees got away with . . .' The Senator shook his head '. . . there wasn't one hell of a lot to start with, son. Just one man's nest-egg in common coin and nuggets . . . No . . .'

No? But, of course, the Senator was probably a rich man. But then . . . if *treasure* was not his objective – ?

The door opened and the young man entered, flushed with conflicting priorities.

'Sir – *sir* . . . We do *have* to go now – with respect, sir.' The priorities resolved themselves. 'It's protocol, sir.'

'Protocol?' The Senator turned the full weight of his displeasure on the young man. 'Hogwash!'

'No, Sir! HRH *and* the Ambassador – *and* the Foreign Secretary – I *have* to insist, sir!' The young man rallied bravely.

The Senator stared at him, then softened before such courage. 'Okay boy – one minute – ' He swung back to Latimer.

'I could meet you later, sir,' said Latimer.

'There won't be any later.' The grey head shook regretfully. 'It's like this, Mister Latimer – I have acquired some papers – some original papers, but mostly some original research by a man who is now deceased.' Now he nodded. 'He was researching the history of one of Billy Sherman's regiments, all the way from when they mustered in Iowa, down through Chattanooga to Atlanta, and from Atlanta to the sea, and then to Virginia. And they were the boys who were at Sion Crossing.' The washed-out grey eyes narrowed. 'And he's got something I want an expert to look at, to see whether it smells right, or it smells wrong.'

Foolish! thought Latimer. 'Then you want a trained historian, sir.'

'No.' The eyes fixed him implacably. 'I want *you*, Mister Latimer. And I want you for two reasons. And one of them is because I think you're the best, and I like the look of you. And the other . . . I'll tell you that one when you report back to me.' He drew a breath. 'But I tell you this, Mister Latimer: whatever you tell me – even if you fail – you'll have a friend in me. And I never forget my friends, Mister Latimer.'

Put like that, it was as much a threat as a promise. But put another way . . . it was both an unrepeatable opportunity to establish his credentials at the highest American level – and an irresistible chance to score a point against David Audley.

'When do you want me to go, sir?'

'As soon as possible. Bob here has all the details – tickets and expense money – ' The Senator waved his hand ' – yes, I know you're not worried about that . . . but it saves time . . . My step-daughter will meet you in Atlanta – she will look after you . . . She will fill you in on the details – the *real* details . . . You can trust her – she's her mother's daughter, by God!' The eyes hardened. 'Just as I'm trusting you now, Mister Latimer – do you understand?'

However foolish it was, it mattered to the Chairman of the Atlantic Defence Committee – *that* was what he had to understand!

'Yes, sir.'

What had he got to lose?

3

Mitchell in London: Mischief

'Curiosity?' James Cable considered his friend not without well-founded suspicion. 'Vulgar curiosity?'

'Not vulgar.' It was not going to be easy, thought Mitchell – not if it was going to be done right. Though 'right', in the circumstances, was hardly the right word for it.

'Idle, then. And isn't that the curiosity which kills cats?' It was certainly not going to be easy. 'Not idle either.'

'What sort of curiosity, then?'

'It's not really curiosity at all.' The one thing that he had going for him, decided Mitchell, was that James Cable was a decent, upright, honourable man, almost an old-fashioned naval officer – a pure Colonel-Butler-appointment. But also, Butler being Butler, nobody's fool either. So, while he took responsibility as easily as he breathed air, nobody was going to push him around.

'Oh?' Cable was one degree away from returning to his report and telling Mitchell to shove off.

'Say "concern" rather. Proper concern, James.'

'Concern for the Honourable Oliver St John Latimer? Get away Paul!' Cable shook his head. 'Not you!'

'Why not? The Honourable Oliver . . . alias Fatso – '

'That's not quite fair. He's not really so bad. And he's damned clever – you must at least concede that, alias "Captain Lefevre".'

'I will concede nothing so far as Fatso is concerned, Lieutenant-Commander . . . Or should I say "Commander", since such obsequious time-serving approbation renders your promotion inevitable? I will concede *that* – I'll even put money on it: you will be carried upwards on his coat-tails when he becomes Deputy-Director.'

Cable frowned. 'You know something I don't know?'

'Very likely. I know he'll be offered the job – much to his chagrin, since he was aiming at higher things. But he'll take it. In fact, he may already have done so.'

'You know too much, Mitchell.'

'So I am often told. *"Larned a little 'fore iver some lads was born, tho' I never sarved in the Queen's Navy, where I'm told yeou'm taught to use your eyes"*.' Mitchell grinned. 'The comings and goings of the last few days . . . and Fatso had a long session with Jack Butler on Thursday. And now there's an envelope addressed to Jack in Fatso's own fair hand, lying in Mrs Harlin's in-tray and marked "Personal" – not "Private and confidential", mark you . . . and not "Urgent" either. Just "Personal". A letter of acceptance – one pound will get you five, Admiral Cable, if you're a betting man.'

'Not with you, I'm not.' Cable was comparing what his friend had told him against what he knew. 'You know both sides of the cards, I'm thinking. I'm but a poor Jack Tar, honest and bluff.'

'More bluff than honest. So tell me – '

'Where does David Audley come into this?'

'He doesn't. David is a man lamentably without any ambition – except to cause trouble for the rest of us . . . by doing his own thing in his own way.'

'But he must have been in line for the top job.' They had been through this many times, but never before with Mitchell's present certainty.

'Then he has been passed over for it – like Latimer. Or he has refused, if they offered it to him . . . which is more likely.' Mitchell stared out of the window. 'Jack Butler will get the top job. After all, he's been doing it quite effectively for two years or more – only a man like Jack would have put up with such a bloody scandalous lack of decision . . . particularly as he hates the job.' Mitchell turned. 'That's the delicious irony of it all: Jack has worked his way up to where he doesn't want to be by sheer loyalty and devotion to duty . . . and, perhaps above all, by actual decency, you know. Old Jack gets results, but he's also above suspicion, so they know he'll never land them with some dreadful intelligence scandal – which HMG must find very beguiling . . . Not least because the Opposition – and the CND, and all that lot . . . they'll be looking for something juicy and nasty. And they won't get it from Research and Development while he's running the show . . . In fact, they probably never thought twice about Latimer and Audley – it's Old Jack for Gold, Silver and Bronze, in that order.'

'But Audley and Latimer are both twice as bright.'

Mitchell made a doubtful face. 'I don't know about that. Jack's no slouch when it comes to plain common-sense – and being honest and honourable gives him one hell of an advantage over most people, 'cause they can never make sense of what he's doing and they lose time coming to the wrong conclusion . . . Say, maybe they're half as bright again. But David doesn't suffer fools gladly enough . . . and he's the original maverick steer that looks like a rogue elephant.' The doubtful face contorted. 'Which we both know well enough, for God's sake! Because he's bloody well nearly done for me a couple of times – and you once, to my certain knowledge . . . It's only because I fancy his wife and adore his little daughter that I put up with him, James – and that's a fact!'

'Or adore his wine cellar and fancy his old-boy contacts?' murmured Cable nastily. 'And Oliver St John Latimer?'

'Fatso? Fatso is a Philistine and a basket-hanger. He probably wears a tartan tie – and Ruskin says that any man who wears a tartan tie will undoubtedly be damned everlastingly.'

'What?' It was fatally easy to lose Paul Mitchell's train of thought. 'A . . . basket-hanger – in a tartan tie?'

'Kipling.' Mitchell waved a cultured hand. 'You go on expensive jaunts to Sweden to learn about Russian submarines – I get sent to Cheltenham, and never when the races are on there either, damn it! But that at least has enabled me to study the Latimer-Audley handicap race – and to brush up on Kipling.'

'What does Kipling have to do with them?'

'Audley means Kipling. He quotes the bloody man all the time, so I'm into the business of out-quoting him – he hates that.' Mitchell grinned again. 'Mr Kind in *Stalky & Co* – he was Stalky and Co's great enemy – I can't work out which of them David identifies with . . . Beetle or M'Turk or Stalky himself . . . he changes rôle most confusingly. But Mr King was their Latin master at the school, and a damn good one too . . . but their enemy. And Oliver St John Latimer is Mr King – Audley's Mr King . . . who wore a tartan tie and a basket-hanger, whatever that means. In fact, "the king of basket-hangers" – Fatso to the life.'

Cable rocked uneasily. 'But our new Deputy-Director – if you're right?'

'Oh – I'm right, *Commander* Cable. And that's what makes my curiosity not idle *cat's* curiosity, but the real *need-to-know* stuff – "intelligence relevant to the Defence of the Realm", if you want the small print of my strictly unofficial request to the Duty Office – ' Mitchell appealed to friendship over duty ' – which I hope, for old times' sake, you won't enter into the log – ?'

Cable looked even more unhappy. 'You tell me *why*, Paul . . . and then maybe I'll tell you *what*. Okay?'

Mitchell thought for a moment. 'Okay?' Then he thought for another moment. 'Last night . . . Fatso phoned you up here – right?'

'Right.' What they both knew could not be denied.

'Right! When has he ever done that before?'

'How should I know?' Already Cable might have an inkling of what Mitchell was aiming at, but he wanted more. 'I'm only – we're *both* only . . . acting duty officers, each of us . . . duty officers – during the holiday period – like now?'

'But you read the log every morning. That's down in the book of words. But it's only routine, because we're not Cloak and Dagger – we're Research and Development. So . . . nobody phones us here, except to find out where somebody else is – and mostly where somebody else is next morning, because there's no hurry . . . We just want to check up on something, or get a second opinion – nothing urgent. So usually . . . *usually*, we don't get any calls at all – *right*?'

Another thing not to be denied. So Cable shrugged.

Mitchell nodded. 'So Fatso phoned last night. And Fatso *never* phones – or never until last night . . . Because he's always doing something far too important – and far too buttoned-up and well-organized and academic – to disturb his dinner, or his gardening, or whatever . . . but nothing *trivial* – not ever . . . That's not his style, James – you know that, for God's sake!'

Mitchell was extrapolating now. But he was doing so from shared experience of the duty log, also not to be denied; and from the assumption that Oliver St John Latimer would not ring in casually, but only in desperation, in some extremity.

'It's out of character, I agree.' Cable shrugged. 'But there are always exceptions to any rule. And . . .'

And hovered between them in the motionless air of the room, because . . . by reason of Mitchell's purely accidental presence in the duty officer's room last evening, they both knew where that led them.

'The American Civil War, James? For God's sake – you gave him something about the *Monitor* – about which you know bugger all except what you read in *The Times* yesterday, or the day before – '

'I know quite a lot about the *Monitor*.' On naval history Cable was not about to let Paul Mitchell bully him: he ought to know as much about naval history as Mitchell did. 'Don't push your luck, Mitchell.'

'Okay – okay! The first ironclad turret-ship! No offence

meant, Commander.' Mitchell retreated. 'But he didn't want anything about that – he wasn't interested in what you offered him, was he?'

'Perhaps not.' They were still haggling over shared intelligence from the previous evening. 'You gave him something better.'

'I gave him mostly half-digested cod's-wallop. And he lapped it up like it was David's Château Pichon-Longueville-Lalande . . . But, if there's one sure thing, it's that Fatso knows sod-all about the American Civil War: he doesn't know Shiloh and Gettysburg and the Shenandoah Valley from any of the innumerable holes in the London-to-Birmingham motorway, for a fact.'

'So what's new?' For a fact Cable shared Oliver St John Latimer's lack of knowledge. 'And you do?'

'Not really. Except that it's a bloody interesting war, I'll say that for it – and I've just been refreshing my memory of it . . . Because it was the standard British Staff College subject in the old days – that at least is the truth . . . Colonel Henderson *was* one smart operator – and that's another fact.' He gestured disarmingly. 'Also . . . when it comes to enthusiastic fire-and-the-sword, the North did a pretty good job on the South – almost as good as the French and the other Europeans did in their civil wars.'

'Mitchell – what are you drivelling on about?'

Mitchell stared at him for a second, and then shook his head. 'I'm drivelling on about Fatso, James – that's all. For him to be interested in the American Civil War was way out enough. But for him to come back to the duty officer – that's not just out of character, it's downright suspicious.' Mitchell cocked his head. 'Because it's something he'd never do unless he really didn't know which way to turn – do you see?'

It was something which had not occurred to Cable the evening before, even when he had turned to Mitchell for help, out of his friend's accidental presence and his knowledge of his friend's knowledge of military history.

And Mitchell had left thereafter, to go drinking and play dominoes . . . Or had he? That was what Cable was thinking now.

'What have you done, Paul?'

'Nothing, my dear fellow! Or, nothing much . . .'

'What did you do?'

Mitchell gestured vaguely. 'I only asked Gammon, down below, about Latimer's call – where it came from –'

'What?'

'It was on an open line – you warned him yourself, old boy. So it wasn't scrambled, or anything like that. I simply asked Gammon where I might contact our Mr Latimer. It was all above board, James.'

'What did he say?'

Mitchell bridled slightly. 'Well . . . he gave me the Oxbridge Club in the end, when I pushed him a bit.'

'The Oxbridge?'

'He gets there sometimes, after work. The drinks are marvellously cheap – you wouldn't know . . . but they are. David goes there too, as it happens . . .'

'You went to the Oxbridge last night?'

'Well . . . yes . . . I mean, not directly after Fatso's call – I had to play this dominoes match first, down the pub . . . and get quite disastrously trounced by those rascally accountants from Procter and Sykes in the Haymarket – at five pence a spot and the drinks. It cost me a small fortune.'

'Why?'

'Well, I think they've got a system –'

'Not the damn dominoes! Why . . . why did you go and check on Latimer? Is that what you did?'

'Yes, damn it! And I've been telling you *why*, James: he acted out of character, and that makes me curious. And when I'm curious I want to know more, that's all. So now I want to know if Fatso's done anything since he phoned – and that's all, too!' Mitchell shrugged. 'It's not much to ask. If I'd been on last night I'd already know.' Another shrug. 'I already know he phoned in again, this morning. But the log says just "routine check". Was it just a routine check?'

It was Cable who was curious now. 'What did you find out at the Oxbridge, Paul?'

'You really want blood, don't you!'

'If I'm going to break the rules I do – yes. What happened at the Oxbridge?'

Mitchell made a face at him, and swivelled his head as though his neck hurt him and he was exercising tender muscles gingerly. 'Exactly . . . I don't know . . .'

'But something *did* happen?' Cable was beginning to worry. 'Come on, Paul!'

Mitchell shook his head. 'I didn't want to push things too far . . . I'm damn certain the Steward there . . . that's Wilberforce, who was a college scout at Oxford before he was recruited by the club committee . . . I'm damn certain he knows more than he's telling – that was one reason why they took him on, because he knows when to put the telescope to his blind eye, as well as when to hold his tongue . . . But you're right: something odd did happen there last night. And there is one thing that I do know.'

'Which is?'

'Howard Morris was there. And at just about the same time that Fatso phoned us – or . . . just about the right time *before* he phoned us anyway.'

'Yes?' That was inviting a cause-and-effect conclusion.

'But he was looking for David Audley – that's what they said at the bar. And there were some rum types swanning about upstairs after that.'

'Rum types?'

'Chaps in ill-fitting dinner-jackets, with bulges in the wrong places. That was all I could get before Wilberforce cut off further communication. "Members' private business is their own" is his motto . . . when someone's slipped a crisp Florence Nightingale into his sweaty palm, of course.' Paul Mitchell gave Cable a jaundiced look.

55

'But David Audley fits very well with Howard Morris. Only . . .'

'He doesn't fit with Latimer?'

'He doesn't fit at all with Fatso. Certainly not well enough to argue about who won the battle of Gettysburg.' Mitchell tried to look innocent. 'So what about this morning's routine call, then?'

'It was just routine. "Any Calls? Any red star post?" That sort of thing. But . . .' Cable looked as though he was tempted to give evil for good, but only briefly '. . . he confirmed that letter in Colonel Butler's in-tray. And he said he'd be unavailable for a few days, but he'd be ringing in at regular intervals.'

'Unavailable?'

They looked at each other.

'Just that.' They both knew that that was another action out-of-character: Oliver St John Latimer was a notorious non-taker of leave, a notorious workaholic. 'So what do we do?'

Mitchell thought hard for a moment, frowning with the effort. 'We can run a trace on his calls, I suppose.'

'It would have to be logged.'

'Which means he'll see it? Point taken.' Mitchell smiled. 'Why should you stick your neck out for my curiosity? But . . . I'm in the barrel here on Sunday, and I don't give a bugger what Oliver St John Latimer sees or doesn't see. So I'll run the trace then.' He nodded at his friend. 'Probably better so, actually – he'll keep for twenty-four hours. And no one'll be able to accuse me of indecent haste.'

Cable stared back at him rather doubtfully. 'You think there *is* something, don't you!'

Mitchell shook his head. 'No. No . . . that would be pitching it too strong by a long way. If it was David . . . now, David is capable of all sorts of eccentricities – as we both know. But Oliver St John Latimer, he doesn't stray from the straight and narrow, so the odds are against.

'A-serving of Her Majesty, Mr Gammon.' He could never quite pluck up enough courage to address Gammon as "Sar-Major", as both Butler and Audley did from the eminence of their military service. 'The ceaseless, sleepless watch, you know.'

'Oh yes?' Gammon studied the duty book. 'But . . . you're not on until Sunday midday – ?' He looked up again at Mitchell, curious as always about deviations from routine; for that, after all, was one of the things he was paid to do. 'How's that new book of yours comin' on, then? The 1915 one?'

Mitchell shook his head. 'I don't think much of that is going to get written this weekend.' He felt in his pocket for the paper he had prepared. 'This is where I'll be the next twenty-four hours, where I can be contacted quickly. Okay?'

'Right you are, sir.' Gammon slid the paper under his bulldog clip, his curiosity satisfied, which was neither vulgar nor idle, but purely professional and quite unconcerned.

The thing was done, thought Mitchell again. Now nature had to take its course, for better or worse.

4

Latimer in America: The Promised Land

It was hot as hell in Atlanta.

And, worse than hot, it was humid – was hell humid? wondered Latimer morosely. Probably it was, since it must be designed for maximum discomfort, and that was a combination undoubtedly achieved here, besides which the very worst that England could manage was laughably temperate. Except that the effort of laughing was beyond him in such an oven.

The heat enveloped him, and three breaths of it were enough – one in disbelief, one in realization and the third only forced on him by the time required to retreat back into the terminus.

From the relative comfort of the interior he took another look around, outside and inside, trying to impose the wretched woman's face from memory on to any of the faces within range. The snapshot had revealed only head and shoulders, so he didn't really know whether she was tall or short, thin or fat. Neither plain nor pretty, and certainly neither ugly nor beautiful, was all memory gave him back . . . although there had been cheekbones . . . ? High cheeckbones, somehow suggesting height and thinness?

He swivelled around, looking for cheekbones, and hoped that she wouldn't be too tall, to the extent that she would be able to look down on him. There were certainly women enough to choose from, all shapes and sizes and ages, some of them quite good-looking, and some of them – more of them, in fact – decidedly plump, even undoubtedly fat. And the men too . . . there were some comfortingly tubby men around, beside whose circumference his own excess inches were unremarkable, if not insignificant –

Damn! He was not meant to be studying *men* (but there

was another splendid fattie; and the way that tall, heavily armed, uniformed guard filled his immaculate uniform suggested that he was also heading for spectacular bulk) – no, it was a *woman* –

The guard started to turn, and Latimer decided to give up his search before he became a suspicious foreign loiterer, the old instinct for unobtrusiveness asserting itself out of the distant past.

He walked meekly to the nearest bench and sat down, tucking his travelling case beside him. Something had gone wrong, but it was nothing to worry about: simply, the wretched daughter – step-daughter – was late, and as this was a big airport, with all the traffic which big airports generated (and, no doubt, this being the home of the automobile, even more traffic here, hard though that was to imagine after Gatwick) there was nothing remarkable in that. And, anyway, even is she never turned up, it was of no real importance, for this wasn't *work*, and was therefore not important. It was, after all, only a favour.

His eye rested on a portly couple chivvying two identically T-shirted children, and wondered what the slogan 'ATLANTA BRAVES' meant. Atlanta had certainly braved General William Tecumseh Sherman, and had been burned to the ground for its pains. But as he could not read the small print on the shirt, the present danger it was braving was lost on him.

Perhaps it was the temperature outside: that would have to be braved sooner or later. Indeed, if that was the seasonal norm for Georgia in late August and early September, then here was an extra insight into what he had been reading about on the plane, which none of his historians had thought to point out. For it had been just about now – the city had fallen on September 6 – that the bone-headed General Hood had contested the place with that egregious hypocrite Sherman, who hated war but was in the direct line from Scipio Africanus at Carthage, via Tilly at Magdeburg and Cromwell at Drogheda, to Hitler at Rotterdam and Coventry and the Allies at Dresden . . . But, regardless of his vestigial memory of historical crimes, if that was typical Georgian weather outside, 1860s and 1980s alike, the siege of Atlanta must have been a truly hellish business for the farm boys in blue and grey, from North and South, Union and Confederate . . . Except that they must at least have been acclimatized from birth to it, with only the fittest surviving – this was Darwin's own lifetime, after all, and he must have observed nineteenth century human beings long before he had set eyes on those Galapagos finches and turtles . . . But . . . it was one thing to plough and sow, and reap and mow – the blue-coated Northern boys from Illinois and Iowa and Michigan in Sherman's armies would have done all those things; presumably, some of the boys from Georgia and Carolina had had negroes to do the cotton-picking, but there must have been many more who had done their own hard work . . . But, whatever they did, none of them had been trained to march and fight and kill each other in such hellish weather, surely?

That was the mystery which had long eluded him, though not with these strangers from Georgian plantations and Senator Cookridge's endless cornbelt, but with his own slightly older peers, and their immediate European ancestors: *what was it like, what was it really like, to get out of the trench and to stand up amongst the bullets? And what had nerved them to do it, in that last second, when the legs took charge, pushing them upwards and forwards against higher reason and lower commonsense alike?*

Well . . . it was something he would never know, even if he dared to make someone tell him, and they tried to do so. For it was not something that could be told, only a thing to be experienced; and he was now past the point, both in years and in seniority, where he would ever acquire such trench-truth. In fact, to be bleakly honest with himself, safely past, since he had no great confidence in his physical courage, but only the gravest doubts –

Stand in the trench, Achilles, flame-capped,
And shout for me

– that was a proper sentiment for braver, younger men, but not for him now, if ever.

And for thinner men, too. He peeked around again surreptitiously, only half-looking for the woman, and felt a small inner glow of satisfaction – even felt, against bitter experience, the beginnings of approval of America. Disapproval of those extra inches in the wrong direction had always been unfair, the more so as in three-quarters of the world a certain fullness of the figure was the hallmark of success and importance and superiority, not of self-indulgence and lack of self-restraint. It had been just his bad luck to live in the other quarter, where fatness was a crime.

But here, at least, he was safe – and doubly safe, because even if the silly woman didn't turn up at all, and the whole trip proved abortive through no fault of his own, it would be of no consequence to his career. It simply didn't matter: that had been the final calculation in his decision, the final safety factor which had stilled the small voice of caution, with the Senator himself merely confirming matters . . .

The Senator had been disingenious, naturally. It was more than that, he wanted: he wanted the miracle itself, just that and no more. Because, if Oliver St John Latimer was allegedly so good, Senator Thomas Cookridge was undoubtedly a winner, and he wanted the lost treasure of Sion Crossing very badly indeed to go to such eccentric lengths to find it.

And that was where the really interesting questions started for Oliver St John Latimer. It no longer surprised him that he had the job, because that was due to a series of wholly explicable accidents in which he had played a starring rôle.

Very simply, David Audley was the perfect and natural

63

choice, not so much because he was an historian, and a foreigner who would bring a fresh approach to an old mystery or even because of his well-known weakness for weird assignments (Audley's overweening curiosity was his Achilles heel: Howard Morris would know that as well as anyone) . . . but simply because he had a proven track-record as a finder of things long-lost. And he, Latimer, was probably only here in Atlanta now because Howard Morris, in his extremity, had led the Senator to believe that, since Audley and Latimer were the brains of Research and Development (which was *true*), then Latimer and Audley were a team (which was palpably and laughably *untrue*).

No . . . but teams and laughter aside (though it *was* a good joke – and all the better for being at Audley's expense for once) . . . *no*, what was truly interesting was the as-yet unanswered question of why Senator Thomas Cookridge needed the Sion Crossing treasure.

He had promised a full and frank answer after Latimer had reported back, but Latimer had long experience of unfulfilled promises and deviously sketchy answers in the aftermaths of assignments, successful or not. However, since he had almost equally long experience of finding answers for himself, for his own satisfaction if not for his advancement, that was not particularly worrying.

In any case, at least it had nothing to do with the hypothetical treasure's intrinsic value. For what little research he had been able to carry out on the Senator, in default of being able to go back to R & D and with time pressing hard, had revealed one thing for certain: the Senator was a very rich man, as secure financially as he was politically. So the vulgar corruption of the profit motive was not something to be feared.

So there must be some other sort of profit involved, in some other and very different currency –

He shivered suddenly, and knew that it was not because of the contrast between the air-conditioned coolness of the terminal and the memory of those breaths of hellfire-heated-air outside. It was the knowledge that the other currencies included among them notes bearing higher "promise-to-pay" legends, in exchange for things which mere money couldn't buy. And . . . *and some of those things were very dangerous indeed, equally if you needed them or if you had them for sale . . . So –*

'Mistah La*tee*mah, sah?'

Latimer focussed on the very clean and well-polished floor of the terminal, at which he had been staring but not seeing a fraction of a second before; and also saw, on the edge of his vision on the floor, a pair of huge and very clean and well-polished and expensive shoes.

He thought . . . *no woman had a voice that deep, never mind feet that size, to fill those shoes* . . . and looked up from the floor slowly, controlling his reaction. And up. And up –

The man was very black. And very thin. But, even more than black and thin, he was very, very tall. He was so tall that it was quite understandable he should be stooping slightly beneath a ceiling ten feet above his head. And he had a huge grin on his face.

It wasn't true that all black men looked the same to white men, just as all Europeans and Chinese were supposed to look the same as each other to each other: he had seen this black men ten minutes before, lounging head-and-shoulders against a wall somewhere – where?

Here, obviously. The question gyrated inside his brain, sweeping all others aside. They could wait –

'Mister La*tee*mah?'

'Latimer.' Whatever was about to happen, it must not be permitted to happen to anyone named La*tee*mah.

'Mister Latimer.' The black giraffe's accent changed, transformed in that instant from Deep South to British.

'Yes.' Latimer frowned before he could stop himself,

65

too many new unanswered questions crowding him. Absurdly, he felt that he had somehow given himself away.

'I'm sorry, sir – I missed you, sitting here.' The black man reached out with an impossibly long arm. 'Your bag, sir?'

'Yes.' Latimer looked down quickly to the hand closing on his bag's handle, then back upwards, conscious that he would still be looking upwards when he had stood up himself. 'Who are you?'

'Kingston, sir.' The black man lifted the bag effortlessly, straightening himself towards the ceiling. 'From Kingston, Jamaica. If you think of Kingston from Kingston then you'll never forget my name, sir.'

Latimer stood up and continued to look up. But he was done with being stupid. 'I was expecting Miss Cookridge. Where is she?'

Miss Cookridge. For a *step*-daughter that wasn't right, but perhaps the Americans had different conventions – that, both in general and in this particular detail, he had not been able to establish, to his present regret.

'Yes, sir – Miss Cookridge.' The black man was already moving towards the exit on legs even longer than his arms, so that Latimer had to hurry unbecomingly to keep up with him. 'She is waiting for us, at the car . . . We were a little late, sir – on the inter-state, there was this pick-up had an argument with a sixteen-wheeler, and we were delayed somewhat, you see.'

The British accent was not quite perfect, but very nearly so –

Then the blast of super-heated humid air, with most of its life-giving cool oxygen boiled away, buffeted Latimer into speechlessness. All he could hope for now was that Miss Cookridge and the car were not far away.

Lucy Hennebury Cookridge? he had turned the Senator's snapshot over, and that had been written on the back of it. And although 'Hennebury' was neither a particularly memorable or melodious name, never mind

66

recognizable in any historical context, it was at least not actively outlandish, like William *Tecumseh* Sherman and General the Right Reverend *Leonidas* Polk, the Confederate warrior-bishop who had stopped a cannon-ball fired by one of Tecumseh's gunners on the retreat to Atlanta –

God Almighty! He was back to marvelling that anybody in his right mind had been able to conduct military operations in such ridiculous weather conditions as this! But that was the other singularly unpleasant thing about military operations down the ages: they had all too frequently been blithely conducted in ridiculous conditions – the mud of Petersburg and Passchendaele, the snows of Moscow and the Ardennes, the humid jungles of Guadalcanal and Kohima, and the egg-frying heat of the Western Desert. They had all agreed on a fine disregard for any sort of day-to-day human comfort, apart from the overriding general discomfort of being killed outright, if not maimed and jolted back to be blood-poisoned by some over-worked drunken surgeon in a cloud of flies. So this, across a few yards of Atlanta car park, was no more than par for the usual battlefield course, give or take a hundred years of progress.

There was a female standing up beside a very battered and quite breathtakingly hideous car – a car hideous even by the standards of cars he had passed already, which all had *consumer durable* written all over them, being plainly designed for the scrap-heap as quickly as possible, their durability rusted and dented and consumed.

Damn! He was letting the heat and his doubts about Mr Kingston of Kingston get to him, fed by his anti-American prejudices! Naples on a bad day could be almost as bad as this; and Kingston was more British than American, judging by that accent; and if his own British car was so much better than all those around him, why wasn't this car park full of British cars – instead of American . . or Japanese?

The woman, though –

God! She was tall, too!

And thin –

He paused, suddenly irresolute because the tallness and thinness of Miss Lucy Hennebury Cookridge was really no more than an extrapolation from that one quick glance at the Senator's snapshot, and on slightly closer scrutiny this woman didn't particularly resemble that one: that one's hair had been fluffed-out in some no-doubt-fashionable style, and this one's was pulled severely back; and this one's collar-bones were apparent, when that one's had been decently covered; and, above all, this one's cheek-bones were hidden behind huge sunglasses, which also blacked out the candid, half-amused eyes which Miss Lucy Hennebury Cookridge had turned on the photographer.

And, in any case . . . he converted his doubt into a turn-back towards Mr Kingston of Kingston, who was no longer ahead of him – who was no longer even beside him –

Mr Kingston of Kingston was performing a strange angry dance ten yards behind him, swinging the case (which was a lot heavier than it looked, with all the books in it which were compressing his two-three days' change of linen) – swinging all that weight wildly as he stamped and twisted.

'Shit!' exclaimed Mr Kingston, angrily.

Latimer stared at the dancing negro. Of course, negroes *did* dance. They sang and they danced, and in the former times of Generals Sherman and Hood they picked cotton hereabouts, and were bought and sold for their pains. And fifteen years afterwards they had caught the British Army on the hop in Zululand, and had left very few survivors to tell the tale, as that visiting Afrikaner colonel had reminded him only recently, in a very different context, to support his view that the British did not understand *blek men*.

'I beg your pardon?' He certainly didn't understand this black man.

'Ffff . . . *dawgs*!' The dance ended with a curious pirouette.

'What?' Latimer could feel the eyes-behind-the-sunglasses hitting him between the shoulders. All appearances to the contrary – and although that rusty consumer durable contradicted the Senator's image – it *was* the same woman, he decided.

Mr Kingston grimaced at him. 'I have just trodden in some dog-shit, Mr Latimer.'

'Oh?' What threw Latimer was the near-perfect Stratford-atte-Bowe BBC English pronunciation. It was almost an Oxford voice: he could have heard it in Fellows' Quad at Oxford – in fact, he had seen Hugh Dymoke execute something like that same dance after stepping in something deposited by one of Professor Gerrard's spaniels, which habitually defecated outside his staircase. Strange –

The negro was staring past him. 'Miss Lucy – '

Latimer junked the memory of Hugh Dymoke, and Professor Gerrard and his spaniels and their calling-cards – all dust now, with Colonel Pienaar's dead redcoats and victorious Zulus – and turned to concentrate on the Senator's step-daughter.

'Mr Latimer.' She came from behind the car, and even in flat heels she looked down on h' i.

'Miss Cookridge.' It wasn't her fault that she was elongated. But somehow the assumption of her step-father's name offended his sensibilities. No doubt it carried more clout, but it was as without pride as a flag of convenience.

'I'm sorry we weren't here to meet you.' She held out a slender hand. 'We were delayed.'

'So I hear.' About thirty, give or take a few years depending on good or bad fortune. And, although he was no expert on the regional accents of America, neither a product of her step-father's corn belt nor a Southern Belle from the Confederate States of America.

'Kingston told you?' She smiled down at him. 'It's our

ridiculous speed limit. At least on your . . . motorways you can outrun the big trucks on the outside lane, and you're safe there anyway. Here they'll come alongside you, and then forget you're there and push you off the road. It can be quite terrifying.'

There was English time in that voice, as well as knowledge of English roads.

'You've lived in England, Miss Cookridge?' It unsettled him to know so little about her – to know really nothing at all about her when by now she might know quite a lot about him: it was something like the reverse of the situations to which he was accustomed.

'Didn't my step-father tell you?' The darkened glass concealed most of her expression. 'About me?'

'Er . . . no, not actually.' Latimer was beginning to sweat beneath his lightest summer suit. 'We didn't have a great deal of time together, as a matter of fact.'

'But he convinced you.'

'Convinced me?' The oven-heat battered Latimer.

'He can be very persuasive.' Her mouth smiled. 'I guess that's an essential political skill. Or would it count as a virtue?'

'Umm . . .' He took refuge behind the non-committal sound while he tried to think. 'I don't know that he convinced me of anything. He did interest me . . .' It was no good: there was sweat under his collar now – he was starting to melt. 'Is it always as hot as this in America?'

She stared at him for a second. 'Oh, Mr Latimer – I'm *sorry* – Kingston!'

'It's probably snowing in England.' Mr Kingston of Kingston spring-heeled past Latimer, as cool as a cumcumber – if there were such things as long black cucumbers. 'Keys, Miss Lucy.'

Miss Lucy threw the keys rather inaccurately, but Kingston fielded them like a West Indian third slip, without apparent effort. And then, mercifully, he inserted them into an immaculate Volvo Estate parked next to the battered consumer durable, tossing Latimer's case into the back and then opening the rear doors with a flourish and a melon-grin which revealed more teeth than Latimer had ever seen before in one human mouth. 'If you white folks will kindly enter *de kay-ridge* it will be mah pleasure an' mah privilege to transport y'll to de ol' plantation.'

Not a Zulu, thought Latimer. But definitely not an ordinary West Indian either, in addition to being definitely a liar: this was a black man as sure of himself and as confident in his tall blackness as Miss Lucy Hennebury Cookridge was in her name and her tall whiteness.

And she was a liar, too – or was he making too much of that false explanation, falling into his occupational hazard of searching for a deeper motive behind what was in reality no more than a social excuse?

Probably. But meanwhile, anyway, the inside of the car was even more swelteringly hellish, full of molten air, excluding all further thought. What he wouldn't give for a pure shivering draught of English winter!

And the windows were closed tight, so that as they moved he reached instinctively to lower his, though more in faint hope than in certain expectation of relief.

Kingston twisted in his seat. 'U-uh, Mister La*tee*mah! Doan you go lettin' in that ol' *Gargah* ay-eer, now! This here car'll cool you down, if'n you give her a chance.'

'Oh, for God's sake, do shut up, Kingston!' snapped Lucy Cookridge. 'I'm sorry, Mr Latimer – Oliver, can I call you? If I'm going to have to apologize all the time . . . Oliver – it isn't just because you're English – because you're a foreigner . . .' She turned the huge dark circles on Latimer '. . . it's because Kingston has this hang-up, you see.'

Hang-up? Latimer was experiencing his own hang-up, trying to assimilate his first encounter with America outside the airport, which he wanted to be a moment of truth delivered from preconception and prejudice. But . . . just as big airports were all the same, so the rushing

71

motorways surrounding them must be all the same; and his images of Atlanta were confused by the only certain pictures he had seen of the place during the last twenty-four hours, which dated from Sherman's wrath-of-God visitation in 1864, full of cannon and stiffly-posed Union soldiery, and trenches, and shell-blasted ruins in war-desolated scenery; and trenches, and this . . . *this* was as far, or even further, from Atlanta in '65 as Berlin in '83 was from Berlin in'45, for a guess!

'Hang-up?' Now that he had raised the window, there was – there *distinctly* was – a breath of cold air on his legs . . . Cold, beautifully cold, air: God bless the Swedes! 'What hang-up?'

'He thinks he's inferior.' Miss Lucy's certainty out-ranked Kingston's. 'South of the Mason and Dixon line he always get like this . . . I think he probably *is* inferior.'

'You *raht*, Miss Lucy!' Kingston slapped the steering-wheel with one hand, then twisted it nonchalantly to overtake an enormous truck with the other. 'Ah doan *think* ah'm inferior – ah *knows* it! Ah'm a *mo-tee*, is what ah am.'

The car shuddered as they overtook the truck, which seemed to go on forever beside them until they were at last free of it, its innumerable wheels screaming alongside Latimer for far too long for peace-of-mind.

'Mo-tee?' The statement invited another question, and if Kingston was in an answering mood so much the better. It was when people talked, seriously or not, that they imparted information. 'What is a . . . motee?'

'Now yo' is askin', Mistah La*tee*mah!' Kingston was plainly delighted with the inquiry. 'See, dere's de *Motees*, an' dere's de *Doodas*. An' dere's de *Moanbacks*. An' ah sho' wish ah wuz a moanback . . . but ah's not.' He shook his head. 'Ah sho is not.'

'Do shut up, Kingston,' said Lucy Cookridge wearily.

'No. Miz Lucy! Better he should know he in *Garga* now . . . de motees, Mistah La*tee*mah – dey in de hotels, wid de white towel over de arm, an' de teapot in de han', an' day sez "Anyone fo' mottee?" An' they pours motee for de white ladies'n'gempmums . . . But de doodas – dey is a heap smarter'n de motees, who jus' down from de trees . . . Dey de ones stan' by de bus-stop an' sez "Hey man, dooda bus stop he-ah?"'

'Kingston – '

'But de moanbacks – dey is the smartest of all – dey like de ones Pres' Abram Lincoln give de guns an' de blue suits to. 'Cept mebbe dey a mite too smart, 'cause dey de ones de Confedrut gempmums done shot at Fort Pillow, when dey catches dem in de blue suits . . . But ah guesses you knows all 'bout Fort Pillow, Mister La*tee*mah, huh?' Kingston turned towards Latimer.

'Kingston!' Lucy Cookridge snapped into the pause, saving Latimer from the necessity of having to admit that he'd never heard of Fort Pillow, or from the temptation of flannelling a lie with the facts that Kingston had given him about what must have been a massacre of negro troops by the Confederates. 'I wish you wouldn't – *watch the road, for God's sake!*'

Noise filled the car. It had been building up while Kingston had been speaking, Latimer realized, but his concern for Fort Pillow had somehow damped it down. But now there was an even more enormous truck beside them, with even more wheels – a great brute towering above them, its high cab ornamented with stainless-steel pipes belching diesel-exhaust like a steam-engine, a thing far bigger than any vehicle he had seen on any motorway, or autoroute or autobahn, a true juggernaut –

Then suddenly his examination of the monster ceased to be academic as it began to move inexorably out of its own lane into theirs, as though they weren't beside it at all, crowding them on to a hard shoulder littered with pieces of tyre-tread.

Latimer opened his mouth, but no sound came out of it.

A piece of tyre-tread bumped underneath them and

then banged frighteningly as it bounced up to hit the underside of the Volvo. The car swerved slightly, then straightened.

'Slow down, Kingston!' ordered Lucy.

The car didn't slow. Instead it suddenly accelerated with a burst of blessed Swedish horse-power which pressed Latimer back in his seat. For a moment the noise enveloping them increased, then abruptly died away, reduced to that only of their own engine as they pulled ahead of the truck.

'Jee-*sus*!' Kingston was holding the steering-wheel with both hands. 'That's one cowboy in a hurry!'

'Fall back,' Lucy ordered. 'Let him pass.'

'No way, lady.' Kingston shook his head. 'I'm putting some road between us.'

'The highway patrol will get us.'

'Better them than him.' Kingston sniffed. 'Besides, if he thinks he can hit seventy, then they probably don't police this stretch much. And another ten-fifteen minutes and we'll be off the inter-state.'

'At this speed we will. You're not in England now, remember.'

Latimer wished he was in England now. For now he would be cool and quiet in his own soft bed, and asleep.

'What – ' his voice croaked embarrassingly ' – what on earth happened back there?'

Kingston chuckled. 'Man – he jus' done clean forgot we wuz they-ah!'

'What?' The negro's return to *Gone With the Wind* language irritated Latimer.

Lucy Cookridge drew an equally irritated breath. 'As I was saying . . . I wish you wouldn't affect that ridiculous phoney accent, Kingston. It isn't particularly accurate, and it certainly isn't funny. And Oliver must find it both boring and incomprehensible.'

Latimer found himself warming to Lucy Cookridge. Or, since *warming* in this pestiferous climate was hardly a desirable condition, 'cooling pleasantly' might be more accurate.

He looked at her gratefully. 'I think I did almost understand, Miss Cookridge – '

'Lucy.' She smiled.

'Ah . . . Lucy. Yes . . . but not quite.' He smiled back, but decided that he didn't want to antagonize Kingston altogether just yet. 'He forgot about us, Mr Kingston?'

'Kingston . . . Oliver.' The black man accepted his olive branch with a suggestion of scorn. 'In the old days it was the engine-drivers who were the romantic figures. The railroads ripped the people off, but there were songs about the trains and the drivers – Casey Jones and all that . . . but now it's the truckers that make the running. Casey Jones would be behind the wheel of one of those big bastards now – "King of the Road", he'd be.'

Latimer frowned. Little boys had wanted to be engine-drivers, so it was said. But the only little boy he had ever known, in the distorted mirror of his own childhood memory of himself, had wanted the Rolls-Royce Merlin engine of a Spitfire to control, not a steam-engine. And who would want to drive an overgrown lorry in his dreams?

'But he nearly killed us. The lorry . . . the *truck*-driver.'

Kingston shrugged. 'That's kings for you, man! They don't kill you, though. They've got bigger things to think about, with all the weight they've got behind them, and how high they are above you . . . They just forget all about you, is all.' Kingston raised his head to look in the car mirror, and the Volvo slowed perceptibly. 'He didn't try to kill us, back there . . . it was just, he was coming up, overtaking us, and we were down there beside him, under his mirror . . . and he's got a lot of truck behind him . . . And he just plain forgot we were still there when he started to move back into the inside lane, that's all.' He shrugged. 'Nothing personal – kings aren't personal, man

Why, he probably wouldn't have felt a thing, just an

75

itty-bitty shake way back behind him – that's why I put my foot down . . . 'cause he'd have side-swiped us with his ass . . .' He paused, and then nodded towards the woods on the roadside '. . . and maybe he'd find a scratch or two when he got to Charleston, or wherever. But we'd have been in that old kudzu, and they'd maybe find us in a couple of months if no one spotted us go in.'

Latimer stared at the woods, which were so heavily blanketed with some sort of thick broad-leaved creeper that the trees on the edge of the road appeared only in vague outline: it would certainly be easy enough to be swallowed up there.

He turned to look back the way they had come. There was only one car in view, and that far behind, apart from the murderous juggernaut in the distance. They had left the built-up edge of Atlanta, with its forest of elevated signs which he had hardly noticed, oppressed as he had been by the heat at first, and then by the need to attend to the conversation. And with it they seemed to have left the traffic, too.

'Where are we going?' He realized as he spoke that he really hadn't the faintest idea where he was, north, south, east or west of the old Gateway to the Confederacy. But the map in his head was over a hundred years old anyway: there might still be places called Decatur and Rough-and-Ready, and there must still be a Kennesaw Mountain and a Peachtree Creek where the Union and Confederate armies had mauled and mutilated each other. But he had seen no such names on any signs, only meaningless and unfamiliar names which hadn't registered, and nothing that stirred his imagination. Yet, of course to be fair, that was usually the trouble with places which were names out of childish history and romantic literature and legend, after they had been swallowed up by the twentieth century. Industrial smog shrouded the Acropolis, and Xanadu probably boasted a large power station; and '*Earth has not anything to show more fair*' certainly did not describe the view from Westminster Bridge in the carbon-monoxide-filled air; so he could hardly expect anything from the environs of Atlanta all these years after General Sherman and Scarlett O'Hara had passed this way – if they had.

'Where we going?' Kingston echoed him, almost derisively, and as though he could hear unspoken thoughts. 'Not far.'

'How far?' There were trees as far as he could see, stretching endlessly and anonymously ahead of them now.

'Just a hoot and a holla, as they say.'

Still more trees, with more patches of all-engulfing creeper, which on second observation seemed rather sinister and alien in its conquests, as though it was just waiting for a chance to invade the road itself, to capture whatever tried to get past it.

He concentrated on Kingston. 'A hoot . . . and a – what?'

'Holla.' Kingston massaged the steering-wheel. 'Holla?'

Latimer frowned. 'A . . . Holla? A . . . *shout*, would that be?'

'A what? Hell, no! Man – a holla – a holl*ow*, is what it means . . . a hoot and a *hollow* . . . like, the next valley, where we turn off the inter-state – okay?'

Not okay. Latimer could see no hill ahead, and therefore could envisage no 'next valley'. There were still only trees, and occasionally the repulsive creeper – was that what Kingston had called 'that old kudzu'?

'But where are we actually going, Mr Kingston?' He persisted almost out of desperation.

'Didn't he tell you – the Senator?' Kingston aggravated the question with deliberate cruelty. 'Hell! He should have done tol' you!' The black hands worked on the wheel again, relishing both Senator Cookridge's failure and Kingston's own play with it. 'Now isn't that something!'

77

'Not exactly.' Latimer was goaded into defending himself. 'I suppose he was concerned to tell me more important things.'

Kingston stared at the road ahead for a moment, and then nodded agreement. 'Yeah . . . that'll be it! He jus' plum forgot to tell you where you was goin' – that's what he did!'

Latimer knew he'd been out-manoeuvred. 'And where am I going, then – ' He looked at Lucy Cookridge quickly. ' – Miss Cookridge – ?'

Lucy Cookridge opened her mouth, but before she could speak Kingston twisted the steering-wheel, and the car sank one-sided on to its springs and shot off the motorway on to a slip-road lifting them up to the right, away from Latimer's own British right-hand drive instinct.

Damn! thought Latimer – *damn, damn!* There had been a sign, way back – *a hoot and a holla* back – and he hadn't even thought to look at it –

'Smithsville, Oliver,' Said Lucy Cookridge.

'Smithsville?' It was such a ridiculous place-name that he didn't want to repeat it, but he couldn't help himself.

'We're not actually going right there.' As she spoke the car twisted to follow the slip-road, between cascades of *kudzu* creeper which blanketed the Georgian trees. 'There's a turn-off before we get there.'

Latimer stared at her, even more lost now. What with the trees, and the slip road . . . and the *kudzu*, and now a turn-off . . . it was enough to make a man wonder how General Sherman had been able to march from Atlanta to the sea, once upon a time.

'I beg your pardon – ?' All he knew now was that the motorway – the 'inter-state' – had disappeared like a dream, with all its dangerous juggernauts.

'We goin' to the Promised Land now,' said Kingston. 'The hill King David done build his city on – an' King David Ben-Gurion done build *his* city on too . . . "*Go round about her, an' tell the towers thereof . . . Mark well*

78

her bulwarks, set up her houses, that ye may tell them that come after . . . For this God if our God for ever. And He shall be our guide unto death" – Psalm Forty-Eight, verses eleven to thirteen – *"A fair place, an' the joy of the whole earth"* – verse two – right?'

'Smithsville?' It was difficult to imagine anywhere so prosaically named as the joy of the whole earth, but they could hardly be going to Jerusalem, the city of those two Davids. And yet, on second thoughts, perhaps that was exactly where they were going, for the early Americans had indulged in a wide variety of inclinations in filling the blank spaces on their maps with place-names. So if there was a Rome, and an Athens and a Corinth as well as a Smithsville and a Brownsville, why not a Jerusalem and a Jericho? 'Do you mean –'

'The Promised Land.' Kingston pre-empted Latimer's question by simultaneously repeating the words. 'Although I guess the Cherokee had a different name for it before the paleface relieved them of it – if it was the Cherokees' Promised Land that'd be just another broken promise.'

Lucy Cookridge sighed audibly. 'Spare us the lecture on the perfidious paleface, please Kingston.'

'Huh! Don't get me wrong –' Kingston directed the car to the right as the road forked, leaving the wider highway for a narrower one ' – I got no time for noble redskins. Load of drunken bums – redskins, whiteskins, blackskins, yellowskins – the hell with them! And yids and wogs too!'

Latimer studied the negro. 'Is there anyone you like, Mr Kingston?'

'There surely is, Mister Lateemah.' Kingston twisted a grin over his shoulder. 'Winners is who I like – black, white, or khaki. All the rest is bleeding-heart crap, about "life, liberty and the pursuit of happiness", an' all that Thomas Jefferson jazz – 'cept one . . .Ain't no rights but one.'

'And that is?' Kingston's silence invited the question.

'To win, man, to win! To get what you can – how you

can, when you can . . . fair means or foul, it don't matter –
it's up to you to do it the way the good Lord made you,
whether you're *Saint* Francis of Assisi or Attila the Hun,
just so you run with the ball . . . And then, what you've
got, you sure as hell don't let the other guy take it away
from you until you're dead. And that's winning, Mister
Oliver Latimer.'

'Meaning "Might is right"?' murmured Lucy Cookridge
disapprovingly. 'You're a fascist, Kingston – a black
fascist.'

'If you say so, ma'am. But I didn't say nothin' about
right and wrong, 'cept that it don't mean a thing.' Kingston shook his head happily. 'Used to be a lot of cotton
round here – you right plumb centre in the land of cotton
now, Mr Oliver Latimer. You know that?'

Latimer looked around him. They had at last broken
away from the belt of trees, endless and boringly green,
which had shut in the motorway: there were still a great
many trees, but there were also some open spaces, and
occasional buildings, and – there was an actual field,
planted with something he had never seen in England –

Cotton? But, even apart from what Kingston had just
said – *used* to be a lot of cotton round here – cotton ought
to have a lot of white fluffy balls on it, surely?

'You won't see any cotton round here, Oliver.' Lucy
Cookridge craned her neck at the negro. 'What was it
finished cotton in the South, Kingston – the boll-weevil,
was it?'

'Lawd, Miz Lucy – ah thought it wuz de Yankees! If'n it
weren't de Yankees, ah doan know. But all de cotton
done grow wes' o' de Missippy now – an' deys got
machines dat works a whole lot better'n de nigras, too.'
Kingston looked over his shoulder at Latimer. 'And that
what I mean. *Autres temps, autres moeurs* – what's right
one time isn't necessarily right forever. Once 'pon a time
cotton was right for Georgia – an' nigras wuz raht fo'
pickin cotton – and slavery was right for Georgia and

80

negroes and cotton, they preached that from the pulpits, so you had better believe it – '

'Watch the road, Kingston,' said Lucy Cookridge. 'And do please stop drivelling . . . I told you, Oliver – he has his hang-up. So he produces this Uncle Tom character of his, if you give him half a chance . . . Just don't let him rile you, that's all.'

They were passing more fields, with more mysterious crops. Perhaps it was what the Americans called 'corn' in these fields, even if it was nothing like the good wheat, oats and barley of his remote childhood? And there were occasional dwellings too, planted behind a scatter of trees, long and low houses with long and low cars in attendance, variously dilapidated. It was nothing like what he had imagined.

'No . . . yes.' He didn't know quite how to react, and he still wanted to know where they were going. But he wasn't going to ask that question again, for fear that it might give Kingston another chance to go off at a tangent on one of his hobby-horses.

'No-yes?' Kingston seized on his indecision. 'Now what's that meant to mean? Do I rile you, Mister Oliver Latimer? Or don't I rile you?'

The challenge – or was it a test of some sort? – was casual on the surface, but something more than that beneath it, Latimer sensed. And putting it directly to himself he was quite suddenly surprised by the answer which his brain supplied, even thought it was vague and incomplete.

'I can't honestly say that you do either, Mr Kingston.' He tried to match Kingston's tone. And if the man was merely trying to sting him, then he might as well sting back. 'With a little more effort you might make me curious, I suppose. But as my work at home doesn't bring me into close contact with persons of your race I still wouldn't know whether you're par for the course these days, or something out of the ordinary, do you see?'

But that wasn't true –

The angle of the car changed. Almost imperceptibly they had been following a gradual rise in the ground on to a plateau. But now the road fell away sharply into a heavily-forested little valley.

But that wasn't quite true, about Kingston. Or . . . it was true that the only negroes he came into contact with were the British versions of Kingston's own *motees, doodas* and *moanbacks*. But what was Kingston himself – and who were the *moanbacks*?

The land on the other side of the valley was higher, and he caught a glimpse of a white building – not a house, by the miniature steeple on it, but a church, he guessed – on the highest point, before trees obscured the view.

But Kingston himself . . . there was something about Kingston, in spite of all the talk, jokey or serious, Uncle Tom-ignorant or Anglo-American erudite, and in spite of the coat-blackness . . . there was something about Kingston that he recognized from his own experience.

A bridge came into view – of course, a valley like this would have a river running down it. Once this had all been King Cotton's land – Scarlett O'Hara's rich red earth, and to support such crops then and such thick vegetation now it must be as well-watered as the Thames valley, if not more so – and much hotter, as he had cause to know.

A bridge – it was not only a narrow bridge, but also a wooden one, almost like something from a cowboy film. The planks rumbled under the car, and his attention was torn apart by another brief glimpse of the little church, now high above them, and an equally brief sight of the river – more a stream than a river – half-obscured by overhanging trees beneath them. Then the trees closed round them again.

'Sion Crossing,' said Kingston. 'We on old Sion land now.'

'Sion?' But of course! realized Latimer. Not Jerusalem,

but *Sion – Zion* – that was the hill of Jerusalem on which the City of David was built, and so the centre of the Jewish and Christian religions as the site of the House of God, and by the psalmists' poetic extension also the Promised Land of Heaven itself! He had said as much himself, to Cookridge, too!

He craned his neck as the car began to climb again. 'Was it a church I saw up there?'

'Sion Church.' Kingston nodded. 'That about the oldest thing they got in Barksdale County now, after Bill Sherman's boys passed this way – the second Sion Church, built by Colonel James Alexander of Sion – James the Third and Last, the *preux chevalier* . . . You dig Colonel James Alexander, Oliver?'

'Yes.' That, at least, had been one name – one fact – that Senator Cookridge had given him.

'Well, that about all there is left of Sion – the church on the hill, an' Colonel James the Third in the history books, an' the other Alexanders that were before him and went down with him.' Kingston nodded again.

'Watch the road!' snapped Lucy, gripping the back of Kingston's seat. 'For God's sake – *watch the road*, Kingston!'

'No sweat, Miz Lucy.' Another hairpin bend whirled the trees around them. 'We're nearly home now – we'll get there – '

'I hope so.' Lucy subsided.

Latimer looked back, through the rear window of the car, instinctively.

'Sion Crossing,' said Lucy Cookridge. 'That's the name on the maps, Oliver.'

The car breasted another rise, on another bend, and Latimer had a sudden and quite unexpected view of Sion Church from ground level, across a wide expanse of well-cut grass on which an irregular line of mature trees stood sentinel.

Kingston slowed the car, to let him get an unhurried

sight of the oldest building in Barksdale County, which General Sherman's men had not put to the torch.

He had crossed into Sion now, thought Latimer. And he could only hope that getting out of the Promised Land would be less confusing than getting into it.

5

Mitchell in London: Pub-crawling

They found Howard Morris in the fourth public house on Audley's Saturday short-list, after a tip-off from the Special Branch.

'Hullo there, David.' The American greeted Audley with a raised palm and a big smile, and no apparent surprise. Then he saw Mitchell 'Oh-ho!' The palm came down to rest flat on the top of the bar beside his glass; and, although the smile stayed in position, the eyes became as dull as pebbles on a dry beach.

'Oh-ho what?' Audley had not been pleased at being taken from the bosom of his family, and the passage down the river had not improved his temper. 'What does "Oh-ho" mean? You can't possibly be pissed this early in the evening. And Dr Mitchell is not unknown to you.'

'Quite right – he isn't, and I can't be.' Morris bowed towards Mitchell. 'The Doctor is well-known to me, both by reputation and through his published works. And I have been drinking, but am not drunk, as your boys in blue would have it.' He smiled again at them both. 'I have been drinking, but I hope to drink quite a lot more before morning, to drown my sorrows, the natives being friendly.' To suit the words he took a drink from a straight pint glass, reducing it substantially. 'At least, that was the plan. Will you have something with me?' He looked at Mitchell.

'Draught Guinness,' said Mitchell. 'Thanks.'

Howard nodded. 'At least you brought something of use to you back from your stay in Dublin . . . David?'

'Dry sherry.'

'What?' The American looked askance at Audley. 'You don't like sherry.'

'I'm not here to enjoy myself. And you haven't answered my question yet: what does "Oh-ho" mean?'

'"Oh-ho?" Oh-ho!' Morris finished his beer, pushed the glass up the bar, caught the barman's eye expertly, and ordered the drinks.

'It's an old Navaho exclamation. You meet one chief on the trail, he's hunting for the pot. But you meet *two* chiefs . . . that means there's a war party out – and it could be *you* for the pot, see?' He addressed Mitchell mock-seriously. 'Metaphorically speaking, of course. Because the Navahos didn't eat people, they were a fairly civilized lot. But "Oh-ho" covers the occasion.'

Mitchell's Guinness arrived. He raised the glass to the American. 'But I'm not a chief.'

'Oh yes you are. That department of yours – it's all chiefs. No Indians at all . . . like All Souls – no students, only academic brass.' Only half a smile this time. 'Your war parties are on contract . . . from other tribes. The more bloodthirsty ones.' He raised his glass back to Mitchell. 'The finest irregular light cavalry of all time . . . But being a military historian you'll know all about that.'

'Balls!' snapped Audley. 'And that's an old Anglo-Saxon expression. We use it particularly when we find strangers hunting in our coverts.'

'Sure.' Morris nodded, as though interested. 'I guess that's the same the whole world over. You need an invitation for that sort of thing.'

'And you have an invitation?'

'No.' Morris shook his head. 'But I'm not hunting. I'm just drinking.' He raised his glass to his lips.

But he hadn't drunk out of his new pint yet, Mitchell observed. He had merely put a line of froth on his moustache.

'You weren't just drinking last evening.'

Howard Morris considered that statement for several seconds before answering. 'I sure as hell wasn't hunting

86

either.' He considered Audley also. 'Within the meaning of the word, old buddy.'

In turn, Audley considered his friend. 'Then I'd like to know what you were doing . . . old buddy.'

Several more seconds. 'If I said it was private – '

'It wouldn't do.' Audley was no longer angry, he seemed almost sad.

'I didn't think it would.' This time Morris took the beer-level down two inches. Then he flicked a glance at Mitchell. 'Presence of young chief mean old chief under orders, huh?'

Against his natural inclinations, Mitchell was suddenly sorry for them both. They had once both been very formidable, and influential too. And, given the right circumstances, they still could be, though Howard Morris was – at least temporarily – out of favour in Grosvenor Square, and David Audley increasingly didn't give a damn either way in Whitehall and elsewhere. But they were also mutual friends of long standing, and old allies longer than that; so, not for the first time, he had probably misapprehended the reason for Audley's recent bloody-minded mood.

'I don't know about the old chief – ' It was useless to attempt to sound sincere, for neither of them would believe that; and it wouldn't have been truly true anyway ' – but this young chief is certainly under orders.' He looked at the American, and then shrugged. 'And you were at the Oxbridge Club last night, Colonel Morris. And you did meet our Mr Latimer.'

Morris nodded slowly, well knowing that it was useless to deny. 'So I was. And so I did.' Mitchell's intervention didn't ease the situation, it merely suggested that the young chief was running the show. 'And if I stuck at that – ?'

'That wouldn't do either,' said Audley quickly. 'We'd have to make trouble for you then, Howard. And . . . the way things are . . . we wouldn't want to do that. But we could. And we would.'

87

'Even if I told you I don't really know anything?'

'We'd have to be the judge of that.' Audley had no choice but to be merciless now. 'Old buddy . . . we've already taken the Oxbridge apart – I'm a bloody member of the club, for God's sake – you know that!' He moved his head slightly, looking away from the American, but not quite reaching Mitchell. 'Old buddy . . . I'm sorry . . . But that's the way it is.'

It was nicely done, thought Mitchell admiringly. The signal between friends, confirming what the American had already guessed; and the regret – that was probably genuine. And both together somehow validated the bluff about the Oxbridge, which they hadn't yet had time to take apart; though, of course, it wasn't really a bluff, because with Audley's weight behind them the club was no problem, so that was merely a short cut to the answers. But it was always an education to see David at work under pressure.

And, come to that, it would be an education to see how the American reacted to that pressure, for Howard Morris was a great pro also, who had counted coup on worthy enemies and had their scalps to prove it; and now that he was up against a friend it would be interesting to observe where friendship's markers were planted. Altogether, it was an educational occasion.

Morris had taken another deep pull at his beer. And that was the word on him now, and it was sad and cautionary: that, even allowing for the fact that he had a great capacity for beer, Colonel Morris was drowning his sorrows somewhat too deeply these days.

Morris put his glass down. '"We could. And we would" – sounds like a threat.' He grinned at Audley. 'But they say that you can die of old age, being threatened.'

'They do. But they also say that those whom the gods wish to destroy they first comfort with foolish clichés to encourage carelessness.' Audley shook his head sadly. 'The Oxbridge, Howard – why not the middle of Piccadilly? Or even Whitehall – that would have been relatively less public. And then we might not have had to oh-ho each other like this. Not so quickly anyway.'

Morris grimaced at Audley. 'Well . . . that was where the old bastard wanted it. I warned him.' Then he cocked his head, as though suddenly curious. 'It hasn't occurred to you that if I *was* up to something . . . or maybe if *he* was . . . then we'd have gotten up to it less publicly?'

The old bastard?

'It did cross our minds – yes.' Audley showed no sign that he too was wondering who 'the old bastard' might be. 'But no doubt you all had your reasons, we decided.'

'Oh, sure.' There was an edge of irritation in the American's voice. 'He didn't want to be late for dinner with His Royal Highness.' He gestured abruptly. 'His goddam' dinner!'

The barman materialized in front of them. 'Yes, sir?'

'What?' Morris blinked at the man.

'Same again, sir?'

Morris looked at him. 'Why not? Okay, Harry – "Through the bottle's dazzling glare I see the gloom less plain".' He nodded at the barman. '"And that I think a reason fair to fill my glass again".' He grinned at Audley and raised his glass. 'My namesake wrote that, you know, David? So here's to Captain Charles Morris, of the army of His Britannic Majesty King George the Third, God bless him.' He drained the glass and handed it to the barman. 'Though I guess the Captain's tipple was port, more likely.'

Dinner with His Royal Highness? That certainly reduced the options in an identification of one old bastard among so many who fitted the description.

'Yes . . .' Audley lifted his untasted glass of sherry and then put it down still untasted. 'But dinner wasn't one of the reasons we were seeking you, Howard – any more than we're interested in King George the Third and the Revolutionary War. It's Mr Lincoln's war we're curious about, aren't we?' He regarded Morris quizzically. 'The War Between the States?'

Morris grimaced again. 'Hell, David! I told you it was private – '

'Not any more, it isn't – '

'I mean, you don't have to ask *me*, goddam' it!'

'I don't see anyone else around to ask.'

'You don't. For Christ's sake – all you have to do is ask – ' Morris stopped abruptly, staring at Audley. '*Oh God*!'

The barman reappeared, with another sherry and another Guiness as well as Howard Morris's umpteenth pint.

'I'll put it on your slate, sir – right?'

'Yeah, Harry. On my slate.' Morris continued to stare at Audley, but did not speak again until the barman had retired. 'Is he all right?'

'He – who?'

'Don't shit me around. Is Latimer all right?'

'So far as we know.' Audley looked at Mitchell for confirmation, then back to Morris. 'Is there any reason why he shouldn't be? The War Between the States is over, isn't it? I thought the shooting stopped at Appomattox Court House in 1865, didn't it?'

'Where is he?' If Howard Morris was lying, then he was a beautiful liar, thought Mitchell as the American spread the question between them with a frown. But then he would be a beautiful liar, of course. 'Is that it? He's gone? And . . . he's gone, and you don't know where?' Morris drew a breath. 'That bitch!'

That bitch?

Now they had an old bastard and a bitch. And a Royal Highness. And that ought to triangulate matters well enough.

'Not exactly.' Audley ignored the bitch. 'That is to say . . . he has gone. And we only have an approximate idea of his whereabouts.' Audley smiled suddenly, almost disarmingly, with one of those rare sweet smiles of his. 'It's funny, really.'

'Funny?' The American said the word, but Mitchell echoed it within himself.

'Ironic.' Audley paused. 'We're not a department with a lot of rules, as you know . . . We have to have room to breathe in – space for a little freedom of action . . . even a little eccentricity, you might say – eh?'

Neither Mitchell nor the American said anything, for Audley was usually the one who needed that sort of room.

'About ten years ago . . . ten years, it would be – Cathy was a new baby at the time . . . I went abroad with her and Faith. It was just a whim – ' Audley shrugged diffidently ' – mostly just holiday, to show Faith the Roman parts of Rome, not those dreadful baroque monstrosities . . . But I did want to check up on something – ' another shrug ' – and . . . there was a bit of quite unforeseen difficulty with the locals there. Quite unforeseen – otherwise, of course, I'd never have taken Faith and Cathy, you understand?'

There was some truth there, as far as Audley's wife and child were concerned. But there was also some considerable understatement, Mitchell suspected, relating to events which had occurred a year or two before he himself had been seduced from the scholarly safety of the 1914–18 War-to-end-all-wars.

'Anyway . . . the point is that I had somehow omitted to tell anyone where I was going, so when things blew up this end . . . which they did with a vengeance . . . there was a certain amount of ill-founded concern, which Master Oliver St John Latimer did his best to transform into departmental panic, for all the world as though I was absconding with the petty cash.' Audley finally nerved himself to taste one of his sherries. A strange expression crossed his face and he scanned the array of bottles behind the bar just as the barman returned. 'They changed the rules after that.'

'Everything okay, sir?' inquired the barman.

'Thank you, Harry!' Audley smiled again. 'A most unusual sherry. Bulgarian, would it be?'

The politeness of the question reassured the barman. 'I expect so, sir. It comes out of a barrel.'

'Just so!' Audley turned back to Morris. 'They tighened up the rules after that, and Oliver St John Latimer is a great one for rules. So I don't doubt he'll be ringing in again some time . . . And, in the meantime, I'm not one to make a crisis, let alone a panic, out of a transitory problem. That's the irony, if you like.'

Mitchell studied the American closely, and was not reassured by what he observed, since the American himself was drinking again. He reached for his second Guinness.

Morris put his glass down, and wiped his moustache delicately with a single finger. 'That's just the little irony, old buddy. There's a bigger one than that.'

'Tell us, Howard.' Audley spoke gently. 'Because we've got two men on each of the exits, and another in the car outside, and as they're all probably on overtime – if not overtime-and-half, on a Saturday evening – I would like to send them home, for the tax-payer's sake.'

'Huh!' grunted Morris. 'But I'm buying the drinks on my private slate.'

'Are you? But then everything you seem to be doing these days is private, isn't it?' Audley leaned across the bar and waved at the barman. 'Private meetings – private reasons – private drinks . . . Harry, could you dispose of these Nicaraguan sherries, and bring me a pint of Colonel Morris's best bitter?'

'Pint coming up, sir!' Harry waved back.

Morris pointed accusingly at Audley. 'You think we're up to something – you do, don't you, David?'

'I don't think any such thing. Mitchell here thinks that – I don't.'

'Mitchell.' Morris zeroed in on Mitchell. 'You know what they say about you, *Doctor* Mitchell?'

That was a challenge not to be ducked. 'That I know too much? That's what I'm always being told, Colonel.'

The reply crest-felled the American. 'They say you're a smart-ass, Mitchell.'

The pint arrived, but the barman looked at Mitchell. 'Anything more, gentlemen?'

The barman knew his job, and Mitchell liked men who knew their jobs.

'I'll have another Guinness. And you can put a pint in for Colonel Morris – and for my friend here.' He nodded at Audley.

The barman studied Mitchell for a moment. 'I know you, don't I, sir – ?'

'You do, Harry.' Mitchell watched Howard Morris.

'Yes . . .' Harry grappled for a moment with his professional memory. '*The Dominoes League* – Mister . . . mister . . . *Paul* – ? Paul?'

'We beat the home side. I had a damn good partner – remember?'

Harry beamed back at him. 'That's right, sir – Mr Procter and Mr Mitchell . . . And your ladies did just as well in the darts match – and your lady was a Miss Elizabeth, right?'

Touché, thought Mitchell. 'I wish she was, Harry.' But there were other matters in hand now. 'And put one in for yourself while you're about it.' He put a note on the bar. 'You see, Colonel, I've been privatized too. This pub's in my territory, that's all.'

The Colonel nodded slowly, adding Mitchell to the full reckoning for the first time.

'But you're right – and David isn't quite right.' They had to hit the American hard from both sides, now that he was in a vulnerable salient.

'Oh . . . yeah?' Morris shied away from another 'oh-ho'.

'Yes. I do know too much. And I don't *think* you're up to something . . . although by "you" I don't necessarily

93

mean you personally.' Mitchell smiled. 'I mean . . . with the old bastard and the bitch . . . We'd like you to put our minds at rest, Colonel.'

That was the old military rule: if you don't want to destroy your enemies completely, because you may need them as allies in the next campaign, then leave them one road open on which to retreat from the stricken field in good order.

Howard Morris looked from one to the other of them, and then at the cheerful Saturday evening occupants of the bar in general. Perhaps he was reviewing the celebrated Special Relationship between his United States and their United Kingdom. And perhaps he was also remembering his own Special Relationship with David Audley, his long-time friend and longer-time official ally. But it was more likely, thought Mitchell, that he was thinking about the heavies outside the two exits.

Harry arrived with the drinks, including his own. And, having swept Audley's sherries from sight, he raised his glass to Mitchell. 'It's *Doctor* Mitchell – that was a good win you had that night Doctor! Cheers!'

Morris fixed a jaundiced eye on him. 'Harry . . .'

'Yes, Colonel?'

'Have you ever heard of *Catch-22*, Harry?'

Harry thought for a moment. 'No, sir. Is it a drink?' He raised an eyebrow. 'A cocktail, is it?'

'Yes,' said Audley. 'It has a hemlock base. Do you have any hemlock?'

Harry ran his eye over the bottles behind the bar. 'No, sir. Would Crême-de-Menthe do?'

'Probably.' Morris sighed. 'Harry, would you give us some privacy? These two gentlemen are about to screw me for all I'm worth. I won't bleed, but it may not be a pretty sight. So bug off, there's a good fellow.'

Harry took them all in, finally coming back to Morris. 'Well – that's life, sir: there's always someone waiting for the chance. Usually it's the tax-man.' Then he brightened.

94

'Just don't forget you've got a pint in with Dr Mitchell – right?'

Morris watched the barman depart. 'With a hemlock chaser . . . Okay, David . . . *so someone's* up to *something*. But not *me* – and I don't know *what*. And that's straight.' He started his latest pint.

Audley drank, and then nodded. 'But you said "Catch-22", nevertheless?'

'Oh – sure! Whichever way it goes, I'm going to lose. Because someone *is* up so something – '

'Someone American.' Mitchell pretended to know a piece of common knowledge, which was either the old bastard's identity, or that bitch's, or both.

'But you were the middleman, old buddy,' said Audley. 'You're not exactly a virgin waylaid on her journey home to the YWCA, are you?'

Morris's features twisted. 'That's not far from the goddam' truth, actually. And I'm about to be screwed, either way – I'm resigned to that.'

Audley leaned forward. 'I could take that as a kind of insult, old friend. We didn't start this, remember?'

'Uh-huh. You didn't start it – I didn't start it. But if I don't come clean with you, you foreclose on my mortgage – ' Morris glanced at Mitchell as though he well knew the author of his misfortunes ' – and if I do . . . then Senator Cookridge will sure as hell have me run out of this town on a rail.'

Senator Cookridge? Mitchell just had time, warned by *if I do*, to hold his expression of well-informed politeness.

'Uh-huh!' Finding no comfort in Mitchell, Morris turned back to Audley. 'So it seems I'm caught between a rock and a hard place, then.'

'Not necessarily.' Audley shook his head quickly.

Cookridge?

'No?' The tiniest flicker of hope crossed Morris's face. 'Go on, David – ?'

Cookridge? *Christ! That raised the stakes!* And, in

raising them, it accounted for the American's resistance to their pressure. And – *Christ*! He mustn't look so hard at Audley to see if he had made the same connection!

He buried his face in his Guinness glass.

'Me?' Audley's voice hardened. 'It's you who should be talking, not me.' He shifted his glance to Mitchell, and then back to Morris. 'And if you're wondering about how long you can stall us . . . we're already into injury time, old buddy.'

'I'll bet.' Morris accepted the situation. 'But what I was actually wondering about . . . is just how much you really know. David?'

'How much do we know?' Audley sniffed at the question, as though he didn't fancy the smell of it. 'We know about the Senator . . . we know about "the old bastard".' He sniffed again. 'We don't know nearly enough about that "bitch" of yours, to be honest.' He flicked a smile at Mitchell. 'And we know a hell of a lot about the American Civil War – or "the War Between the States", if you prefer . . . or "the War for Southern Indepence", or whatever you like. . . . But again, not nearly enough – will that do?'

Morris gave him an evil smile. 'You don't know about Lucy? Now that surprises me!'

Audley gestured abruptly, nearly upsetting the nearest glass. 'Oh, for God's sake, Howard! Friendship is one thing – '

'Friendship?' Morris fired the word back at him. 'It's my neck, buster – not *yours*! And thanks to me, by God!'

'Thanks to you?' Audley frowned.

'This time you owe me – you *really* owe me – my God, you do!' Morris chuckled insincerely. 'You know where you should be?' Morris pointed at Audley. 'You know where?'

'You tell me.'

'Uh-huh.' The finger waved negatively at Audley. 'You tell me where you think Oliver St John Latimer is first. Then I'll tell you where you should be. Okay?'

For the first time Mitchell wondered whether it was all the beer that Howard Morris had taken on board which was talking. But somehow he didn't think it was.

'Very well,' Audley was deadly sober, anyway. 'We think he's in the United States.'

'You think?'

'Cut the bullshit, Howard. He may be there – and where should I be?' Beyond sobriety, Audley was deadly serious now.

'Okay.' Morris picked up the message. 'You should be wherever he is, David.' His mouth tightened. 'Instead of him.'

'Instead?'

'That's right. Instead.' Morris stared at Audley unblinkingly. 'He wanted you – '

'He?'

'Senator Cookridge – now who's bullshitting?' Morris's face twisted. 'He wanted you – the great David Audley, the historian – the finder of lost things – the picker-up of unconsidered trifles . . . the great and good friend of the United States of America.' The finger came up again. 'He wanted *you*, David – and he wanted *me* to get you. So . . . now do you see the joke?'

For a moment Audley said nothing, and they were in a private silence in the midst of the bar's hubbub.

'You mean . . . you disobeyed orders?' The joke appeared to puzzle Audley.

'They weren't orders exactly. He asked me to do him a favour, that's all.'

'Which you didn't do.'

Morris shrugged. 'I did my best, in the time allowed. He wanted you quickly – I went to the Oxbridge because I heard you'd be there. But you didn't turn up.'

Mitchell stirred. 'But Latimer did turn up?' There was something not quite right about this. 'So you approached him instead?'

Morris looked at him. 'Yes, Dr Mitchell. Like they say,

a bird in the hand, is it?' He smiled at Mitchell. 'Or is it Hobson's Choice?'

'He asked for *me*, Howard?' Audley was frowning more deeply now. 'Specifically for me?'

'Uh-huh.' Howard drank some more beer. 'For the celebrated David Audley, no less.'

'Go on.'

'Go on – where?'

'Don't play dumb, Howard.' By the look on his face Audley had reached Mitchell's *unless*. 'Tell me exactly what happened.'

'Okay.' The glass was empty. 'I got a call from him yesterday. I was doing my weekly thing at Grosvenor Square . . . like telling Schwarz what he didn't want to hear, and wasn't going to believe, about Greenham.' The American's mouth twisted under his moustache. 'No matter . . . I got this call, which gave Schwarz a nasty turn, because the Senator farts, and they all smell roses – it was bad news to Schwarz that the Senator even knew of my existence.'

'You know Cookridge?'

'Never set eyes on the old bastard. But he sure knows about me.' Morris paused. 'And he sure knows about *you*, old buddy. Like . . . he knows we have a passing acquaintance, for instance.'

'What else does he know about me?'

'Oh . . . he dropped some names.' Morris glanced at Mitchell for a fraction of a second.

'Go on. What names?'

'Well . . . let's say he knows your wife's maiden name, huh? And there was one of our guys you worked with once – a certain Major Sheldon, who pulled teeth for the USAF down Salisbury-way a few years back – and a few KGB teeth too – remember?' Morris smiled at his friend. 'And he said you were an authority on Civil Wars – yours and ours.'

Mitchell kept his eyes on the American, while placing

half of the last allusion accurately from his own fledgling experience. That had been when he had met Frances for the first time, and the memory was unfailingly painful.

Frances . . . oh Frances, Frances . . .

'Yes?' If Audley had memories, he didn't show them.

'He told me to make contact with his daughter, Lucy. He said she had all the information I needed. I was just to set up the meeting, but she would handle it from there on – I was to get the hell out of it, on pain of death.' Morris gestured. 'Oh, he wrapped it up . . . And he emphasized that it was entirely private, not professional . . . And he put a big cherry on the top of the cake, naturally.' The very white teeth showed under the moustache. 'He let slip that I was the man he trusted to do the job right, not Schwarz. And that there were some chances already in the pipeline – all quite regardless of this little private matter, of course.' Morris signalled down the bar. 'Harry – I thirst.'

Mitchell thrust Frances back into her little English churchyard, and looked at Audley.

'David – '

'Yes.' Audley didn't look back at him. 'It stinks.'

'Like a battlefield on the third day,' agreed Morris.

'So what did you do?' asked Mitchell.

'I did as I was told – inevitably.' Morris reached for his latest pint. 'Who was I to question the Senator's slightest whim?' He tested the new pint, and found it satisfactory.

'So you went to the Oxbridge – ?'

'Not directly.' Morris trusted Mitchell now, on the twin grounds that Audley evidently did so and because he had committed himself, and consequently had no choice. 'With my responsibility for Cruise Security I just naturally had to check up on the Senator's schedule for the evening – just in case the ladies of Greenham might have planned to attend his dinner engagement with His Royal Highness . . . professional etiquette, and all that – ' he put his hand to his mouth ' – pardon! This beer's not absolutely right –

the Senator is a strong supporter of NATO, after all – ' he gave Audley a little nod ' – he is actually quite a sound old bastard, present events apart: for a mid-westerner he shows a surprising grasp of geography . . . meaning, he knows that Europe lies between the Soviet Union and the US of A, more or less, David. Which is more than I can say for some of his colleagues.'

'And?' Audley urged his friend patiently.

'And there was a little private time built into his schedule, before dinner.' Morris nodded. 'It seems he was over here a million years ago, as a mere stripling, dropping bombs from a B-17 on to our West German allies. Which accounts for his nodding acquaintance with the geography of the area, I suppose . . . And while he was taking time off from pulverizing the Third Reich he occasionally came up to the Big Smoke for rest and refreshment, like any red-blooded American boy.' Another smile. 'Cementing Anglo-American relationships – you know.'

'He whored around.' Audley, who just dated from those historical times, didn't smile.

'I thought you were going to say that.' Morris looked pleased. 'A very common British misapprehension – "Over here, over-paid, over-sexed" . . . Actually, he was one of the good Christian boys who played the church organ and sang in the choir, and really did cement Anglo-American friendship. And the lady he came back to see – *allegedly* came back to see – is about a hundred years old, and she really *is* a lady – and an old dragon, too . . . Lady Something-Something, of London W1, who drove an ambulance and dispensed tea and buns from a Church of England tea-and-bun waggon in the Blitz over here.' The smile vanished. 'At least, that's the story officially. Unofficially . . . I rather think he dropped in on Latimer in a private room in the Oxbridge, and talked about the War between the States.'

'You didn't stay to see?'

Morris winced. 'There were some guys I didn't know turned up, to case the joint. So I decided it might not be too healthy to chance my luck.' He finally settled his eye on Audley. 'Besides which . . . I'd already done the deed, David.'

Audley considered his friend without speaking.

The silence lengthened between them until Mitchell could stand it no longer. 'You substituted Latimer . . . Why?'

The eye switched to Mitchell. 'Because he was there, I guess, Dr Mitchell. Like climbing mountains.'

Audley emitted a curious sound. 'Or because you didn't like it?'

'That too.' Morris stared into his beer for a moment, and then looked up. 'I guess I didn't like it – and he was there, and I didn't want to disappoint the Senator . . . supposing I was wrong – okay?' The look zeroed in on Audley. 'I guess I'm justly served, having you screw me like this.'

'Justly served?' Mitchell frowned.

'I shouldn't have done it. The Devil tempted me . . . if it had been David, I'd have told him to see the Senator, and to be nice to him – but to turn the old bastard down flat, whatever he wanted.' Morris shook his head sadly. 'But . . .' He looked at Audley. 'But . . . it being Latimer, I didn't care so much.'

'You didn't trust me, did you?' Audley produced his very rare sweet smile – the genuine one. 'You thought I wouldn't take your advice?'

Morris rocked on his bar stool. 'Christ, David – you've got one helluva bad record for not being able to resist temptation, haven't you! And this was a bloody-near perfect temptation, too – a nice bit of history somewhere – with a first-class ticket to the States thrown in . . . I never thought Latimer would bite – I thought he'd run a mile, rather than go into the field, even if it was a private affair . . .'

'And Senator Cookridge, too!' Audley nodded. 'I'd certainly take a risk or two to get in with him ' He switched the nod to Mitchell ' – he's a new man, and I've never met him. So he doesn't owe me anything yet.' The nod came back to Morris. 'But I would have cleared it with Jack Butler first. I wouldn't just have gone swanning off into the wide blue yonder, as Oliver has done.'

Morris grimaced. 'Well, that would have been a turn-up for the book. But you can't expect me to know when leopards change their spots – I thought you'd go . . . and I thought Latimer *wouldn't* go, anyway – '

'But he *has* gone, Colonel,' Mitchell intervened.

'Okay. So I was wrong.' Morris spread his hands. 'So I don't know what makes Oliver St John Latimer tick – so maybe he's got an eye for a pretty woman . . . I don't know!' He came back to Audley quickly. 'And that was the clincher, David – I knew you'd succumb to the fair Lucy's charms, the moment she lowered her long lashes and showed you her even longer legs. And . . .' He stopped.

'And?'

'And even more when you knew who she really was.' Morris watched Audley. '*Lucy Cookridge* – doesn't she ring a bell?'

'Should she?' Audley plainly disliked being watched so expectantly. 'I told you, Howard, Cookridge is a new man so far as I'm concerned.'

'But – *Lucy*, David – '

'If I don't know the father, I'm not likely to know the daughter, my dear fellow. I'm not a socializer.' Audley waved a hand at Mitchell. 'If she's got long legs it's more likely she rings Paul's chimes of midnight – Paul?'

Mitchell looked at Audley reproachfully. 'What?'

'Well, well!' Morris tut-tutted at Audley, ignoring Mitchell altogether. 'We haven't done our homework very well, have we!'

'We haven't had a great deal of time – the way some of

our alleged friends have been up to mischief. And now we are trying to repair the damage.' Audley took refuge in turn in his beer. 'So what is so special about the daughter that she should ring our bells?'

Morris smiled. 'She's not really his daughter – that's what's special.'

'You said she was.'

The smile became a grin. 'A small deliberate mistake, to test you, my dear fellow.' Morris paused deliberately. 'This whole situation is becoming over-filled with life's little ironies. Like . . . me saving you from a fate worse than death . . . and then, as a result, having my Saturday night ashore spoilt by you.'

Audley inclined his head graciously. 'And my Saturday night, too. Which amused neither my wife nor my daughter – my *real* daughter, that is, of course.' He signalled down the bar. 'But if you'll give me another irony, I'll buy you another drink.'

'Fair enough.' Morris obviously enjoyed playing with Audley when he had an edge. '"Stay me with flagons, comfort me with apples; for I am sick of love".'

'"Raisin-cake", actually.' Audley nodded to Harry.

'Raisin-cake?'

'In the Hebrew. The Revised Version has simply "raisins", but there's a note about the exact Hebrew. The Douai translation is "flowers" – "Fulcite me floribus, stipate me malis; quia amore langueo" – Canticle of Canticles, second chapter, fifth verse. Your "flagons" are only in the Authorised Version. But I wouldn't quarrel with that here in the Admiral Benbow, not tonight.' Audley waited until Harry had recharged the glasses. 'Not in exchange for another irony, anyway.'

'Very good of you.' Morris nursed the glass. 'And you wouldn't be plying me with liquor, would you?'

Audley shook his head. 'I'd never ply anyone raised on moonshine whisky. And I'm perfectly well aware that your head is as hard as your black heart.' He raised his glass.

103

Morris considered Audley affectionately. 'You're a terrible man, David. But that's why you're here, of course. Only . . . you've also got the Devil's own luck, for a damned Anglo-Saxon.'

'Norman, actually. With maybe a touch of Jutish. And I can't say I feel particularly lucky tonight.'

'Uh-huh.' Morris waved his negative finger. 'Being here is lucky for you, I think . . . But okay – you say you don't know the daughter because you don't know the father. But you *did* know him.'

'I did?'

'Long ago. Back in the old days . . . pre-Patrick Felton, pre-Yuri Strelnikov – mid-Philby . . . maybe post-Philby too, just about . . . Long time, David – and that's a fact, by God!'

Again, Mitchell couldn't resist looking at Audley. Long time was right! He couldn't even place . . . Felton and Strelnikov, so they must be ancient history. And Philby – he was right out of legend, the great survivor of that long-stern-chase during the dark years, some of which overlapped Audley's own early service in their own carefully sealed-off section. In fact . . . although the departmental records of that time, so far as they concerned Philby, were conspicuous by their absence . . . David must have been one of the gunners on that stern-chase, too old to be a powder-monkey, but not quite senior enough to have sighted the gun and pulled the lanyard on the uproll – ?

'Oh yes?' Looking at Audley was predictably a waste of time, all the same: the man was not about to give away any sort of expression about those days in the public bar of the Admiral Benbow tavern on a Saturday night. 'Well, I can't say I remember any *Lucy* from those days. But I'm not too good on babies – they all remind me rather of Winston Churchill: not much hair, but they know what they want, and they're determined to get it – my Cathy, for example . . . she was exactly like that, you know, Howard – ' Having shrugged off Kim Philby, Audley

104

smiled at Howard Morris ' – you'd do much better trying to remind me of Lucy's mother. I'm much more at home with mothers from long ago.'

'Uh-uh.' Morris wasn't so easily out-faced. 'If you haven't done your homework, you won't know her either. She was safely shot of him before you knew him.'

Something changed in Audley's smile. It didn't weaken, let alone disappear, but it became curiously fixed, as though a garbled message had reached his face, and the muscles didn't know what to do for the best.

'Macallan.' Howard Morris also observed the change, and he moved quickly to pre-empt Audley himself reaching the name. 'She was born Lucy *Macallan*, David. Remember?'

'Macallan.' Audley repeated the name with such complete lack of emotion that his rage with himself was transparently apparent. 'Bill Macallan – *William O'Reilly Macallan* – of course! He left a family behind somewhere . . . "*I am not a Virginian, but an American*" – he would have said "*I am not a father, I am an American*" – Bill Macallan – Lord! but – ' He frowned at Howard Morris ' – but . . .'

'He's dead?' Morris goaded him.

'That's right. Dead to all intents and purposes, anyway. If not actually dead.'

'Actually dead now. Couple of months back.'

'Is that so?' Audley caught Mitchell's questioning expression. 'Don't look at me – I didn't do it!' He nodded towards Morris. 'Ask him – didn't he have one of those dreadfully incurable and erratic wasting maladies . . . nervous or muscular . . . or both?'

'But who was he?' Mitchell pursued his actual question.

'Macallan?' Audley repeated the name unnecessarily, then nodded again towards the American. 'He was one of theirs. And a top man in his day – a proper little Wyatt Earp, by God!' Pause. 'But a long way back, way before your time!' Pause. 'And he was a long time dying, by

105

golly!' Pause. 'But then he was always a fighter, was Bill Macallan.' This time Mitchell received the nod. 'He'd have made a good frigate captain in your friend Elizabeths old US navy – "Don't give up the ship!" and all that.' He swung back to Morris. 'And so he left a daughter – ?'

'She nursed him, the last year.'

'But she took Cookridge's name.'

'Cookridge brought her up. Married the mother – hell, more than twenty years ago, it would be.'

'Indeed?' Audley registered polite interest. 'Well, Howard, I grant you a little irony there, and perhaps a little coincidence. But it's mostly history you have, it would seem, rather than homework.'

'You're dam' right. *History* is just what I have – American history.' Morris frowned at Audley. 'And since when were you a goddam' expert on it? It's knights-in-armour and feudal system you're into, not our Civil War – since when were you an expert on that?'

'I'm not.' Audley raised a shoulder. 'The last time I opened an American history book seriously was . . . let me think now . . . it would have been about the time Neville Chamberlain was flying to Munich to see Herr Hitler, or thereabouts.'

Christ! thought Mitchell, this was history talking about History: Audley had aged so well, and treated everyone so much in the same way, regardless of age and status, that it was hard to think of him as so old – old enough easily to be his own father.

'Yes.' Audley clarified his recollections. 'We did "Slavery and Secession" in School Certificate. I have a clear memory of mispronouncing something called "the Missouri Compromise", much to my form master's amusement – "Compromise, I made it . . . And there was "the Dred Scott Case", which must have had something to do with the fugitive slave laws – but I can't for the life of me remember exactly what . . . But we didn't actually *do* the war itself – I remember thinking that that was a rotten shame, because it had all the makings of a most enjoyable blood-letting . . . the South wrong, but romantic, and the North right, but repulsive – ' He stopped suddenly.

'Yes?' Morris pounced on the frown.

'Yes . . . I was just thinking . . .' Audley frowned. 'About Macallan . . . *Macallan* was an expert on the American Civil War, if there ever was one – it was his hobby . . . In fact, I remember arguing with him about it once.' Audley lifted his chin and looked down on Morris in one of his most characteristically arrogant movements.

'Uh-huh?' Morris recognized the signal too. 'He was the expert, and you weren't – but you argued with him?'

'Mmm . . . I've never thought ignorance should preclude a good argument. In some ways it confers an advantage – and a good argument is a marvellous way of obtaining information. I learnt a lot about Bill Macallan by arguing with him. And that was even more valuable, as it turned out . . .'

Morris said nothing, but merely waited expectantly for Audley to continue, and Mitchell followed his example. Although, thought Mitchell, what they were learning now about Audley was what Audley chose to tell them.

'But I did have another advantage, of course . . .'

He must have taken his School Certificate, which was now the 'O-level' exam, very young, decided Mitchell. But, of course, he would have been at some expensive boarding school which aimed its bright pupils at Oxford or Cambridge from the moment of their arrival, all small and pink and hesitant. That – although it was hard to think of Audley as small and pink and hesitant – went without saying. He might have been a born scholar, but he had certainly been very deliberately hammered and beaten into the required shape at great expense.

'Yes.' Audley looked for a moment into the smoke-filled air of the Admiral Benbow public bar, projecting the long-forgotten documentary of the Audley-Macallan

Civil War arguments into the haze. 'I'd read *Gone With the Wind* – and he hadn't – '

'What?' Howard Morris slopped his beer, which he'd been in the act of raising. '*Gone* – '

' – *With the Wind*.' Audley completed the title. 'A damn good book! If you haven't read if, Howard, then you ought to have done – and more fool you for not having done so already! If I'd written *Gone With the Wind* – '

' – You'd cry all the way to the bank!' Morris had his beer under control.

'Too bloody right! Except I wouldn't be crying.'

'You wouldn't?' Morris held his beer steadily.

'You better be careful, Colonel.' Mitchell decided to intervene, remembering the contents of one of the rooms in Audley's rambling farmhouse. 'David's an authority on historical novels, from G. A. Henty to Alfred Duggan and Rosemary Sutcliff. He's got shelves full of them.'

After all, keeping a good argument going could be very useful!

'Yeah?' Either Morris was playing the same game by design, or so many pints of English beer had made him reckless. 'Like *Forever Amber*, and – and . . .' He ran out of historical novels too quickly for conviction.

'And *I, Claudius* and *Princess in the Sunset* . . . and *The Last of the Wine*?' Mitchell decided to join the winning side.

'And Mills and Boon?' Morris obviously knew he was fighting a rearguard action, but he wasn't ready to throw his rifle away and run yet – his instinct and training held him steady.

'Nothing wrong with Mills and Boon.' Audley came back to them. 'Charlotte Brontë would have been published by Mills and Boon . . . but Bill Macallan didn't read historical novels – *Gone With the Wind* was beneath his dignity, is what I mean . . . And there's as much real history of the American Civil War in that as there is of the First Crusade in Alfred Duggan's *Night with Armour* – if you read that, and the first volume of Runciman's history, then you can take on all comers, I don't care who . . . So I had enough to take on Bill Macallan, when it came to the American Civil War, anyway. Okay?'

Okay? Mitchell stared at Howard Morris – and Howard Morris was thinking very hard, he could see that.

'Okay.' Morris reached his decision. 'So that was how Bill Macallan reckoned you were an expert years ago, maybe. But it sure as hell doesn't tell us why Cookridge wanted you last evening, *of all people*, David.'

Mitchell continued to stare at the American. He wanted to look at Audley too, but it was Morris who wasn't making the most sense now, after what had gone before. 'But . . . if Cookridge wanted an expert . . . her real father could have told her about David – and she could have told her step-father, maybe?'

Morris looked at him, almost slyly, with an almost cynical expression. 'That's what worries me, Doc – now, anyway.' He turned to look at Audley. 'Though it wasn't that bugged me last evening, David – I just thought you were you, old buddy – and that was enough to scare the hell out of me, you understand? But this scares me more.'

Audley looked at his friend, quite inscutably.

Mitchell looked from one to the other. With honest enemies you had a fair chance of guessing what they were at, but with these two honest friends in different camps it was impossible.

Audley lingered on the American for a few extra seconds, then switched to Mitchell. 'What he means, Paul, is that Bill Macallan and I worked together in the old days.'

The old days?

'Hand-in-glove,' supplemented Morris, white teeth showing under the bedraggled moustache. 'Special relationship.'

The old days?

'Chalk and cheese, Paul.' Audley sighed, and his face hardened. 'We hated each other's guts.'

It had been there before, thought Mitchell: Audley had not mourned the news of the man's death, never mind the onset of that 'incurable and erratic malady' long ago.

But that cleared the way for the obvious question. 'Professional or personal?'

'Both.' Audley regarded him bleakly. 'He was the senior partner – it was after Suez, and we both knew the score after that. So . . . he thought I was a hangover from the decline and fall of the British Empire, which was screwing up the American take-over, to save the world for democracy one jump ahead of Russian fascism – ' he nodded at Mitchell ' – we didn't disagree on everything – that was what made the split between us worse . . . If he'd been a Rhodes Scholar we might have swung it between us, but he didn't make the grade – Christ! maybe that would have done it! I just don't know . . .'

'And what did you think of him?'

'I thought he was an anti-British, anti-Israeli son-of-a-bitch – and more . . .'

'More?' Mitchell knew that Audley was pro-Israeli. That was why he had been hiked out of the Middle East a dozen years earlier, into Research and Development proper.

'A lot more. We were both working in a rather sensitive area.' A look of distaste spread across Audley's face. 'An unpleasant one, too . . . we were witch-hunting for traitors.'

Mitchell observed the distaste deepen, and his own curiosity with it: Audley was not usually so queasy on the subject of treachery.

'Sleepers,' said Audley. 'The really deep ones . . . the Sleeping Beauties who were never going to be kissed . . .'

There was more, and Mitchell waited for it.

'He enjoyed it a bit too much even for my taste,' said Audley, looking away reflectively until his eye finally settled on the CIA man. 'Those were the days of the Debreczen List – remember, Howard?'

Morris looked at Mitchell sidelong. 'A long time ago, David.'

'Yes' Audley stared past him, down the bar. 'Long time ago . . .'

Mitchell could no longer control his curiosity. 'What happened?'

Audley stared at him. 'In the end he found his own name on the list.'

Morris nodded. 'That was the way it looked.' He transferred the nod to Mitchell. 'He was a sick man by then – what he'd got was just starting . . . So they let him go with his pension. No scandal that way.'

'Somebody screwed him,' said Audley. 'And we let it happen – *I* let it happen . . .' He brightened suddenly. 'Let's go and find another pub, and have something to eat – okay?'

William Macallan and *Debreczen*, thought Mitchell. The records ought to have something to say about both of them.

6

Latimer in America:
The Sion Crossing papers

Latimer looked at his watch, and pushed the last of the Sion Crossing papers away, and stared at the blank white wall in front of him.

He felt saturated with information, heavy and soggy with it like a sponge. His head ached slightly, but that was a temporary and familiar symptom of an accustomed condition: all he needed was a few hours' rest – a little exercise first and a little refreshment later – and the headache would be gone, and he would be light and dry again. And then, if there was something of value in all these facts, it would be there inside his head, glinting like specks of gold in the rubbish of the miner's pan.

All the same, he did also feel slightly odd in a new way – slightly disorientated by the confusion of those vanished hours, lost or won in the crossing of the Atlantic, which he had assimilated over the elongated day at his disposal yesterday.

He looked at his watch again. He had arrived here, and eaten a fairly strange dinner, and had worked; and had phoned the office after midnight, and then had slept like the dead in a strange bed for a short time; then consumed an even stranger breakfast. When in Rome – but even the Romans might have baulked at syrup with sausages and bacon, on top of curious little pancakes – wouldn't they? But Kingston had been there, watching him with that falsely casual air of his, so he had pretended that it had all been the most natural mixture in the world for him, not only in spite of its weirdness but also in flagrant disregard for the huge intake of calories it represented.

So one thing was certain: if he established a firm and useful American connection with this favour, he would soon recover all those hard-lost pounds, and become a true Fattypuff again, contentedly unhappy with his silhouette.

He looked down at the scatter of papers on the desk, and then at his own scribbled notes.

There was another certain thing there, too.

He began to move the photo-copied pages experimentally, re-arranging them in the likely time-sequence of their acquisition. If he was right, *that* came first, then *that* (from a different copier), and then *those* . . . or perhaps *those*? As yet, he couldn't be quite sure, but if he had the right inkling of how the researcher's mind worked it was odds-on that the collection had been started long ago and then laid aside. But then the letter from the farmer in Iowa had arrived out of the blue, and the hunt had been revived, with new questions and further research.

When he'd finished there was still a bigger pile of unplaceable material in the centre. But he was more convinced than ever that the dead man had been a professional, and a sharp one.

Indeed, the evidence both of that sharpness and of the man's uncertain health lay before him, in the sequence of underlined facts and in the manner of their underlining.

He bent over the first sheet, and then the others, studying the marks closely. It was undoubtedly a fountain pen which had made those lines, and the hand which had held that pen had been very different from the brain which had directed it: the lines were shaky and uneven, the pressure of the nib varying them from tremblingly spider-thin to splutteringly thick.

So . . .very old, or very sick, or both, that hand had been.

But if that answered one question, it still left the larger one unanswered, which Senator Cookridge had promised to answer in due time, but which Latimer would have liked answered now for his own peace of mind: if, by reason of that pressing appointment, the original researcher could not be at this table, why – *really why* – had a stranger and a foreigner been chosen to replace him? Audley for choice, but Oliver St John Latimer by chance?

Well . . . he stared again at the blank wall, toying not altogether happily with the immodest thought that perhaps they simply wanted the best, which the Senator had given pretty clearly as his main reason, which was galling insofar as it involved Audley first, but flattering after that. Yet, while that was the most likely truth, he was uneasily convinced that it would not be the whole truth. Which meant that he, the very careful and cautious Oliver St John Latimer, had most uncharacteristically allowed himself to be lured far from home into something he didn't quite understand, albeit it was a private matter which must ingratiate him with one of the most influential men in America.

A gentle tap on the door broke his concentration.

'Oliver?'

Latimer automatically scooped up his own notes and pushed them into his pocket. Old habits died hard.

'Come in . . . Lucy.' He stood up.

Lucy Cookridge smiled at him. 'Oliver – you *have* been working hard . . . All these hours – and after you made your phone call your light was still on for at least an hour . . . Do you always work like this?'

He smiled back at her awkwardly, sadly aware of his own inability to deal with pretty girls in general, and tall slender girls who had the advantage of him in both directions in particular. 'That's how work gets done: By doing it.' Why was it that it always sounded so pompous when he was shy? 'I mean . . . I don't have a lot of time – I have to get back . . . and your father – '

'Step-father.' She smiled away the correction. 'You can stay as long as you like. We've rented this place for the whole summer.'

'Yes . . . No, what I mean is . . . I have to get back to *my* work – my job.' He gestured towards the table. 'Your

114

step-father only wanted me to look over all this, and then to recommend possible . . .' he fumbled for the right word '. . . possible . . . action.'. That wasn't the right word, because he hadn't started from the right place. Why was it so easy with men and so bloody difficult with women?

'I think he wants a lot more than that – if I know him. The smile became a wry grin. 'He wants to know where it is – he wants it found.'

'If it exists.' He couldn't help grinning back at her, as though they were sharing a secret.

'Does it exist?' She sounded as though she didn't care either way. But that would make her a most unusual young woman.

'Why does he want it?' That was another question plaguing him. Whatever the Senator needed, it wasn't someone else's long-lost treasures.

'Lord knows!' She raised a bare shoulder. 'Why does my step-father want anything? What does a man who's got everything want?' The shoulder raised itself again. 'Maybe he justs wants what's very difficult to get. Or maybe he'd like some off-beat publicity – there could be a lot of mileage in this, it's the sort of thing the Press would go a bundle on, if they got wind of it, Oliver.'

And maybe that was why the Senator had wanted a foreign stranger digging for him, thought Latimer. Because if the foreign stranger went poking around in Barksdale County, and in whatever archives there might be in Atlanta and Columbia and Richmond, it would be difficult to relate him to the Senator from the Mid-West, certainly. But – so what?

'Does it exist, Oliver?' She came back to her original question gracefully.

'As yet . . . I don't honestly know.' He shook his head. 'It's early days yet – a few hours isn't enough for this sort of thing, even with all this – ' he gestured to the papers ' – but . . . I have my doubts, let's say.'

'What doubts?'

115

'Oh . . . let's say . . . I'd like to know a lot more about the Wolfskin Rifles – the local militia, or whatever the Confederates called it.'

'What about them?'

'Well . . . I'd like to know how well some of them did after the war, for a start.' He blinked at her. 'I seem to remember that there were a lot of new taxes the North imposed on the South – or the Carpetbaggers did . . . If we could find some Wolfskin riflemen who paid their taxes without difficulty, that might be significant.' He blinked again. 'But then, maybe the ones who got the loot left smartly for fresh fields and pastures new . . . so an absence of local prosperity wouldn't prove anything by itself.' He shrugged. 'The thing about research is . . . there has to be a lot of it, usually, to show any results. It takes time, and a great deal of work, and a certain rather unfair spice of luck . . . Which is why there are so many impoverished treasure-hunters in the world.'

She stared at him. 'You think the Rebs could have found the strong-box – the Confederates? Not Sherman's bummers?'

That was the name for Sherman's heavy-handed foragers, but Latimer winced to hear it on Lucy Cookridge's lips. 'I think . . . it's certainly possible.'

'So it's gone.' She nodded slowly. 'That's what Kingston thinks.' She looked downcast. 'And that means you've come a long way for nothing, Oliver.'

Not for nothing, thought Latimer selfishly: either way, Senator Cookridge would have to be grateful. But he didn't want to disappoint her utterly; and, against the odds, the unknown researcher had weighed his own instinct, too – there was that, at least.

'Not exactly nothing.' He searched for something to make her feel better. 'It's . . . it's fascinating material – the letter from the farmer in Iowa, about his great-great-grandfather's story . . . And the Alexanders of Sion Crossing – and the de Brissacs . . . the bride with

116

her dowry from the coast . . . And the way the man who researched it put all that together.' He nodded. 'And the way he set about authenticating the farmer's story.'

'You think that's genuine?' She was still uncertain.

'I don't see why it shouldn't be.' He stopped himself shrugging, and smiled instead.

'But if it's *gone* – ' she made a face ' – and if you've wasted your time . . . That would be too awful!'

This time he could shrug. 'I'm sure your step-father would understand.'

She gestured. 'Oh, *he'd* understand. But . . . he said you're frightfully high-up in the British Civil Service – or the State Department – Foreign Office? – and you're doing him a favour . . . I do think he's got the cheek of Old Nick, Oliver! Apart from which, your wife will miss you.'

That would be the day, thought Latimer. But at the same time he felt absurdly flattered. Pretty girls were rarely so sympathetic in his experience; and *tall* pretty girls looked over his head.

'I'm afraid I'm not frightfully high up. And I haven't got a wife – I only have colleagues, and they certainly won't miss me.' That was God's truth! All he had to do was to remember how Mitchell had spoken to him on the phone only a few hours earlier. 'In fact, they treat me rather the same way as Mr Kingston does, actually.'

'Oh . . . Kingston – he treats everyone like that – you mustn't mind Kingston.' The smile lit her face again.

'I don't mind him. If I was black I'd be a lot worse than that.' The smile warmed him. 'I rather approve of Kingston – if that doesn't sound too patronizing. He's a man of spirit.'

'Oh . . .' His approval of Kingston seemed to confuse her. 'Yes . . . well – would you like something to eat?' She looked at her watch. 'It's long past lunch-time, so you must be starving – ?'

'No.' He resisted temptation. After that peculiar breakfast, lunch would be probably even stranger, and certainly more calorific. 'I'd better not. I have this problem, you see . . .'

'Problem?'

'Yes. I'm trying to lose weight.' He had never spoken to anyone like this. But she was a stranger, and after this was over he would never meet her again. 'I run to fat very easily. I become fat simply by looking at food.'

She frowned at him. 'But you're not fat, Oliver.'

'Yes, I am. Short and fat. Not at all like you.' Now he wanted to defend himself. 'It's a physiological thing – it's rather like trying to keep the tide back: you have to fight it all the time, every day, and you can never win. You just have to cultivate resistence to roast potatoes, and steamed puddings, and thick slices of well-buttered bread – "We shall fight them in the dining rooms, and in the restaurants, we shall fight them in the cafes and the snack-bars – we shall never surrender!"'

Her frown became half-amused. 'Never?' The half-amusement became mischievous. 'That wasn't a white flag I saw at breakfast, then? And last night? . . . Those were just flags of truce?'

'Ah . . . well, in strange surroundings . . .' It had been a mistake to banter with her: now he would have to continue a game which he really didn't know how to play '. . . one mustn't offend one's hosts – it wouldn't be good manners.'

'Of course! Like finishing up your sheeps' eyeballs in Arabia, right down to the last one – and then burping loudly?' She affected serious interest. 'I should have served you hominy grits last evening – and pecan pie . . . But . . . you must have a very miserable life, Oliver – trying not to surrender, except in foreign parts. Or do you travel a lot?'

'No . . . That is to say . . . no, I don't travel much.'

'Don't you?' She looked at him innocently. 'I would have thought that in your line of work you'd always have been jetting around – ?'

He was being pumped. She had abstained last night, and

118

Kingston had tried only half-heartedly, so that he had assumed the Senator had told all. But now he was being pumped – and banter was preferable to that.

'But I do have a rather miserable life. Always having to say "no" to steamed pudding seems to sharpen my tongue. So I'm not very popular with my subordinates.' He sighed. 'And they still call me "Fatso" behind my back.'

'But that's not fair!' Her eyes clouded. 'You're just . . . comfortably plump, Oliver.' She eyed him critically. 'Besides, you shouldn't take any notice of it. If you're not a *Filifer*, then so much the better for you – being a *Filifer* is no fun, anyway.' She smiled at him. 'If you're a *Patapouf* – then *be* a happy *Patapouf* – '

'Good heavens!' exclaimed Latimer, involuntarily.

'Oh no – !' She was instantly embarrassed. 'That doesn't mean what you think it means! I'm sorry! It means – '

'I know exactly what it means, Miss Cookridge.' His surprise equalled her embarrassment.

'No – '

'Yes!' It was quite extraordinary. In twenty years . . . or it must be less than that, but it must be nearly that . . . but in all the years which counted, anyway . . . he had never come across this, which was his own Top Secret Life, shared with nobody. '*Patapoufs et Filifers* – published in English in 1968 – *Fattypuffs and Thinifers,* Right?'

'Golly!' She looked at him incredulously. 'Gosh! I didn't know all that! In English – ?'

'Yes.' He joined her incredulity. Physically she was, of course, a perfect Thinifer – a sharp spaghetti-girl, of spires and minarets and flagpoles. But she lacked the Thinifer's intolerance. 'You've got the original French version – the Maurois? Where did you get that?'

'My father gave it to me. He bought it in Paris.' She blinked at him. 'And there's an English version?'

'A beauty.' Latimer nodded. It was after all a children's book, the story of the Great War between the Fat and the Thin, with its happy ending. It was only real life which was unhappy. 'I'll find you a copy, when I get back to London, and I'll send it to you, Miss Cookridge.'

She blinked again. 'Lucy – please . . . Would you?' She smiled lopsidedly. 'Well, then – you should know – it isn't so easy to be a . . .Thinifer?' She shook her head. 'I was a model for three years, so I know, Oliver.'

He stared back at her.

'I'll bet you never thought of that – what it's like being a bean-pole.' She returned the stare. 'I used to be scared I'd just never stop growing. You know the first thing I used to do at parties?'

Latimer shook his head.

'Sit down. Then boys would come up to me. But the moment I stood up – the only ones who survived that experience were the basket-ball players. And when you've dated one basket-ball player you've dated them all, believe me. Being a *Filifer* is no fun, I tell you.'

It occurred to Latimer that she had actually told him something about herself, which he had been amateurishly slow to explore. 'So you became a model. But that sounds rather exciting – not to say glamorous, even?'

'Huh!' For the first time she used her height to look down on him deliberately. 'I guess you don't know much about modelling? Do you?'

'No.' Latimer quailed for a moment. He had never been so critically over-looked by any woman for so long. But that, of course, was what she'd more or less said only a few seconds before: shorter males avoided taller females, so he was just another case-history. 'No. But I read the colour supplements.' He felt himself unquailing: as André Maurois had demonstrated, the Fattypuffs were easy to defeat, but utterly unconquerable. 'But you don't model anymore?'

'No.' Her mouth tightened. And, in any conventional sense, it wasn't a pretty mouth – it was too wide for convention. And she wasn't really pretty either; but models didn't have to be pretty, they had to be *striking*, with no breasts but good bones – preferably cheek bones and collar bones, so far as he could recall from the colour supplements – and Miss Lucy Cookridge had a total of four of those, undoubtedly. Even, she rather reminded him of someone, who must be one of the colour supplement favourites, at whom he had never really looked very closely.

But now she was not going to help him to any further revelation about her past, after the basket-ball dating and the modelling.

'So what did you do after that?'

The mouth tightened again. 'I nursed my father.'

'Oh?' Senator Cookridge was someone else he still didn't know enough about, although he knew more now than he'd known during that awkward passage in the Oxbridge. 'I didn't know he'd been ill – ?' Then suddenly he knew who they were talking about.

'Not my step-father.' The wide mouth twisted. 'My *real* father, Mr Latimer – Oliver, I mean . . .' she broke off.

'Oh.' If she expected him to know who her *real* father was – if that was what that pause inquired of him, to reveal that knowledge – he must disappoint her. 'Oh?'

'He was ill for a long time.'

'Yes?' He could see that she wanted him to say something more than that. But now that he knew who had researched the Sion Crossing mystery he wanted her to do the talking.

'Yes.' She looked through him for an instant, and then at him. 'He was a marvellous man.'

Her expression reassured him that she had accepted his ignorance. The next time he phoned back across the Atlantic he could ask the duty officer to find out about Senator Cookridge's step-daughter's father; because, the way ruling élites the world over worked, it was odds-on that this relationship had adjusted itself within a restricted circle of names – the more so because she had expected him to know who her father was.

'He was?' He half-smiled at her before quoting.

> '"The Knight's bones are dust,
> And his good sword rust; –
> His soul is with the saints, I trust."'

She looked at him curiously for an instant, almost as
though she was about to frown, so that he began to be
afraid that he had made some crass misjudgement. Then
her expression blanked over. 'I don't suppose you would
have known him?'

He had been revising his earlier guess as she spoke, for
even if the Senator had known the man whose wife he had
married there was more than one catchment area of
acquaintance to consider: the Senator had been successful
in business and domestic mid-western politics long before
he had come to wield power in Washington. But that
question seemed to confirm his guess after all.

'No.' Even though this was painful for her he had to
follow his luck, pressed by instinct and habit. 'He was in
the government service? What was his name?'

She shook her head. 'It doesn't matter. He would have
been before your time, Oliver.'

'Perhaps.' He started to shake his head self-deprecat-
ingly, but his eye caught the papers on the corner of the
desk. For one fraction of a second the rhythm of the shake
was disturbed, during which his brain received the eye's
message and decoded it; and then he caught the rhythm
again. 'Perhaps.' He cocked his head at her. 'But perhaps
not, you know.'

She frowned. 'You know . . . *of* him, you mean?'

'No, not of him. But I think I've met him, in a way.'

'In a way?' That mystified her. 'Where? And when?'

There was no point in mystification for its own sake, not
when he was so close to certainty. 'Last night – this
morning.' He gestured to the papers on the desk. 'Here.'

She looked down at the papers.

122

'This is his work, isn't it?' he continued as her eyes came back to him. 'He gave it to you, all this?'

'Yes,' She sounded almost defiant. 'How do you know?'

He could hardly point to the tell-tale pen-marks of a dying man. 'Oh . . . your step-father strikes me as a man of action, and I've no doubt he's highly intelligent. But a scholar he's not – and I know that there are scholars who are also men of action . . . but I know that type, too . . . No, he's not a scholar.'

She breathed out slowly. 'You were just guessing then?'

'Guessing?' The ache in his head pulsed. What he needed was a breath of air: it was odd how airless this air-conditioned coolness seemed. It would be so easy to show her those underlinings, but that would recall their pain. 'There's a sort of guessing that has its place in scholarship, you know. It's like a ladder in snakes-and-ladders . . . only then you have to go back and check all the squares you've jumped, to find out what's in them. If you're a true scholar, that is.' He offered her a half-smile. 'Sometimes what one thinks is a ladder turns out to be more like a snake.'

She considered that inadequate simile briefly. 'And what had he found – my father . . . ? A ladder or a snake?'

Latimer relaxed slightly. She was no longer pursuing the origins of his inspired guess. 'I can't say yet, for sure. I haven't had enough time yet . . . And I'm not sure that everything's here – is it? There must have been a lot more than this – originally?'

'What makes you say that?'

'Well . . .' Now she was really putting him to the test '. . . I don't believe he started out researching Sion Crossing.' A twinge of irritation jogged Latimer's headache. 'Do I have to tell you what you already know? If he gave you all this . . .'

She smiled with her mouth, but not with her eyes. 'I want to know how good you are, Oliver – if you're as good as my step-father says you are.'

'Oh yes?' Well, what she was going to learn was that if

Ministers of the Crown couldn't make him lose his cool then ex-models didn't stand a chance. 'Why did he give you his papers?' He didn't wait for an answer. 'Okay! He was in the government service, and honest men don't make money that way – and his pension died with him . . . So it was his bequest to you – would that be it?'

She didn't like that: neither the mouth nor the eyes smiled at him this time.

'So why did you then take it to your step-father?' He pressed on deliberately again. 'Because you knew your limitations? Is that it? And you knew it would tickle *his* fancy?'

The smile returned to the mouth. But the eyes were no longer neutral: they were Thinifer eyes, calculating distance and wind-drift and velocity, muzzle-to-target. 'That's bad, is it?'

At least she was honest. And honesty deserved honesty. 'Not at all!' He gave her back her own smile. 'You're quite right – and so is the Senator.' He was drawn to her honesty, even though he liked her less for it. 'Doing him a favour suits me very well: he's a man who pays his debts in full – that's my guess, if you want another guess.'

The Thinifer-look weakened. 'And repaying debts is important, is it?'

'It's what makes the world go round.' He had been too slow to recognize this in the past: it had been what had given Audley the edge over him – the foolish belief that virtue was not its own reward, but would be rewarded with preferment. But now he was wiser. 'Good for good, Miss Cookridge.'

'And evil for evil? And an eye for an eye?' She blinked at him. 'And I wish you wouldn't keep calling me "Miss Cookridge".'

'What should it be, then?'

'My friends call me Lucy. And you still haven't answered my original question – ' She pointed at the papers.

'What did he start with?' He shrugged. 'I'd guess . . . he

was writing a history of the Iowan regiments in the Civil War – ' he raised an eyebrow ' – he was from Iowa, I take it?'

She nodded. 'Cedar Rapids.'

'Indeed?' She was assuming he knew where Cedar Rapids was, although it sounded as though it could be anywhere in America. 'Yes . . . well, there's the sketch of the introduction to such a book here. And it certainly seems to have been a very loyal state in 1861 . . .' He studied the different piles of paper for a moment '. . . It says here "her affections, like the rivers of her border, flow to an inseparable union". So when Mr Lincoln called for a regiment of volunteers they gave him that in a single day, and over fifty before the end of the war, infantry and cavalry – well over 70,000 men, and all volunteers until the summer of '64 . . . And it can't have been an over-populated state exactly, in those days.' He looked up from the sheet of paper. 'And 22,000 casualties – that would be about 30 per cent – including 13,000 dead . . . though I suppose more than half of those would have been from dysentery, eh?' He was supposed to be something of an expert, after all: and he remembered reading somewhere that in spite of the legendary Boer marksmanship three-quarters of the British dead in the South African War had been slain by typhoid, a much deadlier marksman evidently, so that was a pretty safe guess.

'Yes.' She was a little over-awed by him in his expert's rôle, as she had not been in awe of him before, as a Fattypuff stranger in a strange land. 'But it was a very bloody war.'

'Mmm . . .' He must keep her over-awed, if possible. 'Barbed wire and machine-guns – a minor dress-rehearsal for 1914 . . . It's all in Henderson, of course.'

'Henderson?'

Latimer had never thought that he would live long enough to be grateful to Paul Mitchell. 'Colonel Henderson. British military historian in the late 1880s – Staff

College, and all that. Author of the standard work on Stonewall Jackson – and a considerable expert on this war of yours.' Thanks to Paul Mitchell she wouldn't push her luck in any Civil War tests now. 'Yes . . . And so they put most of these loyal Iowan regiments on river-boats, and sent them south? And that would be . . . Mississippi – flowing towards the separated Confederacy?'

She nodded cautiously. 'That's right. And they sent the Confederate prisoners back up the river. There's a great big Confederate PoW cemetery on Rock Island, by Davenport.'

'Is there now?' That was something to take back to England, to give to both Colonel Butler and Paul Mitchell, who shared a ghoulish obsession with war cemeteries and cenotaphs.

'Yes.' Another nod. 'Dad – my father . . . he pointed it out to me once. It's in the middle of the Arsenal – hundreds and hundreds of these gravestones . . . maybe thousands, I didn't count them . . . all in rows in the grass, each with rank and name, and company and regiment – all neat and tidy and forgotten.'

'Indeed?' Latimer acknowledged her memory politely. That she was no Civil War expert herself was reassuring, even though it precluded further questions about the historical details in the papers. But maybe that was also just as well; and, in any case, he was much more interested in the more recently deceased than in the old dead of Rock Island . . . And even more interested in the living, who would by now be jetting somewhere between Paris and Rome on his whirlwind European fact-finding tour.

But she was looking at him questioningly.

'Yes . . . well – ' He sorted quickly though what little he knew about 'dad', which amounted to little more than *government service*, *long illness* and this diversion from Iowan military history to a mystery at Sion Crossing ' – your father was obviously a considerable scholar. But . . . I'd guess . . . not a professional historian?'

126

'No. But the Civil War had always been his hobby, for as long as I can remember.' Her expression, although well-controlled, hinted at a mixture of happy and sad recollections. 'I used to visit him . . . not very often. But we went on trips – mostly to places I don't remember. Except Gettysburg, once.'

'Gettysburg.' Even before his crash transatlantic course in the Civil War, by courtesy of Penguin Books and Professor Bruce Catton, Latimer had heard of Gettysburg: Abraham Lincoln had made a speech at the war cemetery there, which had been poorly received at the time and immortal thereafter. 'Of course. "Government of the people, by the people, for the people".'

'Yes.' She drew a breath. 'He read that to me there. He wanted me to learn it by heart. He said every American should know it.'

'And did you?' She was softening up nicely.

'Did I heck! Not then – ' She caught herself. 'Oliver . . . learning speeches on holiday – and touring old battlefields . . . maybe that's okay for little boys, but it surely doesn't wow little girls, I tell you!' She cocked her eye at him. 'You don't have any little girls by any chance?'

'Perish the thought!' The question caught him by surprise. 'Neither little nor big – I'm not a married man – ' In his turn he caught himself: to be a middle-aged bachelor these days invited the worst sort of suspicion in some people, which those words would seem to confirm. 'Not that I'm against either variety – quite the contrary – *absolutely* the contrary . . . But I do see that . . . ah . . . battlefields might not be to every little girl's taste. No – ' Out of nowhere he remembered suddenly that David Audley had once boasted irritatingly of how much his daughter enjoyed being dragged across battlefields, and through castles and abbeys. Damn the man! And damn the daughter!

'You've just remembered one,' said Lucy.

Latimer blinked. 'One what?'

127

'Little girl.' She gazed at him sadly. 'She must be remarkable. But I wasn't.'

Grrr! thought Latimer. 'I was thinking more of her father, actually.' He sweetened his face to contradict his feelings.

'A friend of yours?'

'A colleague.' He experienced a curious mixture of guilt and exultation. Audley would have enjoyed this little job, for it fitted him like a glove. And it should have been his, too! But for once he had taken something that was Audley's.

'But you like him – I can see that.' She misread his smile wonderfully.

'He's a remarkable man.' The unpalatable truth quite suddenly offered him a undeserved reward. 'In fact, he's probably rather like your father was – a natural scholar in the government service.' That made the next question equally natural. 'What did your father do in the government service, exactly?'

She waved a slender hand. 'Oh . . . something in research – something to do with selecting people for voluntary service overseas I think. One of these Washington agencies with lots of letters spelling a word that isn't in the dictionary – I never could get the hang of it. But he was darn good at it . . . until he got sick.'

Latimer experienced a pang of disappointment. It was no good, that avenue: either she knew better, but wasn't telling, or she didn't know, and couldn't tell. Yet there was still a far more intriguing question remaining which she could answer, and by wrapping it up inside an unimportant one he was perfectly placed to ask it quite innocently.

'Yes, I know just the sort of thing you mean.' He nodded as though satisfied, and then gestured to the Sion Crossing papers. 'And those tell me that he was good at whatever he did. There's nothing like a man's research notes for revealing the quality of his mind – it's like listening to him thinking.'

128

She gave him a pathetically grateful look.

'Yes.' He was encouraged to lay on the praise to an extra thickness. After all, apart from the gratitude it would undoubtedly inspire, it was substantially well-deserved: if the man could achieve this in the extremity of a terminal illness, he must have been quite something in his prime. 'He had a keen mind, did your father.' That was thick enough, coming from a stranger; anything more might be disbelieved, for although she was vulnerable where her dead father was concerned, she wasn't stupid. 'And this . . . was part of your inheritance, was it?'

'Not part of it.' She swayed, giraffe-like. 'Poor old Dad . . . he didn't have much to leave. He just had his pension . . . and he felt bad about that. Although, heaven only knows – Mother was loaded, and Tom wouldn't touch a cent of that, naturally . . . And he's always trying to give me more.' She smiled wanly. 'So this was all of it, Oliver. The family fortune – if I could find it, you might say.'

That was perfect, thought Latimer, inflating 'Tom' to the man he had met in the Oxbridge, the Chairman of the President's new defence committee, for whose favour he had come all this way; she had led him to that crucial question herself.

'Yes, I can understand that, too.' He nodded understandingly. 'It's the same with us. "On Her Majesty's Service" is not exactly the quickest route to treasure on earth . . . so he tried to find a short-cut for you.' He smiled at her, only slightly discomforted by that familiar twinge of self-knowledge and self-contempt. '"Tom" being your step-father, I take it? But how did he come into this?'

She looked at him doubtfully.

'You don't have to tell me if it's private.' He shook his head. 'I've no axe to grind – this is just a favour I'm doing him, and it's none of my business. So you can trust me – but, by the same token, I don't need to know everything, if it's private.'

If that didn't fix the hook, nothing would!

'It's just . . . he knew . . . Dad knew, towards the end, that he wasn't going to be able to unravel everything, you see.' She pointed to the papers. 'It's not all there, is it?'

Latimer considered the papers in their neat piles, and then thought for a moment. 'Well . . . not quite, perhaps.' He could put the whole thing together much better now, he realized: the man had not been mobile, and correspondence was no substitute for face-to-face interrogation. But, much more important than that, he must have been dogged by the fear that he would betray what he was really seeking to his correspondents –

'Not quite.' Suddenly he looked at her with a brand-new certainty. He had written memoranda to intelligence sections, and departments, and agencies, dogged by exactly the same fear – that they would be prematurely alerted to his line of investigation. 'But the signposts are there, sure enough.'

'They are?' She frowned. 'But . . . but, Oliver – all those questions – about the division of Georgia counties, and how the volunteer units were raised in the Civil War – ? And all that nonsense?'

Latimer grinned, and turned to the table to find the sorted pile of material which he regarded as important, in which the specks of gold glinted in the midst of rubbish.

There it was – *Rabbit-trap, Bear-hug, Hound-dog, Sugar-tit, Wolfskin* – 'places holding court are generally called "law grounds"' – and the Wolfskin Rifles, the 184th Georgia Volunteers, had boasted that they pinched their sweethearts' cheeks until they squeaked, and took their liquor straight, and chewed tobacco with the right jaw, and could beat a negro at double-shuffle, and ate red pepper for breakfast and drank gunpowder for supper.

And much more. Starting from those exhaustive lists of Iowan regiments and musterings and personnel, the author had appeared to march southwards, following his Iowans through sickness and health as well as skirmishes

130

and battles and sieges – Arkansas Post and Shiloh, Corinth and Vicksburg, Snake Creek Gap and Kennesaw Mountain, Ezra Church and Lovejoy Station – until the veteran survivors and replacements had finally massed in the ruins of Atlanta for Sherman's bombing raid on the Confederacy, the march to the sea.

But by then the researcher's interest seemed to have expanded to embrace not only the whole of Sherman's army, but also the motley Georgia state militia which was now all that opposed them – an immense pile of facts, out of which in the end the tiny vital clues about the Sion Crossing had naturally surfaced here and there; which had first trapped his interest accidentally, and then roused his curiosity more as he extracted them and united them together, and finally had taken over the whole book, like a cuckoo in the nest.

Well . . . that was what he had thought until a moment ago, *but he had been wrong*!

Sion Crossing had been the beginning and the end of the whole thing, and everything else had been an elaborate blind designed to deceive his scholarly correspondents, and anyone else who might look at all this research without the one vital piece of knowledge which the author had bequeathed to his daughter – that, in the hijacking and dispersal of the loot, *the best part of it had been overlooked and abandoned*!

Latimer squinted at the papers in his hand, and wondered if he himself would have come to that exact conclusion if he hadn't known from the start what he was looking for.

Would he? He had to be honest with himself about this –

'Oliver?' Lucy was tired of being stared at.

'I'm sorry. I was just thinking.' He tried to focus on her, but the question nagged at him.

'Thinking about what?' She was being more polite to him that she would have been to most people, in different circumstances, he decided.

'About your father.' He would have got it in the end,

given a lot more time, because that was what he was trained to do, but also because his mind worked that way, and because he liked doing what he was doing.

'What about my father?' She was nearly at the end of her tether of politeness.

'He worked for your Central Intelligence Agency – or the Federal Bureau . . . didn't he?' Since this wasn't a matter of state security, American or British, he could be honest with her without indiscretion.

That made her frown – as well she might, whether she was very clever, and wanted to deceive him, or not so clever, and knew no better.

'I don't know.' She thought for a moment. 'But – maybe he did . . . I don't know, Oliver.'

That sounded like honesty. And she had no reason to be dishonest, that he could imagine – not when her step-father was involved. For he would never involve the British in any sort of security indiscretion: that was the real safeguard and guarantee in this curious affair.

'But I know. Because I know what he was trying to do now – and how he was trying to do it.' He lifted the papers in his hand, and then put them back on the desk. 'Because I would have done the same, I suppose . . . But I still can't really work out where your step-father comes in, that's all.' Holding to the objective was what it was all about, not simply in peace and war but in life itself. Everything else was self-indulgence.

She studied him with a strange intentness. 'I think . . . I think maybe you won't like it, Oliver.'

Latimer thought that, if she thought that, she was probably right. But he was committed now. 'Try me.'

'All right.' She nerved herself to it. 'Dad knew this man – this Englishman . . . He worked with him, in the old days, you see . . .' She trailed off, with the slightest shade of extra colour touching her well-made-up cheek-bones. But, of course, an ex-model would know how to apply all that stuff they put on their faces –

132

And then, *of course and of course and of course*, he knew what she was trying to say!

'David Audley?'

'Yes.' The well-made-up cheek twitched. 'Dad didn't actually *like* him – he said he was an arrogant bastard – a big clever arrogant bastard . . .'

'Yes?' That was a very fair description of David Audley, as economical as it was accurate.

'But he said he was good – ' she baulked momentarily ' – good at his job, and good at finding things.'

Also accurate. 'Yes?'

'Yes.' She swallowed. 'And he also owed Dad a favour, apparently.'

If that was accurate it was interesting. But it still rang true: Audley was a great one for favours, it was very much how he operated. And, after all, that was how he himself was operating now, however belatedly.

She indicated the papers. 'Dad wanted him to take them over. He knew . . . he knew I couldn't make anything out of them – which is true. But . . . he wasn't *sure* Audley would help me – ' her eyes widened ' – do you see?'

Latimer saw, and to the uttermost part. Although this was exactly the sort of conundrum which would have tempted Audley, that in itself might not have been enough, particularly since the man had been in hot water more than once for indulging his private curiosities in defiance of the rules. It had been the prospect of doing the Chairman of the Atlantic Defence Committee a favour which had made it at once respectable and irresistible to them both.

'Yes, I do see.' He nodded. 'Your father suggested you should enlist your step-father.'

'Right. He knew Tom was the chairman-elect of this new committee. And that meant a European trip pretty soon, with all the hassle over there about the new missiles, he said.' She paused. 'And . . . well, he knew Tom wouldn't refuse me, once he was sure it was all above board – not illegal, or anything. And he said Audley wouldn't refuse Tom.'

Latimer nodded again. That was the final reassurance, on which he'd relied from the start even without knowing all this. And presumably it had only been because the Senator was perhaps a little sensitive about mentioning his wife's first husband – the more so if that man was ex-CIA – that he'd been inhibited from complete frankness in London.

He smiled. 'So everything's gone according to plan – except for me?'

'For you?'

'I'm not Dr David Audley.'

'Oh . . . no.' Her face clouded for an instant, casting a shadow also on his own satisfaction at having finally tied up the last loose ends. 'No. But sometimes I guess a plan can go better than it was planned, Oliver.'

'How d'you mean . . . better?' If it had been a compliment it was at odds with her expression.

'Uh-huh. This Dr David Audley . . . the way Dad remembered him . . . he doesn't sound a very nice man?' The cloud darkened. 'And I think maybe you are.'

No one had ever said that to him. But – so why was she so sad? The contradiction of the words with the look in her eyes confused him, not least because if made him think of his enemy with a detachment he had never achieved before. Because he wanted to agree with her, and yet now that he looked at the evidence it was against him: the truth was that David Audley was undoubtedly well-hated in certain quarters, his own particularly; but he was equally certainly admired and well-liked, and presumably loved also, in others. Even, within the limits of duty and self-interest, he somehow extracted loyalty of a sort from his professional foreign contacts, men like Colonel Howard Morris, and the Israeli, Shapiro, and the German Herzner . . . not to mention the cynical and self-seeking

Paul Mitchell. And he, Oliver St John Latimer, had no one like that on whom he could half-ways depend.

'I think you're wrong.' Even that Thin Red Line, Colonel Butler, who let nothing sway him from the Queen's service, *liked* Audley, even while he disapproved of his unreliability: it was utterly incomprehensible, that. 'And he's extremely clever.'

'Yes. Dad said that.' She looked at him. 'But so are you – and I think Dad would have liked you, Oliver.'

Suddenly, he understood. He had dignified himself, to believe that he had anything to do with her sadness, when it had nothing to do with him at all – when, much more simply, anything which had to do with her father – her *real* father – automatically saddened her. For she had seen him die, and he'd probably died slow and hard while pulling all these papers together as his only legacy.

And, seeing that, he could glimpse much more, about both of them, father and daughter –

There would be love and rage in both of them: love and rage in her father at the unfairness of death, which forced him to use two men he probably hated most, Audley and the Senator, to carry out his plan; and love and rage in her, to carry out his plan with those men when she didn't need his legacy at all. But that, of course, would only make her all the more determined to execute his last will and testament: not out of greed, and for profit, but out of love and rage, and for loyalty.

'I think I might have liked him, as a matter of fact.' In reality that was unlikely, the way he felt about most Americans. But Lucy Cookridge – or whatever her real name was – was an exception to his rules about embarrassingly tall and thin women, not to mention Americans. And a good plan deserved to succeed for its own sake, not to mention the benefits he must derive from doing Senator Cookridge this little favour. 'And, if it's there, I'll do my best to find it, anyway – I promise you that.'

If anything, she looked more unhappy. But his head

ached, and he felt airlessly air-conditioned if not actually cold; and although it would no doubt be hellishly hot and humid outside in the real Georgia of 1983 and 1864, that was where he wanted to be now. He'd had enough of documents, and clues *down*, and *across*, for the time being.

He drew a deep breath, and tried to indicate that he'd had enough of scholarship for the time being, without actually saying so.

'Would you like something to eat?' She misread the signal.

'No. I'd like to take some exercise.' In a way, the challenge now wasn't very different from those he had to tackle professionally, back in England: *first*, the information (which in this instance had been very skilfully assembled, for all that it was still incomplete – as it always was!); *second*, the extrapolation from that information, after the chaff and the waste paper and the red herrings had been blown and thrown away respectively, so that more precise and relevant facts might be sought. And then, *third*, after those facts had been acquired, his own plan of action.

'Oh . . . yes.' She frowned. 'I suppose . . . you want to see Sion Crossing?' She spoke with a curious unwillingness.

'Yes.' It would be oven-hot outside – ridiculously hot, judging by yesterday. But his curiosity about the locations and events of 1864 was even hotter than that now. 'Kingston said you had a car if I wanted it – ' he turned back to the papers ' – and there's a sketch-map here, somewhere . . . and we can't be more than five miles away from where it all happened – ' he had the right pile now, and the sketch-map was in that somewhere, if he could just find it –

There it was! Although those were not her father's marks on it – they were too decisive for that in their reconstruction of 1864 on 1983.

He studied it for a moment, to get his bearings, and then turned it towards her, daring to move closer and getting a whiff of expensive perfume as a reward for his daring.

He drew back as far as he could. 'And I want to go from *there* . . . to *there* – '

All Sion land, on the ridge above Sion Crossing, from Sion Church to Sion itself: it was the Promised Land which he wanted to see for himself now.

7

Mitchell in London: Council of War

'Sit down, Paul,' said Colonel Butler, ever courteous.

It might be Sunday evening outside in the real world, and midday or thereabouts in Sion Crossing; but it was always any time on any working day of the year for Jack Butler, thought Mitchell.

He sat down gingerly, in order not to disturb the enduring remains of his hangover unnecessarily. 'You've heard the tape of my dialogue with Latimer, from this morning, sir?'

Butler was staring at him as though the hangover showed. 'Where's this place Sion Crossing?'

Mitchell collected his thoughts. 'We think it's in Georgia, sir. Not very far from Atlanta. The nearest town is called Smithsville – '

'We?'

'I managed to hunt up a pal of mine who was able to place it. And we ran a trace on Latimer's call – I got the number from him while we were talking. It was engaged while he was on the phone. I'm pretty sure he is where he says he is, sir.'

Butler nodded. 'Who is this friend of yours?'

'He teaches American history.' Although he had drunk several pints of orange juice he still felt dreadfully thirsty. 'In a university up north. He's on vacation at the moment. He's going to call us back when he's got something for us.'

Colonel Butler was unmoved by such evidence of friendship. 'Military history, that would be?'

'What else?' The hair of the dog which had bitten him was the traditional recipe. But the way he felt, there had been a whole pack of them. 'He's what they call "a Civil War buff".'

There was a new file on Butler's desk, under his hand. But he didn't look down at it. 'How did you think Latimer sounded?'

'Like himself.' Mitchell didn't shrug, in case his head fell off. 'A bit stroppy. Not at all worried.'

Colonel Butler gave a single nod. 'That's what I thought. He didn't sound pushed in any way that I could detect.'

'And he phoned in roughly on time.' He couldn't nod any more than he could shrug. 'He obeyed the rules.'

Another single nod. 'So what should we think of that?'

The first thing that Mitchell thought, and not for the first time, was that the comforting thing about Jack Butler was that responsibility came as naturally to him as breathing: that 'we' meant that he was taking it now, whatever happened.

'I think it stinks.' The less comforting thing about Butler was that his virtues encouraged honesty, against better judgement. 'If it was me I'd pull him out.'

'You think Oliver Latimer is up to something?'

Dearly as he would have loved to nod, Mitchell found himself shaking his head, and instantly regretted doing so. 'No. But I think someone is, sir.'

'Who?'

But even honesty went only so far. 'What does David say?'

'I'm asking you, not David,' Butler chided him gently.

Put your money where your mouth is, Mitchell. 'Okay. But he knows Howard Morris better than I do. They're old chums.'

'So this is CIA business, you think?'

The honesty came back. 'Not the way Howard Morris tells it. It seems he doesn't like it either. In fact . . . if you ask me, I think Colonel Howard Morris is a rather worried man.'

'And what is it that is worrying him? Apart, that is, from the involvement of Senator Thomas Cookridge in whatever it is – ?'

139

Ordinarily, Mitchell might have smiled. 'I'd say . . . the same two things that are worrying me now. He stuck his nose into something which wasn't his business. And now his nose is caught, and he doesn't know what the hell's going on.'

'Yes . . .' Sympathy was not within Butler's range of emotions. Without moving the hand covering the file he reached out to the buttons of his intercom.

Nothing happened. The blunt bricklayer's fingers tapped on the file, and then the intercom fingers tapped another number.

'Sir?' inquired the voice.

'Is Dr Audley in?' Butler stared through Mitchell.

'Yes, sir.' The voice didn't need to consult the book. Research and Development was no hive of industry on any August Sunday evening.

'Find him for me.' Butler paused. 'Try Records. Thank you.' Butler stabbed another button and focussed on Mitchell. 'You have no call to worry. You should have spoken directly to me, instead of to James. But that's a minor detail. Just remember that it's always better to be safe than sorry next time.'

'Yes, sir.' On Butler's lips the most banal cliché was somehow acceptable. And also there was the underlying suspicion that beneath that veneer of soldierly simplicity lay all the vast resources of peasant cunning Butler had inherited from his humble northern origins. It was at moments like this that Mitchell always remembered Field-Marshal 'Wully' Robertson, who had risen from the ranks to head the Imperial General Staff of the biggest and best British Army of all time.

Buzz-buzz, buzz-buzz –

Butler jabbed the intercom. 'David?'

'Jack – I'm busy with this dreadful Beast of yours – '

'Come up out of there.' Butler brushed aside Audley's dislike of the wonderful new technology in the basement, which summoned up distilled information on to the screen

140

at a touch of the finger in a fraction of a second. But then, of course, what Audley didn't like was that the dreadful instrument not only logged the user's identity, but also – as a prerequisite of use – the requirement reason as well as the date and time of the inquiry.

'But I haven't finished, Jack.'

Butler swivelled in his chair, towards the screen at his right, and punched its keys confidently. The blank screen came alive, with a pre-ordained list of questions with which Mitchell himself was well acquainted: the dreadful Beast was asking Colonel Butler not only what he wanted, but also by what right and authority he wanted this information.

Butler stabbed a finger at Mitchell. 'You look out of that window, Dr Mitchell.'

Mitchell looked into the pale blue of Sunday evening over the Thames. One day, when he sat in that chair, his unique voice-print would be enough; but, for the time being, Butler had to print his own master's code to satisfy the computer, to override all its prohibitions.

'Right.' Butler released him, and the screen was full of words now – the exact words which Audley must be reading on his own screen far below them. Once upon a time he could have browsed at leisure on those words, when he had at last found them, and no one but he would have known what he had consumed. But now he was betrayed on record.

'For God's sake, Jack – '

'Come up. I've got a print-out of all that. Don't waste your time with it – or mine.' The north-country vowels were undisguised in Colonel Butler's voice. 'And I've got Dr Mitchell here too, and you're wasting his time – you *coom oop*, an' don't argue the toss with me, David!'

Jack Butler had been bullying David Audley for years, as long as Mitchell had known them – ever since they had first looked him over in his own days of innocence. As a subordinate, an equal and now as his master, Butler had bullied Audley, and chivvied him, and protected him, and cherished him; even, until the cause had become plainly hopeless, since Audley would have none of it, old Jack had schemed (as far as he was capable of that sort of scheming) to sit old David in the very chair in which he now sat.

'Oh – all right, Jack! Have it your own way, if you must!' Audley grumbled peevishly. 'You've got my bloody report – you know how much sleep I had last night? You know how late I got home? All the bloody week at Cheltenham – back here Friday afternoon – back on the job last night – back here again now . . . If I was in a trade union I'd be on overtime and double time-and-a-half now, and you couldn't bloody *afford* me – you know that?'

'Up here on the double.' Butler's finger cut off the complaint, and then punched another number on the intercom. Then he looked at Mitchell. 'He doesn't change, does he?'

That was true: the nice thing, and the nasty one, was that David was always David, which was his strength and his weakness. But what was more interesting, was that there was a subtle change in Butler himself: from being Acting-Director he was Director now; and, although he would not have sought that promotion, he had accepted it because it was his duty to obey his sovereign's orders, and that was that.

The intercom buzzed. But the blunt finger first tapped a key in the visual display unit, to bring up more of what Audley had been looking at on the Beast in the basement, before moving across to accept the intercom's call.

'Steeple Horley – Dr and Mrs Audley and Cathy Audley – ?' A childish voice answered the acceptance.

Butler was rolling back what Dr David Audley had been looking at in the basement: the curse of the Beast was that the Director could now recall exactly what any of his subordinates had been recalling out of the department's records, and from those in all other linked computer memory banks integrated with the system and cleared for the Director's scrutiny.

'Cathy?' Butler stopped the screen for a moment, then rolled it back some more.

'Uncle Jack!' Audley's daughter needed no computer to identify her godfather. 'Where's Daddy?'

'That's why I'm phoning, my lass.' Butler studied the screen, then rolled it back further.

'I'll get Mummy – '

'No need to bother your Mother.' This bit of screen clearly interested Butler. 'Just tell 'er your Dad'll be late again, and it's all my fault. She'll understand – right?'

'Oh?' Miss Audley was evidently not such a soft touch. 'Well . . . *she* may – but *I* don't, Uncle Jack . . . Honestly – he *promised* us – he really did!'

'Then he had no right to.' Butler treated his god-daughter as an equal. 'You know what it says in the book – because I've showed it to you: "Duty is a jealous God", it says. And wives and little girls come second to duty. So now I'm busy too – an' I've got little girls of my own – '

'*Big* girls, they are – '

'Aye – an' big girls are more trouble than little ones . . . at least, they used to be.' As he spoke, Butler cleared the screen. 'Now, don't *you* trouble me, my lass – you look after your Mother, that's your job, an' I'll do mine – right?'

There was a fractional pause. 'Yes, Uncle Jack.'

Butler avoided Mitchell's eye. 'Nay, my lass – you don't fret now, eh? I have him here, under my hand – you tell your Mother that – right? So goodbye, then.'

'Good. – ' The rest of Cathy Audley's goodbye was guillotined by the jealous god's finger, ruthlessly.

Marvellous! thought Mitchell. *One day, when I'm old and equally horrible, and if we've held the line for Cathy, maybe I'll say to some god-daughter of mine 'I remember hearing Old Colonel Butler talk to David Audley's daughter, and he said – '*

'What actually happened last night, Paul?' said Colonel Butler.

Mitchell was caught between imagining the distant future and expecting Audley to come barging in without knocking, in the immediate present.

'He'll take his time.' Butler identified half his fear, in allowing for what had been in Audley's report of last night's passage-of-arms, and what hadn't been.

Once again, the truth was called for. 'We tracked Howard Morris down in one of his pubs, sir. And he'd had a fair skinful by then already.'

'Aye.' Butler knew all about Howard Morris.

'David pushed him.' How could he adequately describe it? 'I think they exchanged their own signals . . . And then they stopped, and we went on to another pub, and then we had a meal in another pub, and a lot more to drink. And I'm a bit vague about what happened after that – except that I think David put a watch on him, after we poured him back into his flat after midnight.' Truth. 'I was a bit the worse for wear by then, sir. I came back here and slept if off until Latimer phoned up at the crack of dawn.'

Butler accepted the truth without dismay. 'But since then you haven't attempted to check with the computer about anything Colonel Morris gave you both. Why not?'

Truth? 'I thought about it. But David seems to know all those answers already. And then there was Latimer's call.'

'And you had a hangover to deal with.'

'That too,' agreed Mitchell. 'But I thought you'd rather know about Sion Crossing, anyway.' He stared at Colonel Butler for a moment. 'I suppose I could have inquired about a dead American by the name of Macallan, ex-CIA, and also ex-father to Senator Thomas Cookridge's step-daughter, who apparently has long eye-lashes and longer legs – the step-daughter, I mean . . . And I'd be running a trace on *her*, if David hasn't done that already. Because from what Howard Morris said it looks like she's been *Mata Hari-ing* him and poor old Oliver St John Latimer

144

both on behalf of her step-father.' He watched Colonel Butler. 'But David'll have done that for sure.'

'Yes.' Butler met his scrutiny in the middle of the no-man's-land between them, and drove it back into his own trenches. 'And?'

How much had Audley reported? Well, he wasn't about to play games with Jack Butler himself anyway, Mitchell decided. Friendship did not go as far as that on this occasion.

'David threw in a name which isn't in my book. Before my time, he said . . . but it certainly put the fear of God – or the Devil – into Howard Morris. Because they both clammed up about the job after that, and concentrated on drinking themselves and me under the table.' Mitchell made a face at his lord and master. 'Which they certainly succeeded in doing in my case.'

Butler regarded him unsympathetically. 'What name?'

For a guess, Colonel Butler probably hadn't thrown his heart up the morning after since King George VI had first addressed him as a trusty and well-beloved second-lieutenant all those years ago.

'Debreczen.' Mitchell's tongue felt like a corpse on a three-day-old battlefield.

The console of the Colonel's display unit emitted a nasty little beeping sound, and a light on it flashed red, to offer a transmission. Butler poked a key, and the screen filled up with words again. Someone, somewhere, had been busy this early Sunday evening, and knew where the Colonel could be found.

Butler was reading the screen. 'Debreczen?'

'A place or a person, but probably a place. "Debreczen List" was what he actually said – "from the Debreczen List". Sounds like anywhere east of the Oder-Neisse line. Though I suppose it could be a mining town in Pennsylvania.'

Butler finished reading, and methodically put the words back into the Beast's memory before turning to

Mitchell. 'Debreczen – yes. It's a place.' He nodded unhelpfully.

But such unhelpfulness was a challenge. And that was perhaps what it was meant to be. 'Well, when you're through with me I can always go and try my luck in the basement.'

'You could try.'

There was a distinctive *thump* on the door. In the absence of the presiding dragon-lady outside. Audley had penetrated to the Holy of Holies by himself, ignoring the red lights on the way while taking his time. But the last red light was physically impassable.

Another *thump*. That was Audley, for sure: not a light-handed man, he had never merely knocked on a door in his life, preferring to pummel it with the soft side of his clenched fist as though to warn those on the other side that he was about to come in whether they liked it or not.

Butler pressed another of his buttons, to release the lock.

'Come in, David.'

Audley came in frowning, and Mitchell was half-pleased and half-frightened to observe that he looked somewhat under the weather. Over the years, Faith had done her best with him, but there was still no one who could wear good suits more scruffily: he looked as though he had slept in this one – in fact, he looked curiously as though he'd stepped straight out of one of Matthew Brady's Civil War photographs, unpressed and unshaven and unwashed. All that was needed was a stovepipe hat, a chewed cigar and the strong smell of whisky.

'Christ, Jack – one of these days I'm going to take a sledgehammer to that bloody contraption of yours in the basement!' Audley gave Mitchell a grimace. 'I swear I will! I'll boil its chips, and serve them up mashed.'

Butler sat back. 'It's been tried before. The Luddites tried to smash the industrial revolution. It didn't work then, and it won't work now.' He folded his arms. 'You'll be the one who gets mashed – like Ned Ludd.'

146

Audley gave him a sidelong look. 'You think progress can't be held up? Ask Attila the Hun – and ask the National Graphical Association, Jack. They've not done too badly.'

Butler sniffed. 'You read too much ancient history – and you hobnob with too many journalists. Besides . . . I thought our Two-Four-Thousand was commonly known as "The Beast", not as "a contraption"?'

'Huh!' It must be a matching hangover that was making Audley so vulnerable. But Butler was handling him with more authority, also; and the sooner Audley accepted that fact, the better for both of them. 'And so it is – a beastly contraption! It's a Jabberwock, Jack – and it needs a vorpal blade to go *snicker-snack*, and the sooner the better, before it dishes us all!' Plainly, Audley had not got the message yet. 'You know what it did to me?'

Mitchell stole a glance at Colonel Butler. But Colonel Butler was still looking as nearly benign as he was capable of looking. Which meant – friendship aside – that the Colonel understood the Two-Four-Thousand Beast's limitations, and how he needed Audley to work with it . . . even though he must know exactly what it had done to cause offence.

'It refused to give me what I wanted.' Outrage, rather than amazement, sat on Audley's brow. '"Not available", it said – a bloody machine! "Not available", when I know that half the stuff that's *not available* is what I damn well put into the files myself! *A contraption*, Jack!' He pointed accusingly at Colonel Butler. 'If you'd said "Not available" – damn it, I could have argued with you . . . but you wouldn't have said that – but . . . *contraption* – is that the shape of things to come, now you're boss? How soon before the Beast is the organ-grinder, and we're all just the monkeys?'

Butler unfolded his arms. 'I'm the organ-grinder. And the sooner you understand *that*, the better. What it won't give you is what I don't intend it to give you – or anyone else.'

Audley cooled. In fact, he cooled so quickly that Mitchell found a whole new set of reasons why Butler needed Audley as well as the Beast.

'Okay.' Audley gave his friend his coldest smile. 'If you think I can't reconstruct Bill Macallan's last years from my own sources . . . then *up yours*, Jack! Because I've got contacts who'll talk to me, who wouldn't give your Beast the time of day – okay?'

Mitchell glanced at Colonel Butler uneasily, in the knowledge that he had just lost a bet with himself. Because it wasn't *Debreczen* which had been embargoed, wherever it might be, but the long-time-a-dying Macallan, the Senator's wife's first husband, on whom Audley's curiosity was centred.

'I don't doubt it for a moment.' Butler was never as polite with Audley as with the rest of mankind, but he was always more long-suffering.

'No.' And Audley, for his part, was more quickly defused by Butler than anyone else. 'But when you do, my redundancy letter will be in the post, eh Jack?' He shook his head. 'I'm sorry, Jack – you're right, and I'm wrong . . . I'm Captain Swing, if not Ned Ludd . . . But that Beast of yours *is* a beast . . . And after last night I'm a bit fragile –' he looked at Mitchell ' – when you get to my age you don't get drunk so easily, Paul . . . you just begin to feel your age next day, and that isn't pleasant.' He smiled. 'How do you feel?'

He was with two very dangerous old men again, thought Mitchell. And it was because they were both good men – old-fashioned *good*, as well as good at their job – that they were so very dangerous.

'Don't ask, David!' No pretence was required. 'At the moment I feel your age rather than mine, if you must know.'

'Yes. Boozing is so *tiring*.' Audley switched back to Butler. 'But we were only doing our duty, Jack. Old Howard Morris is a First Division drinker, but he'll not be

148

thinking straight for twenty-four hours. And, short of taking him into custody, that was the best we could do.'

'And what will he be doing then?' Butler leaned forward.

'He'll start trying to put two and two together. And then, as he would put it, the shit will be in the fan, I rather think.'

Butler frowned. 'But he's out of favour. So what weight does he carry?'

Audley shook his head. 'He's only out of favour so long as he doesn't draw on his capital. If he wants to push it all the way back to Washington, then they'll start to take notice. Because then they'll remember just how damn good he is – Bradford knows that, and Bradford knows me as well, and when Howard throws me in Mike will start taking him very seriously. Because they'll both be able to put Macallan into the picture, Jack. And I'd guess Macallan is dynamite.' He paused. 'With Senator Cookridge as the fuse in the dynamite . . . They'll be into bomb disposal, with those two.'

'But *why*?' Butler stared at Audley. 'Where's the sense?'

'Search me! But when someone sets a bomb where's the sense? All I've done is buy a little time – and all I know is that we've got a bomb and a fuse. And Oliver St John Latimer may be sitting on top of it, studying the American Civil War and scratching his backside. That's all *I* know, Jack.' He gazed at Butler innocently. 'The Beast wouldn't give me any more – remember?'

Butler pushed the file across the table. 'It's all in there. I was going to give it to you anyway. I just didn't want anyone else to look at it.'

Audley didn't touch the file. 'What's in there that's new?'

'Nothing. That's the whole trouble.'

Audley looked down at the file, and then back at Butler. 'He wasn't doing anything? What was he doing?'

Butler's face set hard. 'He was dying, David. That was what he was doing.'

'I know that. He'd been dying for years, off and on.' No one could be more brutally honest than Audley when he set his mind to it. 'He'd had a lot of practice.'

'He knew it this time.'

'Well . . . that's something.' Audley cocked his head.

'The daughter nursed him. Lucy Cookridge.'

'Why Cookridge? Why not Macallan?'

'That was the mother's doing. Cookridge brought her up as though she was his own.' Butler paused. 'And the word is that Cookridge is clean.' Another pause. 'Deep vetted.'

'By whom?'

'Bradford. They gave us that before he came over. He's cleared all the way up. Debreczen included.'

Audley nodded. 'Bradford's about the best there is.' His nose wrinkled. 'And that makes it . . . contradictory, Jack.'

Mitchell knew he was out of his depth, but he was tired of being part of the furnishings. 'Why contradictory?' he inquired.

'Because it means a man like Cookridge isn't going to play silly games – mischievous games,' snapped Butler. 'Not with this department's new deputy-director.'

'Not with *anyone* in this department at the moment, Paul.' Audley gave Mitchell his evil smile. 'Not even with *me* – not when we're about to take the first delivery of Cruise missiles. And the way Central America and the Middle East are shaping up . . . troubles they've got enough to complicate their relations with us in the coming months, without . . . what Jack likes to call "silly games".' The smile grew more evil. 'And certainly not at Oliver's expense, much as that would delight me personally.'

Butler sat up. 'And troubles *I've* got without *you* playing games, either.'

'Perish the thought, Jack!' Audley scrubbed his face clean. 'I am all too well aware of Oliver's value.'

'David – '

'I even know that old Fred Clinton recruited him at least partly to demonstrate that I wasn't the only fish in the sea – I do know *all* that. And now he will undoubtedly be your strong right arm, when you've licked him into shape – I know *that* too, Jack.' Audley was doing his best to sound sincere. 'But the fact is that at this moment he is out there somewhere, quite on his own. And, if I may say so, he's no single-handed sailor – he's an organizer and a planner and a trap-setter . . . In fact, he's even less of a field-man than I am.'

Mitchell frowned at him. 'But David . . . if Cookridge is okay . . . do we really have anything to worry about? Apart from which, Oliver's no fool.'

Audley raised a finger. 'Ah . . . now that isn't quite what I said, young Paul. Because, given the right circumstances – or the wrong ones, if you like – *anyone* can behave foolishly, including the cleverest of us . . . you, me . . . even Jack there – we all have little weaknesses. And if they catch us on the wrong day, or even the wrong moment . . .' He shook his head. 'What made Caesar go to the Forum? What made Napoleon put that idiot Ney in charge of his cavalry at Waterloo?'

'And what is Oliver Latimer's Achilles heel?'

'That's easy.' Audley didn't look at Butler. 'In our relationship I have to admit that I am the aggressor – I am almost unfailingly rude to him, as you know.'

That was undeniably true. With Latimer, Audley managed to make even his politeness offensive.

'He probably has many good qualities. But he has one extra ingredient I can't abide – "Ingredient X".' Audley smiled suddenly. 'Or, at least, I can't abide it in my alleged peers, let's say. I don't mind it in the next generation, so long as it is decently concealed.'

God! thought Mitchell. That smile was for him!

'Ambition.' He couldn't resist the word.

'Yes.' Audley turned back to Butler. 'Last Friday, of all

days . . . I'd guess he was somewhat depressed, if not totally surprised and disappointed. And then Senator Thomas Cookridge appeared to him out of the blue, Jack. What a chance! And what a feather in his cap – in his new cap – to bring you Senator Cookridge's friendship and gratitude! The wrong moment – the right temptation maybe?'

Mitchell stirred. 'But now we're back to Cookridge again. And if Cookridge isn't up to mischief – '

'*Cookridge* may not be.' Audley swung towards him again. '*But someone else could be*.' He shared the idea with both of them. 'Cookridge is a new man – a Mid-Western domestic politician called to the colours . . . Christ! I've never set eyes on the man – I only know what the Beast agreed to tell me . . . Okay – so Mike Bradford has checked him out, and he's pure white driven snow, all the way from the Arctic to the prairie . . . But that means he's mixing with some very dicey characters now, who've maybe put one over on him – who knows?'

Butler chewed on that for a few seconds. 'So . . . what *do* you know, David?'

For a moment Audley stared at nothing, which was suspended in mid-air over Colonel Butler's desk.

'I know that Howard Morris is one scared *hombre*.'

Butler glanced at Mitchell. 'That's one.'

'And it's a big one. Because old Howard is one part Apache . . . or Navaho, or some pesky redskin – he claims all sorts of different tribes, according to how it suits him . . . But he has got a gift for smelling danger when the palefaces only smell the sagebush. And he smells it now.'

'So that's one.' It was to Butler's credit that he was prepared to accept the CIA man's one-part-indian nose, thought Mitchell. It was not the sort of warning the average British redcoat normally credited.

Audley's lips compressed. 'And I know that this – whatever it is – was designed for *me*, not Oliver.'

152

Butler caught Mitchell's eye again, but this time interrogatively.

Mitchell leaned towards Audley. 'Would you have fallen for Senator Cookridge, David? Out of the blue – Senator Cookridge?'

The lips compressed again. 'I don't know.'

'Come on, David,' Mitchell pressed him.

'I don't know.' Audley was pressing himself now. 'But . . . probably not, on balance.' He gave Butler a slightly embarrassed glance. 'I've had a few spots of bother, going off and doing my own thing . . . And with Jack just confirmed in the hot seat there, it maybe wouldn't have been quite cricket . . .' He brightened suddenly, and came back to Mitchell '. . . and the American Civil War isn't my period really, you know. "Slavery and Secession" in School Certificate umpteen years ago and *Gone With the Wind* wouldn't have been enough to tempt me – apart from the fact that I'm fairly busy in Cheltenham, as it happens.'

'How about gold?' said Butler.

'G – ?' Audley had started to sit back, satisfied with his answer's dishonesty. But *gold* stopped him. 'Gold? What gold?'

Butler nodded at Mitchell. 'Mitchell put in an inquiry about Sion Crossing. There was an answer which came in a few minutes ago, and they put it on screen for me.' He looked directly at Mitchell.

'What gold?' Audley cut in irritably. 'And where the hell is . . . Sion Crossing?'

'It's approximately where Oliver Latimer is at the moment: Sion Crossing in Georgia, David,' Butler informed him mildly. 'It's near Smithsville.'

'Oh yes?' Audley controlled his impatience. 'Smithsville?'

'Smithsville is the nearest town . . . or village. General Sherman burnt the place in 1864. And Sion Crossing, too – that was a big cotton plantation.'

153

'Indeed?' Audley's apparent lack of interest was now a sure measure of his annoyance. 'Well, Sherman burnt lots of places, didn't he?'

'Yes, I believe he did.' Butler allowed himself a small measure of gratification. 'It was in that film, wasn't it – ?'

'Yes, Jack. It was in that film.'

'Yes . . . well, it seems at some point in time before that, when there was still fighting around Atlanta, one of the banks there shipped out what they'd got in their vaults. But it only got as far as Sion Crossing. And that was the last anyone saw of it.'

Audley waited. 'Yes?'

'It was plundered by the Union army, apparently.'

'And?'

'That's all Mitchell's Civil War expert has come up with so far.' Butler turned to his screen and tapped a series of instructions into it, his lips moving silently as he recalled the correct sequence of commands for retrieval. 'Isn't that enough for you?'

From where he sat, Mitchell could see the screen fill up. Butler's fingers hovered over the keys again, and then transmitted another sequence, which brought the printer alongside the screen to chuntering life.

'Enough?' Audley took in the scene with undisguised suspicion.

Interesting, thought Mitchell, punching the tableau into his own memory for future reference: the bright mind, restless and inquisitive and encyclopaedic, resisting the new technology, seeing it as an enemy and not a liberator – seeing it as the very Beast of Apocalypse . . . for it had been David who had named Colonel Butler's computer.

The printer ceased its tuneless song, and Butler ripped the printout from it and handed it to Audley.

'I think so.' Butler simply dropped the print-out on his desk when Audley failed to accept it. 'You do have something of a reputation for striking gold when you look for it, David – actual as well as metaphorical, I seem to

154

recall?' He paused. 'And Senator Cookridge has access to such information. So now we can guess at what he's after – and why he wanted you.'

Audley's face twisted. 'Sod that! It isn't Cookridge I'm worried about – it's Bill Macallan.'

'Bill Macallan's dead and buried, David,' snapped Butler.

'Aye! And a-mouldering in the grave, Jack,' Audley snapped back. 'But his soul – or his daughter – may very well be marching on, to trip us up.' He shook his head. 'I don't like it at all.'

'What don't you like?'

'Coincidences, Jack. That's the third thing I know for sure – *coincidences*. And I don't like coincidences any more than Howard Morris does. Okay?'

That was the truth of it, thought Mitchell: Howard Morris wasn't scared because he had some tincture of Red Indian blood in his veins which gave him an unfair advantage over the palefaces, with their computers and their atrophied instincts. Much more simple, he shared some special knowledge with Audley – and, from the expression on his face, with Jack Butler too.

But not with Paul Mitchell. 'What coincidences?' He let them share his question.

'I worked with Bill Macallan in the old days, Paul.' It was Audley – predictably – who answered him. 'I told you last night.'

'And quite improperly.' Butler shook his head at Audley. 'And in the middle of a crowded public bar . . . Sometimes I despair of you, David. I really do.'

'And sometimes I despair of you, Jack.' Audley was aggressively unrepentant. 'You accuse me of being over-secretive – and then you sit on all your eggs like a broody hen . . . Besides which Harry Randall was watching over us from behind the bar, anyway. So we were probably more secure in the Old Ben last night than we are now.'

'But Dr Mitchell is not cleared for Debreczen.'

155

'No? Well, you'd better clear him double-quick then . . . or put him in chains, because he knows about the bloody place now,' snapped Audley. 'Christ! Jack – he *ought* to have known . . .' Then he weakened suddenly. 'Where is Senator Cookridge at this precise moment?'

'About midway between Paris and Rome.' Butler's arms were feeling their way into the coat of responsibility, which was a garment of many colours.

'But you can hardly ask him what the hell he's been up to, in any case.' Audley thought aloud. 'Short of grossly insulting him . . . and I wouldn't like to be the one to do that . . .'

'No.' If Audley could think aloud, so could Mitchell, decided Mitchell. 'And not when we don't even know that he is up to something.'

'But someone's up to something, Jack.' Audley, at least, was certain. 'Howard Morris scared for *one*. And Howard scared for me – that's two. . . And me and Bill Macallan and Debreczen – that's *three* for coincidence, Jack.'

It was time to push his own interest, decided Mitchell. But all he had to work with was what Audley had irresponsibly let slip last night: that Debreczen was something to do with deep-cover communist sleepers – the agents which the Russians caught when young, and salted away for the future, when they had risen to positions of power and influence.

'Where's the coincidence?' He rounded on Audley. 'For Christ's sake, David – what did you do, once upon a time?'

Audley faced him. 'I screwed it up, young Paul – that's what I did!' But then he shrugged Mitchell off. 'Jack – did they ever rehabilitate Bill Macallan?'

'Not really. No.'

'But some of them never really believed he was crooked – Goldberg, for one . . . and Bradford had his doubts – Bradford even more than Goldberg: he always maintained

156

Bill had been framed . . . In the last year – *last year* – when Bill was dying . . . did either of them go back to see him?'

Butler bridled at that. 'We're not sure.'

'So Bill might have known what happened last year.' Audley turned to Mitchell. 'It's like this, Paul: Bill Macallan and I worked together years ago, in the Debreczen thing – and if Jack doesn't want to tell you about that in detail, that's his privilege.' He fixed Mitchell with such an innocent look that it was clear he didn't want any further public revelation of just what he'd said the night before.

Okay, thought Mitchell: *let's make that one you owe me, David!*

He looked questioningly at Colonel Butler.

'In due course, Mitchell.' Butler wore his "need to know" restriction face. 'It was a very sensitive affair.'

'It was damn near impossible.' Audley's bitterness not doubt concealed relief. 'We were sent to find needles in a very large haystack. And, what made it worse . . . maybe it was the job, or maybe it was something else . . . we hated each other's guts.'

A pair of clever arrogant bastards, more likely – each of whom probably regarded himself as the senior partner: when Anglo-American relationships went wrong, that was one of the standard foul-ups. And with Audley's temperament that would have been a high-risk occurrence in the old days.

'But you did actually find two needles,' said Butler.

'So we did. And then we lost both of them again.' This time the bitterness was genuine, Mitchell estimated. 'Mine allegedly committed suicide, and' Bill Macallan's was sniped at long range. And that was another coincidence.' Grimness now, not bitterness. 'What old Fred Clinton said . . . was *one* might be bad luck, but *two* smelt like treason – like an inside job. So we were both for the high-jump then . . . But I happened to be one of Fred's own special appointments – he and I both knew I was true blue, you see, Paul.' Audley gave Mitchell a lop-sided smile. 'So it had to be Bill Macallan, by simple arithmetic. Two minus one equals one.'

'But nothing was ever proved,' said Butler.

'*We* couldn't prove anything, is what you mean, Jack.' Again he looked at Mitchell. 'The truth is we wanted to fix him one way of another . . . In the end, his own side did it for us. Someone dug some dirt on him.'

'What sort of dirt?'

'Oh . . . he was a poor man, and he had money he couldn't quite account for. And there were one or two other things . . .' Another shake, almost regretful '. . . enough to break him, but not enough to bury him. So he got his pension – ' Audley looked at Butler quickly ' – but they never did rehabilitate him, did they?'

'No.' Butler's face was suffused with doubt. 'But you're right, David: there were those who thought he'd been railroaded, if not actually framed.'

'To use their own expressions . . . yes.' Audley nodded. 'So it could be that he kept in touch . . . somehow.' He came back to Mitchell. 'And that's the whole point now, Paul, you see?'

They were talking about the stuff of history, thought Mitchell, remembering his own First World War researches. Because, with the past, truth existed on so many conflicting lines and levels. There were *the facts*, which was what had actually happened, so far as that could be established, because even facts were never absolutely certain. But then there was *the why* and *the how*, which were both infinitely more nebulous. In the end the only certainty was the result.

'All those years ago,' said Audley. 'And Bill Macallan was a back number – invalided out, officially . . . and genuinely.' He paused. 'And then last year we got a Debreczen tickle. In fact, we hooked someone who'd been on the inside at Debreczen, on the staff there – an Irishman – '

'David!' said Butler sharply.

'Oh – *Christ*, Jack!' Audley rounded on him. 'If you really don't trust him, we might as well pack up and go home.'

Butler sighed. 'It isn't a question of trust – as you well know. It's a question of procedure. There are a lot of names in the Debreczen file – the ones with question marks, remember?'

'Well, let the Beast look after that.' Audley pointed at the equipment at Butler's elbow. 'It's good at censoring things.'

'Debreczen isn't in the computer yet.' Butler turned away from Audley. 'I'm sorry, Mitchell. This has nothing to do with you personally.'

'That's okay.' Mitchell smiled helpfully. When Audley was in this mood, he was apt to be self-destructive, and that wasn't a mistake he himself was about to make with Butler. 'No problem.'

'Okay, okay!' Audley raised a hand. '*No* Irishmen – forget I said "Irishman", even though half the world knows what happened last year – *their* quarter as well as ours – ours including the CIA *and* the BND . . . but – okay! So you want me to go on, Jack – without Irishmen?'

'If you can manage to do so prudently – yes.'

Mitchell caught himself almost frowning at Colonel Butler, the man's refusal to explode was so remarkable. For he was by no means always equable, and he certainly wasn't awed or afraid of anything that walked upright on two legs under the sun. So there must be a reason –

He looked at Audley. 'Stop pissing around, David. You were trying to explain a coincidence for me, weren't you?'

'Yes . . .' Audley eyed Butler balefully '. . . "no Irishmen" is really rather appropriate . . . yes.' At last he came back to Mitchell. 'So Debreczen was "a sensitive affair" while you were still a scrubby schoolboy smoking furtive

159

cigarettes behind the sports pavilion. And I've hardly thought about Bill Macallan since that time.' The jaw tightened. 'But the Debreczen came up last year – late last summer . . . And we nearly had it again, but we screwed it up. Because I had a man . . . a man who could have told us all about it. And I lost him.'

Butler stirred. 'We all lost him.' *They* lost him, too.'

So the Irishman was dead. But, more than that, this was why Audley was so unmanageable – "*I screwed it up!*" And Butler being understanding only made matters worse, of course: the Colonel was trying to damp down glowing embers with a bucket of petrol.

'Yes.' Audley glowered at them. 'And that suited them just fine.'

Mitchell was trying to remember what had happened late the previous summer. He had been doing the ground-work for the Cheltenham deep vetting with Del Andrew . . . and Audley had been on one of his elongated leaves, allegedly researching a learned article for some old professor's *festschrift* . . . But then Audley *had* turned up, out of the blue, to take the whole thing over from them at Cheltenham.

'No. It didn't suit them fine,' Butler disagreed. 'They didn't know how much he'd told you before . . . he had his accident.'

Audley *had* been in an odd mood at Cheltenham, remembered Mitchell. Not exactly chastened, but not quite the usual self-confident Audley. Although, of course, he had soon recovered from that.

'Which was in fact sod-all.'

'But they don't know that.' In his private debate with Audley, Butler changed the past tense with the present! 'They know we never identified all the men who attended those Debreczen courses, David.'

Debreczen –

'But there's your coincidence anyway, Paul.' Audley shrugged. 'Old times – new times . . . After last year I

160

don't like being reminded again of Bill Macallan so soon, even if he is dead. And I don't think Howard Morris liked the reminder either. Because – '

The buzzer on Colonel Butler's console cut off the rest, but Butler took no notice of it. 'Because, David?'

'Howard was in on our Debreczen business last year, Jack – remember? The same coincidence must have occurred to him, you can bet on that.'

'Perhaps.' Butler touched the console. 'Yes?'

'Cable here, sir. We've got something you ought to see . . . hear, I mean, sir.'

Mitchell felt a bit guilty about poor old James, who had done his duty, and had been rewarded with extra work for his pains, as a result of his own machinations. But then James was Royal Navy and old-fashioned, so he probably didn't mind – he probably hadn't even made the connection.

'Very well, James.' Butler thought for a moment. 'You'd better come on up.'

James, thought Mitchell – to Butler James was always *James*, while he was usually *Mitchell*. So he didn't need to feel too guilty, on second thoughts.

'But it's still all hypothesis.' He found himself arguing against the real existence of the mystery he had raised, playing the devil's advocate against himself. 'If Senator Cookridge is above suspicion . . . and he simply wanted David to unravel an historical conundrum for him?' And if it was all a 'wolf-wolf' nonsense, which he had irresponsibly cried in the hope of embarrassing Oliver St John Latimer, he would have done himself no good at all! But the logic was inescapable. 'Howard Morris was the obvious man to soften up David. They'd have told Cookridge that in Grosvenor Square . . . And the rest – it's more hypothesis than coincidence, really.'

They both looked at him, but he couldn't make out what they were thinking. What he had to remember was that they were a couple of very wily old birds, and when

161

they were together their different virtues more or less cancelled out their different vices.

'Of course, I don't really know whether Debreczen is animal, vegetable or mineral.' Better to hedge his bets, therefore. And it was the memory of Debreczen, from long ago, that was ruffling their feathers, like the memory of some legendary monster –

> Far, far beneath the abysmal sea . . .
> The Kraken sleepeth –

He assumed his inquiring expression. 'Would Oliver know about it?'

Audley looked at Butler. 'He'd know about Debreczen well enough. But he wouldn't connect Lucy Cookridge with it.'

That just about worked out, Mitchell computed. Latimer was a few years younger than Audley, but he'd joined the service a year or two before, poached by old Sir Frederick from the Treasury. In fact, in those far off days and in very different spheres, Audley and Latimer had been the old boy's *enfants terribles* of intelligence research.

The buzzer at the door announced James's arrival: James was not a door-pummeller.

'I didn't remember her, Jack.' Audley ignored the buzzer. 'And I was a hell of a sight closer to Macallan then he ever was.'

The same mental print-out advised Mitchell that Audley knew a lot more about Debreczen than Butler did, notwithstanding the Beast's embargo. Because back in those deeps of time Butler had still been a serving soldier, at the uncomfortable sharp end of the retreat from empire.

'Yes.' Butler released the door lock, and waited for James Cable to appear. 'Well, James – what have you got?'

162

'Something rather odd, sir.' James advanced to the desk in order to deposit the file on it. 'I thought you'd want to know.'

'What does "odd" mean?' Audley had never been impressed by James's impeccable manners. 'Uneven? Singular? Exotic? Bizarre? Egregious?'

Butler drew the file towards him, opened it, frowned, and then closed it before Mitchell could steal a glimpse.

'What's Mulholland got to do with this?'

'Sir – '

'Mulholland?' Audley sat up.

Butler looked at Audley. 'What do you know about him?'

'Geneva. The non-aligned conference in '79.' Audley could always be relied on to know more than he ought to. 'Sweden in '81. And he was working for the French then.'

It was an AF dossier, that file. So Mulholland – wasn't that a good Scottish-Irish name? – was a freelance . . . *a condottiere* whose lance was anything but free, going rather to the highest bidder. But the Scots and the Irish had always been drawn to other people's quarrels, no matter whose.

'Angola last year – working for the South Africans.' Audley grinned. 'The Boers paid him in gold, so the story goes. And he earned every ounce of it. He's a hard man, is Mulholland.'

Butler transferred his thunderous frown back to James.

'I didn't think you'd want him on screen, sir. Not with his record.'

So James didn't trust the Beast either! Under his armour of dutiful naval innocence, James was no slouch. Which, of course, was why he was here now.

'Yes.' Butler was neutral again. 'Just answer my question.'

'Yes, sir.' Lieutenant-Commander Cable's battle-flags fluttered proudly. 'Further to your instructions of yesterday, I had the passenger lists of all American flights checked for Dr Latimer's name – '

'We know where Dr Latimer is, James.'

'Yes, sir. But last night, when Audley came back, we added Miss Lucy Cookridge to the search, with the same priority.'

'That was me, Jack,' said Audley. 'We don't know a single bloody thing about Miss Lucy Cookridge – and that's a fact.'

'We do now.' Considering that he must have been up half the night, James was as chirpy as a sparrow, thought Mitchell enviously. But that was because his liver was in better condition.

'Did she come in with the Senator?'

'No, Dr Audley. She same in two days before. On a Baltimore flight – but Baltimore connects with a lot of Delta flights from Atlanta. And she went back to Atlanta on the flight before Dr Latimer's.'

'And Mulholland?'

'Yes – ' James rolled an eye at Colonel Butler, and was rewarded with a nod ' – that's where I ran slap bang into the Special Branch . . . In fact, I've slapped a "hold" order on their report, and they're arguing with Chief Inspector Andrew at the moment – '

'They made him on entry?' That part of Butler which was not disturbed by Mulholland's appearance was reassured by the Special Branch's efficiency, Mitchell suspected from the Colonel's tone.

'And exit. He came in on her Baltimore flight, and went out on the same Atlanta one.' James nodded. 'He's on the pink list, so they were scared in case he made contact with anyone dodgey, naturally.'

Naturally. One swallow didn't make a summer, and pink list characters – the soldiers-of-fortune who had no sacred cause except to find another paymaster – were regular birds-of-passage through London, en route to their next job. It was only when they started to transact business locally that the Branch went into top gear.

'And did he?'

'No, sir. At least, not so far as they're aware.'

'Was he with her?' Mitchell advertised his presence again.

James brightened, friend to friend. 'Who else? He is a minder, after all – and in the Rolls Royce class: bloody expensive, and the noisiest part of him is his wrist-watch.' The Lieutenant-Commander very nearly smiled. 'If I wanted to keep my daughter safe in foreign parts, and I could afford the best . . . I'd hire Winston Spencer Mulholland, Paul.'

Butler leaned forward. 'What evidence?'

'Adjacent seats, sir.' James had been expecting this question. 'Booked at the same time. Same hotel – also adjacent rooms, with connecting door. And he never let her out of his sight . . . except when she was dotting in and out of the embassy in Grosvenor Square . . . presumably to see her step-father, sir.'

'He didn't go in?'

'No, sir. But he's probably a bit leery of having his name and number taken by them, with his record.' James blinked. 'Not that he's got a bad conscience, or anything like that – don't get me wrong, I mean.'

'What d'you mean?'

James drew breath. 'There's nothing against him, at least not in our book. And he came in on his own passport, bold as brass.' He cocked his head at Butler. 'I mean, he must have reckoned he'd be spotted – he's a professional, as Dr Audley so rightly said . . . And that means he used us for extra insurance, for whatever he wanted to insure the Senator's daughter against.'

'Which was?' Butler pursued his question. 'What did he do?'

James spread his hands. 'He just watched over her, sir – '

'So what did *she* do?' Audley cut in.

James was not so happy now. 'Well . . . she went to the embassy, several times . . . And she went to Selfridge's, presumably to do a bit of shopping.' Distinctly not so happy. 'She dined in her room at the hotel – '

'So they watched *him*.' Audley paused. 'Not *her*.' He looked at Butler. 'So we don't bloody-well know what *she* did, is what that means, Jack.'

James took another breath. 'Not quite. Because we know she didn't go to the Oxbridge on Friday night. The last night she stayed in the hotel.'

'And Mulholland?'

'He was there too. And then they both flew out very early next morning.'

Audley looked at Butler. 'Just one phone-call – to let her know that Oliver had taken the bait. One of Cook-ridge's heavies could have tipped her off. On an internal line there won't be any record.'

Mitchell unwound again. 'But why, David?'

Audley raised an eyebrow. 'Why? Christ, Paul – I don't know *why* – *I just know Mulholland*, that's all. And that's enough.'

'Because he's an expensive bodyguard?'

Audley made a face, 'Well . . . that would be enough to frighten me – if it's a minder she needs.' He leaned forward, and pushed the Mulholland file up the table towards Mitchell.

MULHOLLAND, Winston Spencer AF/A4*/238

He noticed that Colonel Butler was not objecting. So MULHOLLAND, *Winston Spencer*, whoever he might actually be, was at least less sensitive than DEBREC-ZEN, wherever the hell that might actually be, or once have been.

'Have a look,' invited Audley.

Suddenly Mitchell felt bolshie, even against his better judgement. Maybe Colonel Butler wasn't playing games, because that wasn't his style; and although James knew more than he was saying, he was merely keeping his own counsel, which was fair enough – it was impossible to dislike James. But David Audley *liked* playing games.

'No.' He kept his itchy fingers away from MULHOLLAND, *Winston Spencer*. 'You tell me, David.'

Audley looked sidelong at Butler, which advanced Mitchell's feelings from bolshie to bloody-minded Stalinist.

He pointed to the file. 'Sir – I can read a file as well as the next man. But it takes time . . . and if Leonard Winston Mulholland frightens David, who seems to know all about him . . . then what is he doing to Oliver Latimer in Atlanta?'

Audley nodded quickly at Butler. 'He's right, you know, Jack. Mulholland changes our terms of reference.' He transferred the nod to Mitchell. 'You don't fancy "hypothesis" so much now, Paul – eh?'

James Cable made one of his polite naval noises, to attract Butler's attention.

'Yes, James?' Because he was not the most assertive of men, James only coughed when he had something to say.

'Sir . . . I agree with Dr Audley – and Dr Mitchell.' He switched to Audley. 'I'm thinking . . . would you recognize Mulholland if you met him, Dr Audley?'

Audley looked down at the file for a moment. 'If I wasn't expecting him . . . probably no.' He frowned at James. 'Not in Atlanta, anyway . . . But then, I wouldn't recognize Miss Lucy Cookridge either – or Senator Thomas himself, come to that . . . No, I only know of Mulholland accidentally – *incidentally*, if you like. He's never preached in my parish.'

'Yes.' James came back to the Colonel. 'That's what I thought. So Dr Latimer certainly won't know him. He may not even know *of* him. And, as Dr Audley says . . . in Atlanta – ?'

What *Atlanta* had to do with Winston Spencer Mulholland, particularly, defeated Mitchell. But, of course, there had been Irishmen and Scotsmen enough, and Scots-Irish, in the Old South in the days of the Confederacy: the peerless General Patrick Cleburne, who had died with his boots off at Franklin because he'd just given them to a bare-footed infantryman, had learnt his trade as an Irish cavalryman in the British Army.

So now *need to know* outranked *playing games*, anyway.

He reached for the Mulholland file.

'He's right,' said Audley. 'Oliver may be damn good, but he won't know Mulholland from a hole in the road, let alone be able to handle him.'

Mitchell opened the file.

'I ought to be out there,' said Audley, pointing at Mitchell almost simultaneously. 'With Paul to mind me, maybe – '

Mitchell's attention to the contents of the file was momentarily diverted by this suddenly-enticing idea: he had never been to Atlanta – he had been to Gettysburg, and had seen the rising ground on which Pickett's charge had withered away, to file in memory with the killing grounds of Hastings, and Agincourt, and Mont St Jean at Waterloo, and the quiet villages of the Somme and the Ancre, and the D-Day beaches . . . But he had never climbed Kennesaw Mountain or marched in the wake of Sherman's army in Georgia.

'After all. I was *meant* to be out there, Jack.' Audley leaned towards Butler. 'Oliver – he's no more than a bloody *accident*, because Howard Morris had a rush of blood on the head, and took second best . . . *I* should be there, Jack – because *I'll* get the message, whatever it is – don't you see?'

More to the point, *what was happening now at Sion Crossing* – that was what Mitchell saw –

'No, sir!' said James Cable decisively.

Mitchell's attention was further split, away from the file again, by both Audley's and Butler's reaction.

'Why not?' Butler's mouth opened, but Audley got in first.

James, quite typically, wasn't stampeded into answering, but took his time to arrange the ships of his task force where he wanted them, to get his Harriers into the air before the missiles arrived. And that gave Mitchell time to look at the first page of the file.

The picture hit him first – full-face, side-face – enlarged long-distance, not mug-shot posed for the camera –

'Dr Audley's right: he was meant to be out there.' James nodded.

Winston Spencer Mulholland was a negro: he was black as the ace of spades –

'There isn't enough time to get him out there now, even if that's what you want sir.'

Winston Spencer Mulholland. Born Kingston, Jamaica, 5 May 1945 –

Mitchell accelerated to multi-dimensional reasoning: born near VE-Day in 1945, Mulholland was *Winston* for the same reason that innumerable British girl-babies had been *Diana* recently, and German boy-babies *Adolf* back in the early 1940s –

Irrelevant –

'There never is enough time,' said Audley. 'So that's a good reason for never doing anything, James.'

'I wasn't suggesting we shouldn't do anything, Dr Audley.' James Cable looked down at Audley. 'I am merely advising against you going to the United States at this time.'

'And I am merely asking why not?' Audley's tone became deceptively casual, and Mitchell tore himself away from the grinning black face in the file.

'You are fairly well known, David.' said Butler gently. 'In certain circles.'

As little golden-haired children trailed fleecy clouds of glory and innocence, so David Audley was the thunderbearer of trouble and strife in a clear sky when he came unannounced, that was what the Colonel meant, thought Mitchell.

'So my card's marked.' Not even David could argue with that. 'So what about Oliver St John Latimer's card, then?'

'Dr Latimer isn't so well known in America – '

'Damn it! He's the new Deputy-Director, man!' Audley changed his tack. 'His unlovely mug-shot will be on the wall from here to Timbuktoo by now – whatever he does, wherever he goes, some poor sod will be paid good money to ask "*Why*". So what difference will I make?'

James composed his expression to one of pure innocence. 'Wouldn't the two of you constitute what you would call "unlikely coincidence", Dr Audley?'

Ouch! thought Mitchell. Old James was sharper than usual this morning.

'Besides which . . .' James let go of Audley like a terrier dropping a dead rat, in preference for a live quarry '. . . Wing-Commander Roskill is in the United States at the moment, sir. He's actually lecturing on the Falkland Islands – on V/STOL air superiority tactics – at Annapolis . . . And we do still have an emeritus link with him – we can use him, and trust his discretion – '

'That's ridiculous!' exploded Audley. 'Apart from the fact that Hugh's got a game leg, and can't go marching through Georgia the way he goes up and down like a yo-yo in a Harrier – apart from *that*, the Americans know all about his background. So you'll only be substituting one coincidence for another, is all that will achieve.'

'I have readied Wing-Commander Roskill therefore, sir.' James ignored Audley. 'I've prepared a hot-line SG, scrambled on his personal key, telling him all we know. And I have laid on private air and ground transport for him, so he can be on his way from Atlanta to Smithsville in a couple of hours. All he needs is the G-word from you, sir.' At last he came back to Audley. 'And with one-and-a-half legs he's still better than most people with two, Dr Audley.'

Audley glowered up at James, and Mitchell thought

. . . *beautiful* – and *beautiful* not only because it was always good to see James at work, but also because that work was cutting David down to size, which never did any harm.

'Quite right!' Butler gave James and David that fleeting glance of his which transferred all responsibility to him, as he reached for his hardwear, to activate the Beast's executive rôle. 'In the circumstances, Hugh will do very well.'

Mitchell watched the G-word tapped in, from Whitehall to Washington, and Washington to Annapolis, to launch Hugh Roskill off his comfortable pad towards Smithsville, and Sion Crossing.

'Jack – for Christ's sake – this is mine!' Audley cracked under the pressure of technology, which had taken away from him the chance of arguing his way into the forefront of the battle. 'Oliver's there – and it should be *me* – and now you're putting *Hugh* there . . . and it still should be *me*, Jack.'

'Yes.' Butler stared at the screen, waiting for the Beast to reply. 'Of course it should be.'

'Jack – '

'Shut up, David . . . there's a good fellow.' Butler waited another second, until the Beast accepted his order. Then he came back to Audley. 'That's done, then . . . Now – what was it?'

'Cancel it, Jack.' Audley tried to be casual. 'All you have to do is make it *NG* not *G* – Oliver isn't up to this sort of thing . . . And this is my can of worms – you know *that*, too.'

'Sir – ' began James.

Butler cut him off with a peremptory hand. 'You're quite right, David: this *is* your thing – Cookridge wanted you, and you knew Macallan . . . and, for all I know, you're probably an expert on the American Civil War – '

'I'm not, actually. But – '

'It doesn't matter. You can probably relate it to medie-

171

val history somehow . . . But it doesn't matter – ' Butler refused for once to be overborne ' – it *is* perfectly your thing . . . *And that's why I'm not giving it to you.*' He turned to James Cable. 'Right, James?'

'Yes, sir.' James was obviously vastly relieved to be understood. 'We don't know what they're at, is the way I see it. In fact, we don't even know who *they* are – '

'So we may lose Oliver St John Latimer?' Audley still wasn't finished. 'And . . . I admit I hate his fat guts, but it would annoy me rather more than somewhat to have them spilled out unnecessarily – I've enough on my conscience as it is . . .' Suddenly he smiled. 'Besides all of which I've never been up-country from the coast in those parts, and I can provide you with a perfectly good cover. There's a very distinguished scholar I've corresponded with – he lives in a little town not so far from Atlanta . . . one that Sherman missed, so it's full of the most delightful ante-bellum houses, and charming people to go with them, by all accounts . . . and, Jack, he does just happen to be the world authority on the Mint Julep, you see . . . And I really won't be missed at Cheltenham for a few days – '

'*No!*' At the best of times Colonel Butler was not a man to be disarmed by a smile, and least of all by one of David Audley's smiles. 'You haven't been listening to a word anyone's been saying, damn it!'

'Yes, I have. You don't want me to go because someone planned it that way. I think that's a bloody good reason for going – now we know about it.'

'I'm not going to say "no" again, David. I have other work for you – and for you, Mitchell.' Butler's gaze lifted to James Cable. 'Where is Senator Cookridge as of now?'

'Rome, sir.'

'Okay.' Audley shrugged. 'But I wouldn't leave Oliver to Mulholland's tender care if I were you.'

There was something about that "tender care" which made Mitchell look down at the file on his lap.

Winston Spencer Mulholland was still grinning at him.

172

He looked as though he hadn't a care in the world. But then, if he was as expensive a bodyguard as James had indicated, he was obviously on top of his job. So –

A name leapt out of the page – then another –

Mitchell's eye raced through the passage. And now there was another name he recognized.

'Christ!' he exclaimed, and looked at Audley.

'That's right.' Audley nodded. 'For "minding" he charges hours worked plus expenses, with a bonus for delivery alive on an agreed date. But for killing it's always a lump sum in advance.'

8

Latimer in America: On old Sion land

Latimer followed Lucy Cookridge down the passage from the air-conditioned coolness of the study into the more temperate climate of the immense living room.

His head didn't ache so much now. After all, it had been a useful morning's work, topped off by his successful handling of her mild interrogation; and there was this reassuring living room, with its well-filled bookshelves and its elegant furniture and colour scheme, and its pots of exotic greenery sprouting up to the ceiling or cascading onto the tiled floor. The absent couple from whom the house had been rented were clearly persons of taste and respectability; and somehow that, even at the remove of temporary occupancy, bestowed even greater respectability on Miss Cookridge and on the curious mission he had undertaken.

For it *was* a curious mission, and he still had the feeling that there must be more to it than he knew – more perhaps than he had seen, and more than Lucy Cookridge had revealed; in fact, the night before, in the uncertain moments of not-quite-asleep, he had felt very far alike from home and from the certainties and safety of his ordinary life, with its carefully calculated beginnings and ends. But he no longer regretted his actions.

'Kingston?' Lucy smiled at him as she called the name. 'Where are you?'

Latimer returned the smile. He had known then, in that moment of doubt last night, how far he had strayed on impulse from his accustomed path. And he had never been a creature of impulse . . . which might very well account for young Mitchell's irreverent curiosity about his whereabouts during that routine call.

'Kingston!' Lucy craned her neck towards the dining area.

Latimer studied the bookshelves. Lucy had said last night that the owner was an academic, and the study had been full of scientific work. Here the range was more catholic . . .

He could not honestly quarrel with Mitchell's curiosity, he decided. And when he got back to England and took up the Deputy-Director's reins he might cultivate that young man. Because, properly channelled – channelled away from David Audley's erratic influence – that young man had possibilities. All Mitchell needed was discipline.

'Miz Lucy!' Kingston's voice came from far away.

Now . . . *Kingston* was a much more equivocal character: there was more to that man than met the eye, and maybe a lot more. But, in the meantime, he felt at peace with the world.

'Come here!' Scarlett O'Hara herself could not have sounded more imperious; at least, out of earshot of her mother, who would have admonished her not to raise her voice so at the house-slaves!

'Ah's a comin'!' The reply mimicked Miss O'Hara's command, out from the slave quarters.

Lucy made a face at him. 'But in his own time . . . But never mind, Oliver. I'll have him drive you – he's going to town anyway . . . So he can show you where to go, and then he can wait for you on his way back.'

But a slave Kingston certainly wasn't, thought Latimer. That baffling manner of his, by turns argumentative and then deferential, sometimes that of a mocking – and self-mocking – inferior, and then more like a well-informed and well-educated equal . . . there was no pinning the man down at all, except to be sure that he was more than he pretended to be.

And that was another thing the new Deputy-Director would have to zero in on: they must recruit coloured personnel now.

'Kingston! We're waiting, darn it! Where – '

'An' ah's a comin' – ' Kingston barged through the swing-door from the kitchen, with his accustomed grin on his lips and an automatic pistol in one hand ' – you want something to eat, huh?' He pointed the pistol at Latimer.

'No. Oliver wants to see Sion Crossing. So you can take him in when you go, in Fat Albert . . . And, for heaven's sake, do stop playing with that wretched thing before you shoot someone with it!' Lucy gestured irritably. 'Is it loaded?'

The negro returned Latimer's expression of horror with one of mischievous delight. 'Hell no, Miz Lucy!' He opened his other hand to reveal an oily rag and commenced to polish the pistol. 'I wouldn't clean a loaded gun now, would I? That's the way accidents happen.' Almost impossibly, his grin widened. 'I just can't bear a dirty gun – like my Ma couldn't bear a dirty kitchen . . . She just couldn't stand for anything to be dirty, an' that's the truth – always polishing and cleaning, she was, you know. Oliver.'

Latimer took a grip on the anger which had swiftly succeeded fear inside him. The man had seemed to behave with abominable carelessness, but he couldn't be sure of that – or at least not sure enough to risk humiliation by expressing outrage. For David Audley had caught him in the past with just such deliberately simulated excesses, albeit never with anything so crude as firearms, for which they both shared an aversion.

He frowned as he thought of David Audley. Why was he continually thinking of that wretched fellow? Perhaps it was because it should have been Audley standing here now? Or was it because – however aggravating the conclusion might be – Audley might have known better how to handle this black man?'

'Don't you fret! I wouldn't have shot you, Oliver.' Kingston misread the frown. 'Not unless I'd wanted to.'

Two of a kind, thought Latimer suddenly. One black

and one white, and utterly different. *But two of a kind, nevertheless*!

'I wasn't thinking of that.' The identification relaxed him. 'I was thinking . . . do you always carry a gun? Is that an American custom still – like in the cowboy films?' That was much better; it even had possibilities. 'Were there any black cowboys – historically, I mean?'

Historically was nice, too: after all, he was here – and David Audley should have been here – as an historian.

'Not my gun.' The smile didn't disappear, but it wasn't quite so wide. 'This is one of Professor Booth's equalizers – '

'Where did you find it?' Lucy cut in.

'In the g'rage.' Kingston stuck the pistol into the waist-band of his jeans and produced a ring of keys from his pocket. 'In the locked drawer in the work-bench.' He jingled the keys. 'That's four he's got, so far . . . One in the bedroom – one in the drawer over there – ' He pointed towards a low table beside the fireplace ' – an' the squirrel-rifle in the cupboard . . .an' this little ol' piece.' He tapped the pistol. 'Like the Professor's ready for uninvited guests, wherever he may be when they come visiting.'

'Good God!' exclaimed Latimer. Somehow, the idea of a professor armed to the teeth was more shocking than the armoury itself.

'There may be more.' Kingston brightened. 'You see, you're quite right, Oliver – it *is* an old American custom. You can get yourself shot here a whole lot easier than most places . . . It's written down in the Constitution – the Right to Get shot . . . though they call it the Right to Bear Arms.' The brightness increased. 'You being a historian would know that – it dates from when there was open season on British redcoats . . . and then red indians and buffalo. And when all of them were shot, that just left us to shoot up each other. But it's all properly divided up.'

Latimer couldn't help himself. 'Divided up?'

177

'Sure. If you got a badge, then it's law enforcement. If you haven't, all you need is a sharp lawyer an' some extenuating circumstances. Or . . .' Kingston pointed at the window '. . . if there's a lot of trees around, an' some poor four-legged animals too – *an*' it's the right time of year – that's a hunting accident, and you won't do any time at all. You just got to get it right, that's all.'

'Kingston!' Lucy bridled at this litany of death. 'It isn't like that at all! Don't listen to him, Oliver – '

'Honeychile – it is!' Kingston shook his head. ''Cause, a few years back, if you wuz a nigger here'bouts – you wuz just in the wrong place at the wrong time . . . It ain't so *now*, in that partic'lar sub-division, I grant you – if Oliver was to shoot *me* they'd probably throw the book at him . . . less'n there's a good sheriff round here – and there *are* some good sheriffs in the South now, I grant you that, too – Okay?'

Lucy frowned. 'He *is* good – '

'Sheriff Rinehart?' The negro cocked his head at her. 'He's smart – that's for sure!' The sidelong look came to Latimer. 'Keeps his eye on strangers, is what she means . . . Knows who Miz Lucy Cookridge is, if you're a betting man you could make money on *that*, if I was willing to give you odds – okay?' He grinned. 'All you gotta remember with guns, Oliver, is that it's *concealed* weapons that are bad medicine.'

A different world, thought Latimer. The same, but different – and all the more different for its sameness. But then a thought struck him. 'Why does . . . the Professor – Professor Booth . . . why does he have all these weapons?'

Kingston raised a hand. 'Self-protection.'

'From what?'

'From whatever – from whoever.' Self-protection appeared to be self-evident to Kingston. 'Man's got a right to protect himself – a stranger comes round the back, an' doesn't knock at the door, he better have his hands empty, that's all.'

It was a different world, thought Latimer. Of course, the negro was trying to frighten him with exaggeration, no doubt to see how he reacted. But it *was* a different world nevertheless – and all the more menacing because of its obvious similarities.

'You'd shoot him, would you?' All the more reason to keep his cool.

'No he wouldn't!' snapped Lucy.

Kingston grinned. 'Not if he was running away, maybe. But if he was trying to get in . . . you bet your ass I would.'

'Even if he had no weapons?'

'I wouldn't wait to find out . . . An' after that . . . if he hadn't – I guess I'd just go round to the wood-shed an' get the little axe. An' I'd put it in his hand.' Kingston nodded. 'An' I'd say "Hell, Sheriff – when he come at me with that deadly weapon, ah wuz real scairt, an' ah feared for mah life!"'

A different world. But the truly horrible thing was that there were beginning to be dangerous places even in England now, where the jungle was encroaching all the time.

He shook his head. 'I see . . . Yes, well . . . guns don't particularly interest me at this moment, Mr Kingston, as I don't intend to break into anyone's property. All I want to do is go for a walk along the ridge above the river, from near the bridge and the church to where the old plantation house used to be. Would that be possible?'

The negro studied him. 'Sion Crossing, you mean?'

'If that's what it's called – yes.'

'Uh-huh . . . all that land . . . Sion Crossing – old Sion land . . . Sure, there're paths all along the top, 'bove the stream.' The negro nodded. 'No problem – no problem 'cept it'll be a mite warm for a cold-blooded Englishman just now.' He estimated Latimer critically. 'Might melt you down some – might be more than you could take.'

The memory of yesterday's oven temperature, thus crudely recalled, still radiated uncomfortable heat. But after that challenge to his ability to withstand it Latimer could not have backed down even if he'd wanted to.

'You underestimate us.' He couldn't look down on the man physically, but he had an historical advantage. 'We're quite accustomed to ridiculous temperatures. One of my ancestors fought on Delhi Ridge for four months in the Indian Mutiny, a few years before your Civil War – 120 degrees, and no cover, before the rains . . . and cholera after that. I should think he'd regard your ridge at Sion Crossing a good place for a picnic, Mr Kingston.'

Kingston's mouth opened for an instant, then rearranged itself in its almost-habitual grin. 'Is that a fact? Hell – but of course it is!' He looked at Lucy. 'It's like in that song –

> Mad dogs and Englishmen
> Go out in the midday sun –

– you abs'lutely raht, Miz Lucy – it doan bother him none!'

Latimer, in his turn, looked at Lucy. 'What?'

Lucy looked daggers at Kingston. 'I didn't say anything –'

'Yes, you did – you once said other countries has a climate, but the English Limeys . . . they just got *weather*, an' they don't do nothing about it 'cept complain, an' they take everythin' else for granted, whether it's good or bad, 'cause it's *foreign*, an' there's no point in trustin' it, or worrin' about it – they just ignores it, like it wasn't there – is what you said, Miz Lucy.'

'I said no such thing.' Lucy looked at her watch. 'And, in any case, are you going to Smithsville or not? Because if you aren't, then I'll have to take Oliver to Sion Crossing . . . Well?'

Kingston rolled a glance at Latimer. 'You don't want

nothing to eat? 'Cause I was fixing to make you something really Southern – ' The glance lowered offensively to
Latimer's stomach.

'Oliver wants to see Sion Crossing,' said Lucy acidly.
'He can wait for his dinner until supper.'

Latimer looked from one to the other, if anything even
more confused by their relationship. It seemed to him that
in some ways Kingston was the family retainer – a
competent chauffeur and a meticulous man-about-the-
house . . . meticulous even to the point of unlocking
locked drawers, and cleaning the pistols he discovered
therein, as well as calmly battening down and securing
everything last night. But he was also more than that . . .

But this was a different world, he had to remember that
now . . . So okay – not only as a chauffeur and a man-
about-the-house – but also as a cook – as a cook,
Kingston's performance last night, with that okra dish, as
well as this morning, with that extraordinary breakfast,
was enough above average to make him wish that he'd
swallowed his pride just now, and settled for dinner
(which was presumably lunch), instead of supper (which
was presumably dinner, in a civilized world) –

But it was too late now.

The garage of the Professor's house was enormous, and
filled with all the equipment of American husbandry and
do-it-yourself technology . . . and, along the back wall, on
the other side of which lay the enticing blue lagoon of the
swimming pool, a work-bench with drawers; in one of
which drawers there had been an automatic pistol – he had
to remember that, in order not to compare all this too
unfavourably with the less sophisticated hardwear of any
equivalent British upper middle-class establishment,
where burglars could not be shot down in their tracks.

And two cars – yesterday's Volvo, and a curious vehicle
which looked as though it had been slightly over-inflated
from a sleeker design to distort the angularity of modern

181

European drawing boards, so that it was almost bulbous in outline.

Kingston slapped the roof of the curious vehicle, flashing that eternal grin. 'Okay, Oliver?'

Some sort of reply was required to that – some sort of reply was always required when Kingston addressed him. 'This is "Fat Albert", is it?'

'This Fat Albert – ' Kingston massaged the unmasculine curve of Fat Albert's roof ' – this *Missus* Professor Booth's mode-of-transport . . . We go to Smithsville, we always use Fat Albert – the Professor, he drive the Volvo to Columbia, 'cause that's his car, an' they know that there . . .But, Smithsville – they know Fat Albert better here 'bouts, so we drive Fat Albert here – okay?'

'Oh?' That dichotomy of the Volvo and Fat Albert, and of Professor and Mrs Booth, baffled Latimer; was the Professor a more dangerous driver than his wife – or a better one? 'Yes?'

Kingston bobbed his head. 'Maybe I oughta take you there first, only Miz Lucy sez no . . . They got a big parade there, this weekend, all dressed up like you never saw . . . But mebbe we can do that this evening, huh?'

'A parade?' But, of course, Americans were always parading: they had pretty girls in short skirts who marched at the head of bands, tossing batons and flags into the air above them: that was why American parades were so much more successful than British ones.

'Uh-uh.' Kingston shook his head. 'You oughta see the war memorials they got in the square, Oliver – that's what you oughta see – you bein' a Civil War man, you see.'

'Oh?' The identification momentarily threw Latimer. He had just started to admonish himself for being unjust to his own country: the British did some parades better than anyone – the stiffly formal ones, like the Trooping of the Colour, and the Royal occasions . . . But it still had to be admitted that the Americans were far superior on more popular occasions – and although they must have their

182

riots, he could never recall having read of *American* football hooligans –

But Kingston was looking at him curiously across Fat Albert's roof –

'Oh . . . yes?' What had the man said? Not parades – but war memorials . . . '*you being a Civil War man*', of course! But what was really disorientating him was this unaccustomed need to play a rôle: it had been years since he had had to do anything like this, pretending that he was something that he was not. And that uncomfortable conclusion pricked another discomfort, of which he had been aware the moment he had stepped into the garage, but which he had tried to ignore.

'What's the matter?' Doubt succeeded curiosity on the negro's face. And when he wasn't grinning, or at least smiling, it revealed itself as a face not architect-designed for laughter: somewhere far back in that bloodline, maybe before some enslaved ancestor in the Americas, there had been an original Kingston whose mouth had been cruel and whose eyes had been watchful – whose sneer of cold command had put the fear of dark unknown gods up his Dahomeyan or Ashanti subjects.

'It's nothing.' He shivered in spite of what he was about to say. 'I was just thinking that it's pretty warm in here.'

'Warm?' Kingston relaxed. 'Man – if you think this is warm . . . maybe you should go back inside . . . You get on the ridge there – ' He had opened Fat Albert's door on the driver's side, but now he slammed it again ' – maybe you should wait 'til tomorrow morning, 'fore the sun come properly up, huh?'

'No.' Once again the challenge made him more resolute. Besides which, the sooner this charade was over, and he was safe back home, the better. 'No . . . You said . . . war memorials?' He opened the passenger's door decisively.

'Okay. It's your funeral.' Kingston re-opened his door, and folded his height to enter Fat Albert.

Latimer followed suit almost gratefully, only to find that

183

Fat Albert's interior was no improvement. Instinctively he tried to wind down the window.

'Doan do that, for chrissake!' exclaimed Kingston.

Latimer pretended he had been reaching for his seat-belt. 'War memorials, you said?'

'That's right.' Kingston hurled Fat Albert out of the garage in a shower of gravel. 'You know 'bout them? You got them in England, huh?'

It was on the tip of Latimer's tongue to reply that England had bigger and better war memorials than America, and more of them going back to wars which Kingston had never heard of. Because – damn it! – there was one outside that hotel in Cheltenham, where he'd stayed that last GCHQ time, which listed the local dead of Britain's last official war against Russia, back in the 1850s, which had once been adorned with captured Crimean cannon – cannon subsequently melted down, together with most of the town's iron railings, for use against Hitler in 1940.

'Yes, we have a few.' He curbed his tongue. Admitting to more and bigger war memorials was not far short of claiming more and bigger lunatic asylums. 'So what?'

'Man, they got *three* in Smithsville, for Barksdale County.' The negro spun the wheel and the gravel spurted again. 'One's for '41 to '45 – mebbe twenty-thirty names, plus a few more they added for Korea and 'Nam . . . an' there's still plenty of room for more – ' Fat Albert bucked as they left the drive for the road ' – and then there's one for the first war 'gainst the Krauts, back in '17 – '17–18 – the First World War, okay?'

It was a very open road, hemmed in by trees but with not a car in sight. He had imagined America as the land of the car, but so far, except for the maelstrom of Atlanta airport (which had not been so very different from Heathrow or Gatwick), it had been more the land of trees. But then, it was a vast country and he'd seen but the tiniest and perhaps untypical part of it.

'The 1914–18 War.' Mitchell would have liked that correction. 'The Great War, we sometimes call it.'

'That so? Well, it wasn't so great in Barksdale County. Got a big memorial . . . statue of this guy wearin' one of your funny steel helmets, like a soup-plate, on his head . . . but ain't no more'n a dozen names on the whole damn thing.'

'Indeed?' Latimer remembered irrelevantly that Colonel Butler was morbidly fascinated by war memorials. Perhaps the negro shared that same rather unhealthy interest, unlikely as it seemed. But at least here was something he could take back to England with him, to tell the Colonel about. For lack of any common interest outside work, making small talk with Butler was usually quite beyond him. But now he had American funerary monuments to offer. 'Very interesting.'

Kingston gave him a suspicious look. 'That's not what's interesting, man – hell no! It's the third one – the Confederate one – that you oughta see, for chrissake!'

Damn! Latimer shook himself free from extraneous thoughts about Colonel Butler and the afforested nature of the Land of Cotton. He was *A Civil War man* – and it had taken hardly a minute for him to forget that, and he damn well mustn't forget it again!

'Of course – yes . . .' He dredged into the information acquired during recent study '. . . that would be for the Georgia militia units who fought Sherman's men hereabouts, I take it . . . as well as from the regular regiments in the main armies?' He returned the suspicious look with one of false expert knowledge. 'I've always thought that the Governor – Governor Brown – was quite disgracefully obstructive over the use of the local militia. But then, if you're fighting for the rights of individual states, you have to concede the right of any individual state to be obstructive, logically, I suppose . . . Only, in the South's case, a defensive strategy was bound to fail eventually, given the disparity of resources, so long as Lincoln could hold the

185

North together – ' God! What was he saying? But that was roughly what the *real* experts appeared to have said, including Miss Lucy Cookridge's anonymous real father, so far as he could make out; only . . . they had also hedged their bets at the same time –

'Uh?' Suspicion gave way to – was it mystification or boredom? – as Kingston took his eyes off the road to study him again.

Well, either would do. 'But, then again, a defensive strategy *might* have worked . . . It *was* the era of defensive warfare – from Sebastopol – ' Simultaneously the image of the Cheltenham Crimean War memorial superimposed itself on what Lucy Cookridge's real father had written ' – though Plevna and Paris – and even Port Arthur – ' Where the hell was *Plevna*? He'd never heard of it! ' – to Gallipoli, and the Somme – ' He could see that Kingston had heard of at least some of them ' – and Verdun.'

'Plevna?' Fat Albert swerved slightly as Kingston glanced at him, and then began to slow down. 'What's that?'

Fat Albert was slowing even more – was actually coming to a halt, nosing on to a grassy hard shoulder beside the road – with *Plevna* still unidentified –

'Yes.' Latimer decided that Plevna was a place, since all the rest of them had been geographical. 'The siege of Plevna . . . But, you know, if the Confederacy had maximized its defensive capabilities – if General Johnston had had enough men in the West, to cover Sherman's flanking movements . . . Because Johnston was probably a better general than Sherman, given half a chance, you know – remember Kennesaw Mountain – ?' It was undoubtedly boredom now, in Kingston's eye, thank God!

'I'm sorry, Mr Kingston – I'm disgressing.' But that, at least, was an authentic touch: asked a straight question, historians usually disgressed to other periods of history to cover their ignorance. 'You were saying . . . the Confederate war memorial in Smithsville – ?'

'Yeah.' Mercifully, the negro abandoned Plevna. 'Well, there's a lot of writing on it, at the front, about "The Cause", an' "the noble sacrifice" an' "patriotic devotion", an' all that – ain't no room for another line. An' no room on the other three sides, either.' He looked at Latimer.

'Yes?' Latimer waited.

'Names, Oliver. It's all covered with names – must be a thousand of 'em – mostly widows 'n orphans in Barksdale County hundred years back – an' old maids.' Kingston shook his head, and turned away to scan the woods on his left. 'All because of "The Cause" – helluva thing . . . Me, I don't go for causes.' He craned his neck to study the roadside behind them. 'No way!'

Latimer frowned at the back of the negro's head, and thought that he would like to know a lot more about the man, as well as the phenomenon of colour itself. The trouble with an utterly absorbing specialization – the trouble with knowing more than anyone else about certain areas of the KGB's operations in Western Europe without having to consult Colonel Butler's new computer – was that he knew so little about most other things, not excluding everyday life as well as all things American: he was as specialized as a giraffe or a polar bear – and at this moment he was as far away from his own specialization as from the African bush and the Arctic wastes.

'What do you go for, Mr Kingston?'

Kingston didn't turn around. 'Whatever I'm paid to go for, Mister Latimer . . . Did you see a sign back there, just round the bend behind?'

'No. I was listening to you – '

Kingston turned at last. 'You got that sketch map, huh?' He waited for Latimer to produce Lucy Cookridge's father's map of Sion Crossing. 'Thanks . . . yeah – I think we're just about *there* – on the edge of the ridge, where there's a path . . . You stay here, an' I'll go look – okay?' He opened the car door.

Latimer studied the map while he waited for the negro

to return. With the trees all around, except for Kingston's location of their position, he might have been anywhere in Georgia. But, if Kingston was correct, the road would fall away towards the stream just round the next corner.

There was a certain confusion about all this *Sion* nomenclature. What Kingston called 'Sion land' seemed to be everything beyond the bridge, on this side of the water: that must be the original extent of the old Sion Crossing plantation, where the trees had reconquered the original cotton fields over the last century, since the outriding raiders of General Sherman's wrath-of-God army – 'the Bummers' – had devastated everything worth devastating in a twenty of thirty mile swathe on each side of the main line of advance towards the Atlantic, tearing the rich heart of the Confederate States of America to pieces in the process.

So . . . hereabouts, on Sion *land*, there had been Sion *Creek*, and Sion *Church* – he had seen both of them yesterday, as he had descended in the car to what he had thought of as Sion *Crossing* – with the site of the old Sion Crossing House of the Alexander family hidden in the trees somewhere along the ridge, to his right – to his right *then*, but to his left *now* –

But in fact, *Sion* had been the abbreviation for all the different ingredients of the whole, which (according to Lucy Cookridge's father, whose scholarship could certainly be trusted) had derived from the original James Alexander's vision of his promised land, when he had brought his worldly goods across the creek nearly two hundred years ago – worldly goods which included wife and sons and slaves – to dispute possession with the last Indians here.

He heard the crunch of Kingston's large feet on the edge of the road behind him, on the passenger's side of Fat Albert. But this time he would not attempt to lower the window: it was no longer cool inside the car, but it would be far beyond warm out there.

Sion Crossing was what it all had been: the red earth on this side of the creek which old James Alexander had grasped in his hand as his own, although it didn't belong to him except by his own law, just as William the Bastard had taken England nearly nine hundred years before – by right of conquest!

Kingston opened his door, and a draught of super-heated air entered Fat Albert.

'Okay!' Kingston grinned. 'This the place, Oliver. Jus' back there, there's the path . . . You follow that, an' keep the creek on your right – go by the church mebbe half-mile, an' there's the chimneys still there somewhere, jus' by the path – mebbe more'n half-mile, I can't say for sure, 'cause I ain't never bin that far . . . But where the chimneys are – that's where the house wuz.'

Latimer climbed out of Fat Albert, and felt the heat embrace him. But there was no going back now: he had offered up his St John ancestor, who had sweltered on Delhi Ridge in an even more dreadful temperature: compared with Delhi Ridge, Sion Ridge was nothing.

'Okay?' Kingston enlarged his grin.

'Yes.' Latimer slipped out of his English summer jacket, hanging it casually over his shoulder 'Fine.' *God!* he thought. *Not fine – had Lieutenant Marmaduke Arthur St John really served the guns on Delhi Ridge, to breach the Red Fort, while battered by this sort of ridiculous heat?* 'Fine.'

'Okay.' Kingston gave him an old-fashioned look, as though reading his thoughts, and at the same time esti-mating his ability to withstand high summer at Georgia. ''Bout an hour, say? Meet you here, same place?'

'Very well.' If Lieutenant Marmaduke Arthur St John could fight, then Oliver St John Latimer could walk – that was the least he could do. 'About an hour, then.'

'Fine.' Kingston echoed the word cautiously. 'But . . . now, don't you go off the path – right?'

Latimer looked at him, askance. 'What do you mean?'

189

'I don't mean nothing, really. But there's mebbe some old snakes in there, off the path . . . But they won't do you no harm . . . But there's poison ivy – an' sumac – an' you don't want to take hold of that . . . Like, mebbe you wouldn't want to take hold of stinging nettles in England, huh?'

Latimer glanced at the forest. 'What d'you mean?'

Kingston shrugged, still smiling. 'Jus' keep to the path, that's all.' Another shrug. 'Jus' remember – this is Georgia, not Hertford-shire okay?' Suddenly his expression clouded, and he gestured towards the woods. 'What I mean is . . . if you're not used to it, that poison ivy'll sting you – that's all . . . So don't think you're back home, is what I mean – huh?'

Latimer tore himself away from the innocent-looking forest. Stinging nettles were fair enough – they were a well-remembered minor childhood hazard . . . but *snakes* –

'What sort of snakes?' He had to conceal his gibbering irrational fear under what he hoped sounded like a casual inquiry: Kingston would assuredly make a meal of the cowardly truth. 'Poisonous ones?'

'There's some are. Big ol' rattler now – you leave him alone.' The innumerable white teeth flashed. 'The Professor . . . he got a big ol' black snake I seen near the okra patch, in the veg'table garden back at the house – *he* won't do no harm . . . Man, you jus' got to watch where you put your feet, that's all . . . Hell – I remember, when I was boy, way down south from here, after we left Jamaica . . . I was out in the swamp, catchin' frogs with a flashlight – I caught myself a water moccasin – a cottonmouth – instead . . .' Kingston chuckled at the hideous memory '. . . jus' behind the head I ketched him. An' he wound himself all around my arm . . . I had to unwind him an' *throw* him – an' I can tell you I throwed him clear out of the swamp!'

'Indeed?' If the man was setting out to terrify him, he was doing rather well, thought Latimer bitterly.

'But that was *my* fault, you see,' confided Kingston. 'He was only out there catchin' frogs – jus' like me – ' he looked at his watch quickly. ' – Hell! I got to go . . . you jus' keep to the path, Oliver – an' keep the creek on your right goin', an' on your left comin' back – an' you'll be jus' fine . . . An' I'll be waitin' here for you . . . 'Cause I'm fixin' to cook you a real Southern Supper this even' – all dipped in corn-meal an' fried in hog-lard in a black ion skillet . . . An' you're gonna like that jus' fine. . .'cause that'll be real soul-food!'

Latimer watched Fat Albert disappear in a haze of blue exhaust-smoke, and with mixed feelings. He had the feelings that the negro had been mocking him with hog-lard, which made him feel decidedly queasy, and . . . snakes . . . which made him feel queasier still. But he couldn't be sure.

He sighed, and turned back down the road, to look for the path into Sion. Two things he could be sure of, there were: he felt absurdly lonely, and before long he would feel extremely hot. In fact, he wished now, and very heartily, that he had not allowed himself to be so easily talked into this expedition, when he could so easily have pleaded jet-lag.

He eyed the woods doubtfully. He could find the path, and walk along it for a few yards to some safe clearing, and sit down for an hour. But that would not help him escape this ridiculous heat, which seemed already to thicken the very air in which he moved: not even that memorable heat-wave in Rome in '72, when David Audley had so nearly over-reached himself, had been like this . . . And he had been a dozen years younger then.

But . . . to yield to that temptation would be to expose himself to his own self-contempt, which was as inescapable as the heat itself. With that as the alternative there was no choice left, even though this was not so much a sweating temperature for Fattypuffs as a melting one:

191

better to walk and melt, testing himself against that hallowed St John battle honour of Delhi Ridge . . .

He walked.

It really wasn't so very different from some anonymous side-road in the anonymous English midlands – except for the cicadas loudly doing whatever it was they did.

And except for the heat.

There was a path –

There was also a fence, complete with barbed-wire. But someone had uprooted it here, and trampled it down, and the path beyond was tolerably well-trodden.

He looked at his watch, and decided to play down the line, for self-respect's sake: he would walk for half an hour, as far as he could, and would then turn around and walk back – to Kingston, and to whatever it was that Kingston purposed to dip in corn-meal and fry in hog-lard, however revolting that sounded.

He negotiated the fallen wire and started walking.

A few yards in he remembered *snakes*, and found himself a fallen branch for protection, just in case Kingston hadn't been kidding him.

Through the trees, turning in a belated attempt to memorize his route, he caught a glimpse of the little white church, away behind him on his right now, which had been on the highest point of the ridge above the wooden bridge when he had crossed yesterday – Sion Crossing and Sion Church . . . *'We on old Sion land now'* . . .

He walked on a short distance, but when he turned again to look back the white spire was already lost from view among the trees. This surprised him a little, because the woodland around him was not really dense, with its spindly younger saplings struggling haphazardly between the more mature trees.

He had always liked trees. Once upon a time, in the days of hope, he had even learnt about them in an amateurish way with suburban enthusiasm: autumn in Oxford, in the Parks and Mesopotamia and the Botanic Gardens – and in Broad Walk before Dutch Elm disease – had been unforgettable, and autumn had been his favourite time of all.

He looked around. Whatever the ridge had been like *then*, in Sion Crossing's age of elegance, all this had grown up naturally over long years: it was probably what the experts called 'climax forest', the stabilized terminal growth which the landscape supported when untouched by man, which only such natural agencies as fire and storm could substantially change. And it was like, and yet not like, any such wood in faraway England: there were trees he thought he recognized – a walnut there – and others he almost recognized – there were several varieties of oak, but no *English* oaks . . . and some he could only guess at – was *that* the famous hickory, only imported into Europe . . . and *that*, so much less spectacular . . . dogwood, maybe?

For a moment he was tempted to investigate one of the larger and more unfamiliar trees, but then he noticed the ivy and vine-like creepers which crawled over the forest floor and climbed the tree. The ivy looked innocent enough, and probably was innocent; and the vine-like thing might even be the Scuppernong of which he had read somewhere, which produced the native American grapes . . . but . . .

Anyway, regardless of poisonous snakes – and there were probably none of them within miles of him: they were more likely Kingston's little joke, designed to prevent him getting lost by keeping him to the path – regardless of such hazards, he had no time for natural history. It was history-book history he was supposed to be smelling out here, on old Sion land.

He paused again, arrested partly by the sudden fear of getting lost in this wilderness, and partly by an irritating feeling of inadequacy. But, of course, he couldn't really get lost: there was the path, ahead of him and behind him, and all he had to do was keep to it; besides which, although the woods hemmed him in, the land to his right did seem to fall away quite steeply now, presumably to the creek far below which had once been old Sion land's boundary on this side of the plantation.

No . . . he couldn't get lost here and now, on this path with the creek to his right, in 1984. *But in 1864 . . .*

He stood stock-still, almost wanting to hear some sound, no matter how far distant, to remind him that it was 1984, not 1864. But the woods were utterly silent, without a breath of wind, as though held by the heat. And the silence and the heat together only combined to remind him that nothing whatsoever had happened here since then until now, while the world outside had changed beyond all recognition.

He shivered at the idea, and was at once fascinated by that phenomenon: that it was possible to be hot and sweaty on the outside and yet cold somewhere deep inside, like a chef's *Bombe Surprise* –

He shook his head at the ridiculous analogy, and started to walk again. It was an age since he'd tucked into a *Bombe Surprise* – and he wasn't even hungry for once, although he ought to be – but such unlikely fantasies suggested to him that the flight had confused his time-clock, leaving him light-headed and susceptible to foolish notions.

He looked again at his watch, trying to estimate time against distance, and was disappointed that so few minutes had passed since he had left the road. He could hardly turn round yet, to retrace his steps, without having found . . . whatever there was to find, which had once been the beating heart of the great Sion Crossing plantation. And his own self-respect (apart from Kingston's likely scorn) ruled that out, anyway. Better by far to go on, and make Kingston wait, than to turn back prematurely and admit failure.

And yet . . . *what was he looking for?*

194

He came back to that irritating sense of inadequacy. It would look well enough in his report to Senator Cookridge to minute some facile window-dressing aside . . . *'With regard to the actual location of these events, I have examined the terrain, between Sion Church and the site of the Sion Crossing house – '.* But how would that advance his final recommendation? Because, after all, that recommendation would be made solely from the documents and hypotheses which Lucy Cookridge's father – *real* father, had amassed, which had nothing to do with this tangled woodland.

He stopped again, and looked around, helplessly aware that he hadn't the first idea of how to conduct a treasure-hunt. No doubt Audley would have known how to do that –

Damn it to hell! That was his own fault: it was Audley who should have been here, and he only had himself to blame for having twisted that well-laid plan out of true!

He felt the sweat prickle under his shirt. Regardless of his error of judgement, Audley wasn't here, but he was. And, regardless of crude technicalities, he was Audley's equal in the rational assessment of information any day of the week – *that* was what he had built on. Even . . . even without Audley's special advantages, he could do *better* than Audley – right?

Right!

So . . . he had not come far enough – so he would go further until he had at least sorted out in his own mind what he was supposed to be doing here – even, however annoying the thought might be, what Audley himself might have been doing, which Lucy Cookridge took for granted.

Of course, there was nothing really to see. And even if he found the ruins of the old Sion Crossing great house there would still be nothing to see of the slightest value. He had heard *ersatz* historians, like young Mitchell, speak of their great battlefields lovingly, as though the horrors which fascinated them were still eloquently there. But the truth was that time very quickly restored the bloodiest field to innocence, even if the world had been changed on it. He had himself raced over young Mitchell's dreadful stamping grounds along the motorway to Paris, travelling in minutes over the boring farmland which the bravest of the brave had taken years to cross; and he had watched French children splash and paddle happily between high tide and low tide on the Normandy sands where the sons of Mitchell's soldiers – and the great-grandsons of Lucy Cookridge's father's soldiers, Union and Confederate – had also splashed and paddled and died, leaving not the slightest mark.

It was all an illusion, this – a pointless return to the scene of the crime – a fraud perpetrated by military historians to pad their expense accounts and their tax returns: the truth of *then* did not exist *now*, on the ground, but only in the carefully sifted records, cross-checked and treble-checked and critically analysed, and the expertly-interpreted photographs. The truth was always there, somewhere, for those who had eyes to see and knowledge to understand – the truth was there even in default, crying out by its very absence: that was how he, Oliver St John Latimer (and *not* David Audley), had first identified, and then broken, the KGB's *Vengeful* operation, by God!

He started to walk again.

There was no rational reason to be here except that it was the done historical thing: to recreate the *then* one self-indulged oneself for form's sake (and to inflate expenses) by pretending to consult the *now* before coming to a decision –

Or, in this case, before consulting the practical treasure-hunting experts, with all their gadgets, about the economics of sweeping this climax-forest wilderness for what first-rate research and logical deduction suggested *might* still be planted between Sion Church and the Sion Crossing house.

Might?

Latimer frowned at another unidentified tree. For a man of Senator Cookridge's wealth the treasure-hunting game was plainly not worth the effort, never. mind the curiosity-value of the headlines . . . for he had no need of publicity. But if he was bent on indulging his stepdaughter, then the self-indulgence of the rich and powerful was its own justification . . . and the lesser mortals who pandered to it took their profit from that gratification, as he was doing now.

But that only brought him back to the original problem: somehow he had to play this silly historical game, although the wilderness was still only a wilderness, which looked for all the world as though nothing had ever happened in it beyond the natural cycle of the seasons, endlessly repeated.

He slowed suddenly, at first hardly knowing why in the continuing silence; and then, almost to his surprise, he found himself reading what must be his own thoughts, though they had an oddly external feeling, as though they had come from outside him.

He halted, and began to listen to the silence.

It seemed to him that, although appearances were truth, appearances were also deceptive. For it was *not* true that nothing had ever happened here: men had fought here, long ago . . . all those years ago . . . very young men mostly – Sherman's Iowa farmboys and the Georgia farmboys of the Wolfskin Rifles, teenagers with a stiffening of veterans – transformed by their different uniforms into victorious invaders far from home and angry defenders who had seen their homes burning . . . they had stalked and killed each other in these very woods, in the same heat, long ago. And although their fighting had not been of the slightest importance in any wider scheme of things – a mere footnote to a footnote, far less important in history than the fate of Scarlett O'Hara's Tara was in fiction – for the dead, Sion Crossing had been a greater battle than Gettysburg and Waterloo, than Bosworth Field or Bunkers Hill –

Was that what he was really thinking? Or was there something else inside his mind, in a corner he couldn't quite reach – ?

He wiped his palm across his sweaty brow, and shook his head to clear it. Whatever it was – it was foolishness, mere light-headed imagination!

He looked at his watch again. Twenty-seven minutes – in three minutes he would have won his own release, no matter what that negro said.

He drew a long breath. And no matter what Kingston said, it didn't matter: he didn't like these woods, and would be glad to be out of them. For, although they were just woods, they were too quiet and too lonely, and too far from home.

He looked ahead.

Nothing – trees –

Then he frowned.

Damn, damn, *damn* – there was *something* – something not a tree, high up there on his left, ahead, glimpsed through the trees: another step might have concealed it . . . but he had not taken that step, and could not unsee it now, it was there, and it was not a tree –

Unwillingly he went forward to confirm the bad news.

Not a tree . . . but a chimney-stack – ?

Another dozen steps set the matter beyond doubt: it *was* a chimney stack; or that was what it had once been, for, with no house around it, it stood deceptively taller, like an ivy-coloured obelisk in brick set in the midst of an irregular collection of mounds the shapes of which were equally blurred by ivy.

The path skirted the mounds. And there, less obvious, was the overgrown stump of another chimney, with some of its fallen fragments still visible at its base.

He had come to the Sion Crossing great house at last.

And this, of course, was always how it was with great

burnings: the fire stripped away the body of the building, the higher debris bringing down weakened walls to leave the more solid chimneys, which had not only been built stronger for their height but were by nature fire-resistant. Indeed, the rest of the house might have been all wood, the most abundant material available – he could remember now having glimpsed white-painted wooden houses yesterday, some of them even substantial enough to boast two-storey columns at their porches.

But there were no fallen columns here, that he could see . . . except that this must be the back of the house – ?

He turned towards the creek. Only a few yards, and then the ridge fell away steeply: without the trees there might well have been a splendid view from here, down and across the valley, in the great days of Sion Crossing . . . with the lawns and a tree-lined avenue sweeping up to a neo-classical columned front – a front on the far side like Ashley Wilke's Fair Oaks?

Belatedly, he remembered Lucy Cookridge's sketch-map, which he had stuffed into his pocket back in the study.

It was as he remembered it, yet there was a detail on it which he had noticed without remarking on at the time, but which was now intelligible to him.

There it was – *Old Road*. But the path along which he had come, though the shortest distance between the bridge and the site of the house, had undulated up and down along the shoulder of the rising land above the stream – it would have been quite unsuitable for a road in the days of horse-drawn carriages. So the original route to the Sion Crossing house had been along an old road which branched off the modern highway in a wide curve, approaching the house first at an angle and only straightening for the final run-in up the avenue.

That must be how it had been . . . And, of course, that fitted in exactly with Lucy Cookridge's father's material, and his interpretation of events –

199

Latimer's lip curled. In spite of himself, he was now playing the game. And, ridiculous though it was, it was not altogether unamusing. Or, at least, it might have been amusing if the theories had been his own, out of his own knowledge and research rather than another man's. But it would be foolish of him to be annoyed with himself for knowing nothing about this whole period of history, beyond what he could remember from a novel read long ago, and the film of the novel which he had once seen. His only foolishness had been in the Oxbridge, in letting himself be tempted in the first place!

No. *No* –

The path carried on, but there was a smaller path – hardly a path at all, but more a series of occasionally used footholds – leading up the nearest mound into the midst of the ruins between the chimneys.

No . . . since he was here, since he had come all this way, he could not turn back now. He had to see what there was to see.

He took the minor path gingerly, fending off what was probably perfectly innocent ivy with his stick, climbing step by step up into the ruins. At least there were no stinging-nettles: an English ruin would have been thick with them in such a place as this, at the tail-end of high summer.

It was disappointing. For there were no ruins, only the chimneys and there were still no ruins . . . no ruins, no fallen columns, no hint of former lawns and avenues of trees.

Trees, there were. Trees in the ruins, and trees all around it; it was just . . . mounds and chimneys in a wood in the middle of nowhere.

And it was so small . . . It was not *a great house* at all – it had never been a Tara or a Fair Oaks, Sion Crossing: it had been . . . it had been (he looked around him, estimating the distance between the chimneys, the area of the mounds) . . . it had been maybe a small manor house, maybe a large farmhouse – ?

Was this really the great house at Sion Crossing? Had he got it wrong?

Or had he got it right – and all the rest was the enlargement of travellers' tales and romantic fiction – Tara and Fair Oaks and Sion Crossing alike? He had seen larger *Roman* sites at home – at Lullingstone and Bignor, and at Chedworth, near GCHQ at Cheltenham – than this! This was so *small* – there had been no sweeping staircases between these chimneys on which southern belles in crinolines could pass each other gracefully!

He felt absurdly cheated, and the deception which historians practised angered him, which had so nearly fired his imagination: here, in this pathetic farmhouse ruin, he wished David Audley stood in his place, as he ought to have done, to test his *history* against *reality* –

He slashed his stick savagely at the nearest inoffensive sapling to punish it for his disappointment, and the sound behind him coincided exactly with the action and the thought, too late to stop either. But the sound overprinted itself on the thought, conjured up *rattlesnakes*, and twisted him round, with his stick at the ready to defend himself.

Behind him, looking directly at him, there was a Confederate soldier, with a levelled rifle –

9

Mitchell in London: Clutching at straws

Mitchell waited to the very edge of outright disobedience, in defiance of the spirit of Colonel Butler's orders, in order to catch Audley before he left. And then, from the thunderous expression on the man's face as he emerged from the lift, he almost doubted his judgement.

But not quite, so he braced himself. 'Hullo, David.'

Audley emitted a growling sound, like an old dog, who'd lost his best bone. 'So what do you want?'

'Nothing. I was just – '

'If it's Debreczen . . . you can have it: it was the finishing school for the deep sleepers.' An awful travesty of a smile accompanied the gift. 'As of now, the Beast's got all the details somewhere in its vile maw, which it will vomit up to you on demand. Jack depressed the necessary instruction before he cast me into the outer darkness.' Audley sighed. 'So he trusts you. And much good may it do you – more than it has done me, I hope, anyway – ' He started to move past Mitchell before he had finished speaking.

'No – ' Mitchell had to swivel and skip to keep up with him ' – I was just going to suggest – '

'Suggest?' Audley checked and faced him. 'You know what I've got to do tonight? I've got to fly to Rome – that's what I've got to do. So I'm not in a suggestible mood.' He glowered at Mitchell. 'So don't suggest anything. Just tell me what you *want*, Paul.'

Judgement was one thing, decided Mitchell. But grovelling was another. 'A bit of commonsense is what I want – I realize that common courtesy may be beyond your range . . . I'd *like* that, but after ten years I don't bloody well expect it.' He stared at Audley without flinching, and watched the big man's face harden for an instant – and then collapse into embarrassment.

'I'm sorry, Paul.' Audley raised a hand – that inevitably grubby hand, with its schoolboy inkstains on the fingers – and went on to scratch his head with it. 'Rome in August . . . even without Senator Cookridge . . . and what I've got to ask him – I shall have to crawl, damn it!'

Mitchell experienced a mixture of emotions which simultaneously elated and depressed him, quite confusing him with their contradiction. Audley had taught him . . . well, a lot, if not everything over those ten years . . . but he had never been quite sure whether he loved the man or hated him – he loved Faith, and he adored Cathy . . . but his relationship with Audley had been in some sense feudal, with obligation and self-interested expectation cancelling out all the bullying and the double-crossing, leaving no room for any definite emotion.

Audley tried to grin at him. 'He'll probably send me away with a flea in my ear . . . And that's only if he even agrees to talk to me – ' He finished scratching his head, and looked at his ink-stained hand with critical distaste, as though he wished that it didn't belong to him.

The man could have had the job Latimer had got – for the asking . . . In fact – damn it all to hell! – he could probably have had Butler's job, and with Butler's help, if he had stirred himself to get it.

'So what do you want?' Audley abandoned his hand.

For the first time Mitchell thought of Audley as *old* – *old* now, from this moment, past any of the promotions which he had inexplicably scorned: from this moment they were *equal* . . . *equal* – except that now *he*, David Audley, was going nowhere . . . except where he wanted to go, on his own terms . . . and he, *Paul Mitchell*, intended to go up, on whatever terms he could get.

Audley managed that grin at last. 'Something in your best interest, at a guess?'

Mitchell had just been about to substitute a certain

203

grudging affection for whatever he had felt before. But instead he advised himself that, as an enemy, David might still be more dangerous than Jack Butler and Oliver St John Latimer rolled in one.

'Mutual self-interest, let's say.' He shrugged. 'I've got something to trade about Sion Crossing, David.'

The grin vanished instantly as Audley looked past him, towards the guard's cage at the entrance. 'That sounds fair enough.' He came back to Mitchell. 'There's a pub I know. I'll buy you a beer.'

'That was what I was going to suggest in the first place.' They drove, with Audley giving instructions.

Over Westminster Bridge, down Lambeth Palace Road, past Lambeth Bridge . . . the Albert Embankment . . . past Vauxhall Bridge –

'Where the hell are we going?'

'Turn left here. I like a bit of privacy when I'm trading.'

They were into a maze of mean streets, maybe still on the edge of Vauxhall, maybe South Lambeth.

'Stop here.' Audley pointed. 'Park over there – in that little yard.'

Mitchell watched him wedge a piece of plain white card in the windscreen. Over the years, David had done a lot of odd trading, with a great many equivocal contacts. So this was probably as much out of habit as necessity.

'There now.' Audley pointed down an even meaner street. 'No one'll lift your car from here. But we have to walk a little.

Mitchell followed him. It was psychology, even more likely, designed simply to unsettle him before putting him back in his place.

They passed two grimy corner-pubs before Audley found the one he wanted – an even grimier one, which looked as though it hadn't seen a lick of paint since the end of the war – the Boer War.

Mitchell looked up, at the sign above his head: there was a soldier on a horse, waving his sword, crudely painted and with no name.

'The Marshal Ney.' Audley held the door for him. 'Better known hereabouts as "The Frenchman". There was a Frenchman owned it . . . oh, about a hundred years ago, whose grandfather was one of the Marshal's boy-soldiers at Waterloo . . . Or, strictly speaking, he inherited it from his wife, who was the landlord's only daughter – or was it his widow, Tom?' He addressed the last half of the sentence to the man behind the cramped little bar.

'Widow, Dr Audley.' The man bared a set of impossibly white National Health teeth. 'I told you – they done away with the old boy between them, the woman and the Frenchman . . . Pints, is it?' He accepted Audley's nod, and then flashed his NHS tombstones at Mitchell as he drew the beer. ''E was a sailor, the Frog was – with 'is eye on the main chance . . . an' she was it.' He placed the straight glasses side-by-side on the unpolished bar, which was as white as the holystoned deck of an old sailing-ship. 'An' then he done away with '*er* too, they reckon – drowned by the bridge, she was . . . an' got the pub, an' changed the name.' He accepted Audley's money without taking his eyes of Mitchell, as though he was checking him against some private rogues' gallery. 'An' married the skivvy wot worked for 'im.'

'And got away with it?' It was obvious, but he had to say something.

'Aaargh . . . well, that depends wot the skivvy was like.' The man blinked, as though the checking was complete. And that only left the filing-for-the-future-reference. 'Like, she knew too much . . . but 'e couldn't drop 'er off the bridge too – even the Ol' Bill might've smelt a rat then . . . An' she was a local girl – the other two, they was from 'cross the river, see . . . Naow, 'e knew when 'e was laughin' – them frogs isn't stupid – the way they gips us in the Common Market . . . Right, Dr Audley?'

205

'Right, Tom.' Audley looked round the bar, which was empty except for four old men playing crib in the corner. 'Can we be private now?'

'Ah?' Pure pleasure suffused the man's wizened face. 'Double or quits? Ten minutes?'

'Fifteen.' Audley watched the publican produce a pack of dog-eared cards from under the bar. 'You cut, Paul – and you look at *me*, Tom, when you cut – right?'

Mitchell cut the cards.

Four of Diamonds. Damn!

Tom stared at Audley, and cut the remainder.

'Two of Clubs.' Tom shook his head at Audley. 'Born to be hanged, you were, Dr Audley.' Then he looked at Mitchell, without looking at his card. 'Don't know you. Gotta proper name, 'ave you, Paul?'

'Dr Mitchell to you, Tom,' said Audley quickly. 'And on our side. And he went to the same university as your younger daughter – for all the good that has done him . . . which is precious little, to date.'

Mitchell felt complimented. Or, at least, if he could find the bloody place again, that he'd got a safe house of a sort.

But Tom shook his head. 'A good *eddication* – waste o' time, Dr Mitchell. But at least you're lucky at cards – '

The door banged open, to reveal a large youth, with others behind him.

Tom straightened up. 'The other door, mate.' He pointed to his left uncompromisingly. 'An' the first drink's on the house – if it's not shorts. Right?'

The youth filled the doorway, struck dumb with surprise.

Tom raised himself up another inch. 'You fancy buyin' a round for the Old Bill then, sunshine?' he challenged the youth.

Mitchell was caught for an instant between studying Tom and wondering what the large youth would do. But then the door was swinging shut, and the youth had vanished as though he had never occupied it at all. And Tom was giving him an embittered look.

Again, he had to say something. 'Unlucky in love, Tom – that's me. What did your daughter read at univeristy?'

And that, too, was a mistake. 'Mathematics. An' she's too bleedin' clever to do my accounts now, is Miss Christ Church College.' Tom pointed towards the corner furthest away from the unconcerned crib players. 'You got *fifteen* minutes to do your business at my expense, Dr Mitchell – ' he jerked his head towards the clock behind him ' – fifteen minutes and runnin' . . . and you better not be so lucky next time.' He raised the flap of the bar and waved a dog-eared square of cardboard at Mitchell as he made his way towards the door.

'*Temporarily closed*'. Mitchell just managed to catch the hand-scrawled legend, '*Use Salloon bar*'.

Audley took up the two pints and led the way to the corner furthest from the crib-players, who had shown little interest in the proceedings. The bar had a curious smell, Mitchell noticed; he had caught it earlier when he'd come in, but it was not so pronounced up at the bar. He hoped that it was the Thames, but had the uneasy feeling that they were too far away from the river for that, in which case it was the drains.

'Tom's a rotten loser,' confided Audley. 'He reckons to finger the Queen of Spades out of that pack, nine times out of ten . . . and I won last time, too – that's what's bugging him.' He smiled lop-sidedly at Mitchell. 'But this is a good pub, all the same – it's one of Jake Shapiro's actually, so you can rely on the beer as well as the security . . . The only reason it isn't full is that Tom's so dreadfully rude to the customers, if he doesn't like them at first sight. He's got an index-linked pension from somewhere, as well as a punch like a sock filled with sand, so he's no respector of persons . . . You should be complimented that he said "next time" – that's a rare accolade . . . Although it may be because he was unlucky in love too . . . I don't know.' He eyed Mitchell innocently. 'How is the fair Elizabeth these days?'

'She was well.' Mitchell watched Tom retrace his course from the door. 'When I last saw her.'

'Fourteen minutes,' he admonished them, before disappearing into the *salloon* bar on his right.

'A bad loser,' murmured Audley. 'A good man, but a bad loser, as I say.'

'You're not such a good loser yourself.' After that crack about Elizabeth, Mitchell felt resentful. 'When's your plane?'

'Not yet awhile.' Audley drank some of his beer. 'I should have bought you a Guinness, shouldn't I? But never mind – this is a good brew . . . Yes, you're quite right. I've never become reconciled to failure . . . Although it's very unBritish, if I can't win I don't like to play at all.'

'And you think we're going to lose now?'

'I think . . .' Audley pointed to Mitchell's beer '. . . I thought you were thirsty – ?'

Mitchell drank, and remembered Colonel Morris from the night before. 'Very nice.' He drank again. 'You think?'

'I think . . . we may already have lost, Paul – is what I *think* . . . But what I *know* . . . is that I don't really know what game I'm playing, you see.' Audley drank again.

'Senator Cookridge's game, surely?'

'Is that so?' Audley's voice was frosted with disbelief. 'Now, that's what Jack Butler thinks – because he's shit-scared of the Americans . . . And I don't blame him for that, in these particular circumstances – in his shoes I'd be just as scared.' He smiled. 'Things always look different from the top. In those trenches of yours, where we are at this moment, one has to do one's duty, and obey orders regardless – *Serve God, honour the King*, and end up hanging on the old barbed wire . . . Poor old Jack! He knows he's got to take a larger view of the proceedings, but he can't forget about that barbed wire all the same . . . So, in this instance, he's got the egregious Oliver St John

208

Latimer in some trench in Georgia – Confederate or Union, it doesn't matter . . . It's just that Oliver isn't trained for trench warfare . . . But, now that he's been promoted, there'll be a scandal if anything untoward happens to him. So that's one thing to worry about . . . And if no one scuppers Oliver in America, old Jack's going to have some hard words for him when he gets back – ' the smile became wickedly genuine ' – Oliver St John Latimer behaving like David Audley is really the most unkindest cut of all: it's like the Labour Party asking for more Cruise missiles – or calling for the de-unionisation of GCHQ at Cheltenham, say?'

Mitchell retreated into his beer. So that, among other things, was what Audley was up to in Cheltenham, was it?

'And, worst of all, he knows sod-all about Cookridge.' Audley sighed. 'Except that if Reagan is re-elected in '84, then the Senator is going to be a Very Important Person indeed – like, one old man trusting another old man of the same type . . . So Senator Cookridge could be calling the tune over here by '85, or '86 – and who the hell is Senator Thomas Cookridge, I ask you – eh?'

They really were into high policy now, far away from events in Sion Crossing in 1984, never mind 1864. This was the other dimension of decision-making, so hideously removed by that 'larger view' from the life-and-death affairs of the poor devils in the trenches!

'That's my job now – to check up on Cookridge.' At the same time, what Butler had set him to do no longer seemed so stupid to Mitchell. Indeed, it could be crucial, even. 'Whatever I get . . . I'm due to phone you in Rome tomorrow morning David.'

'Oh yes?' Audley didn't seem much comforted by that prospect. 'Well, I wish you the best of British luck!' His eyes clouded. 'Does Jack know anyone who can give you the low-down on the Senator? Anyone in London?' Audley's expression became as innocent as when he'd mentioned Elizabeth. 'Because, if Howard Morris doesn't know – because if *he* doesn't know – ?' Suddenly the innocent-clouded look dissolved. 'I tell you, Paul – the Foreign Office is bloody useless. The only man they've got who knows the blighter from Adam is sailing a trimaran in a single-handed race somewhere. And they don't even know how to ask him the question, never mind get any sort of answers, without broadcasting it across six continents . . . I can give you that for free – I tried that this morning, and I got a dusty answer . . . All you'll get from them is facts and figures, nothing more.'

Mitchell's moral dropped another point on the scale. 'There are SGs scrambled to Washington at the moment, to our people there. And there's a chap at Cambridge who knows him – I've put a "search" out for him.'

Audley said nothing for a moment, yet Mitchell could read his thoughts exactly.

'I'm sure you're doing all you can.' Audley nodded. 'But it's too bloody late, if you ask me.'

'You mean . . . we haven't got a prayer.' Mitchell nodded.

'A prayer is about all we have got. We can pray that we've imagined all this from start to finish – that all Senator Cookridge wants is a professional opinion from an unbiased third party that this . . . this Sion Crossing treasure – gold, or whatever, still exists, and can be found.' He nodded back at Mitchell. 'That sort of initial professional advice, from someone who isn't going to be in on the actual search, is perfectly correct procedure – sensible procedure, too . . . Because most treasure-hunters are consumed with a mixture of greed and enthusiasm, so their judgement is usually defective. You need a cool, dispassionate approach for that sort of thing – I know, because I have been involved in one or two little treasure-hunts, as you know, Paul.' He drank, and nodded again. 'In fact, I would have been a natural choice for Sion Crossing – as you yourself have pointed out . . . So the Senator was well-advised . . . but in this instance –

unlucky, shall we say?' He half-smiled at Mitchell suddenly, and frowned at the same time. 'Or perhaps not, as the case may be, since Oliver might well make a perfectly adequate consultant . . . good logical mind, used to handling unreliable information . . . a bit short on imagination, but that's not a fatal defect when it comes to treasure – better a devil's advocate than a dreamer . . . Yes, Oliver could well earn his fee, you know.' He nodded once again.

Mitchell frowned. 'His fee?'

'Oh – I'm sure he's not seduced by the thought of money.' Audley cocked his head knowingly. 'To do Cookridge a good turn could well be better than money in the bank.' His eyes narrowed thoughtfully. 'Yes . . . I think, if Cookridge had come to me, I might very well be in Sion Crossing by now, one way or another.'

'Even after knowing about Mulholland?' The black face grinned in Mitchell memory.

'Ah . . . well, now . . . I might not have known about Mulholland.' Audley thought for a moment. 'Yes . . . you see, that's just possibly the one place where this operation didn't go according to plan – if it *is* some sort of operation . . . which, on balance, I think it has to be.'

'But surely it went wrong when Howard Morris chose Oliver instead of you, David?'

'Same thing. Just related cause and effect.' Audley nodded. 'Let's suppose old Howard *had* met me in the Oxbridge, and popped the question – and suppose I *had* agreed to meet Cookridge.' He shrugged. 'I'd hardly have refused, because it would have been much too interesting . . . so then Cookridge pops *his* question – '

'But you said you'd have checked with Butler, David, then?'

'Ah . . .' Audley bridled '. . . but that doesn't mean we wouldn't have taken the bait.' He gave Mitchell a sly look. 'You shouldn't have started digging then . . . And we'd never have checked with anyone – I'd have said to Jack:

"Here's a marvellous chance to get in with this fellow Cookridge, about whom we know sod-all at the moment – you can spare me from Cheltenham for a few days – I'll be back in no time at all."' Audley smiled. 'It would have made good sense . . . And I've never been to Georgia – I know the theory of the Mint Julep . . . I've drunk an Oxford version of the South Carolina recipe from the Trapier cup at New College, even . . . But one of Rick Harwell's juleps served "on location", as it were – that would be something to remember, Paul!'

Audley's eyes closed momentarily, and Mitchell thought *when it comes to doing the right thing for the wrong reason* –

Then the eyes were open, transfixing him. 'And Jack would have bought that – because it makes sense. In fact, if Oliver had gone to him with the same story he would have bought it, though he wouldn't have let Oliver go . . . *In fact*, Oliver behaving out of character is the real and only place where this operation has come unstuck – otherwise, it's a quite damnably clever little piece of logical planning, when you think about it – ' He stopped abruptly.

And there, of course, was the cause and effect, thought Mitchell: *it was only because they had been baffled by Oliver St John Latimer's eccentric behaviour that they had dug deeper – had cornered Howard Morris and checked the flights to America* –

'Whereas now we've got Mulholland,' he said.

'Miss Cookridge led us to Mulholland.' Audley looked at him, and then through him into the deep of his own memory. 'But it was Howard who gave us Miss Cookridge – and it was Howard who connected her with Macallan . . . Although he might well have assumed we'd already got both of them . . .' Audley continued to stare into his memory. 'Was that for friendship's sake? Or was that because he was scared? Or was it deliberate policy?' Audley frowned.

'He knew Macallan would remind you of Debreczen, David,' said Mitchell.

Audley focussed on him. 'Debreczen – of course! You're absolutely right, Paul Mitchell . . . if he'd been an Englishman, and they'd kicked him up into the Lords, he'd have been Lord Macallan of Debreczen, by God!' He nodded approvingly. 'Quite right!'

'But where does Cookridge come in? Because he doesn't mean Debreczen – ' Mitchell stretched Audley deliberately ' – he means Macallan's ex-wife and daughter. And that's not exactly a friendly connection – it's more like an unfriendly disconnection, David.'

Audley shook his head. 'But Sion Crossing means the Civil War, and there's a connection there. Because the Civil War was always Bill Macallan's hobby – that I do know!' Then he shook his head again. 'But then Macallan was bed-ridden in Iowa for months – or years – before he died. And Iowa's a long way from Georgia.'

'I can get him closer than that,' said Mitchell.

'What?' Audley concentrated on him. '*How*?' And then caution overlaid the flash of eagerness. 'Or is this your stock-in-trade, Dr Mitchell?'

The sudden half-mocking formality marked the man's acceptance that the ten-year-old pupil-teacher relationship was over for him too: they both knew they were equals now.

'Not really, Dr Audley.' In that instant Mitchell decided that it was enough to have made his point implicitly. With Latimer as deputy-director he might need Audley as an ally in the coming months, and Audley wielded influence with Colonel Butler and others out of all proportion to his position. 'I don't think we have to trade with each other. I only said that to get you out of the office.'

Audley contemplated him for a moment, as though he too was making a longer appraisal of their future relationship. 'Just as well! Because I haven't got anything to trade with you – now that you've got full access to The Beast.'

Then he straightened up. 'Though don't you go getting the idea that The Beast knows as much about Debreczen and Macallan as I do, my lad . . . At least, so far as the old days are concerned. Because most of what it's got is mine, and I didn't put everything in it, by golly!'

'Of course.' Mitchell recognized his chance. 'And the same applies to Sion Crossing now, David.'

Audley's eyes narrowed. 'What's that supposed to mean? Didn't this pal of yours put over the details? I thought Jack was reading 'em off from that screen of his?'

'So he was.' Mitchell nodded. 'But my pal didn't put everything he'd got into it.'

'Why not?'

'Because he's a friend of mine – because I told him to put over the history.' Mitchell gazed at his teacher innocently. 'But I also told him that if he picked up anything that wasn't history he was to keep that for me alone.' He smiled at Audley suddenly. 'You once said that common knowledge spread power too thinly for it to be very useful, David.'

'Disgraceful!' Audley concealed approval behind insincere disapproval. 'Did I say that?'

'You did. With many other anti-social doctrines.' Mitchell nodded. 'I have been very badly trained, I suspect.'

'Evidently.' Audley was as susceptible to flattery as anyone – except Jack Butler. 'So what was Bill Macallan's connections with Sion Crossing?' He raised an eyebrow. 'I take it you've been through to your . . . friend again? Does he know what you do?'

'Yes.' Mitchell drank some of his beer. 'He has a fair idea.'

'And he's reliable?'

'Absolutely. And as a teacher of American history he has a lot of contacts over there.'

'Even in Sion Crossing?'

'Not exactly *in* Sion Crossing. But the story's quite well-known, it seems.'

'Yes.' Audley nodded. 'Treasure stores usually are. It's

the treasure itself which is elusive. Was it a king's ransom – a great treasure?'

'No. That's really the point, David. You see, by '64 – 1864 – there wasn't a great deal of hard cash left in the Confederacy. There was a lot of paper money – and bonds, and such like.'

'Uh-huh – naturally . . . "Promise to pay" rubbish, yes – Scarlett O'Hara's father invested everything in the "Glorious Cause", as I recall. Like our National Savings and Victory Bonds in the last war – if Mr Hitler had won, all that would have been waste paper. And Mr Lincoln *did* win.' He nodded once more, but then frowned. 'But Senator Cookridge must be after gold, not paper, surely?'

'Not this gold.' Peter's facts and figures came back to Mitchell. 'The whole of the Confederate treasury, that Jefferson Davis sent out of Richmond in '65, only amounted to about a third of a million – in gold, that is . . . there were millions in paper – but there was actually more private gold in that convoy, from the Richmond banks. Nearer half a million, maybe.'

'From Richmond . . . in '65.' Audley looked past him, at the clock. 'But what has that got to do with Sion Crossing in '64?'

'Nothing – directly. Except that Jefferson Davis's gold was also plundered. At a place called Chennault Crossroads, in Georgia. They got some of it back, and the lawsuits about possession went on for years afterwards.

'I still don't see – '

'What my . . . contact says, if that Chennault Crossroads is just an historical footnote to the war, David. And Sion Crossing is just a couple of lines on the end of it – a footnote to a footnote. Calling it "treasure" is ridiculous, he says. At the most there was no more than 20,000 dollars in gold and silver, and that's stretching it. The rest was paper.' He met Audley's frown. 'Chickenfeed, David.'

Audley blinked. 'Gold's never chickenfeed, my lad.'

'Chickenfeed to Senator Cookridge. Not worth the effort – particularly as it most likely doesn't exist anyway. Because the local militia tangled with Union foragers there – some of it was recovered, but most of it went into the soldiers' pockets.' He shook his head at Audley. '"Tipu's Treasury" at Mysore. And after the battle of Vittoria in Spain – and the Summer Palace in China . . . never mind Chennault Crossroads in '65, or Sion Crossing in '64.'

A corner of Audley's mouth twitched. 'And Germany in '45 – you have a point, I agree.' He twitched away the memory of Germany in '45. 'But *somebody* thinks this is worth Oliver St John Latimer's time – somebody thought it was worth *my* time, damn it!'

'Yes.' They had come to it. 'And not just your time.'

Audley concentrated on him. 'What d'you mean?'

Mitchell experienced a curious twinge of memory of his own past. 'You remember what I was doing when we first met, David?'

'You were . . . writing a book.' For a fraction of time Audley's expression softened. 'I have a copy signed by the author – remember?'

'But that didn't pay the bills, while I was writing it.'

'No.' Audley knew the economics of historical writing better than most. 'You were a leg-man.' He smiled. 'You did the donkey-work in the archives for those blessed with more of the world's goods – or who had comfy academic tenure, and lots of other irons in the fire. Right?'

'I was a researcher.'

'And a good one.' Audley nodded. 'That was one of the reasons why we hired you.'

'Yes.' "One of the reasons" was a most delicate way of putting it. 'Well . . . my contact, he uses researchers in the States. He's been working off and on for several years on a biography of Nathan Bedford Forrest.'

'Oh yes?' Audley took a second to work that out: he was much better on medieval horse-soldiers than their

216

mid-19th century Confederate descendants. 'You mean Professor Welsh does?'

There were a lot of ways Audley could have known about Peter Welsh: he could simply have asked Colonel Butler whose Sion Crossing information had been fed into the Beast. But what he was signalling was for Mitchell to cut the crap with him.

Very well, thought Mitchell. Their time was almost up, anyway. 'He had a good one in Atlanta. A lady by the name of Wright – Mrs Holly Wright. She was an ex-librarian whose husband ran out on her, and left her with two children . . . And they don't pay librarians much, so she branched out . . . Peter thought a lot of her, because she was bright, as well as accurate and tenacious, so he paid top rates.'

'*Had*?' There wasn't a hint of softness in Audley's face now.

'She wrote to him, the last time, to say she'd got this commission from an old buff in the mid-west, to trace the route of a particular Iowan regiment in Sherman's army. And though the money wasn't all that good, it could be quite long-term, because the man was some sort of cripple and couldn't do any of his field-work.'

'The last time?' Audley was adding two-and-two fast now. 'What happened?'

'Actually, it wasn't quite the last time – that was the last letter. But she sent him a card, David.'

'From Smithsville?'

'From near there. There's nothing photogenic at Smithsville – she always used to make her own cards, with pretty postcards or photos of her own. So . . . this one was of an historic old church – an ante-bellum one that survived the war. The Sion Crossing Church, it was.'

'What happened to her?'

'She had an accident, David – a road accident – ' Mitchell accelerated to forestall Audley's mounting exasperation. ' – they found her upside down in her car, in the trees off the inter-state one morning. Her sister wrote to Peter Welsh . . . It was a dead-straight highway, so they reckoned some damn great truck had maybe shouldered her off, and didn't stop – maybe didn't even know . . . It happens like that out there. Sometimes they don't even find the wrecks for weeks.'

Audley thought for a moment. 'That does sound suspiciously like Mulholland. He likes an accident . . . And you're sure Welsh is reliable?'

'Peter Welsh?' Mitchell was taken aback. 'Good God – what d'you mean? He's just a friend . . . we were up at college together.'

'Famous last words! You asked him about 1864 – and he gave you a fatal accident in 1984. That was good of him.'

'So he's got a suspicious mind. I told you – he knows I work for the Government now. He thought what happened to Mrs Wright was a curious coincidence, in the circumstances.'

'In the circumstances we're up to our necks in coincidences. And this is the final one.' Audley looked at his watch. 'We're into extra time – if Bill Macallan hired someone to look at Sion Crossing, and that someone had a fatal accident – and Winston Mulholland *specializes* in fatal accidents . . . than that's way beyond coincidence, Paul.'

And when Oliver St John Latimer was unknowingly following in Mrs Holly Wright's footsteps, thought Mitchell. *Christ!*

All the same –

'I only see Peter Welsh once in a blue moon. And I got in touch with him this time. I've no reason not to trust him, David.'

'Yes.' Audley was only half with him. 'And he's your vintage, not mine . . . we can check on him later . . . It's Bill Macallan I'm worried about – *Bill Macallan . . .*'

It was no good saying *but he's dead, David* again, he had to accept that if Bill Macallan could still worry David

218

Audley from the grave then there was something to worry about.

'Why, David?'

'Why?' Audley shook his head quickly, as though to clear it. 'Yes . . .' He concentrated fully on Mitchell. 'The trouble with the passage of time, Paul Mitchell, is that it leaves one behind, pickled with one's memories . . . You don't remember Bill Macallan – and, come to that, neither does Jack Butler . . . he was playing soldiers somewhere when I was playing silly buggers with Macallan. So Macallan's just a man in the "dead files" to both of you – and the same with Debreczen – Just a bit of history, like Sion Crossing and General Sherman. But I remember them both – they're not history to me, they're *experience* – and bitter bloody experience, too!'

Audley looked at his watch again, and Mitchell decided that it was better to say nothing.

'Debreczen was a KGB place in Hungary, way back.' Audley looked at him. 'It wasn't in the town, it was in the woods some miles away – in an old Hapsburg hunting lodge, not too far from the Russian border . . . The Germans trained their Brandenburgers there for the Russian front – their Long Range Desert-SAS deep-penetration groups – so it was all wired-up and developed when the Russians took it over in '45 . . . And *they* used it in the early '50s – the Russians – to coddle their deep sleepers . . . Not your run-of-mill agents, Paul: they were the *really* deep penetration agents, whose job wasn't to betray anything, but only to be respectable and successful, and rise in the system – in government and politics, or in business and the trade unions – until they were policy-makers . . . Or, even, if they weren't so successful, they could help to organize for the next generation after that, because they'd be so clean they'd always be able to set up safe-houses – that was the Debreczen thinking.'

Audley observed Mitchell's expression, and grinned. 'Well, we got a line on this . . . from the inevitable

219

defector . . . eventually – ' the grin suddenly became painful ' – by which time, for the same reason, they'd closed it down. So . . . all we knew was that a series of individuals had been individually processed – *number* unknown, *name* unknown . . . there never were names at Debreczen . . . nationality, *various* – British, American, French, German, Ruritanian . . . All we actually knew for sure was that they'd been away from whatever they usually did for about a week, *and they hadn't been where they'd said, but for about a week they'd been at Debreczen* . . . Maybe they'd been climbing in the Alps, or studying the Renaissance in Florence, or skiing in Austria – or taking pictures of bears in Yellowstone National Park . . . *But actually they hadn't been* – okay?'

Mitchell could see. And he could also see that without some creature like the Beast . . . he could see endless paper-work, for a start.

'And I got the job.' The memory was evidently bitter. 'I think old Fred Clinton thought it would cut me down to size – Oliver would almost certainly have done it much better, because he wouldn't have worried, because he's got the soul of a clerk in a counting house . . . But *I* got the job – and I can vividly recall spending a week on a likely lad who claimed to have been studying Romanesque churches in Burgundy, or thereabouts . . . but who was actually screwing his best friend's girl in a hotel at Cannes, as it turned out – *and* got her pregnant and married her, which only made it worse . . . At least, that's what I *think* – but I'm not sure.'

'Why aren't you sure?'

'He refused to talk. So there were five days I couldn't trace, somewhere between Cluny and Cannes. I think he was screwing *her*, somewhere in Provence. But I certainly screwed his chances of promotion, because of those lost days . . . And I ruined six other men, because I had to put a question mark beside their names – and two of them were undoubtedly innocent – and they weren't promoted either. I only got close to one genuine traitor, and he shot himself before I could pick him up – or maybe *they* did if for him . . . I had the feeling they were ahead of me. But it was a bloody disaster either way – I told Fred that every time I got warm, the effing KGB would get there first, but mostly I was just putting black marks against innocent names, and they were laughing their Russian heads off . . . Maybe I was wrong, but I told him I wanted to quit, anyway.'

'So what happened?'

'I was lucky, actually. Old Fred took a civilized view. He realized I wasn't as clever as he'd thought. And I also think he was pleased – secretly pleased – to discover that I still had a vestigial conscience of a sort, maybe.' Audley made a face. 'He once told me that his special nightmare was that he'd wake up one day to find he was running a British replica of the KGB. He said – ' Audley stopped abruptly.

Mitchell turned. Tom had appeared again behind the bar, and was raising the flap.

'That's it then, Gents.' He strode past them. 'This bar's going public again.'

Mitchell leaned towards Audley. 'But what about . . . Bill . . . you-know-who – ?

Audley waited as Tom unbarred the door and recovered his sign.

'Can we have another five minutes, Tom?'

'You already owes me a good five minutes, Dr Audley.'

'God will reward you, Tom, in the hereafter.'

Tom banged the flap down. 'I hope not! I'll be servin' drinks to you in the Other Place if 'e does, like that black bugger in the pome. So the answer's "no"!'

Pome? Mitchell gave Audley a baffled glance as Tom vanished into the *salloon* bar. 'What black bugger?'

Audley chuckled. 'Come on, Paul –

> 'E'll be squattin' on the coals
> Givin' drink to poor damned souls,
> An' I'll get a swig in Hell from Gunga Din!

221

– Tom's a Kipling-fancier, like all good men.'

Damn! 'But I'm a Macallan fancier at the moment, David.'

'Yes.' Audley stood up. 'But I ought to phone Jack after what you've told me – '

Mitchell sat firm. 'We had a deal, David. Remember?'

Audley sat down again. 'All right. But quickly.'

'Quickly, then.' He was under orders for *Cookridge*, Mitchell told himself. But if Audley's mysterious fears were well-placed he needed to know about Macallan.

Audley drew a breath. 'Bill Macallan was the American end of the Debreczen inquiry. But for Anglo-American reasons we worked in tandem for some of the time.'

There was a hint of unwillingness there. 'Go on, David.'

'We didn't hit it off – I told you last night . . . Chalk and cheese – damn Yankee and effing arrogant Limey . . . The cards were stacked against us, Paul: he'd ridden one of Patton's Shermans – the tank, not the general – out into the wide blue yonder while I was slugging it out in the Normandy *bocage* . . . I thought he'd had it *easy* – and *he* thought I didn't measure up – he thought my heart wasn't in the job . . . Maybe he was right at that – I don't know . . .'

It had been a bad scene, certainly. For Audley to mention *tanks* was something out of the ordinary: the massacre which had been Audley's war was pretty much a closed book, unmentionable.

But tanks had nothing to do with Debreczen. 'But you worked together on Debreczen?'

'Yes. We didn't hit it off on that, either . . . This was after Burgess and Maclean and Co – and the ones we don't mention, of course. But . . . I suppose I understood them better than he did – I hated them, but I was also sorry for them, maybe – like, *there, but for the grace of God, goes David Audley* . . . If I'd been at Cambridge ten years – fifteen years – earlier, in the wrong place at the wrong time – *who knows*?' He gave Mitchell an anguished look. 'Christ! If I'd commanded a tank in Spain – would it have been an Italian tank or a Russian one? You tell me, Paul – ?'

The pub door opened. There was a pretty blonde framed in it, who seemed to be surprised that the bar was so empty, and whose mother hadn't been born when the tanks of that other long-forgotten civil war had tested each other on the Ebro and the Jarama.

The little blonde was propelled into the bar from behind, by a brunette –

'David – '

'Okay.' Audley glanced up at the girls and their followers. 'Bill was different – I used to argue with him – I accused him of having the same attitude as the orthodox clergy had towards heretics in medieval times – during the Albigensian Wars.' He gave the group a friendly nod. 'In fact, I said he was like Arnald-Amalric of Cîteaux at the seige of Bèziers in 1209 – when the soldiers asked him what they should do with any good Christians captured in the storming of the town he's supposed to have said "Kill all: God will know His own".' He turned back to Mitchell. 'Arnald-Amalric became Archbishop of Narbonne in 1212 – or maybe it was 1211 . . . He was Papal Legate in 1209.'

The group's curiosity wilted under the onslaught of medieval history and it took sanctuary at the bar.

'To which Bill instantly replied "Well, that was one guy who knew his business, then". Which really just about sums him up. All you have to do is substitute patriotism for religion – he didn't hate Russians nearly so much, because they were only doing their job and they were fair game . . . But *American traitors* . . . and to a lesser extent the British too – they profoundly offended him. That was *heresy* – ' The door opened again ' – that would have rated the thumb-screw and the stake, in his book. if he'd been allowed to use 'em, Paul.'

'But he got the sack, David.'

'Yes.' Audley stood up and started towards the door. 'It's getting too crowded here.'

It was getting dark outside.

'Why did he get the sack?' persisted Mitchell, following him.

Audley looked up and down the empty street. 'If I'm going to call Jack we'd better get our skates on.'

'When's your plane to Rome?'

'Never mind the bloody plane.' Audley started to walk. If Rome could be avoided, it would be, thought Mitchell. But knowing Colonel Butler – and knowing that Macallan was dead, but Cookridge was alive – that was a faint hope.

'Why did Macallan really get the sack?' He measured his stride against Audley's.

'It was inevitable, really. For one reason or another.'

'What reasons?'

'He wouldn't give up. We gave up – but he wouldn't . . . When he put a name on his list – a possible name, mark you . . . not a probable – he got his teeth into it . . . It wasn't "Guilty until proved innocent", it was "The-more-innocent probably the-more-guilty" – Arnald-Amalric would have loved him in the siege-lines at Bèziers and Carcassonne and Montségur!'

Audleys stride was three inches longer than his. 'That was a reason?'

'Too right it was! He started to offend people – and some of them were people with influence . . . apart from being innocent – this was after McCarthy, remember – Debreczen broke after him: that was one reason why it was kept so firmly under wraps . . . So he made a lot of enemies.'

One reason . . .

'Yes?'

'Yes – ' Audley nearly cannoned into him as they turned a corner ' – and some of his enemies really were his enemies – '

'What?'

224

'I told you – he wouldn't give up . . . so he got a real Debreczen graduate in the end – dead to rights . . . Whisked him out of his posh Wall Street office before you could say "Jack Robinson" – or "Kim Philby" . . . A genuine Ivy League blue-blooded bastard – over there – ' Audley pointed to a gap in the badly-lit street.

It was where they had parked the car 'Yes?'

'Got him in a safe house near Washington, just south of the Mason-and-Dixon line – way down South in Dixie – ' Audley faced him across the car ' – let's go.'

'What happened?'

'Some safe house!' Audley placed both hands on the roof of the car. 'They were softening him up gently, when some idiot let him walk in the garden to get a breath of air . . . Wide open countryside – I know the place, and they measured the distance afterwards. It was seven hundred yards . . . They say some buffalo hunter hit an Indian with a long rifle at eleven hundred . . . Well, the KGB got this chap at seven-hundred, right through the heart. Let's go, Paul.'

'No.' Mitchell had the keys in his pocket, so at last he had the whiphand. 'That should have established his credit, David.'

'Oh . . . it did – it did.' Audley took his hands off the car. 'Open up.'

'Not until I know why Macallan was sacked. We had a deal.'

Audley looked at him for a moment, then smiled. 'So we did. But I don't have much time. So . . . open up, and I'll tell you.'

He had to leave the man something, decided Mitchell as he inserted the key. 'You want a phone?' There probably wasn't an unvandalized public phone for a mile.

'No. Take me back. Jack will be worshipping the Beast – I'll try him face to face. Bugger the plane!'

Mitchell manoeuvred the car into the empty street, and then put his foot down. Audley intended to win by cheating – by missing the plane and chancing his luck with Colonel Butler.

'If I miss it I won't blame you.' Audley read his mind with disconcerting accuracy. 'No need to kill us both on the way to Armageddon. Just take it easy and drop me by the Cenotaph.'

'Why did they sack him, David?'

'It was a combined operation, really.'

'Combined?' He slowed down.

'Yes. Anglo-Russian-American. That's about as combined as you can get, wouldn't you say?'

'How did they combine?'

'We didn't actually combine, in a formal sense . . . but we worked towards the same end independently . . . And God blessed our consensus in His own inscrutable way.'

There were the flashing lights of an accident ahead, blue and red.'

'Get in the other lane – we'll cross the bridge,' said Audley.

'That's a fair old blasphemy – ' Mitchell swung the car outwards ' – even by your standards, David.'

'Maybe.' Audley refused to take offence. 'But it didn't seem like that at the time. But . . . maybe you're right.'

Suddenly Mitchell remembered his own past – *the thin Yorkshire drizzle misting the green-and-grey landscape, when Frances had died for him –*

He swung the wheel again, regardless of all the lights, and an angry car-horn protested behind him –

'Steady on!' Audley sat up beside him.

'Sorry – ' Mitchell addressed the car behind and Audley together, quite uselessly ' – sorry!'

Audley settled back. 'We do get things wrong, you know, Paul. In fact, we very rarely get them all right. And we just have to trust in our luck, and let the dead bury the dead.'

He couldn't possibly be thinking of Frances – he wouldn't have said that if he was, for God's sake!

Audley sat up again. 'What I meant was . . . Bill got sick for the first time about then – it was the first twinge of this disease he had, you see – Paul?'

Maybe he *had* remembered – but belatedly – ?

'Okay.' Sympathy was something Mitchell didn't need. 'So that was God. So what about the rest of you?'

They had reached the other side of the bridge: he turned carefully, watching everything behind him as well as ahead.

'The Russians set him up – at least, that's what I think now . . . They wanted him out, after that . . . after he'd shown that he was dangerous.' Audley was eager to explain now. 'There was some money in a bank which he couldn't account for – somebody who looked like him had deposited it, and he couldn't disprove it, and he had no money of his own . . . It wasn't *proved* – ' Audley sat back, and stared ahead ' – but the people he'd offended applied his own rules to him – they implied he was taking back-handers to put names on his list . . . And that wasn't *proved*, either, but there was this implication that the Russians were trying to use him to discredit good up-and-coming red-blooded Americans – the very thing I'd suggested to Fred, when I was trying to get out of the Debreczen operation, in fact.'

The Mother of Parliaments reared up dark and empty – the law-givers were away holidaying with their wives and families and mistresses, while Colonel Butler was minding the shop for them, with the help of the Beast, high up ahead.

'They thought he was in with the Russians? Although you say he was a super-patriot?'

'Yes . . . well, there was a certain irony there. Because one of the fellows he'd been hounding was also an extremely patriotic type, and Bill had argued that this was a cover – the best cover of all, he suggested, so . . . what was sauce for the goose became sauce to cook the gander in.'

227

Mitchell looked for Boadicea in her chariot: only the British would celebrate the destroyer of their capital with a statue in its heart.

'But you didn't think that, David.'

Audley caught sight of Boadicea. 'Aren't you going the wrong way?'

'James is digging Cookridge contacts for me. He may have someone by now.' And, of course, Elizabeth would be in for her night-shift, with any luck. It was no good dwelling on the guilty memory of Frances. Life had to go on. 'I said I'd come back –'

He took his eyes off the red tail-lights ahead for an instant. 'But you scuppered him all the same, didn't you, David?'

Audley said nothing.

'Didn't you?' He almost missed his turning.

'We didn't exactly scupper him. But we might have been able to do something *for* him . . . and we didn't.' Audley paused. 'We let him cook.'

'We . . .' Mitchell waited for the steel door to obey his signal '. . . meaning *you*, in this instance?'

'Fred took the decision.'

The door lifted.

'Fred took the decision.' Audley tried the statement again, as though he wanted to be convinced by it. 'Bill Macallan wasn't any friend of ours. We didn't owe him anything – he hadn't done us any good turns, and he likely wouldn't in the future. If he came out smelling of roses . . . the fact that we'd helped him wouldn't have influenced his judgement . . . and he might have gone to the top.'

'He was an honest man, in fact.' Mitchell found a parking space near the lift.

'So was Arnald-Amalric of Cîteaux.' Audley turned to face Mitchell. 'But you're right: *I* let him cook – *I* advised Fred that he might harm us . . . that he was probably innocent, but certainly dangerous – dangerous to innocent

228

people in the present and dangerous to Anglo-American relations in the future. Yes.' He raised his chin. 'Is that what you want?'

'Not quite.' He was a little sorry for Audley, but not very sorry. Everyone had to live with the guilt of their decisions. If they couldn't they should try to live on a desert island. 'You think you were wrong now – do you?'

The chin went up half an inch. 'About not helping Bill Macallan? No – not altogether . . .'

'He wasn't innocent?'

'Oh – he was innocent – ' The chin came down ' – but he would have done us a mischief sooner or later. And it's the Anglo-American accord which underpins NATO. And it's NATO which allows people to have tender consciences, and to slag America off to make them feel good.' He shrugged suddenly. 'Sorry to teach you to suck eggs. But Bill Macallan was a casualty in that war – and rightly so . . . And, of course, he was quite the wrong man to handle the Debreczen thing – I wasn't wrong there, either.'

'Why was he wrong?'

'He enjoyed his work too much. By the time he'd put the fire out he would have burnt the house down.'

The logic of that was surprising. 'So you were the right man for Debreczen, David.'

'Yes.' Audley looked away from him, and the unnatural light in the underground car park caught the lines on his face and beginning of stubble on his cheek, making him look a hundred years old. 'That was the worst decision I ever made – that was where Bill Macallan was right: *I didn't measure up* . . .' Audley came back to him. 'I've thought a lot about Debreczen since we got a sniff of it again, last year, Paul. And I botched that one, too . . .'

Mitchell felt like a boy who'd turned over a stone to find creepy-crawlies, and had found a hole full of rattlesnakes.

'I should have stuck to it, when we still had a chance. And Fred should have kept me at it – he should have given me the resources the job needed . . . Stopping secrets getting out – pre-empting Soviet operations – that's peanuts compared with what we might have achieved if we'd nipped off the Debreczen graduates in the bud . . . the long-term investments – that was where Bill Macallan's instinct was dead-right, you see – ' He blinked at Mitchell. 'Time's up, Paul: *This bar's public*, as Tom would say – '

Mitchell got out of the car. 'Cookridge, David?'

'Maybe.' Audley slammed the door. 'But we won't find out that by asking him to his face. If Cookridge is a Debreczen man we've got to take it slow.'

He had done Audley an injustice in thinking he merely didn't want to fly to Rome in August, thought Mitchell.

Audley looked at his watch again. 'I can try to change Jack Butler's mind, but I don't rate my chances. Because that would mean writing off Oliver St John Latimer at Sion Crossing, and I don't think he'll stand for that – from me.'

'How long have we got?' Mitchell allied himself to Audley with the pronoun. 'When's your flight?'

'Two hours and thirty-one minutes, I've got.' Audley half-smiled. 'You've got until ten-thirty, Rome-time, tomorrow morning. But as for Oliver – poor old Oliver's probably run out of time by now – '

There was a note for him in the guards' cage – not an official slip, with its flimsy filed for future reference, but a sheet of white notepaper in James Cable's nervous scrawl, in a private envelope.

'*PLM –* '

He couldn't read the first word after his initials: there was no word in the English language resembling *Brediably*, which was what it looked like, more or less –

'*PLM – Brediably, the FCO is still useless*' – the elongated snake-like squiggle had to be "useless", on the basis of David Audley's own description of the Foreign and Commonwealth Office's performance in moments of crisis –

Predictably!

230

Mitchell looked up from the scrawl. The duty-man in the guards' cage was dutifully noting the time of Dr Mitchell's arrival and the delivery of the message from Lieutenant-Commander Cable to him, to no possible purpose.

'*PLM – Predictably, the FCO is still useless. And, what's worse, they've now begun to react to our inquiries about TC*' –

TC was Senator Thomas Cookridge: once you got into James's hieroglyphics they were just about decipherable, and a Rosetta Stone was not required.

'*– about TC. So, instead of help, we've received an order not to prejudice Anglo-American relations by investigating his private life, pending ministerial clearance*' –

Blast! thought Mitchell. They should have thought of that contingency. But maybe Jack Butler *had* thought of it – and had chanced his arm nevertheless, balancing Oliver St John Latimer's well-being against the possible repercussions . . .

And, in Butler's place, what would he have done? It wasn't even as though the FCO was really being unreasonable: even Howard Morris had been scared of Cookridge; and . . . which was perhaps the final irony . . . no one much liked Oliver St John Latimer, who had brought all this on his own head, anyway!

'*– pending ministerial clearance. Which order I have temporarily scanned with my blind eye –*'

God! James had faced a more immediate dilemma, and had applied Nelson's famous rule of disobedience –

'*– blind eye, leaving it in my own pending tray, and going off duty –*'

But why – ?

Suddenly the scrawl had all his attention: for James, of all people, to flout the rules – to *Engage more closely* when the plain order was *Disengage* –

The next word was unreadable –

No, it wasn't: it was 'because' –

231

' – *because I have the contact we need. Meet me at my mother's flat off the Park, and we'll brief you. If you're not there by 2030 I'll go to see her myself* – '

Mitchell took two steps and punched the lift button.

The lift took an unconscionable time, and the duty-man was looking at him.

'I've got a date with a lady, sar-major,' said Mitchell.

'Ah!' The duty-man sat down, and started to enter Dr Mitchell's time of departure.

Mitchell looked at the message again, and then at his watch.

Lady was right. But what the devil had James Cable's mother got to do with Senator Cookridge and Sion Crossing?

10

Latimer in America: Meeting the Man

'Shuddup!' said the Confederate soldier again, not very eloquently. But the steadiness of the rifle made up for his lack of eloquence: Latimer had never in his entire life had any sort of firearm pointed at him for real, and this third attempt to argue with it died on his lips, still-born.

The first time had not been much better – it had been even more inadequate, for he had not been able to get out any meaningful words before the Confederate soldier had behaved as though he really existed.

'Oh – !' What did one say to a figment of the imagination? How did one address an impossibility? 'Hullo – ' Was it morning or afternoon? It felt swelteringly hot and deathly cold at the same time, beyond rational calculation. 'Good afternoon – '

'Shuddup.' The illusion spoke, and it was no longer a figment of imagination: it gestured with its rifle. 'Move.'

Latimer moved: whatever the thing with the rifle was, the rifle was not to be argued with.

He swung round, towards the continuation of the inadequate path through the ruins, automatically pushing aside the leaves which impeded his advance with his stick. But then, two steps further on, he couldn't believe in what he was doing.

He turned back, hoping that it wouldn't be there. 'I'm sorry, but what – '

'Drop it!' The thing *was* there – the rifle *was* there, pointing at his chest. And he could feel everything around him, as it had been before: the trees and the chimneys, weight of his coat on his arm . . . even the oppression of the heat and the stillness of the woods . . . it was all there, even though it was incomprehensible.

'*Drop it*!'

His hand released the stick: it *was* a Confederate soldier – yet it was *real* –

'*G'warn – move*!'

Latimer moved again. Whatever the man was – and he couldn't be a Confederate soldier, for that was against reason – the implacable will behind the rifle was real: he could almost feel the bullet inside it, straining against the pressure of the finger on the trigger and the propellant in the cartridge – the imagined force of that was too strong for argument.

The path led him down from the ruins; and then it continued through the woods, offering him no choice, meandering between the trees.

Where was he now? The marked path on the sketch-map had not continued past the ruins, so although there had been other features on the map beyond that point, he had not bothered to memorize them. All that was certain was that they had left the line of the creek somewhere behind them. Perhaps if he could look at the map again . . . but somehow he didn't think that fumbling in his pocket at this moment would be an advisable action.

And yet . . . and yet all this was *crazy* – the Confederate soldier, with his little grey képi crushed on his head and that nakedly hostile expression on his face – even his own instinctive certainty that the man's levelled rifle was no joke, any more than it would have been for one of General Sherman's Iowans – it was not merely crazy – it was *impossible* –

The rifle?

He slowed down deliberately, and turned back towards the Confederate with exaggerated care, holding his coat in one hand and spreading the palm of the other to show his peaceful intention.

'Look – I think there must be some mistake – '

No more argument. The rifle had been rock-steady, and as ready to kill as the look which went with it. But Latimer had seen what he wanted to see.

It was a modern rifle.

He was not dreaming, and he was certainly not in some science-fictional time-warp triggered by the lingering vibrations of the explosion of violence and fear and pain which these quiet woods had once experienced, the pulse of which he had almost imagined he had felt as he had approached the ruins of the Sion Crossing house. That had always been no more than a malignant trick of the mind played on him by the unfamiliarity of his situation and his foolish actions.

The Confederate soldier was a real man – and he had to stop thinking of him as a *Confederate*: he was no more than a man in fancy dress –

Oddly, that was almost a relief. But it was only a relief for an instant. Because the rifle *was* real: it was not a military weapon . . . it was no more a modern military weapon than it was an ancient Springfield or Enfield, or whatever the Confederates had once carried: it was a light hunting rifle of some sort, complete with a telescopic sight – the weapon of a man who meant business.

But what business? What conceivable business, ancient or modern, could a man in fancy dress have here in the woods of Sion Crossing which required the gun-point hold-up of a perfect stranger?

Two related answers at once presented themselves, neither of which was particularly reassuring: he had chanced upon a lunatic who affected fancy dress (and the man had certainly not looked very bright) . . . and this was America anyway, where even cultured academics were armed to the teeth, so why not lunatics?'

But then another explanation occurred to him.

He had been asking himself all along why Senator

Cookridge had gone to such trouble to recruit an Englishman to unravel his mystery treasure-hunt, and had come up with all sorts of excuses and explanations. But he had known in his gut all along that there had to be more to it than that – and he had let himself be bamboozled and deceived, against his better judgement –

Where there was treasure, there would always be other treasure-hunters – that was a childishly simple piece of logic.

There had even been straws in the wind, which he had shrugged off: Kingston had lied to him at Atlanta airport, pretending that he'd arrived late when he'd actually been watching him covertly for half an hour – possibly to identify others interested in his arrival?

Even . . . even from Lucy Cookridge's father's papers he could deduce another clue, which he had stupidly ignored. Because . . . there had been more straws in the wind in them . . . to suggest that someone else had been researching Sion Crossing not merely from the documents, but in the field: there had been two or three gaps in the narrative sequence – tell-tale gaps in retrospect, indicating unlisted but very precise first-hand observation –

Either, someone had been in Sion Crossing before him . . . or someone had come close to it, and hadn't liked the odds: because – by God! – he'd seen reports like that from agents in the Soviet Union, who'd stumbled on intelligence which was out of their class and too hot to handle –

In this case, the analogy was ridiculous . . . but the rule was the same: *Pull out the small man to safety, and cut the contact; move in a bigger man from a different direction, unconnected with the small man, and let him pick up the threads for himself, if the dividend justified the risk –*

But that couldn't be the case here – the analogy was altogether ridiculous: Senator Cookridge might be a new man on the Anglo-American scene, but he surely wouldn't hazard a senior British intelligence officer on some crazy private enterprise of his – the Anglo-American scandal of that would surely ruin him if it went wrong, and there was no conceivable dividend which would justify the risk, surely –

Surely?

He had been telling himself that from the start. But that rifle was pointing at his spine now, even more surely.

Christ almighty! There was another Confederate soldier, who had risen up from nowhere, beside the path ahead of him!

Not a rifle, this time: with this Confederate they were moving from hunting rifles to machine-pistols of the smallest and most lethal variety – and to a two-way radio in the hand which did not hold the weapon.

The new fancy-dress man said something into his radio, as he circled to the right, presumably to give himself a clear field of fire.

'Ah gott'm,' the original fancy-dress man informed his comrade unnecessarily in a broad Southern accent.

'Where?'

'Down by the ol' place. He ain't from round here, Joe.'

The second fancy-dress man studied Latimer for a moment. Then the transmitter came up to his face again. ''kay – sure . . . White – maybe five-eight, five-seven . . . say 'bout one-seventy . . . age . . . maybe fifty . . . hair brown – got that?'

'Joe – '

'Shuddup, Willy.' The man Joe kept his eye on Latimer as he listened to the radio. 'No – ah said *five-eight, five-seven – one-seventy* . . . What?' He frowned at Latimer. 'Hell no! Hair brown – no glasses . . . Like ah said – he's short an' fat . . . an' he looks scared like he's set to shit himself.'

The name of the machine-pistol came to Latimer. It was

an Ingram, like those supplied to the SAS Special Squads. And where the first man's hunting rifle could kill him from afar an Ingram would cut him in two at this range.

Joe was still watching him. 'He say who the hell he is, Willy?' It sounded as though he was relaying a question.

There was a moment of tongue-tied silence. 'He ain't said.'

'My name's Latimer,' said Latimer quickly. 'Oliver St John Latimer . . . I – '

'Drop the coat.'

Latimer let go of his coat. The Ingram was pointing at the ground in front of his feet, which allowed for the upwards movement if it was fired one-handed: it would cut him in half vertically in that case, with its rate of fire. Released from the weight of the coat his hand automatically raised itself.

'Move away – *not that way, goddam' it* – '

Latimer froze.

'Other way . . . easy now . . . *stop.*' Not for a second did Joe take his eyes off him. 'Willy – see what he's got.'

Latimer moistened his lips. He wanted to say something, but his mouth had dried up. But he had to get his brain into gear first, in any case. Not his mouth.

'Hey – he's got a map, Joe!' Willy spoke as though he'd struck gold in finding the sketch-map.

Joe said nothing.

'An' – an' he's got cash money – twenties – fifties . . . shit – he's got maybe three-four-hundred bucks – '

Joe's jaw tightened. 'He got a name?'

'What?'

'Try the inside pocket. He'll have credit cards.'

'Credit cards?'

'Look for a name, Willy – anything with a name.'

'Sure – okay . . . *Hey!*'

'What you got?'

Latimer knew what Willy had got.

238

'Man – *he's British* – hell, ah *thought* the way he talked was funny – '

'*What you got*?' Joe controlled himself. 'Jus' tell me what you got, Willy.'

Willy paused to assimilate what he'd got. 'He told you raht – "*Mr O. St J. Latimer*", it sez.'

'What sez?'

'It sez – little blue book – "Mr O. St J. Latimer . . . *British Passport* . . . *United King-dom of Great Britain and Northern Ireland* . . . *N 676986*", it sez, Joe.'

'Look inside the book, Willy. What's it say there?'

'Sure . . .' Willy studied the passport. 'It's got a lot of writing – N 676986 – Mr Oliver St John Latimer – that's been writ in, the name – '

'Turn the next page.' The radio came up. 'Yeah – we're okay . . . Yeah, he's safe . . . Jus' you hold on . . . you get the next page, Willy?'

'Uh-huh . . . Got his picture – an' that's him sure 'nough . . . It sez . . . it sez "*Occupation – Civil Servant . . . Place of Birth – East Grinstead . . . Date of birth – 9.3.1934 . . . England . . . height – five-foot eight-inches . . . eyes – blue –* ' Pause ' *–* an' he's sure as hell been around – '

'Okay – shuddup – ' Once again the radio came up, as Joe repeated the contents of the passport into it.

Latimer was trying to think, but what he had so far been able to work out had not been reassuring. Because although Americans were all armed to the teeth he could not convince himself that Ingram machine-pistols were standard domestic equipment, even in darkest Georgia: there was surely no country in the world which permitted private possession of such weapons.

So that made Sion Crossing somewhere special. And it had to be somewhere special *legal* . . . or highly *illegal*. And in either case he was now in very deep trouble indeed, that meant.

'Okay.' Joe had transmitted his message, and had

received instructions in return. 'He got anything else in his pockets – no? Okay, then . . . feel him up then . . . An' put your gun down first, Willy, an' watch yourself . . . Because he's maybe a pro, the man sez – okay?'

Maybe a pro?

Latimer submitted to a search, from behind.

'Legs too, Willy.' Joe nodded. 'All the way down to his ankles, that's right.'

Maybe a pro?

''Kay?' Joe still didn't relax. 'Ah'll take it from here, then . . . You go back to your spot, Willy, an' snug down there an' keep your eyes skinned . . . An' put the cash-money back – put it *all* back, jus' where it come from.'

Maybe a pro revolved inside Latimer's head. That was certainly what he was, though not within Joe's terms of professionalism. But then . . . what sort of pro was Joe himself?

It was the Ingram which most obviously set him apart from his comrade. But there was more to him than that deadly professional little weapon: the two of them spoke alike, genuinely in that distinctive Southern speech of theirs, which Kingston had falsely affected off and on, but which came from them as naturally and musically as the very different accent of Highland Scotsmen from Kyle of Lochalsh; and their inexplicable Confederate fancy-dress was identical, which by itself would have made it hard for him to take them seriously now.

Except . . . it was *not* just the Ingram: there was an attention-to-detail and a cat-on-hot-bricks wariness about Joe which reinforced the Ingram dreadfully, tagging him with the same label as that worn by the special breed of men who operated on both sides of the Ulster border, whom he had briefed a couple of years back.

'Mistah Latimer – ' Joe caught him embarrassingly in the midst of his scrutiny, with a look of his own as cold as his voice ' – you jus' put your coat back on, nice an' easy . . . an' we'll go see the man – okay?'

The man?

The heat of the day enclosed Latimer, as it had done all the time, though he had been too pre-occupied to feel it since Willy had come upon him from nowhere, in the ruins of Sion Crossing. But now there was also the heat of the private fires beneath Joe's coldness, which frightened him.

The Man?

He could play the game of innocence now, but it would be useless: argument and bluster would at best only prolong the agony, and there was no point in that. And, at worst, neither the man Joe, nor that frightening weapon of his, were amenable to time-wasting games.

Besides which . . . all games were over now, which he perceived too late he had been playing from the start: Senator Cookridge's game, and Colonel Howard Morris's game, which he had played back in England – had played because of cretinous miscalculation and professional greed; and now Lucy Cookridge's game (and Kingston's too?), which must be part of the same game.

He put on his coat and followed the direction of Joe's nod meekly, without argument.

And, besides which, there was *The Man* –

It was extremely odd, thought Latimer.

He knew that he was very frightened, but that didn't surprise him: he had been frightened before, *physically* frightened, and more than once . . . frightened at school, when he had been forced to climb dangerous cliffs, and to do other unnatural things like that, which other boys had enjoyed doing . . . and frightened more recently, in that near-accident on the motorway . . . So he knew himself for a coward, where flesh and blood was concerned – *his* flesh and blood, anyway – just as he was *not* a coward in any other respect, when decisions had to be taken.

But this was different: this was genuine physical fear, because he was being threatened now, as he had never been threatened before – which the man Joe had seen in his face.

But this was not the same fear as those other old fears,

so well-remembered: it was real enough – it was not a minor part of what he felt . . . but it had to share his consciousness with a mixture of anger and curiosity.

The woods were still all around him –

Anger . . . because this was all his own fault – he had been deceived, but he had let himself be deceived: he had known it, too – so that wasn't so surprising.

But *curiosity* – what was odd was that curiosity was still so strong, in relation to *fear* and *anger*!

He wanted to see *The Man* – he wanted to do that almost as much as he was frightened for himself, and angry, with himself, for being here – on the end of Joe's gun.

There was something through the trees ahead – something white – ?

His curiosity instantly receded, and he felt his spirit begin to weaken: there was something unhealthy about that curiosity, on second thoughts – a man didn't need to plunge his hand into the flames to discover the properties of fire –

Joe growled something unintelligible from behind him, but the meaning of the sound was all too plain: whether he wanted to meet *The Man* or not was not a choice programmed into Joe's orders: willing or not, curious or not, frightened and angry or not, he was going to meet *The Man*, that sound meant.

The trees fell away, on either side, and the white blur resolved itself into a house – a house set in well-cut lawns, unnaturally green, with banks of bright-flowering unEnglish trees setting off the green-and-white.

For an instant the scene almost took Latimer's breath away, not so much because it was surprising, as because it *wasn't* altogether a surprise: it was something he had never expected consciously, but it was quite unbelievably like another house which had never existed.

242

He was looking at the great house of Sion Crossing, as he had imagined it!

His feet walked, remembering Joe, while his mind tried to accommodate what he saw.

It was a wonderfully elegant house – it wasn't really like any house he had actually imagined, at second glance, because it was not like any house he had ever seen; so it was neither Tara nor Fair Oaks, never mind Sion Crossing.

It was a house built for hot southern weather – for this very heat – long before air-conditioning: it was a house built inside a square of Corinthian columns holding up its wide overhanging roof, with cool shadowed verandahs all around it at two levels, raised ground floor and first floor.

That was how Sion Crossing ought to have been . . . but – what had made it momentarily more unbelievable, until recent memory reasserted itself – it was also Sion Crossing true-and-false, with Confederate soldiery in attendance.

But recent memory was almost instantaneously stronger, enough to destroy the illusion: reality was behind him, and there was only more fancy-dress ahead of him, with 1984 playing 1864 for some childish reason of its own, in a game in which he had no part.

The fancy-dress men reacted to his approach – two, three . . . and now a fourth appearing from behind a bright red-flowered bush – taking up their weapons, but then relaxing as they saw Joe behind him.

'What the hell?' Joe's voice was sharp with sudden anger. 'For chrissake!'

The man from behind the bush ceased studying Latimer. 'Huh?'

'For chrissake!'

'Joe – ' The man passed out of Latimer's line of vision ' – who you got there?'

They were well out on the lawn now, and with Joe's anger behind him Latimer felt himself hurrying towards the house in spite of the appalling heat.

'Joe – '

'Shuddup! Shuddup an' listen – ' Joe drew a breath ' – Willy's back there, by the ol' place, but ah want someone down by the creek with a sight of the bridge – ' another breath ' – so you get the hell down there, an' you doan take your goddam' eyes off'n that goddam' bridge . . . an' anythin' crosses it – an' ah mean *anythin*' – you call in Control right away – *you got that*?'

There was a pause. 'We . . . we got trouble, Joe?'

A matched pause. 'We got trouble? You jus' think . . . anythin' gets 'cross that bridge – anythin' on wheel, anythin' on legs, anythin' that goddam crawls – an' *you* got trouble – that's for sure, if'n you doan call in. An' that'll be all the trouble you'll need – okay?'

'Sure, Joe – '

Sure, Joe: the man from behind the bush had got the message. But there was also information in it for Latimer, and he knew he was badly in need of information, any scrap of it, with the house only twenty yards ahead now, cool and elegant and tree-shaded, and very frightening.

These were not fancy-dress men, for all their grey uniforms and brass buttons and silly little képis. They were guards – and they were *armed* guards . . . and they were on the alert for trouble.

But what sort of trouble? *And why* – ?

The little knot of Confederates by the steps up to the ground floor verandah had evidently picked up the vibrations of Joe's anger, if not his actual words: they had unrelaxed themselves into readiness again, although they looked as though they weren't quite sure what they were ready for, any more than Latimer himself did. All that was apparent was that they shared his fear of the man with the Ingram machine-pistol.

'For chrissake!' The original anger had decayed into

244

contempt during the passage of the lawn. 'Y'all got rocks for brains?'

Latimer stopped at the foot of the steps. Somehow, although no one had worn those uniforms as real soldiers for over a century, they had the look of real squaddies wilting under their sergeant-major's scorn, as their great-great-grandfathers might have done outside another house at Sion Crossing. But perhaps that fancy originated in the cold suspicion that there were real bullets in their rifles.

'*Jee*-sus – Jee-*sus*!' Joe swept a glance across his hoplites and selected a target. 'Ronnie – for chrissake – you should'a bin watchin' the gate by now, not takin' part in a goddam' convention! The Man pays you – an' you're tryin' to prove somethin'? You tell me?'

The youngest of the juvenile trio stiffened under the blasphemy, but the eldest shuffled half a step nearer to Ronnie, as though defensively. 'Shit, Joe! We gotta be in town, for the parade – ' he looked at his wrist-watch, an anachronism below the pale blue cuff of his grey uniform coat ' – like, we gotta be there *now*.' He looked up again, and caught Latimer's eye accidentally for an instant, and then transferred the look back to Joe. 'How we gotta be *there* now an' *here* too, the same time – huh?'

Latimer felt his soul contract. In that instant of contact he had not even been a blue-coated Iowan prisoner from Sherman's army from long ago, let alone a prisoner-of-war protected by any more modern convention. He had simply not been anything requiring human recognition, neither to be feared nor pitied.

'Huh?' Joe reacted predictably. 'You tryin' to blow smoke up my ass, boy? We got intruders an' you wanna play soldiers in town, an' take time off to feel up Di-*anne* when you through flag-wavin' – that it?'

Ronnie's defender opened his mouth to deny the allegation, but he was a breath too late to pre-empt Joe's follow-through.

'You get the hell over by the smoke-house, where you oughta be now – an' you doan let *no one* in there, less'n ah tell you – not if it was the goddam' Governor of the State . . . not if Di-*anne* was t'come showin' that cute little fanny of hers – Do ah make mahself plain?'

Very plain, thought Latimer. And there was more useful information there too, in the plainness. Joe was a professional burdened with low-grade local help . . . or maybe it had been carefully chosen for the lack of curiosity which went with low intelligence. But that was beside the point –

'*Then for chrissake move it!*' Joe broke the moment of acquiescent silence, galvanizing Ronnie and his comrade in opposite directions and leaving the last member of the trio standing petrified in front of him.

The point was that these mock-Confederates had been *expecting* trouble of some sort.

'As for you . . .' Joe shook his head speechlessly, in the manner of sergeants down the ages in the presence of insuperable stupidity.

The youth blinked nervously. 'Ah'm t'set . . . an' ring the house bell if'n ah see anythun – you said.'

Joe studied the youth for a moment. 'You rung the bell then, sonny?' He nodded up the verandah steps towards the big white door.

The youth stared at Joe for a second, his hands clenching and unclenching on the rifle in them. Then he gave the door a quick glance, as though he was seeing it for the first time. 'But . . . but . . .'

'You see anythin'?' asked Joe, not unkindly. 'Comin' 'cross the lawn jus' now – anythin' – ' he nodded at Latimer ' – like him, mebbe?'

The youth blinked at Latimer, and then at the wide empty lawn, and then frowned at Joe. 'Ah saw you, Joe.'

It suddenly came to Latimer why they were all wearing uniforms. Kingston had said something about 'the parade', and Joe had referred to 'playing soldier in the town' and 'flag-waving.' And, of course, the legend of the Old South and the Lost Cause was still cherished by the descendants of the Confederates – and Americans loved parades, even more than Frenchmen did.

'Ah saw you, Joe,' repeated the youth.

Something else came to Latimer, quite unbidden. Long ago, with all the men away at war in Virginia and Tennessee, there would only have been old men and young boys like this one to defend Sion Crossing from Sherman –

'You see *anyone* – you ring the bell, sonny,' said Joe. 'So you go ring it now, like ah said.'

But . . . *to hell with Sherman and fancy-dress Confederates – that was not what all this was about – it couldn't be –*

'Okay, fella – go on up,' ordered Joe.

The big white door opened for them before Latimer had reached the top of the steps. Under the verandah it was hardly less oppressive, but only a few steps took him into the doorway and a blissful air-conditioned coolness – if there was a heaven, it was air-conditioned.

It wasn't dark inside the house, but for a moment it seemed so, until his eyes accustomed themselves to deliverance from the glare outside. But it was chiefly the wonderful chill: he was still bathed in sweat under his coat, but at least he could think again.

There was a man on his left – a man who was not an *ersatz* Confederate, but a twentieth century civilian, in twentieth century shirt-and-tie.

'Mr Latimer?'

Dr Livingstone, I presume? he might just as well have said.

'Yes.' The thought-processes were accelerating. Whatever was happening, he had one thing going for him: he was not here on official business, so he had nothing to hide and nothing to protect, and nothing whatsoever to risk his skin for. In fact . . . *whatever was happening, he was an innocent bystander*!

'I believe you have a passport?' The twentieth century

man resolved himself into a middle-aged, medium-sized American. 'May I see it please?'

American? If an American, from a long way north and east of Sion Crossing. But, from wherever, at least polite.

'Of course.' There would be time for protest, but it was not yet come, with Joe still at his back.

'Close the door.' As the man took his passport he addressed Joe more curtly. 'Thank you, Mr Latimer.' The voice readjusted itself for Latimer.

He couldn't place the accent at all: it was neither the Queen's English nor the President's American – it was statelessly educated.

Rimless spectacles – hair without a trace of grey, but maybe dyed: chief accountant in a middle-sized multinational, rather than a civil servant, Latimer estimated, speculating a little wildly . . . a civil servant might have spoken as politely, but there would not have been an extra edge of menace deep down, which this man had.

'Thank you.' The passport was not returned with the thanks. 'You have a map, I think?'

Was this the moment to protest?

No.

'I have a map – yes.' Latimer felt in his pockets, unsure where Willy had replaced the map. 'And I have a wallet and four hundred and fifty dollars – do you want them too?'

'Just the map, Mr Latimer, if you please.

Having taken in the man, Latimer used his next ration of time to take in the man's setting.

It wasn't quite Tara – the staircase fell short of a Scarlett O'Hara sweep . . . But, although it must have been built in the generation after the original Sion Crossing house had gone up in flames, it owed nothing to Victorian gothic taste: it had a pleasing style of its own which he couldn't identify at all, except that it seemed to lean more to the eighteenth century than the nineteenth . . . Only, that didn't fit at all with his brief reading of post-Civil War

Georgia – the Georgia of Reconstructions, in which the vulgar Carpetbaggers had displaced the old families . . . the old families like the Alexanders of Sion Crossing, which had been extinguished by the war.

'Would you come this way, Mr Latimer?' The man gestured towards the staircase which Latimer had been admiring only a moment before.

Latimer just managed to take in the rest of the entrance hall, which filled the centre of the house. There were packing cases to his left – but they gave no hint of arrival or departure –

'This way, Mr Latimer.' The second time there was an edge of command to the politeness.

Was this *The Man*? If he was, he didn't fit this Sion Crossing any better than the Carpetbaggers fitted it: he was an *organization man* of some sort – a professional very different from Joe, but nonetheless professional.

But . . . on balance, not *The Man* – ?

Latimer ascended the staircase. At the second turn there was a window which gave him a brief view of an avenue of trees at the front of the house, to the end of which the half-witted Ronnie had been despatched. Then the final stairs and the landing were ahead of him, with a choice of passages and doors.

'Straight ahead, Mr Latimer.'

There was a door ahead, pale oak like the other doors and the panelling: it looked at though some vandal had once painted it all, and then it had all been decently stripped down to reveal the original fine grain by some later owner whose taste matched his wealth.

'Go on in.'

Latimer opened the door. They were at the back of the house again after that double-turn on the staircase: over the first storey verandah he could see the lawn across which Joe had so recently marched him at gunpoint. But it wasn't a bedroom, for there was a fine walnut desk with a comfortable leather chair behind it to his left, and . . . and

249

there was a matching chair to his right, out of which a white-haired man was staring at him.

The Man?

Latimer decided to break first. Having come here with an Ingram at his back he could by no stretch of the imagination consider this a friendly meeting. But, even though he well knew the fate of innocent bystanders in the barbarous twentieth century, that was the only rôle he could play, because that was what he actually was.

'Good afternoon,' he said to the white-haired man.

'Sit down, Mr Latimer,' said the polite man. 'There is a chair to your left.'

Latimer allowed the white-haired man some more time in which to react, but received only a blank look of unrecognition. Curiously, although the man in no way resembled Senator Cookridge either in features or physique, he was reminded of the Senator without knowing why. Perhaps there was a *type* of American, beyond a certain age, and well-groomed and expensively-suited, just as there was a *class* of Englishman – ?

The eyes left Latimer's face for an instant, shifting to the polite man.

'No.' The slightest shake of the head. 'No.'

He had not been identified – any more than he could make an identification: Latimer himself agreed with that conclusion.

'Sit down, Mr Latimer.'

Latimer moved the chair. There was nowhere for it which would give him a simultaneous view of them: either by accident, or more likely by design, they had achieved the classic interrogation positioning.

And, more than that, he was already in two minds about them and slightly disorientated, no longer certain as to which of them – was *The Man*. In fact . . . *in fact* (and the fact was very disconcerting), he had never been caught so exactly in the rôle of nut between the nutcrackers: in the last ten years he had always been part of the nutcracker itself – in the last five he himself had been something like *The Man*!

But he *mustn't* let himself be disconcerted.

He sat down meekly.

'What sort of . . . "civil servant", Mr Latimer?' The polite man arranged his passport and the map neatly on the desk.

So there was going to be no mercy: it was *First Service* on the centre court at Wimbledon on the last day.

Latimer looked deliberately at the white-haired man. 'In so far as it's anyone business . . . I'm an economist, actually.'

'An economist?' The polite man was still polite. 'You have economic business here?'

Latimer looked at him. 'I have no business here. I was looking at the ruins of the old Sion Crossing house, and a man threatened me with a gun. And then another man threatened me – and that's why I'm here, Mr – ?' He cocked his head. 'Mr – ?'

'Economists do not read notices, then?' The question wasn't shrugged off, it was ignored.

Notices?

'They do when they see them.' Play for time. 'What notices?' But even as he played, the beginnings of a very nasty suspicion started to form in Latimer's mind. 'What notices?'

The rimless spectacles gave nothing away. 'There are notices at all the entrances to Sion land – to all this property – warning unauthorized persons to keep out, Mr Latimer. They are large notices – they are most explicit.'

The nasty suspicion was becoming as large as the notices, and almost as explicit. 'I didn't see any notices.'

'I find that hard to believe.'

So did Latimer. 'I found a path – ' *Kingston must have known* ' – and I followed it. I didn't see a notice.'

So he was here because Kingston intended him to be here –

'Yes.' The polite man smoothed out the map in front of

251

him. 'But then . . . you must have passed the church, Mr Latimer.'

He had carefully been routed on to a path which did not pass the church. He had been set up.

'Not exactly.' No other interpretation was possible: *he had been set up*. 'I saw the church through the trees. I think I must have taken a short cut, somehow . . . If I've trespassed, then I'm sorry.' He had to get away from the notices. 'I only wanted to see the ruins.'

'Why? There is nothing to see, Mr Latimer.'

That was better. Latimer smiled from one to the other. 'If you're interested in the American Civil War there's a lot to see.' He spread the smile on the white-haired man. 'I didn't know it was still going on, though . . . Those men in the Confederate uniforms – is that something to do with the parade in Smithsville today?'

The white-haired man did not resemble the Senator in more ways than features and physique, he decided. Where the Senator had exuded bonhomie and confidence, almost like an actor giving his audience what they expected, this man cared nothing for his audience. Rather, he was hostile and he was so full of doubt that he almost looked frightened.

So he was not The Man!

'And you are interested in the American Civil War?' The polite man's disbelief was not quite so polite this time.

'That's why I'm here.' Latimer grimaced suddenly. 'Or . . . that's why I was *there* – at the ruins – yes!'

'So?' The not-so-polite man touched the passport. 'English economists are interested in the American Civil War?'

'I don't know about economists . . . but you obviously haven't read Henderson's book on Stonewall Jackson – ' But he could do better than that! ' – or Sir Winston Churchill's *History of the English-Speaking Peoples* – ?' The bastard might not know Colonel G. F. R. Henderson

252

from a stone in Stonewall Jackson's wall, but he could hardly shrug off Winston Spencer Churchill, by God!

'Ssso?' Behind that hiss the politeness was wafer-thin now. 'Sir Winston Churchill was interested in Sion Crossing?'

'No.' Latimer wished he could remember what Winston had written in the American chapters of Volume Four, which he had long ago skipped through more as an act of piety than from either interest or need. 'But he wrote about General Sherman in Georgia – ' That had to be safe! ' – and Sherman's men burnt Sion Crossing, as I'm sure you must know – '

But the look on the man's cold accountant's face suggested quite the opposite. So he turned to the white-haired man. 'He burnt Sion Crossing – ' Sherman himself had no more burnt Sion Crossing than King George III had burnt Washington, but the guilt was about the same ' – as you know.'

At least there was something there, in the look the-man-who-wasn't-The-Man gave to the-man-who-might-be. And if it wasn't recognition, it at least had a hint of doubt in it.

'As you know – ' If that was the way it was, then he must capitalize on their greater ignorance: he must encourage them to dismiss him as an enthusiastic idiot ' – though, of course, the Sion Crossing episode isn't historically important in itself, I admit . . .'

He felt himself suspended midway between their doubts. So, at all costs, he mustn't lose momentum – he must flannel convincingly – as he had once done in Oxford tutorials –

'Geographically . . . *geographically*, it was on the very edge of Sherman's line of march, although the house was burnt.' Another more recent memory surfaced. 'But . . . Catton – Bruce Catton . . . he described the march as a nineteenth century equivalent of a twentieth century bombing offensive – ' The memory opened up an even more promising line of bullshit ' – and, as an economist, I'm interested in the economic effects of such calculated destruction . . . the devastation not only of the Atlanta industrial complex, but also of the agricultural heartland of the Confederacy – '

The opening of the door behind him was half welcome and half unwelcome. He didn't really know whether Georgia had been the agricultural heartland of the Confederacy. It had grown cotton in Scarlett O'Hara's time, for the mills of Lancashire in England; but, with the Northern blockade, cotton would have been useless . . . and . . . could corn be grown in cotton-fields?

He felt he was running out of his inadequate stock of knowledge far too quickly for comfort. On the other hand, they both still looked slightly bemused.

But then Joe appeared on his left, seeming ridiculously out of place in his crumpled Confederate uniform beside the bespectacled man's neat city suit.

'Yes?' The man frowned slightly.

Without a word Joe placed a piece of paper on the desk, beside the passport.

The bespectacled man studied the paper for a long moment. Latimer waited, expecting to receive the next glare, but was disappointed when the man studiously avoided him in preference for Joe.

'Is there any word from Smithsville?'

It was Joe who looked at Latimer.

'Is there any word from Smithsville?' the bespectacled man repeated the question sharply.

Joe shrugged. 'We only got a coupla boys there 'fore we got word about him – ' he jerked his head at Latimer ' – an' less'n we got the others in there's no way we can cover the town worth a damn.'

His face twisted. 'Not that ah'd set any store on any of those useless little bastards out there.'

A nerve in the bespectacled man's cheek twitched. 'They know strangers when they see them.'

254

'Strangers – hell! The whole goddam' town's crawlin' with strangers . . . f' the parade.' Joe shook his head. 'Mebbe if ah wuz there . . . an' mebbe Jack – he knows what t'look for . . . But ah got him on the bridge, 'cause we need a good man there – ' He looked at Latimer suddenly. 'Ain't he strangers enough for you, for chrissake?'

The bespectacled man himself looked at Latimer at last, and his lack of expression was not reassuring. 'You have all the approach roads covered?'

'Damn right, ah have!' Joe accepted the questions. 'But ah wouldn't count on boys t'do man's work, if that's what you want – huh?' He gave Latimer another look, coldly appraising, and then came back to his master. 'He's the one, then?'

The bespectacled man stopped looking at Latimer. 'We will bring the departure plan forward, as a precaution.'

'To when?'

'To . . . immediately, shall we say?' The man watched Joe, and so did Latimer.

Nothing changed in Joe's face except his eyes, which went as blank as if a light had been turned off behind them. 'That'll be mebbe an hour – ' Joe looked at his watch ' – if that's the way it is – ?'

The bespectacled man seemed satisfied. 'Yes.'

Joe looked at Latimer. 'And him?'

'We have matters to discuss . . . Mr Latimer and I.'

Latimer didn't like the sound of that. And, from the way the white-haired man had stirred and sat up during the exchange, and now from the look of apprehension on his face, neither did he. In fact . . . although it must be a trick of light, or maybe it was a reflection of his own fear . . . but in fact the man seemed to have aged shockingly in the last minute. The lines on his face seemed deeper, and there was a hint of silver stubble on his cheeks; his well-cut suit hung on him as though it was too big – or as though he had crumpled inside it under the pressure of a

255

world which had suddenly become a size too small for him.

'My friend – ' The bespectacled man also seemed to have caught the change in his colleague ' – of course, you will have things to do? But we have an hour . . . and you are not unprepared.'

The elderly man levered himself out of the chair and stood up slowly.

The bespectacled man glanced at Joe. 'What are you waiting for?' he snapped. 'You know what to do.'

'Sure.' Joe looked at Latimer, '*And him*?'

'I told you. I will ring when I want you.' The man – *The Man* – waited for Joe to withdraw. Then he turned back to the old man. 'Do not despair. He is competent, and we are well-prepared – we are efficient . . . as you have cause to know.' He projected calm confidence at the old man. 'And you know also that we have talked of this moment, my friend . . . It is not a time of shame and defeat – it is a time of victory, and of honour and recognition to come.'

The old man's face was grey. He stared at The Man for a moment, and then at Latimer. He no longer appeared to be frightened, but Latimer saw that he was on the far and darker side of fear, beyond hope, for which there was no word in the dictionary.

'I have things to do,' the old man said to himself.

'And we have things to do,' said The Man.

Latimer waited.

'So, Mr Latimer . . .' The Man collected Latimer's belongings into a neat pile on top of the paper Joe had delivered. 'So you are here because . . . long ago Sion Crossing burned – yes?'

The trouble with that was that it was true, more or less if not quite, thought Latimer.

'Yes.'

And the trouble with that – *the trouble even with the exact truth* – was that it was not going to be good enough.

And that was a far greater trouble. In fact, it was the last and greatest trouble of all here and now. Because, although he didn't know who this man was, he knew *what* he was now – he knew the type as well as he knew Joe's type. So he knew, even more surely than he had known with Joe, that he was fighting for his life.

And he had one hour in which to fight for it –

> Now hast thou but one bare hour to live,
> And then thou must be damned perpetually –

Or maybe less than that –

He shook his head, and tried to smile disarmingly. There was the desk between them, and he was no fighting man anyway. And then there was an armed Confederate on the verandah below, never mind Joe somewhere in the house behind him; and the woods were crawling with other armed men. And he was half a world away from any help.

'No?' The Man correctly interpreted the smile as surrender.

'Not exactly.' He had to play the cards in his hand, but he had only one trump. And in this game instinct inclined him to lead with it. 'Do you know Senator Cookridge?'

God! It was a high trump – he could see that from the surprise in The Man's face. Had he played it too soon?

'I know . . . *of* him – yes?'

That was something to be built on. 'I've known him for years. Tom and I ware old friends – we share the American Civil War as a hobby, you see.' The lies came to him like old friends repaying long-forgotten debts. 'He was in London just recently, and he asked me to do him a favour.' The more he could hint at his own importance, the more The Man might be inhibited. 'I first met him when I was over here as the Prime Minister's economic adviser in '75 . . . and then, after that, when I was with the embassy – that was when I got to know his family.' He shrugged, self-deprecating. 'I'd never have met the President, but for him . . . so I owe him a favour or two, even apart from friendship – and apart from how jolly interesting this Sion Crossing business is, you know . . .' He gestured vaguely, as though to something they shared.

'What favour?' The Man had recovered a little too quickly for comfort, in spite of all his name-dropping.

'Well . . . you know the Sion Crossing story – ?

'Tell me, Mr Latimer.'

Latimer frowned. 'But you must know – ? Surely – '

'*Tell me*, Mr Latimer – if you please.' The steel glinted through a hole in the velvet.

'Well . . . there was the gold shipment from Atlanta, in '64 – you really don't know?' Latimer feigned incredulity.

The Man's face became implacably hostile.

'Very well – all right!' Latimer couldn't pretend not to have seen that anger, with the seconds ticking away. 'There was this shipment of valuables from the Atlanta bank, when Sherman's army started to encircle the town . . . But it wasn't very big – most of it was worthless paper, in fact . . . And it only got as far as here – at Sion Crossing, anyway.'

The Man seemed to be holding himself in check. 'Continue.'

'Well . . .' He had to get Lucy Cookridge's father's facts right '. . . then some of Sherman's bummers came here, when his army was marching to the sea – '

'*Bummers*?'

'Foragers.' For the first time Latimer really relieved that The Man knew less about the Civil War than he did. 'Their job was to sweep up all the supplies for the army, and then to burn what they couldn't take with them.' He searched for an analogy. 'Like the Germans retreating through Russia in the last war – "scorched earth", I think it's called . . . But it's an old military tactic – the Romans were experts at it . . . Latin *vastare*, "to lay waste" – '

'Come to the point, Mr Latimer.'

'That is the point. A party of Sherman's men came here to take the food and burn the house.' He blinked at the man. 'You've seen the ruins in the woods?'

A single nod. 'So they burnt the house. So?'

'Ah . . . well, you see, it wasn't quite as simple as that. You see . . . Tom Cookridge has been doing this reearch – Tom and I, that is.'

'On Sion Crossing?'

'No . . . at least, not to start with. He – we . . . have been following this Iowan regiment, which fought all the way from Chattanooga to Atlanta, and then from Atlanta to the sea. And these foragers were from that regiment. And . . . we've been collecting original materials – letters and diaries, and such like. And stories that have been handed down . . . And we've got this particular letter, which contains the real story of what happened at Sion Crossing.'

'The real story?' There was a curious expression on The Man's face. 'What story?'

'About the Sion Crossing treasure. They'd buried it in the garden, for safety. But when the soldiers came . . . There was only this one woman in the house, and two negro servants – the men were away at the war, the slaves had all run off . . . But she couldn't bear for them to burn the house, so she offered them the treasure instead – to show them where it was in exchange for sparing the house.'

'But they did burn the house, Mr Latimer.' The Man looked at his watch.

'Yes. But that was because one of the servants had gone to get help – there was a Confederate militia company that had just passed through, and wasn't far away. And they arrived just as the Iowans had recovered the box. So there was a fight – that was when the house burnt.' Latimer nodded. 'It was a running fight. The Iowans were outnumbered, and they had to get back across the river – the creek – where their comrades were. And the box was too heavy, so they broke it open, and shared out the old coins . . . Or rather . . . they just grabbed what they could, and ran like hell.'

The Man nodded slowly. 'And – ?'

'The Confederates killed several of them, with the gold on them . . . In fact, they probably got the ones who tried to take the most gold.' Latimer shrugged.

'And that is the real story?' The Man stirred behind the desk.

'*No* – that's the *official* story,' said Latimer hastily. 'That's the story everyone knows, you see.'

The Man looked at him. 'It is not true?'

Latimer saw that he was not really very interested in the question, or in the story itself, true of false, and felt a pang of depair.

'Yes – I mean, *no* . . .' If he couldn't appeal to The Man's greed to support the big names he had dropped then he had nothing left at all.

'Yes . . . or no?' The Man seemed slightly amused. 'Are you trying to delay me, as the lady of Sion Crossing tried to delay the . . . bummers, Mr Latimer?'

'What?' Latimer fought his despair.

'Come to the point, Mr Latimer. The real story?'

'Yes.' The real story was all he had. 'The letter we had . . . it was from a farmer in Iowa. It was a story he had from his grandfather, who'd had it from his father.'

'His father?' The Man was playing with him. 'His grandfather's father – ?'

'His father's grandfather – ' *Damn*! ' – he was the soldier who carried the box. He was there when they broke it open – he saw what was inside.'

The Man nodded. 'He saw the gold – so?'

'There was the gold, and a lot of paper money – useless Confederate money . . . and documents – he didn't know what they were, and he didn't care.' Latimer remembered Lucy Cookridge's father's conclusion. 'He was seventeen years old, and he was straight from his

260

father's farm at Cedar Rapids – he was probably barely literate.'

The Man raised an eyebrow. 'And these documents were important?'

Latimer drew a breath. 'He didn't care about the documents. But there was a small tin box full of beads, and he had a little sister back in Iowa. So he took a handful of gold coins and the tin box. And . . . they were trying to get to the bridge, by the church, but the Confederates had it covered, so they had to swim the river . . . So he stuffed the tin box between the roots of a tree down by the creek, because he couldn't get it into any of his pockets, and there wasn't room in his knapsack – he had his spare shirt in it, wrapped round a big piece of bacon he'd taken from the house.'

'A prudent soldier!' The Man looked at his watch again.

So they had come to it at last.

Latimer drew another breath. 'The woman who tried to trade the treasure for the house was Marie-Louise Alexander of Sion Crossing. She had three brothers – Simon was killed at Antietam in 1862, Richard died in a PoW camp on Rock Island in '64, and James was killed in the trenches at Petersburg in '65 – he was the eldest. And Marie-Louise died of small-pox in Savannah in '66, at her grandparents' home.

'A tragic story.'

'Their parents both died before the war.'

'Then they were fortunate. Your time is almost up, Mr Latimer.'

'Their parents were James Alexander, of Sion Crossing, and Marie-Louise de Brissac, of Charleston. And Marie-Louise de Brissac's dowry chiefly consisted in the de Brissac pearls, which were brought out of Haiti in 1798. They were also known as the *Stupor Mundi* pearls, because they were so perfect. There's a description of them in Samuel Tracey's *Southern Aristocracy*, and the word he uses is "breath-taking". And they were last seen

261

in public at the christening of Simon Alexander in 1844 . . . After that, there's no recorded sighting. But Professor Tracey thought they'd been sold in aid of the Confederate war effort.'

The Man nodded again, but very slowly. 'But you think that is not the case?'

'I think . . .' But it was what Lucy Cookridge's father had thought. But that didn't matter! '. . . I think Professor Tracey didn't do his homework properly. Or . . . let's say, I don't think Colonel James Alexander loved the Confederacy enough to give his pearls to it – even though he died for it.' It was good, sound research, after all, even though it was all second-hand, to be taken on trust. 'And I also think that an Iowa farm-boy might not know pearls from child's beads when he saw them.' Latimer sat back in his chair. 'That is what I think.'

The Man reached under the table. 'So . . . the child's beads are still in their box, somewhere down by the stream?'

They had come to the very last card. 'No.'

'No?' The Man frowned.

Latimer pretended a sly confidence which he certainly didn't feel. 'I said "down by the creek". But I'm not quite as foolish as that.' He smiled. 'I'd say . . . I'd say that, without me to guide you, you've got no chance of finding them. Or . . . say, given about ten years, and the right equipment, and enough men . . . maybe you could, at that. But maybe not even then.'

The door opened behind him. Joe must have been waiting for his call, to come so quickly.

'That is what you think?' The Man didn't look at Joe. 'And do you know what I think, Mr Latimer?'

What Latimer thought was dust and ashes: his last card had been no better than all the others.

'I think that you have told me a good story.' The Man didn't expect an answer. 'Even, perhaps, in other circumstances it might have been good enough – a beautiful story . . . But then, I would expect no less from David Audley.'

'From – ?' Latimer felt his mouth open.

Oh, sweet Jesus Christ! Now, simultaneously, he knew everything and he knew nothing – he knew only that he was lost – that he had been already bought and sold from the beginning!

'From who?' The story about the chick running round the yard after its head had been cut off was true: he could still form words, even though he had nothing to say.

'We expected Dr Audley. So you confused us for a little time, Mr Latimer.' The Man separated Joe's message from Latimer's belongings. Then he looked up again. 'But not for long.' He touched the passport. 'Though I am perhaps a little surprised that you travelled on your own passport. It would hardly have changed matters . . . but it did make them easier for us.'

The facts in the man's statement clicked in Latimer's brain like the tumblers in a combination lock, one after another.

They had expected Audley. (And, if there was nothing else that he really understood, at least he could account for that, damn it!)

They knew who he was. They had not known it at first, but now they knew it exactly. And it had taken them less than half an hour to obtain that direct knowledge. And that, in the peculiar setting of Sion Crossing – and even though he still couldn't guess the reasons for his betrayal – narrowed the field to a dreadful near-certainty.

But somehow he had to fight, even though he had no weapons.

'I know Dr Audley. I've served on two committees with him.' His voice seemed to come from a long way off. 'But he's . . .' He frowned. 'Surely he's . . .?' It wasn't really difficult to feign incomprehension: even it if wasn't believed it was nonetheless the truth.

263

'He's . . .?' As The Man trailed off Joe fidgetted as thought tired of the charade.

'He works for the Ministry of Defence.' It was no good denying what was already known. 'I suppose it's no good me saying that I haven't the slightest idea what you're talking about?'

'No good at all. Dr Audley works for RD3, and he is your colleague, Mr Latimer.' The Man regarded Latimer intently. 'Indeed, if our information is correct, you will shortly be more than that. In which case I must congratulate you, Mr Latimer.'

Latimer stared back at him. *The Americans*?

The Man smiled. 'A well-deserved promotion, to be sure!'

The Man was being polite again. In fact – *dear God*! – in fact The Man was almost deferential!

So The Man was, for a near-certain guess, a senior KGB controller on the American circuit. Only the Russians could know so much and transmit it so quickly and securely!

Latimer's hold on reality weakened. The Americans would not have been so polite – they would have been justifiably angry with a poacher on their estate. But it would not have been a killing matter for them – *as it must be for this polite and deferential man* –

He must not panic. Indeed, perhaps he had another card to play after all –

'Your information is . . . as good as always, shall we say?' He almost bowed. 'But, as regards Sion Crossing – '

The Man cut him off. 'Don't disappoint me. Mr Latimer! For you to have come here . . . and with the exact cover story that we expected from Dr Audley . . . perhaps that was admirable, but it was also very foolish – very foolish!' He chided Latimer with a shake of the head. 'You could have come to harm, believe me – very grave and permanent harm.' Another shake. And then he looked up at Joe. 'You have a reliable man?'

264

Joe and Latimer exchanged the same incredulous glance for half a second. 'I can mebbe find someone.'

'Find him.' The Man regarded Joe uncompromisingly. 'He must see that Mr Latimer comes to no harm – is that understood?'

Joe looked at though it wasn't understood at all, but he nodded nevertheless.

The Man looked at his watch. 'It is ten minutes to the hour. Your man will take Mr Latimer to the old boat-house by the river. If Mr Latimer attempts to escape, or makes any hostile gesture, he is to be killed. If he does not . . . then he is to be released in exactly two hours from now – *unharmed.*' He studied Joe. '*Unharmed* – you understand?'

Joe shrugged. 'If that's what you want . . . okay.'

The Man gave Joe a terrible cold look, which chilled Latimer at second hand. 'You misunderstand. It is not what I "want" – it is *an order.* So . . . the one way, or the other, is how it will be. And on your head. Is *that* understood?'

Latimer watched Joe shrivel.

'Yes, sir,' said Joe.

Unharmed – ?

The Man switched to Latimer just as the unbelievable sweetness of the word was percolating from surprise to belief in his brain. But even with belief – *relief* – there was a swirling incomprehension – *why* – ?

'We are not barbarians.' The Man seemed to read his thoughts. 'And you have heard my order, Mr Latimer. So that should be enough for you.'

It was – and it wasn't, thought Latimer. Because they *were* barbarians. But they weren't stupid . . . and now, at least, he did not intend to be stupid either.

'Yes.' It was more than enough: it was a reprieve from a death sentence for an unknown crime which he had not committed – *it was life!*

'Good.' The Man drew the telephone on the desk

towards him. 'Then . . . farewell, Mr Latimer. I think we shall not meet again.'

It was life –

Latimer retraced his way across the landing towards the staircase, with Joe behind him.

But was it really life? . . . The presence of Joe at his back made him suddenly less certain. Because . . . because they *were* barbarians . . . and that exchange could have been a rehearsed play to make him more tractable –

He started to descend the staircase.

But . . . they were *not* fools, on the other hand: to kill someone as senior as he was now – and as they knew he was – without overriding necessity would be an act of inviting counter-sanction, and therefore one requiring the highest clearance, surely?

He turned the corner of the staircase.

Surely? He had to repeat the thought in order to stop his legs folding under him. Because there was nothing he could do to prevent whatever was going to happen –

But why?

There was a clatter of something falling beyond the back door ahead of him. As he reached the foot of the staircase he turned towards Joe, uncertain of what was required of him.

Joe opened his mouth exactly as the door opened, and his eyes left Latimer, and no words came out.

The change in Joe's expression jerked Latimer's attention back to the doorway.

Kingston, naked to the waist – Kingston grinning his melon-grin, as ever – Kingston holding a tray of groceries awkwardly – naked to the waist and grinning – was framed in the doorway in that slow-motion fraction-of-a-second –

'*Mull –*'

The word from behind Latimer was swallowed up in a fierce *thump-thump* which seemed to come out of the tray of groceries, which almost simultaneously lifted and scattered itself in a suddenly accelarated blur of motion.

The echo of the word, and the *thump-thump*, and a crash of sound behind him were all part of the same continuous noise which ran together, and then merged with the individual sounds of the groceries hitting the floor – the sharp *crack* of tins and bottles among cardboard packets of cereals and washing powders – with the louder and sharper *crack* of something striking the treads behind him and bouncing down and skittering past him and across the floor in front of him –

It was the Ingram machine-pistol – !

'Okay, Oliver – ' Kingston fielded the Ingram like Gary Sobers in the slips, with the hand which didn't hold the silenced pistol ' – let's move it, then – '

11

Mitchell in London: Lady Alice remembers

Mitchell fumed outside the block of flats for a full five minutes, until Audley arrived. And even then it took Audley a couple of extra minutes to decide what sort of tip his taxi-driver deserved, and then to find it among the coins in his pocket, which appeared to be foreign to him.

'David – this is bloody unpardonable!' Mitchell fired first, and fired low. 'This is my show – and you're coming damn close to pulling rank on me . . . and when you really haven't got any rank to pull, actually.'

Audley looked at the coins remaining in his hand. 'You know . . . I think I gave the blighter too much – you saw the way he perked up just then? I think I must have slipped him one of those utterly unspeakable pound coins, you know – and that would be *damnable* – '

'*David* – '

'Yes?' Audley put the coins back in his pocket, and peered at Mitchell owlishly. 'Yes . . . you are quite right, dear boy.' He adjusted his spectacles. 'That is . . . quite right that it is your show. And also quite right that I haven't any rank to pull on you any more . . . But if you want to play the game like that, then that's the way I'll play it too. Only I must warn you . . . there is a drawback.'

The obvious drawback, thought Mitchell, lay in the differences between them: Audley was not only considerably older, and more experienced, and richer . . . but he was also unhampered by ambition. Or . . . he was only hampered by the ambition of continuing to do what he liked doing. But even that was really more a self-indulgence than an ambition.

'You think you'd win all the time?'

'Not *all* the time.' Audley smiled. 'Most of the time. But that wasn't what I was thinking about. I was thinking . . . if you want to hitch your wagon to Oliver St John Latimer's star you really ought to make sure that he's still alive first.'

If that was what Audley thought, then there was no time to reject the slander. 'You think he isn't?'

'I think we've been taken for a ride, is what I think. Although I still don't know where we're going.'

'Is that what Colonel Butler thinks?'

'Ah . . . now, I haven't actually consulted Jack on the matter.' Audley bridled slightly. 'I found a message from young James waiting for me, informing me where you were going . . . And I got to thinking about everything we've been doing since Oliver took wing.'

'Shouldn't you be taking wing, talking of wings?'

'Yes . . . pretty soon.' Audley nodded, and looked at his watch. 'It would be dreadful if I missed that plane, wouldn't it! That would get me into hot water with Jack, I shouldn't wonder . . .'

Poor old Jack! thought Mitchell. In the terms of the Industrial Relations Act, David Audley was already long past his First Verbal Warning, and innumerable Written Warnings, far beyond First, Second and Final: his penchant for disobedience was as legendary as his instinct for elusive truths no one else had seen.

'Maybe I'll still catch it. But if I don't it won't be your fault, anyway.' Audley smiled again. 'So shall we go and talk to Lady Marshall meanwhile, Paul?'

They went into the building.

It was a very expensive block of flats: it had something like a hotel reception, but with the extra security which went with the expense.

'Dr Mitchell and Dr Audley for Lady Alice Marshall-Pugh,' said Mitchell.

The porter behind the desk sized them up, and for once

Mitchell tried to look as though his doctorate was medical, brought here via Harley Street.

'Yes, sir.' The sizing up and the appointments book didn't quite give them the *nihil obstat*. 'Dr Mitchell for Lady Alice. . .' The porter gave Audley a hard look '– Dr Audley?'

Audley's call to James Cable had come – must have come – after James had set up this meeting. But the porter's suspicious scrutiny of him took Mitchell by surprise.

'Yes.' He considered David himself. It was certainly true that he didn't look like what he was, with that battered face of his. And his shirt was somewhat crumpled, and his tie was old and had been knotted in anger (and the porter could hardly be expected to recognize its exclusive rugby club colours, which probably accounted for the battered condition of the face).

The man came back to him. 'Dr Audley, sir?'

Mitchell decided on half-truth. 'Dr Audley is my senior consulting colleague,' he said stiffly.

'Just so, sir.' Like all good porters, the man wasn't overawed. 'If you'll excuse me for a moment – ?' He retreated into a cubicle to his left, even though there was a phone right in front of him.

'He doesn't like the look of me, does he?' murmured Audley. 'And . . . not that I blame him . . . what's so special about Lady Alice Thingummy?' He glanced sidelong at Mitchell. 'And it's Lady *Alice*, is it – not Lady . . . Thingummy – Marshall-Pugh?'

'She was a duke's daughter.' Mitchell watched the porter watch them both as he spoke into the phone in the cubicle. 'She married Marshall-Pugh before he was knighted.'

'And who the hell was he?'

'Fertilisers – ' Mitchell just had time to hiss the word as the porter emerged from his sanctum.

'Ah!' Audley gave the porter a haughty look. 'In the

270

shit, of course – she married money! Where there's muck there's brass, as they're always saying.' The look focussed on the porter. 'Now, what seems to be the trouble?'

The porter gave Mitchell a bleak look. 'If you'd care to take the lift to the right, sir. It will open when you reach your destination.'

They went to the lift.

Audley shrugged. 'It's a commentary on the state of London, I suppose . . . when it's almost as hard to get into Lady Alice's pad as it is to see Jack Butler. *O tempora, o mores*!'

The lift doors opened.

There was one important thing, thought Mitchell – and there was one more important thing –

'How have we been taken for a ride, David?'

Audley stared at the blank wall of the lift. 'My dear Paul . . . when you're taken for a ride you usually never know until it's far too late. So probably it's too late now . . . All I know is that someone has hatched a damn good scheme – and I know it's damn good because it's got a variable factor in it, which is the hallmark of excellence.'

'A variable factor?'

'That's right.' Audley continued to study the false veneer of the lift wall. 'No plan devised by man ever goes according to plan. Nothing ever goes exactly right, and you can't foresee what is going to go wrong. So you have to build in variables – tolerances, if you like . . . But you can never build *on* variables, because after the first thing goes wrong there's a sort of geometric progression – the first disaster multiplies the possibility of the second by twenty, and any of those multiply by fifty . . . So you have to be lucky as well as beautiful.'

The lift stopped, and Mitchell stared at Audley for a second. Then the doors quivered, and opened.

They stepped out into a tiny enclosed hall, with an elegant little table bearing a plant which could do without sunshine and a water-colour which looked genuine and was all the better for the lack of sunshine.

'Don't ring the bell,' said Audley. 'This chap had bad luck from the start: he got Oliver instead of me – and because of that he got you, and because of that he got all of us . . . ferreting around, to find out what the hell Oliver was up to . . . Although he was also lucky in a way, because Oliver didn't do what he ought to have done. But that's just good luck balancing out bad, the way it tends to do – although no bloody computer can ever work that out precisely.'

Mitchell waited without speaking, even though he had the feeling of a time-clock ticking against them.

'This chap was *good*, though. Because even though we got into the act far too quickly, we still only threshed around among ourselves, to get information . . . And even though it wasn't *bad* information – like what you got from your Civil War contact, and what we both got from old Howard – even what came out of that bloody awful instrument of Jack's . . . All good stuff . . . but where has it got us?' Audley examined the door. 'Ring the bloody bell, Paul.'

There was a bell-button beside the door, with a little speaker above it. Mitchell pressed the button. 'It's got us here, David.' He looked at Audley. 'Or . . . it's got *me* here . . . for all the good it may do. But I'm still a bit hazy about your exact interest – ?'

'No? Ring the bell again.' Audley pointed. 'I thought we were digging into the antecedents of the Simon-pure and somewhat enigmatic Senator Thomas Cookridge?'

And that was an inadequate answer, thought Mitchell. 'I hardly think Lady Alice Marshall-Pugh is going to add to the store of knowledge. At least, not knowledge of any use – if James's dear mum has got her dates right, she may be an old friend of his, but she's not an old flame. And she didn't even get to see him Friday either – he stood her up in preference for Oliver, and more pressing business.'

'Very true! This is a long shot. Ring the bell.'

'A very long shot.' Mitchell didn't ring the bell. 'And even if she has anything of the slightest interest . . . and always supposing that she'll let it slip to a perfect stranger . . . I can signal you in Rome, David.' Mitchell shook his head. 'It really is a rotten excuse for missing the plane – it isn't really a long shot, it isn't a shot at all.'

The speaker emitted an electric crackle. 'Who's there?' inquired a quavering voice.

Mitchell stared at Audley for a moment, then shook his head. 'Dr Audley for Lady Alice Marshall-Pugh,' he said in his most reassuring voice in reply.

'Oh . . . Just a minute – thank you!' Faintly, through the thickness of the door, there came the rattle of a chain.

Audley nodded. 'A very long shot – I agree! But that's why I like it: it's the first bloody thing we've done that's crazy enough not to have been foreseen by whoever put this thing together.'

The door opened.

'Oh dear! I'm so sorry to have taken so long, Dr Mitchell – or is it Dr Audley?'

Mitchell found himself looking down. Lady Alice was tiny and bird-like – there was no such creature in imagination as an elderly London sparrow . . . sparrows neither lived to be old, nor did they wear pearls at their throat . . . But here was just such a little bird, nevertheless.

'It's all these chains, you see.' She smiled at him. 'We have a new one which the man said is made with some special new metal, and nothing can cut it . . . Dr Mitchell?'

'Yes.' At least she wasn't scared of him. 'Lady Alice?'

'Oh no! I am Miss Wall, Lady Alice's companion. Please come in, Dr Mitchell – and Dr Audley, of course.' Miss Wall gestured to admit them both into the flat.

Mitchell looked around with a curious sense of recognition, almost dêjà-vu. It was a big flat, if the size of its entrance hall was a clue to the rest of it – much bigger than his mother's new pad in Dorking. But it had the same atmosphere of widowhood, and the cramming of the best of accumulated possessions of a lifetime, which had once graced an entire house, into a much smaller space.

The difference was that these possessions were in an altogether different class from Mother's. Where hers were middle-class memories, with a scatter of heirlooms, these were genuine treasures jammed together: pictures on the wall, hung three-deep so that there was precious little wall; opulent eastern rugs almost too big for their floor; and that table, on which there was a dangerous concentration of what looked like Meissen figures, would look well in a Sotheby's catalogue.

Audley took a step past him and peered incautiously across the Meissen collection, at a water-colour behind.

'Samuel Atkins,' said Audley. 'My wife tried to get me to buy one of those recently. It seemed rather expensive to me. But this one's a little peach, I must say.' He nodded down at little Miss Wall, unsmiling, almost irritably. 'The trouble with most amateur collectors is that they always see the light about ten years too late.'

Mitchell cleared his throat. 'Miss Wall – Dr Audley.'

'Oh yes!' Miss Wall simpered at Audley. 'I should have known *you*, Dr Audley!'

Audley frowned at her discouragingly. 'Indeed, madam?'

'Oh yes – ' Miss Wall looked quickly at Mitchell, and then back at Audley ' – it was silly of me . . . it was that wretched chain, though – Lady Alice remembers *you*, naturally.' She indicated a door to her left. 'Shall I lead the way?'

As they followed her Mitchell gave Audley a look of mingled hatred and suspicion.

Audley spread his hands and lifted his shoulders in feigned innocence. 'Search me,' he murmured.'

Shit! Thought Mitchell, as he followed Miss Wall.

The room beyond the entrance hall was the entrance hall writ large, because if was larger, and the treasures in it were larger and more numerous, the loot of a lifetime's trade on fertilisers as yet undistributed by death duties.

But it was not the treasures which mattered –

'Ah, Dr Mitchell?'

Lady Alice Marshall-Pugh, tastefully arranged in the midst of her loot, was something more substantial than her companion, and perhaps older, but altogether ordinary otherwise, without the adornment of pearls and as plain as a pikestaff.

'And Dr Audley.' Lady Alice's eye was not so ordinary: it was sharp and suspicious, where Miss Wall's had been welcoming.

'Lady Alice,' agreed Mitchell quickly, before she could further recognize Audley. 'I believe Lieutenant-Commander Cable has telephoned you – or was it Lady Cable – ?'

The sharp and suspicious eye concentrated on Mitchell. 'It was Edna Cable.' She nodded. 'Who is an exceedingly stupid woman. But she did phone on behalf of that boy of hers, who has been three times blessed – he has his mother's good looks, his father's brains and his grandfather's exquisite manners.' She gave Mitchell another nod. 'If he had Edna's brains I doubt very much whether he would have been working with you, Dr Mitchell – ' She switched back to Audley ' – and especially with *you*, Dr Audley.'

Audley had been unashamedly examining the contents of the room, casing it like a burglar. But now he gave Lady Alice his attention.

'We are as God makes us, Lady Alice.' His lip twisted unbeautifully. 'And if I understand your companion correctly God has presently given you the advantage over me.'

She liked that, thought Mitchell. And, however annoying that might be, it was a useful thing to know – that she liked being given as good as she gave.

'Which is just as well for me, if what I hear about you is true.' She teased him. And, thought Mitchell, she was as plain and as irresistible as his darling Elizabeth, by God! 'Sit down, gentlemen, please.'

'I don't know what you've heard.' Audley acknowledged her game with a slight shrug. 'But it's probably all true. And more and worse besides.'

It had gone far enough, decided Mitchell. She had heard about David Audley from someone, somewhere. But the Audley-Marshall-Pugh bisecting social circles had no bearing on their business now.

'Lady Alice – ' He demanded her attention. ' – I'm sorry to disturb you like this, at this time, quite out of the blue. But we have pressing business.'

'You do not disturb me, Dr Mitchell.' She turned to him with obvious regret at having left Audley unanswered. 'I am a bored and useless old woman – the thought of you coming to me with pressing business is quite enchanting, actually. I can hardly wait to be brutally interrogated under some obscure clause of the Official Secrets Act – ' She cocked an eye at Audley ' – I can always complain to the Labour Party, or to the National Council for Civil Liberties – or to the Editor of the *Manchester Guardian* newspaper . . . I'm sure they would have what my late husband used to call "a field day", whatever that means, with my case. And my expensive lawyers would also be overjoyed to visit me in Holloway Prison, too.'

'Allie!' exclaimed Miss Wall. 'Do stop talking nonsense!'

'Nonsense, Sam?' Lady Alice mocked her companion's concern. 'Dr Audley only deals with very serious matters. You might very well be called on to pack an over-night bag before he's finished with me – '

'No!' An old lady's fun-and-games were one thing, thought Mitchell. But Winston Mulholland was something very different: Winston Mulholland wasn't fun-and-games at all. 'I believe you are acquainted with Senator Thomas Cookridge, Lady Alice – is that correct?'

'Paul – ' began Audley.

' – Shut up, David.' Cosy games were not real life: he had played cosy games with Frances once upon a time, and Frances lay in a country churchyard because of it. 'You know Senator Cookridge, Lady Alice.'

'Yes, I do, Dr Mitchell.' Quite suddenly Lady Alice gave him all her attention.

So now he had to get it right. 'I'll be frank with you, Lady Alice: we have a situation which worries me.' Instinct, as well as what James's mother had said, inclined him to trust her. 'We have a man out in the field, far away from here, in what may be an exposed position – he may be in great danger.'

She was thinking hard now. 'How does this concern Tom – Senator Thomas Cookridge, Dr Mitchell?'

'We don't know. But it does concern him somehow – that we do know.' The danger lay also in her friendship with the Senator, so he must involve the man more closely. 'It could be dangerous for him too.'

The effort of thinking made her look older and more frail. 'What is it that you want to know?'

It was the exact question which had been bugging Mitchell ever since he'd received James Cable's message: *what did he want to know? What could Lady Alice tell him?*

Audley seemed to pick up the vibration of his doubt. 'You've known him for a long time, Lady Alice – the Senator?'

'Yes.' She shifted uneasily between them. 'Tom and I are very old friends . . . When he's in England – or I'm in America . . . we never miss each other.' She seemed to contract within herself. 'We first met more than forty years ago now.'

'During the war?' Mitchell moved into the gap.

'Yes. He was with the American air force – he was a bomber pilot.' Her expression softened. 'He was a fine young man . . .'

'B-17s?' Audley took the next gap.

'Flying Fortresses – would that be . . . B-17s?' She paused, but neither of them spoke. 'He was on all those raids when they took those dreadful losses. But when he'd finished his tour of duty he wouldn't go home . . . It was 1943 – that was when I met him . . . My son had been killed by then, flying from Malta. And my husband was with the 14th Army, in India . . . And into 1944 – when the doodlebugs and rockets came over . . . He used to come down to South London, where I was driving my ambulance, when he was on leave. He used to say that I kept him out of mischief – he had a girl waiting for him back home, he said, so he didn't want to be put in the way of temptation – those were his exact words, "put into the way of temptation." He was a dear boy!'

She chuckled, almost cackled, at the memory, and Mitchell tried to estimate her age more exactly. Lady Cable had described her as *ancient* (and Lady Cable must be the wrong side of sixty), to which James had added *but not senile* (and she was certainly a long way from that). But if she'd had a son killed at Malta . . . and that would most likely be between '40 and '42 . . . she must certainly be well into her eighties. So she must have been mid-fortyish when –

'Which was quite ridiculous, of course – he was a very *proper* young man, very serious . . . He was really rather more *proper* than I was . . . But that was his upbringing, which had been strict Protestant – or was it Presbyterian?' She fixed that sharp eye on Mitchell. 'No matter – it was the sort of upbringing which caused him to fear being "put into the way of temptation" anyway. He preferred to be put into the way of those wretched doodlebugs, you see.' She sat back suddenly. 'In fact, I remember him spending a whole afternoon tinkering with my ambulance, to make the engine run more quietly – American boys were so *good* with engines . . . my poor Andrew never really knew one end of an engine from another, even though he did fly

Spitfires . . . *No*, you see, it was those doodlebugs Tom was worried about, for my sake – what they called the "Flying Bombs", you remember?' She paused for a moment. 'But, of course, you won't remember – you're far too young! She switched to Audley. 'But Dr Audley will recall them – that nasty little motor-cycle noise? And then it stopped, just as though it had been switched off – and then you had a minute to find somewhere safe . . . They used to say it was *four* minutes, but it never seemed like that to me . . . And then there was this enormous *bang*, when it exploded – and I always used to feel so *grateful* that it hadn't come down on top of me . . . and then so *ashamed*, because it had come down on some other poor innocent person.' She cocked her head at Audley. 'You remember the doodlebugs, Dr Audley?'

Audley nodded politely. 'But I was on the other side of the Channel then, Lady Alice. Though I did see some V-2s later on, in Germany – the rockets.'

'Oh – they weren't nearly so frightening. You never heard them at all! Or . . . you only heard them afterwards – if you didn't hear them, that was because you were already dead. So they were like an Act of God – at least that's what I always thought.'

She gave them both a satisfied nod, as though to settle the matter. And Mitchell thought: *There she sits . . . and if anyone gives her a second thought, it'll be "boring old bag". But this boring old bag once drove an ambulance under fire in the Age of the Guided Missile, by God!*

'Yes, of course.' Audley nodded, exuding respect and polite interest. 'But now . . . about Senator Cookridge – '

'Ah! Yes – I was telling you about Tom!' she nodded back at him. 'Yes – '

Mitchell felt half-ashamed with himself for being side-tracked by his own romantic reaction of her World War Two reminiscences. Audley was right: they weren't getting anywhere fast –

'That was the trouble!' She wagged a wrinkled finger at

them. 'Tom worked on my engine because if was too noisy, you see.' She looked at them expectantly.

'Too . . . noisy, Lady Alice?' inquired Mitchell.

'That's right. When I was driving it I couldn't even hear the doodlebugs when they were passing overhead. So I couldn't hear them when they *stopped*.' She smiled triumphantly. 'But when Tom had finished with that eingine . . . well, then I had time to stop the ambulance, and jump out and crawl under it.'

Mitchell didn't dare look at Audley. 'And . . . and you've been friends with him ever since, of course.'

'But he didn't marry that girl back home – ?' Audley took up the relay-baton.

'Oh yes he did. Of course he did – a lovely girl! My husband and I were at the wedding – a lovely girl.' Her face didn't change. 'But she died, she died . . . you know, I have seen so many people die, who were my contemporaries . . . But it's the young ones I can't bear to lose . . . And Tom was broken-hearted. So that was when he really concentrated on making money. And then on those politics of his – very complicated, like an Irish horse-sale – which, I think, is why those Irishmen do so well in American politics . . . He always tells me about it, when he comes to see me – you really wouldn't believe what they get up to: it makes our people look quite like amateurs.'

Mitchell leapt in quickly, before she could elaborate on the intricacies of American poltical horse-trading. 'But he married again – didn't he?'

'So he did.' She nodded agreement. 'Another nice woman – his Patricia would have approved of her.' Another nod. 'He asked me about it, and I listened to him – he was worried about the memory of Patricia – and I said to him: "She sounds a very nice woman, and Patricia would take that as a compliment that you're tried marriage once, and you liked it, so now you're going to try it again."' She shook her head. 'But she died too . . . Poor

280

Tom – lucky in war, and almost everything else. But . . . *Poor* Tom!'

'She'd been married before, hadn't she?' Butter would not have melted in Audley's mouth. 'The second wife?'

'Yes. But most unhappily.' Her brows knitted. 'A most obnoxious man . . . There was a daughter – pretty little thing, but as thin as a bean-pole, and *so* suspicious of poor Tom, who's ten-times better than her proper father . . . Yes – ' She stopped suddenly.

'You knew him then, did you?' The butter still sat on Audley's tongue. 'What was his name? Mac-something?'

It wasn't good enough: Mitchell could see that from the look on her face. But he had to do what he could.

'Macallan, David.' He pretended to jog Audley's memory. 'He was with their embassy over here – oh, way back . . . in the economic section. I think he's dead now. He retired donkeys' years ago, anyway.'

'Yes?' If Audley had noticed the change in her expression he didn't show it.

'No,' said Lady Alice. Then she wagged a thin finger at little Miss Wall. 'Pass me the cigarette box, Sam. Or, better still, light one for me.'

Miss Wall registered genteel shock-horror. 'Allie, you know you're not supposed to.'

'Light me one, and don't witter. The doctor said I could have one to celebrate good news, and that's what I'm doing. Must I get it myself?'

Audley leaned forward. 'Good news, Lady Alice? Do share it with us.'

'I will, Dr Audley, I will.' She watched Miss Wall light up. 'Just light it, dear – don't smoke it . . . Thank you.' But then she turned to Mitchell, not to Audley. 'He's dead, is he?'

It was no use playing with her. 'Yes.'

'And that's good news?' There was a hint of steel in Audley's question.

'Isn't it?' She hardened her voice to match his. 'Oh . . .

281

come now, Dr Audley! I know *you* – you were pointed out to me once, at a meeting of the Atlantic Friendship Society, years ago, by someone who knew quite a lot about you . . . And I never forget a name or a face.' She drew on her cigarette. 'William Macallan – I know quite a lot about him, too.'

'Indeed?' Audley paused. 'I'd be enchanted to know how.'

'Very simply. Because I am what you both take me to be – and what I have said I am: an old friend of Senator Thomas Cookridge.'

'And he told you about Bill Macallan?'

Another puff. 'Why should he not? We have a relationship which is rewarding to us both. We owe each other nothing . . . except perhaps he once saved my life, and perhaps I delivered him from temptation. We can do each other no harm – we have always lived in different worlds, and it amuses us to exchange confidences. We have the wonderful advantage of having no relationship except affection and esteem and trust, quite free from self-interest.' A last puff, and then she stubbed the cigarette out. 'Will that do, Dr Audley?'

'Very well, Lady Alice.' Audley smiled. 'So now tell us about Macallan.'

She thought for a moment. 'An obnoxious man.'

'So you said.'

'And ruthless.'

'And clever. We know that.'

She considered them both. 'You were a historian once, Dr Audley . . . And you, Dr Mitchell?'

'The same, Lady Alice.' Mitchell shrugged. 'It must be an occupational hazard.'

She nodded. 'Yes. I can see you have something in common. But I think you may share something else . . . I always imagine men in their correct centuries. My husband was a Victorian: he would have loved building the railways. But you are both eighteenth century Englishmen, I think.'

This game had to be played. 'Both rotten with port? And we lost the American colonies?' Mitchell grinned.

Audley glanced at him. 'I can stand that quite easily – ' Back to Lady Alice ' – but I always see myself as a medieval man . . . and I can never forgive myself losing Bordeaux to the French – all those vineyards?'

'Stuff and nonsense!' Lady Alice cast a longing look at the cigarette box. 'Your patriotism is civilized by reason. But William Macallan was a sixteenth century man – he could have served either the Protestant cause or the Catholics, but his patriotism was a fanatical faith. His ends always justified the means.'

Audley cocked his head. 'And this irritated Tom, did it?'

'It did more than that. That wretched man pursued Tom – he thought he was a traitor – ' She pointed at the box ' – light me another, Sam – go on . . . My Tom a traitor!'

A chill settled on Mitchell, so that he couldn't look at Audley.

Miss Wall lit the cigarette obediently, and Audley took it from her and passed it to Lady Alice.

'A traitor?' Puff. 'I first met Tom after that raid on the German balls – ' She saw Mitchell's face, and waved a hand at him ' – ball-*bearings* – when he lost half the squadron . . . and I've seen him press his face into the road under an ambulance – ' This time she caught Audley's expression. ' – *You* think I don't know when a man's lying to me, through his teeth, I know . . . because you couldn't tell when all those wretched men in the Foreign Office were lying to you!'

Audley wasn't going to take that lying down. 'They can be pretty good liars, Lady Alice, you know – '

'What do you know?' Scornful puff. 'You never had a woman talking to them – how do you say it? *De-briefing* them? And not on the pillow beside them, either . . . *really* talking to them . . . over forty years, and never missed a time to talk too, not once . . . *No* – he wasn't a traitor then, and he isn't a traitor now, if that's what you're on about.' She gave him a sharp nod. 'But that Macallan – *he* could have been a traitor – *he* would have sworn black was white if it suited him . . . And that's what I told Tom, when he came to me years ago – I said "Don't try and defend yourself, he'll love that. You take the war into his country – if you know what you are, you try and show that he isn't what he claims to be – you look for some of his dirty washing, and throw that in his face."'

Audley's hand had come up to his face. 'God bless my soul!' he exclaimed, and looked at Mitchell.

But there was something niggling Mitchell –

They weren't going to get anything out of her: to her Senator Thomas Cookridge was as far above suspicion as he was to Colonel Howard Morris of the CIA –

But that wasn't it – ?

'Have you ever heard of Sion Crossing?' said Audley, obviously animated by the same despair.

'Sion Crossing?' She frowned.

'S-I-O-N Crossing?' repeated Audley.

That wasn't it –

'S-Y-O-N – Syon House, I know . . .' Sion Crossing threw her. 'That's the Somerset-Northumberland house – Robert Adam interiors and Capability Brown landscaped grounds – what?'

'In Georgia, Lady Alice,' said Audley. 'In the United States – or the Confederate States, more correctly. It was burnt down in the American Civil War.'

Now he had lost her – and she had lost him – completely: he was an eighteeenth century Englishman talking about a nineteenth century American house.

'Did Senator Cookridge ever talk to you about the American Civil War?' Audley pursued his line of inquiry like a doomed infantryman pulling at the unbroken German wire.

'No.' She was quite lost now. 'Why should he?'

284

Something came to Mitchell, but unformed in his mind. 'On Friday . . .'

'No.' She was positive about that, anyway. 'He was on about his speech on Friday.' She was torn between them. 'He'd never made a big speech over here – and this new job of his is a great responsibility . . . He wanted to mention the war, when he was over here. But he had to make a speech in Germany on Tuesday, and he couldn't make up his mind about how they'd take it – his own people had given him conflicting advice, the way civil servants always do – ' She stopped as she saw their faces – *as she saw her own sudden doubt reflected in their greater doubt –*

Mitchell looked at Audley.

'What's the matter?' said Lady Alice.

Audley was looking at Mitchell.

'I'm sorry, Lady Alice . . . but – ' The unformed thing in Mitchell's mind formed, and then distorted itself, and then formed again in sharp focus ' – you say he came here on *Friday*?'

'Yes.' She frowned at him. 'Where else would he go?'

'On Friday evening?' It sounded stupid, it was so simple.

'Of course.' Her look and her words were both edged with pride. 'He always finds time for me, whenever he comes over. He never misses, I told you.'

Never –

'On Friday?' Audley was afflicted by the same stupidity. 'At what time, Lady Alice?'

'What time?' She thought they were both mad. 'Well . . . I suppose it was just about seven.' She thought for two seconds. 'He was short of time – is it important?' But one look at them was enough. 'He went straight to the embassy from Heathrow, and he changed there . . . and he came to me . . . for about half an hour – maybe a little longer – he was afraid he might be late, but it was more important to get the speech right – the bit about the war.

285

And I said that the Germans would understand that when he spoke about the horror of it he knew what he was talking about . . . And after that he went straight to his dinner.' She turned to Miss Wall. 'Right, Sam?'

'Yes, Alice.' Miss Wall nodded. 'He had all those bodyguards with him. I was quite frightened of them!'

'Christ!' exclaimed Audley.

Mitchell stood up. 'Can I use your phone, Lady Alice, please? *At once* – ?'

'Over here,' she gestured to the table beside her. 'Or in my bedroom, if you want privacy – Sam will show you, Dr Mitchell.'

No nonesense: she might not understand what had passed between them, but she sensed its urgency.

Mitchell circled her chair to reach the phone. It didn't matter what she heard: there was not a moment to be lost, and he wanted Audley to hear what he said. And these two old ladies weren't going anywhere as of now.

He dialled the right number. The table was piled with books, and he observed that she was into sixteenth century history, which did not surprise him: that analogy between Queen Elizabeth I's spymasters and spies – Walsingham and Throckmorton, and Gresham . . . and Maitland and Melville and Leigh, and all the rest of the tortured doubles – and their twisted allegiances –

The number answered, and it was Elizabeth, of course – his own not-quite Elizabeth.

'Robertson here. Please clear this line.' There was also an empty glass on the table, and an ashtray with two cigarettes stubbed out on it, and several bottles of pills. On the top of the books there was a note=pad with a ball-pen attached to it. On the pad was written "Edna", then "James", and then "Dr Mitchell" underlined.

It wouldn't take long, because Elizabeth was efficient. Also, it was the first time he'd ever used an emergency code-name to her.

Audley caught his eye. 'You might scramble a line to

Washington Station, while you're about it,' he advised casually. 'It'll save time.'

Mitchell nodded. He must get the procedure right too, otherwise all hell would break loose around their ears, with all sorts of funnies alerted, from the Bomb Squad to the SAS.

'Line cleared,' said Elizabeth. 'Please state origin of call, Mr Robertson.'

'Thank you.' Mr Robertson's "All Clear" signal resided in those innocent words, repeated. 'Thank you.'

Just enough time for an intake of breath. 'Are you all right, Paul?'

'Quite okay, Elizabeth.' He took heart from her unofficial concern. 'Embarrassed, but quite okay. Origin of call is Flat 7, Macmillan Gardens, 037–98842, the residence of Lady Alice Marshall-Pugh. Two requirements: Clear a priority scrambled line to Washington Station for onwards transmission to Wing-Commander Roskill – he should be somewhere in Georgia by now, but he'll be checking back at frequent intervals, so they'd better be ready to tape Colonel Butler's instructions for instant action, and no messing – understood?'

'Yes, Paul – understood.' Elizabeth was not normally so meek. 'Understood.'

Her very meekness steadied his: she was picking up his implicit panic signal, and that was humiliating. 'Also . . . I'd like to have a word with Colonel Butler, if that's *possible*, Elizabeth dear.' He tried to recapture his own normal voice.

'It's possible.' She was not deceived. 'Hold the line.'

He caught Audley's eye again, and observed that Audley was nodding. 'Tell Jack to abort Oliver at once – ' With what was rare delicacy for him Audley cut off the advice with a shrug ' – Sorry, Paul – your show . . . But that's what I would *advise*, is what I mean.'

Mitchell managed a smile. It was like the soldiers all remembered: some commands were rewarding, and others weren't. Platoon commander and company commander were all right, because they were at the sharp end; and battalion commander was okay because he was father of the family; but nothing else was worth having until you got to the top and could conduct the whole orchestra of an army. And they were both uncomfortably somewhere in the middle now.

'I have Colonel Butler for you now. I am putting you through. Good luck, Paul darling.'

That was something anyway –

'Butler here.' The Colonel's voice blotted out the echo of *darling*. 'Mitchell?'

'Sir!' Mitchell stood to attention mentally. Butler liked things clear and concise. 'I am speaking from the flat of Lady Alice Marshall-Pugh, off Regent's Park. She is a close friend of Senator Cookridge. He had an appointment to meet her on Friday evening, before he gave his speech at the Savoy.'

Audley nodded at him again. 'It was in my report.'

'It was in David's report.'

'Yes.' Pause. 'He met Latimer instead. So?'

'Sir . . . She says he met her as arranged. So Latimer met someone else. Cookridge couldn't have been in two places at once.'

Pause. 'Are you telling me Cookridge has a double?'

'No, sir. Not a double. Latimer's probably never met Cookridge.' Another encouraging nod from Audley. 'Hardly anyone over here has. A general resemblance would have been enough – if Colonel Morris said it was Cookridge, anyway . . .'

Pause. 'You think Lady . . . Lady Marshall-Pugh is reliable Mitchell?'

Mitchell looked down at Lady Alice, who was observing him with rapt attention. At this short range he could smell old age mixed with Chanel No 5. Then he looked at Audley, but this time the big man hadn't picked up any message.'

So it was up to him, to his judgement. Which was fair enough, because he'd started it all.

'Either she is, or Morris is,' said Butler harshly. 'You can't have both.' Butler paused. 'And I have just been informed that you've cleared a line to America – is that correct?'

'Yes.' The combined weight of time and distance, and of the equivocal events of the past forty-eight hours, pressed down on Mitchell. *He had always thought of himself as so clever – but when it came to the crunch he wasn't at all –*

'Speak up, man!'

He saw Audley looked at him, and suddenly he heard Audley's voice in his memory: *it was a damn good plan because it fitted together loosely, allowing for elements of bad luck –*

'No, sir.'

'No – ?'

'Colonel Morris got his instructions by phone. He never met Cookridge. He could have been deceived also.' But it didn't really matter: what mattered was the smell of the whole thing – and the presence of Winston Mulholland in it – and the fact that James Cable had come up with Lady Alice only as a long shot. 'We have to get Oliver out of there, sir. Whether the Americans are in it or not – it doesn't matter. I think she's okay, and I think we've been set up somehow. And Oliver's at the sharp end, and he doesn't know it. So we've got to get him out.'

Pause. 'Quite right, Mitchell.' This time it was Colonel Butler who was nodding at him, though from far away. 'The SG is on the way – to the Americans as well as the Wing-Commander. And I have also sent minders to your present location, to seal it up. When they arrive you are to come on in. Right?'

Mitchell only gawped at the receiver for a second. Because, with The Beast there beside him, Colonel Butler could tap out his instructions with his fingers while his ear and his mouth were otherwise engaged. It was only technological.

'Yes, sir – '

Click.

'Well?' inquired Audley, with a supreme effort of politeness. 'Did he buy it?'

Mitchell smiled reassuringly at Lady Alice before turning to Audley. 'He's sending in the Marines.'

'Good.' Audley stood up. 'And the whole Union Army, I hope . . . Lady Alice – since you know so much about me, perhaps you will permit me to call on you again by appointment, to take you out to lunch?' He cocked an eye at Miss Wall. 'With Sam . . . to put you both right about any slanders which may have been spread about me?'

Lady Alice inclined her head graciously. 'Dr Audley . . . we shall look forward to that with great pleasure.'

Audley's eye came back to Mitchell. 'In a little while I may phone you at the office, as from the departure lounge at Heathrow. And I confide that you will cancel my flight, Paul.'

'Is my Tom safe?' inquired Lady Alice. 'You owe me that, Dr Mitchell.'

'Quite safe now, Lady Alice. And . . . I hope you don't mind, but we will be giving you a bodyguard for tonight.'

'Oh, dear!' exclaimed Miss Wall. 'A . . . bodyguard!'

'Don't witter, Sam!' snapped her mistress. 'At our age – we should be so lucky!'

12

Latimer in America: The Contract is fulfilled

Kingston fielded the Ingram from the midst of his super-market purchases with one hand, while the silenced pistol in his other hand covered the staircase above and behind Latimer and the hallway on his left in a narrow arc. Then the slightly blood-shot eyes in the black face switched to the doors on each side of him.

Latimer himself stood rooted to the spot, terrified first by the pistol as it passed and repassed him, and then by the sight of Joe tumbled in death on the landing behind him.

'Cmon – move it, man!' Kingston clutched the Ingram to his naked chest as he backed towards the open door, while his eyes and his pistol quartered the hall again. 'We got to get off Sion land!'

For another half of a fraction of a second Latimer's mind and his legs refused to move. Then they both accelerated him towards the doorway.

'Get the rifle – ' Kingston's final instruction caught him as he passed the negro and the light burst all around him.

The Confederate guard was wrapped round the corner of the balustrade on the verandah at the top of the steps, his legs sticking out stiffly halfway across them, with his rifle lying on the grass at the bottom.

As Latimer stooped to take up the rifle, already uncertain as to what to do next, Kingston passed him at the run, leaping half the flight in one bound, and was already way across the open space as he straightened up. And then he was no longer uncertain.

The trees were a thousand miles away, and the house reared up behind him as he ran, leaving his back naked.

But it was too late for arguments and explanations – he had to *run*.

There was bushes, bright red-flowered, to his left – and Kingston was turning, no longer holding the pistol, but with the Ingram held two-handed, sweeping left – and through him – and right, to cover his rear . . . Kingston had dropped to one knee, and was looking back, as though he didn't exist, oblivious of him –

The trees were so far away, and then only with their thin scattering of leaves, and he had never run like this in his life, through hot and cold, outside him and inside him, towards a winning post which seemed unattainable –

He plunged into the beginning of the forest, at the end of the lawn without stopping – trees were obstacles, but anything that wasn't a tree could be burst through regardless, compared with what lay behind him.

Where was he going?

But that was not what was immediately important, any more than rattlesnakes and poison ivy were important: covering ground was what was important – there was no path, but any direction which was not backwards was the right one –

We got to get off old Sion land – swerve left, swerve right – just keep running!

A stray branch whipped his face, starting tears and nearly blundering him into a thicker patch of undergrowth. He skidded in a shower of leaves, almost losing his balance as he twisted his direction – the bloody woods were all alike, and every way was suddenly indistinguishable –

Which way? Tears and sweat blurred his vision.

He drew a shuddering breath, and was conscious of the rifle in his hands for the first time: he had picked it up on the negro's order, but it had been no more than a stick of wood to him. Now it was a rifle – but it still might just as well be a stick of wood for all he could do with it: even if he had ever been any good with guns, he could hardly see now.

He brushed the sweat from his face with his sleeve, and

blinked to clear his sight. He had to get moving again – but which way?

Then there was another sound in his ears, over to his left.

He swung the rifle towards it, blinking again to concentrate his partially-restored sight, and saw – saw with an overwhelming wave of relief and gratitude – the black shape of Kingston bobbing and weaving through the trees not far away.

'The creek, man – ' the negro signalled urgently ' – make for the creek!'

The creek of course! That was the nearest and most obvious boundary of old Sion land. When they reached that they would at least know where they were, and whatever Kingston had in mind then, it was better than the near-panic in his own brain.

There was no time to argue anyway, for the man was already ahead of him, running like a gazelle.

Latimer's aching legs carried him forward. As he fended off branches with the rifle he felt an arrow of pain in his side which made his gasp: he had not had a stitch like that for years – not since the agony of those dreadful house-runs at school, when he had been the fat little boy at the back of the run –

'*Come on, Latimer! Don't let the House down!*'

Latimer swore silently at the memory as he ran –

'*Come on, Latimer! The way to beat a stitch is to run it off!*'

They had all had longer legs, and he had always come in last: this was only history repeating itself unbearably –

History repeating itself: long ago the Iowans had run through these woods, making for the creek!

At last the land was changing – it was no longer dead level, but was falling away ahead of him. Yet now Kingston was changing direction, no longer taking the shortest route down the slope, but veering away to his right, in the direction of the bridge. *But the bridge was guarded –*

He tried to shout, but it was useless: the arrow had fallen

from his side, but he had no breath left for shouting. His chest hurt, and he could hardly take in enough air, and what he could take in burnt like fire. And he was wringing wet with sweat, as though he'd already been in the river.

It was no good: he couldn't go on, and he wouldn't go on – not that way, into danger!

And besides, he didn't owe Kingston anything. It was illogical to think of the negro as having saved him: Kingston had delivered him into danger, and then into greater danger when the first danger had receded – he owed Kingston nothing except suspicion.

His legs were carrying him downhill. The stream at the bottom there was probably not very deep, and even if it was, it was not very wide anyway. And he was sick and tired of being led by the nose.

'Where you going, man?' Kingston's voice was only slightly breathless. It was more surprised than breathless.

Latimer looked up towards the voice. Kingston's naked chest was shiny with sweat, and it rose and fell with deep controlled breaths.

'Where you going?' repeated Kingston, steadying himself on a tree with one hand. But it was the other hand which steadied Latimer: the Ingram in that black hand was still as much a persuader as it had been in Joe's.

'They – ' He struggled to control his own breathlessness ' – they have – men – covering . . . covering the bridge.'

'You don't say?' The grin was only slightly smaller than usual. 'Man, they got men all over.' Kingston nodded past him down the slope. 'Got an old boathouse down there, covers the creek for half a mile either way nicely.' He jerked his head in the opposite direction. ''Nother guy by the bend can see up the creek this way, an' down to the bridge. Like, interlocking fields of fire, as they say. Maybe more by now . . . Though losing Joe'll throw them some.' The grin widened. 'Make them trigger-happy too, though.' This time the nod was towards the rifle in Latimer's hands. 'You any good with that, Oliver?'

'Not much.' It was no good pretending.

'Uh-huh.' Kingston didn't seem surprised. 'Well, you jus' squeeze the trigger when you have to. 'Cause they won't know that.' Grin. 'We go on a piece, an' the creek's not too wide, an' there's good cover on the other side. Okay?'

It was not at all okay, but it made sense as far as anything did, leaving aside the traffic jam of questions in Latimer's mind.

'Okay?' repeated Kingston.

'Okay.' There wasn't time for questions. All that was certain was that Kingston knew more about the defences of Sion Crossing than he did.

'Okay.' Kingston pointed up the slope. 'You keep your eye on the top – you see anything on the skyline, don't holler – jus' tap me on the shoulder an' give me the rifle. An' if I hit the dirt, you hit it too.' He looked at Latimer critically. 'Gimme your coat.'

'What?'

'Jus' give it me, man.'

Latimer watched, at first uncomprehending, then in horror as the negro swept aside the leaves at his feet and proceeded to rub his best lightweight jacket in the red earth.

'What –'

Kingston looked up from his work. 'Get some of this dirt on your pants – an' your face. White face – pale suit like this . . . they show up too good – go on, man! Better to be a mite dirty than a lot dead – *go on*!'

Latimer set about ruining his trousers. The sweat-sodden materials stained easily, as also did his sweaty face if his hands were anything to judge by. It seemed only natural to complete the job by wiping them on the front of his shirt, and he thought insanely *if I ever come out of this I'll never be able to look at the red fields of Devon again* –

'That's jus' fine, Oliver man.' Kingston returned the wreckage of his jacket. 'You hit the dirt now, you jus' like part of it. Let's go, then.'

295

Latimer followed him at a steady dog-trot through the trees, his mind still whirling with questions while he divided his attention between keeping up with the negro and casting fearful glances up the slope.

He was committed to trusting the man now –

There wasn't quite a clear skyline above them, there were too many trees for that; but there were patches of light between them –

It didn't make sense. *Nothing* made sense –

As he moved, so the trees above him on the slope moved, each one differently relative to its distance from the others in a constantly changing pattern; and since he couldn't keep a continuous watch anyway . . .

They had deliberately sent him into Sion Crossing – Kingston and Lucy Cookridge both – knowing what that meant, while making sure he didn't know . . . *But why?*

The slope was steeper here, and there were outcrops of grey rock which he had not noticed before –

And then Kingston had come back, obviously at great risk to himself . . . *Why?*

It didn't make sense. But then . . . for Senator Cookridge to set all this up made even less sense: whatever the outcome – even if it was hushed up, and even if he was blamed for his own ill-considered actions – whatever the outcome it was bound to cause serious Anglo-American trouble – *the man Joe was certainly dead . . . and The Man himself* – who the hell was he?

Just as he was about to take another useless look up the slope, Kingston dropped behind one of the outcrops, and signalled him down urgently.

Latimer flung himself down on the leaves and wormed his way to the safety of the rock, trying to keep the rifle out of the dirt. The one advantage of having ruined his suit, he decided, was that its preservation was no longer one of his worries: the preservation of himself was all that mattered now.

'I think we got company ahead, up near the path – you jus' keep low,' murmured Kingston.

The advice was superfluous. From where he cowered close to Kingston, Latimer watched the negro slowly raise his head above the rock, and then just as slowly lower it.

'Yeah . . . Johnnie Rebs up there,' Kingston turned his attention to the slope below them.

'Have they seen us?' whispered Latimer.

'Uh-huh.' Kingston shook his head. 'Guess they found Fat Albert near the church, where I left it for them. With any luck they'll be expecting us to be heading that way. But our way's thataway.' He pointed down the slope. He grinned at Latimer. 'We hug the dirt, we'll get down okay.'

Latimer had caught his first glimpse of the river below him. 'And after we get across?'

'There's a track on the top. Miz Lucy'll be waiting for us.' Then the grin diminished. 'Jus' let's get over first, hey?'

Latimer watched the negro slither away from him. Apart from a grovelling concern for himself, which was indistinguishable from fear and could easily become terror if things went wrong, he couldn't analyse his feelings for Kingston adequately. The long black bastard had got him into this, but he was now trying to get him out. And it was hard not to worship the ground he slithered on for that reason.

It was his turn now. And he had come a long way in a short time from being frightened of snakes and poison ivy: there were worse things than both in Sion Crossing, and things which had a hostile interest in him now.

Where Kingston had slithered with a certain serpentine elegance, even when hampered by the possession of the Ingram, he managed the journey down quite without grace, in a series of undignified stages and with discomfort to his backside and damage to his hands.

But it was done at last, past one final weathered outcrop

297

to where the negro lay at the water's edge, crouched beside the spreading roots of a tree which shaded the river.

River? It hadn't looked wide enough for that description when he'd observed it from the bridge. But here and now, looking across if from old Sion land to the true promised land of the other side, it looked more like the Mississippi in flood, in Latimer's imagination. Or . . . because of its smooth unwelcoming olive-green surface . . . more like the great grey-green greasy Limpopo, which was the home of crocodiles.

But Kingston was looking past him, with both hands on the Ingram.

'Man . . .' Kingston listened for a moment '. . . if they ain't heard you by now, they ain't gonna hear you ever.'

Latimer held his breath and listened. But the woods above them were as silent as they had always been.

Then he looked at the water again, and wondered which of them was going first. If the choice was his, he thought, he would not be able to make up his mind. Rather, he would prefer to be neither first nor second, but to stay here until nightfall.

But, on the mature consideration of five seconds, that was equally frightening. In the dark, that water would suck him down and lose him forever.

'What are you waiting for?' he inquired.

The eternal grin. 'Man . . . Oliver, you are a glutton for punishment!'

'What do you mean?'

Kingston gave the slope a last look. 'I mean . . . this is not quite where I wanted to cross. Like . . . a little way further up, it's closer to the bridge. But I reckon they'll be watching the road from there – or maybe Fat Albert, if they can see him.' He bent down, to look up and down the river. 'But from here . . . from here they've both got a fair shot – from the bridge *and* the boathouse.' Grin. 'This is the beaten zone, where the field of fire interlock.'

Latimer stared at the negro. There was a world of professional frontier-crossing experience in that statement, even if Joe's fate had not been at his memory's call.

But on whose side?

Well – *on his side at the moment, anyway*!

'So what do we do?'

Shrug. 'We wait for two-three minutes. If they've spotted us from above, we'll see or hear pretty soon – and then we'll both go like hell, okay?'

'And if they haven't?'

'Then I'll go across first, in my own way. And they won't see me.' Suddenly Kingston wasn't smiling. 'Then I'll be in the shallows on the other side, waiting for you. And I can take out the bridge or the boathouse – or I can frighten the hell out of them, an' spoil their aim – with this little sonovabitch, Oliver man.' Kingston patted the Ingram. 'This is something extra, that'll make the Johnnie Rebs think twice, is Joe's weapon.'

Joe . . .

Latimer looked at the negro. 'Why did you kill him?'

Kingston gave him back the look. 'It was jus' bad luck Oliver.'

That was an understatement, if ever there was one. And most of all for Joe. 'Bad luck?'

The black shoulders moved slightly. 'Joe Walker . . . *he knew me*, Oliver. We – we had some times together, way back . . . And he was a good man, was Joe. A top man, even . . . We were lucky back there, is what I think.' The shoulders moved again. 'He must have been thinking about something else – like maybe you, Oliver, huh?'

They had both been slow, thought Latimer – he, Oliver St John Latimer, as well as Joe . . . Walker. Because, in spite of all the differences of race and style, Kingston and Joe were – had been – a matched pair.

'They were going to let me go, Kingston.' He watched the negro. 'They weren't going to kill me.'

'Uh-huh?' Kingston seemed to lose interest. Instead he

put the Ingram down carefully and began to feel in the pockets of his jeans. 'Is that a fact?'

As Latimer watched, the negro produced a clasp-knife from one pocket, and a fresh handkerchief and a carefully wound-up piece of string from the other. He replaced the handkerchief and grinned at Latimer again. 'You ever a Boy Scout, Oliver?'

The edge of scorn in the grin flicked Latimer on the raw. 'They're getting out of this place, you know.'

'Uh-huh?' Kingston unwound the string and methodically cut two equal lengths from it, returning the remaining bit and the knife to his pocket. Latimer saw that the pistol with which he had killed Joe was jammed in his waist-band.

'They're leaving,' said Latimer.

'That figures.' Kingston nodded as he knotted the pieces of string and attached them to the Ingram, to make a crude sling. 'They didn't reckon you were on your own – they just waitin' to hear the cavalry trumpets, man.' He hung the Ingram round his neck, grimacing as the string cut into him.

'They were going to shut me up in the boathouse,' said Latimer.

'In the boathouse?' Kingston gave up trying to adjust the sling, and turned back to Latimer. 'Man – they were sure as hell going to shut you up, I'll buy that.' Grin. 'That Joe . . . he was careless back there, no denying that . . .' He shrugged. 'But jus' don't you depend on that when you go into the water – okay?'

Latimer stared at him open-mouthed.

Another nod. 'He had a few old boys he worked with – he had a lot of contacts . . . not like that kid on the door, that thought *ah wuz jus' a dumb nigger lost his way* – ' Kingston rolled his eyes and feigned an expression of vacant possession ' – man, if I'd known Joe was here I wouldn't ever have agreed to come back, no matter what, I tell you!'

300

Before Latimer could think of anything to say to that the negro was no longer looking at him: he was scanning the slope above very carefully, slowly from left to right.

'No . . . if he's got any of his old boys posted, that were with him in 'Nam, an' one or two other hotspots – ' Left to right slowly, then back right to left ' – then, if they know what happened up at the house by now, we're livin' on borrowed time, an' you had better believe that, Oliver.'

There was no answer to that. Instead Latimer's eyes were drawn to the expanse of the river behind Kingston. The trees on each side overshadowed its banks, but sunlit water between their shadows looked wider than ever.

'That's right!' murmured Kingston. 'You any good underwater, Oliver?'

Latimer thought of his laboured breast-stroke and noisy uneconomic crawl, and shook his head wordlessly.

'Okay.' Kingston's voice was suddenly soothing. 'No sweat . . . I guess you're smart in other ways . . . but right now we both got to get off old Sion land – okay?'

Latimer tried to judge the distance between the shadows. 'I could get halfway, perhaps.'

'That's fine.' Kingston nodded. 'Because I can go all the way, an' I'll be in the shallows waiting for you, like I said.' Reassuring nod. 'You go halfway, an' then go like hell – odds are they won't even be looking.' Reassuring grin. 'Me . . . I'm jus' careful because you are a very valuable commodity now, Oliver – they still got C.O.D. back in England?'

Cash on Delivery?

Huge grin. 'Okay, Oliver?'

It was still oppressively hot, even in the deep shadow, and Latimer could feel his clothes sticking to his body. It was only deep inside him that it was mid-winter in England, before the postman called to delivery his C.O.D. parcel.

Cash on Delivery!

'Is that . . . .? Why you did come back for me?'

Kingston drew a deep breath. 'Shit, man – change of heart, is one half of it – ' Another breath ' – an' goddam' error of judgement, the other half – ' Another breath ' – ask me again on the other side, okay?' He turned away from Latimer, slipping into the river as soundlessly and naturally as an otter.

The water was waist-deep at once. Bending down to water-level, Latimer saw for the first time that they were on the apex of a bend in the river, where the flow must have scoured the bottom. And there, altogether dread-fully near, was part of the lower structure of the wooden bridge.

As he turned in the other direction to search for the boathouse, Kingston came round to him again.

'Keep an eye on your back, man – ' Another of the rhythmical breaths ' – you see something – ' The narrow black chest expanded again ' – don't wait, jus' go, man!'

Latimer took a quick fearful look behind him – trees all unmoving among the rocky outcrops all the way to the broken skyline – and was then pulled back to the river.

Kingston was further away, still in the shadow but almost shoulder deep. And then the shoulders lifted – and he was gone, with only a gentle swirl of green water, and a swiftly vanishing shadow beneath the surface, lost in the greenness.

Latimer thought: *Oh God! I can never do it like that – can I?*

And then – *Keep an eye behind you* – because he was alone now, on old Sion land, which was no longer the Promised Land – the Promised Land was on the other side, in the land of the living –

The woods up the slope were as silent as ever, but horribly menacing in their stillness, as though they were only waiting for the avenging Confederates to come roaring out upon those long-dead plundering Iowans –

The rifle was in his hands. He looked down at it, but it only caused him a moment's doubt, before he came to an

302

Iowan decision: he couldn't swim with it, and crossing that water was all that mattered.

He turned back to the river. It shouldn't take Kingston long to –

The open stretch was no longer quite so oily-smooth. As he stared at it, the sunlight winked suddenly on a swirling eddy which rippled the surface two or three yards beyond the shadow of the trees, as though a great fish was turning just beneath it: it must be so shallow there that –

In that instant the eddy broke into waves, and the waves boiled into spray as Kingston burst into the open, threshing wildly!

Latimer's jaw dropped as he watched the negro struggling for another instant in the broken water against an invisible enemy. Then the man vanished again, leaving behind him a centre of turbulence from which concentric waves spread out.

But the commotion beneath the water continued, and Latimer's own imagination swirled in horror and helplessness to match it, quite unable to comprehend what was happening.

Then Kingston came up again, and as he did so a burst of gunfire which seemed to come from every direction shattered the silence of Sion Crossing.

Latimer threw himself to the ground beside the tree at the edge of the water, hugging the earth in terror as the echoes of the shots reverberated up and down the valley. His face was only inches from water-level, and his mind was so empty that all he could register was the sight of the corrugated water rippling towards him from the centre of the river. Then there was another shattering burst of fire, and the river beyond the ripples burst into spray.

His eyes closed instinctively and his body tried to sink into the unyielding earth as he flinched against the noise, wtih his mind past fear because it was beyond reason. He thought, as he had thought only once before in his life, and as desperately, and as hopelessly, *Mother, take me away, please take me away* –

There was a *plop* outside him, in the unacceptable world of reality. And then another sound, unidentifiable.

His eyes opened as they had closed, without orders.

The horrible river was still there, darkly rippling in the foreground, sunlight-flashing in the unfocussed distance. Then, beyond horror, the dead rose from the surface out of the ripples, black and glistening.

'Help me, man – ' Kingston lurched in the water as he threw out an unnaturally long black arm, with its pale obscene palm, in supplication. 'Help me – '

Latimer froze, sickened with shock as well as fright.

'Help me – ' The rest of the appeal was lost in incoherent bubbling as Kingston submerged.

Latimer's sickness suddenly included himself, and without understanding what he was doing, or why, he swung his body sideways, into the water, pushing outwards and twisting towards the point where Kingston had gone down.

The coldness of the water shocked him, but only for an instant, because it wasn't really cold at all. Then his hand – his hands – encountered yielding rubbery flesh.

Half dragging, half lifting, he manoeuvred Kingston to the tree roots, the water lightening his burden, but the mud under his feet dragging him down.

Getting the man out of the water was more difficult; but suddenly the dead-weight stopped blowing water and started helping him – at least, helping him at first, but then hurting him as a sharp edge of the Ingram, which still hung round the man's neck, cracked against his head painfully.

Then Kingston was lying on the bank, and he was still in the water – *and the ridge was still behind them both, and they were both still on old Sion land* –

Kingston groaned, and then arched his back and shuddered . . . And then rolled slightly sideways, towards

Latimer, and raised himself on his elbow, the river water running down his face and off his shoulder.

The bloodshot eyes blinked vaguely at Latimer, and then cleared.

'You gotta run, man – ' Kingston's face twisted in agony ' – gotta run!'

Run? The order simultaneously confused Latimer and comforted him. Anything was preferable to the river behind him . . . but run . . . where?

'Not the river –.' Kingston misread his doubt ' – they got a box-net in it, with a trip–warning, like the East Germans have . . . I shoulda thought of that . . . Guess – getting careless – like Joe . . . huh?' A travesty of the old grin mocked the man's pain. Then he concentrated on Latimer. 'Take this . . . off my goddam' neck – you take it – go back the way we came – don't try the bridge . . . Gimme my gun . . . Zap anything that moves . . . If you go *now*, you jus' might make it, man.'

There was blood mixed with water on the black chest: there was a hole two inches above the right blue-brown nipple, from which the blood oozed steadily – and there was more blood on the arm which dangled slackly across the chest.

Kingston wasn't going anywhere: that arm was broken for sure – and if that was an entry-wound in the chest . . . where was its exit?

'Go on, man!' Kingston snarled the words, as though he'd lost patience with an idiot. 'I got a goddam' contract on you!'

The lukewarm water around Latimer was cold again now, as he reviewed his chances dispassionately. It seemed to him that – having not worked at all – his brain was now working overtime, in a dispute with itself, picketed by foolish inclination against intelligent self-interest. But perhaps inclination was not so foolish after all: just as he could not swim that river now, even if Kingston had told him to do so, so he doubted his ability to make it to safety through the woods, even with the Ingram to help him.

'Go on – don't shit me – ' Kingston plucked ineffectively with his good arm, on which he was leaning, first at the Ingram, then at the butt of the pistol in his waistband. '*Go on* – '

'No.' Once made, even a wrong decision was better than indecision. It wasn't an Iowan choice any more: he couldn't cross the river now, even if the whole Union army was waiting for him on the other side . . . But if *The Man* was pulling out, maybe his Confederates wouldn't fight so hard when their commander had abandoned them . . . And, in any case, he couldn't face those woods again – he was too frightened, and too exhausted! 'No!'

'What?' Kingston's eyes clouded.

Latimer hauled himself out of the water, quartering the slope above him as he did so, as Kingston had done – left to right – right to left.

Nothing . . . nothing?

But there would not be *nothing* for long, if that was an East German trip-warning net in the river: the bloody People's Democratic Republic had refined such devices to a fine art on land and in water alike, so that those bursts of gunfire could have been either human or automatic, there was no telling; all that was certain was that they would now know exactly where the attempted crossing had been made!

He lifted the Ingram off Kingston, and hung it round his own neck. Then he took the black man under the armpits and started hauling him towards the safety of the outcrop of rock just above them.

'*Aaarhg*!' The man protested and twisted convulsively as he was moved, and as the Ingram bumped his face in turn.

'Shut up.' It was a release of a sort to tell someone to do something at last: at least, if he was being stupid, he was his own fool now!

He lowered the shoulders as gently as he could, although there was no time for tenderness, and then turned his attention to the Ingram.

He had never handled a weapon like this – he hadn't held a weapon at all for years, but *they had discussed the arming of the police with rapid-firing arms, back in Uncle Jim's time, and he had voted against it –*

It was smaller than the Heckler and Koch, but it was the same animal; single shot – varying after that from rapid to unimaginably fast, to exhaust the whole magazine at a touch.

'Don't be a fool, man.' Kingston had recovered enough from his rough handling to understand what was happening.

The weapons specialist who had given evidence to the committee had brought his samples with him, extolling their different virtues and emphasizing their simplicity. But Latimer remembered being more interested in their political implications then their technology. Now he wished it had been the other way round.

'Listen – ' began Kingston.

'Do be quiet, Mr Kingston,' said Latimer. It did *look* fairly simple; and, since it had been designed for simple soldiers, perhaps it was. 'I'm not going anywhere. I'm staying right here with you.' But he would have liked a bit of practice first, to make sure; this way, if he got it wrong, it would be too late.

'You wanna be a hero or something?' Kingston quite misread his motives, but sounded angry rather than grateful. 'You're not going to do either of us any good . . . I'm . . .' He reached across his chest with his good arm '. . . I'm all bust up inside . . .' He touched his shoulder tentatively '. . . but you still got an outside chance, Oliver.' He nodded. 'But this ol' nigger's had it, man.'

Ridiculous, thought Latimer suddenly: *ridiculous* that he was fiddling with this beastly thing – and Kingston was *ridiculous* . . . and that they were both here like this – that was the most *ridiculous* thing of all!

'No.' He giggled, even though it wasn't in the least funny-ridiculous. 'I do not want to be a hero – this is all like *Alice in Wonderland* to me, Mr Kingston – or *Alice Through the Looking-Glass* . . . "I'm very brave generally – only to-day I happen to have a headache" . . . You see . . . I'm just like the oysters in *The Walrus and the Carpenter*, Mr Kingston – "Some of us are out of breath, and all of us are fat" – do you see?' He found himself giggling again, and forced himself to stop. 'How do you work this wretched thing?'

Kingston stared at him for a moment. Then he nodded slowly. 'Okay, Oliver – hold it up so I can see it . . . a bit more – that's fine.' He nodded again. 'No sweat . . . Now, that little catch is the safety catch – right . . . An' that's the change lever – a single shot, automatic an' cyclic . . . okay? Whatever you do, don't put it on cyclic. You got thirty-two rounds, an' on cyclic that's two seconds' worth . . . Only, it's on additional safety right now . . . So jus' twist the cocking handle through a right-angle – that's fine . . .' He grinned at Latimer. 'You done jus' fine. So now put the change lever on automatic. That's twenty seconds' worth . . . Now . . . you jus' put it down here by me, an' you crawl on down an' get the rifle – okay? But first, you gimme my little gun – like, it's got snagged on my trousers . . . huh?'

Latimer eased the automatic pistol from Kingston's waistband, and put it into Kingston's hand.

'Fine.' Kingston held the pistol weakly. 'Now, go get the rifle, Oliver man, like I said.'

Latimer slid down the slope obediently to retrieve the rifle from where he had left it beside the water. Getting the rifle made good sense, he thought. With the Ingram, and even more certainly with the pistol, he doubted that he could hit anything at less than point-blank range. But with a rifle, anyone could hit anything provided he pointed it accurately, held it steady, and squeezed the trigger gently.

It was only when he was coming back that he remembered something else Kingston had said in the heat of that first moment on shore.

He stopped abruptly, on knees and one filthy hand, the rifle held awkwardly in the other, and stared back up the slope towards the negro.

'I got a goddam' contract on you!'

Kingston had moved slightly, half on to his good elbow, as though to lift the wounded side of his body off the ground. His pistol was held in his good hand, and it would only need a slight movement of the wrist to bring it to bear on a target below him.

As Latimer stared at the black man in mute horror, quite unable to save himself, Kingston raised his head slightly to stare back at him.

'You seen something?' Kingston scrabbled with his feet suddenly. and tried to turn towards the edge of the outcrop of rock. 'Aaargh!' The effort of twisting brought a grunt of agony from him, and his head sank almost to the ground.

Latimer scuttled up the last few yards to reach him.

'No – it's all right.' He tried to rearrange the wounded man. 'It was nothing.'

Kingston drew a deeper breath which ended in another shiver of pain as the expansion of his chest reached the damage inside it. Then he blinked at Latimer as though to clear his vision, and grinned again, but weakly. 'Man, I'm never going to understand you, Oliver . . . but we gonna give the Johnny Rebs a run for their money, huh?'

'Yes.' If talking was going to keep Kingston conscious, then that was what he must do. 'Even though you had a contract on me?'

The question had the desired effect; Kingston's eyes lit up. 'Shit, man! That wasn't to kill you – that was to keep you alive, jus' back there!' He shook his head lopsidedly. 'You worth good money on the hoof . . . although I *never* should have made that deal, I tell you – that was one *big* mistake!'

Latimer concentrated on him. 'You were hired to keep me alive?'

'Not at first – hell, no!' The big mouth twisted contemptuously, as though the question was a stupid one. 'Ol' Bill Macallan paid good money for me to look after Miz Lucy, an' fix things for her, the way she wanted them – to hire the guys she needed to do what had to be done . . . to get *him* to Sion Crossing – the big fella . . . what's-is-name – David – ?'

'Audley.' A terrible certainty took away the question mark. 'Audley – David Audley.'

'That's the guy.' Lopsided nod. 'A real bastard . . . Ol' Bill owed him a score . . . An' if he was killed here, at Sion Crossing, then the shit really would be in the fan . . . No way the Brits would ever let that one go – there'd be hell to pay in Sion Crossing if the Comrades took him out on old Sion land – you get it, Oliver?

Latimer hadn't quite got it. But whoever 'Old Bill' was . . . and 'Old Bill' must be one of David Audley's many enemies from long ago . . . but there would never be any shortage of them, by God!

'Yes.' He had got it suddenly: 'Old Bill' was Bill Macallan – and Macallan was a name which rang bells now, from long ago – and now Macallan had purposed something dreadful to happen at Sion Crossing, involving David Audley . . . *and something dreadful was now happening – but it was happening to him, not to Audley –*

But something else was happening; it was a bee buzzing in his head, and the sound of it was mirrored in Kingston's sudden frown.

'They got a boat on the river, Oliver,' said Kingston. 'You got to take him out – they get us from the river, we got no chance man – '

It was the snarl of an outboard motor, away behind up-river.

Latimer reached for the Ingram.

'No!' Kingston gestured with the pistol. 'Take the rifle, man! We need Joe's gun when they come through the woods.'

Latimer obeyed automatically: he was still holding the rifle, and all he had to do was to release his foothold on the slope to slither backwards down it, almost noiselessly along the tramlines of his earlier passage.

Down by the water's edge the trees which had protected them with their overhang now obscured his view inconveniently. But the big tree was still there to protect him, and he shrank against it: raising the rifle as he did so.

Safety catch off!

The snarl of the outboard motor came closer –

It was bolt-action. He worked the bolt, and an unfired round sprang out.

The sound changed, almost dying away altogether, and he caught a blur of movement through the leaves as he slammed another round into the chamber.

It wasn't real: it wasn't happening to him –

It was a shallow-draught punt-like boat, with one man at the back controlling it, and another standing up halfway along, with an assault rifle in his hands, scanning the river ahead of him.

They thought they'd got their man – they were slowing on the spot where Kingston had been netted – they were turning towards him – the moving target suddenly steadying –

Beyond reality and unreality, Latimer thought *and they were right: they had got their man* – and thought of Kingston behind him as the sights zeroed exactly on the armed man's chest and he squeezed the trigger – *oh, so gently, so very gently* –

The rifle kicked and deafened him, and the man was plucked out of the punt as though pulled from behind, with his own weapon spinning up into the air. And he was already working the bolt again desperately as the engine

311

snarled again, and the man and his gun hit the water in two splashes, one tremendous and one hardly noticeable, but both distracting him as he fired again –

Missed, damn it!

The boat was accelerating, and weaving, and the leaves were already unsighting him as he worked the bolt once more, and fired again, and missed again, and worked the bolt again –

No! Unless – but he had fired before the message reached his brain – useless –

His ears were ringing, but the great splash in the river was smoothing itself out into widening ripples, just as it had done when Kingston had been hit: even as he watched the dancing sunlight on it winking at him it was already becoming innocent again, as though nothing of enduring interest had occurred – as though all that had happened had been a man falling out of a boat, over-balancing as he might have done on the Cherwell or the Isis on any summer's afternoon at Oxford.

But this time the man didn't shoot up out of the river again blowing water and shaking spray from his hair and swearing and laughing in the same breath to hide his embarrassment, as he had once done beside the meadows: this was another river in another time –

There were sounds outside him, he could hear them calling him back . . . not only the departing racket of the outboard motor knocking echoes up and down the valley, but also Kingston's voice from behind recalling him.

He pushed himself away from the bank and up the slope again, on heels and elbow, away from the no-longer-innocent flash of sunlight on the water.

'You got him?' Kingston's voice was hoarse.

'Yes.' But that wasn't quite true. All these years, such things had been academic, and carefully vague. Now he had to be exact. 'One of them.'

'One's enough. They won't try that way again.' Weak approval. 'Next time they'll come over the top.'

Next time? He turned towards Kingston.

'You did jus' fine.' The black face had a stretched look, with the sweat on it standing out on dry skin. 'They'll come slow, an' they'll be scared shitless . . . Ain't no one likes to get killed, even when he knows why . . . So they'll come *real* slow.' Kingston lay back carefully. 'We got some time now.'

Time to do what? He stared at the rise and fall of the blood-stained black chest. What was the point of buying time which they would have to repay in full?

Kingston stirred. 'You get up here, Oliver man.' He waved the pistol, summoning Latimer back to the security of the outcrop. Then he nodded and grinned. 'Okay?'

Latimer surveyed the negro uneasily. Apart from the hole in his chest and the useless arm there was blood soaking through the tightly-stretched jeans on his thigh, which he had not noticed before, although he couldn't see any wound.

'Yes, Mr Kingston.' In the circumstances the man's attempt to encourage him was belittling, however admirable. 'But how are you? Is there anything I can do?'

Grin. 'Winston.'

Latimer frowned. 'Winston?'

'Winston . . . That's my name. Like . . . Oliver *St John* Latimer – Winston *Spencer* Mulholland – okay?' Nod. 'My pa was a Yankee nigger, but my Ma was from Kingston – a *British* nigger . . . When I was in Savimbi's army, there was this Pole who'd got an ol' British passport . . . An' he used to say to me, "*Vinston, my fren', ve British most stick togezzer*" – you dig that?'

Winston Spencer Mulholland?

Latimer tried to smile. 'Is there anything I can do?'

'Not a thing, man. I'd like a big drink of river-water, but I don't think that'ud be a good idea.' Winston-Kingston thought for a moment. 'Maybe if you could wipe my face . . .?'

Latimer felt in his pocket. His handkerchief was already soaking wet, if not exactly ice-cold.

'That's great . . .' Winston approved the clumsy treatment. 'For a little fat guy, you're okay, Oliver. I'm jus' sorry I'm not going to collect on you.'

'You're not?' Latimer didn't know whether it would be better to leave him alone, or to encourage him to talk. But he seemed to want to talk.

'Hell no!' The same irrepressible grin: the man would die grinning, if he got a chance! 'They'll take us . . . If Joe was around they'd have done it already. But . . . they'll try coming over the top . . . An' then they'll get smart, an' flank us . . . Maybe roll grenades down, to scare the shit out of us . . . Won't do us any harm – they'll just go on rolling . . . But they'll scare us.' He nodded calmly at Latimer. 'Real pity, when you're so valuable.'

Latimer opened his mouth, but no words came.

He tried again. 'I am . . . am I?' Only that wasn't really the question. 'Why?'

''Cause Miz Lucy had second thoughts.' Kingston became mockingly-serious. 'Like the soldier got a medal for saving this girl from a fate worse than death . . . An' they ask him how he won it, an' he sez "Hell, ah changed ma' mind" . . . So I'm drivin' along, mindin' my own business, an' she overtakes me in the Volvo, an sez "We can't do it to him, Winston" . . . An' I sez to her "We jus' done it to him, Miz Lucy – why not?" An' she sez to me "Because he's not David Audley, Winston".' Kingston rolled his eyes at Latimer. 'If you ask me, I think *she* thinks you're *cute*, Oliver – like tall girls sometimes take a shine to little fat guys . . . no offence?'

'No offence,' said Latimer automatically. She had bloody-well killed them both, but that was all he could think of saying.

'Uh-huh . . . Maybe you should take a look over the top – okay?' Kingston eased himself slightly.

'Are you all right?' Latimer leaned forward with the damp-warm handkerchief.

'I'm fine.' The negro nodded the filthy rag away. 'I don't really hurt yet . . . Take a look, man – we got a big score to settle, remember!'

Latimer lifted his head slowly above the rock. And then lowered it, and shook it.

Kingston-Winston nodded. 'I told you! They are *scared*, man – they reckon we're a real mean combat group, so they not queuing up to win any medals, you can bet on that!'

One little fat guy . . . and one dying black man, thought Latimer bitterly: *it would be funny if it was not so finally ridiculous*.

'You were saying . . . she changed her mind?' He had to keep Kingston talking – and he had to stop himself thinking.

'She sure as hell did.' Nod. 'An' that wuz my big – *big* – mistake, Oliver man . . . I should have said "Well, you hire the US Marines, Lucy honey. 'Cause I'm not goin' into that Confederate-KGB hornets' nest for any cute little fat man."' Pause . . . slow shake. 'But I was *greedy* – an' that's the whole trouble with private enterprise – when it's tax-free it makes a man *greedy* . . . So I said, "That's a bad scene in there – I go in there, it's a double-contract when the banks open tomorrow.' Another shake. 'That was a *mistake*, man!'

'Yes.' It had been several sorts of mistake, thought Latimer: whatever Joe had actually planned to do it had been a mistake. 'Yes, I can see that.'

'Damn right!' This time it was a nod. But it was a nod which was cut off in mid-nod by a sudden spasm of pain. 'I . . . I should have asked *treble* . . . A man can get hisself *hurt*, doing deals on the side – *greed makes you careless*, the Pole used to say, *so you multiply the fee by the risk to inhibit the contracts* – okay?'

The man was weakening, and he was also beginning to

ramble into aspects of their predicament which really didn't matter. Although . . . since their predicament was terminal, nothing really mattered now, thought Latimer bleakly.

But there was still a vestige of curiosity.

'Why is Sion Crossing so dangerous, King – *Winston*?' He leaned towards the negro.

The black chest expanded. 'You don't know?'

'You tell me, Winston.' Latimer took another look over the rock.

'Man . . . they say this ol' guy . . . Robbins . . . Roberts . . . *Robinson* – ' The eyes closed.

For a moment Latimer thought he'd gone. But then the chest expanded again. 'Robinson?'

'Gen'l Robinson . . . his army out there – ' The eyes opened again, focussing on Latimer ' – but I guess you know better now, eh?'

Robinson? Who the devil was Robinson? He thought wildly of Cookridge, smooth and authoritative . . . And then – *the old guy* – was that the frightened old man back in the house? Was he Robinson?

Another name hit him again suddenly, from out of the recent past and from the recesses of much more distant memory, both of which had been overlaid by other things –

Macallan?

Nothing he had ever read or heard of was ever quite forgotten, that was his skill and the source of his confidence.

'Macallan, Winston – Macallan?'

Winston – Kingston – grinned. 'Bill Macallan, huh?'

Long ago . . . long ago . . . hadn't William Macallan been the CIA man they'd sacked? The one who'd worked with Audley on some ultra-secret business? It had all been carefully hushed-up, but –

'What about him, Winston?'

'Shit, man!' Winston started to chuckle, and then checked himself. 'This is all his idea – don't you get it?

Cash-money in advance on the contract – you still don't get it?'

What had he read recently about Macallan? It was something utterly unimportant among the digests and bulletins which came to him by routine from outside his terms of reference, which he skimmed through in the last half-hour of every working day, as a matter of careful duty.

'Mac – ' It came to him: the imperishable imprint of the photo-copied page, which he'd consigned to the shredder with all the other dross, which could always be summoned up again from the computer if he needed it. 'Macallan's dead, Winston – '

Not just the cold certainty of memory cut him off, but also a dreadful certainty of the future: *he had thought that these woods had frightened him because of his knowledge of the fear and death they had witnessed in the past. But, could it be . . . could it really be . . . that this red earth also carried the imprint of the future for those who were about to experience it – of his own death as well as Kingston's?*

No. That was impossible! 'Macallan's dead, Winston.' He refused to believe what he was thinking. 'He's *dead*.'

Lopsided nod. 'Damn right, he is! But his money's in my woman's account, man – an' that sure as hell isn't dead!'

Latimer stared at him, trying to encompass the idea of Macallan's death and his living memory.

'Hell . . . it don't matter now, anyway,' said Kingston conversationally. 'but . . . we get Audley here, Bill Macallan sez – we get him here, snooping in Sion Crossing, an' he gets wiped out . . . an' we leave a trail a mile wide . . . an' then the Yankee trash in Washington gotta take notice of that – no way the Brits gonna lose *him*, an' let it go . . .' The eyes rolled at Latimer, still blooshot but no longer bright. 'Only, it was you, Oliver, an' I'm real sorry 'bout that – sorry for both of us . . . But I guess we both

317

got careless, an' that's the way it goes man . . .' The negro seemed to struggle for an instant with that thought, as though he wasn't quite resigned to its philosophical implications. 'Still . . . we gonna shit them up between us, Oliver man – we really gonna shit them up, eh?'

Something registered outside Latimer, beyond Winston Spencer Mulholland. But, at the same time, something broke inside him in total bitterness.

He had once heard Mitchell tell of the volunteers of his 1914–18 War – the cream of all those nations which had been poured out in the mud of the trenches – all the glory of the arts and the sciences, lost with men like Asquith's son *pro patria*.

But he wasn't even going to die like that, with even that excuse for dignity – he was going to die because of bad judgement, as a substitute for a mere decoy.

The sound outside him came through, and he knelt above the stone, raising himself.

There were men out there – away to his left, and above him – one of them was just a few yards away –

Oh, Jesus!

He started to lift the rifle in his hands. But then a sobbering irrational rage with himself threw down the rifle and plucked the Ingram from the leaves, fumbling with it as he raised it.

The thing bucked and burped convulsively as he squeezed it, and bits of tree fragmented as the man in front of him seemed to dissolve in the flying pieces.

He swung the thing towards a second man, further away, and squeezed it again, but it only jerked at him for a fraction of a second, and then became inert.

He squeezed it again, but it was useless, and he heard himself cry out in panic as he threw it down, reaching for the rifle again.

Click –

He sobbed, and worked the bolt.

Bang! It jolted in his hands, barrel towards the sky –

318

Joy!

He worked the bolt again – *Bang*!

What was he firing at? The woods swam – trees blurred with movement – he had to have a target –

His vision cleared. There was movement out there, but it flitted and twisted though the vertical lines of the trees before he could sight on it –

Bang!

He had fired at something again, but it was far away now – it had been there, but not there, even as he had fired.

WORK THE BOLT –

Now there was nothing: nothing but trees and ringing echoes in his ears, and the silence of the woods was flowing back down the hillside, past him to the river.

He wanted to shout at them, but couldn't shout. Instead, he tried to ask himself how many unfired cartridges there were in the rifle, and didn't know the answer.

Maybe none. But there was still Kingston's pistol, he remembered. And the man's hand was slack: he didn't mind giving up the pistol.

'Mr Kingston?' He shook the black shoulder.

No reply. He was alone now.

He waited, holding the pistol up at an awkward angle on the edge of the rock, his mind empty of all thought.

Eventually there were distant noises.

Crack-echo-echo . . .

Then – *tearing-bang-crack-bang-crack-echo-counter-echo* into infinity, down away past him, and back again – meaningless bursts of gunfire echoed and re-echoed along the margins of Sion Crossing. And his spirit stretched until he couldn't hold the silly useless pistol, and he couldn't cry either for himself or for Kingston, but thought only of long cool drinks of tap-water gushing out into the long tall glass he kept on the shelf above the draining-board in his kitchen, a million miles away.

* * *

Eventually, when thirst was already beginning to be just another illusion, there came a *rackety-rackety* engine noise; which he thought he might have heard before, but which came nearer this time, until it was quite insistent, with another noise which gradually repeated itself, until it resolved itself through the sound of the engines as a loud-hailer –

'OLIVER – OLIVER LATIMER – STAY WHERE YOU ARE – THIS IS HUGH ROSKILL – STAND FAST, OLIVER – THIS IS HUGH ROSKILL – '

Later there were other words, in another and very different voice, altogether less sympathetic, as the helicopter flew back along the valley above the river and the trees –

'THIS IS THE SHERIFF – LAY DOWN YOUR ARMS – HEAR THIS . . . LAY DOWN YOUR ARMS – THIS IS THE SHERIFF – '

By the time Hugh Roskill's voice came back again, louder and lower, Latimer's head had reached the rock, and the pistol was where the Sheriff wanted it to be.

'OLIVER – OLIVER LATIMER . . . STAND FAST – WE'RE COMING TO GET YOU OUT – OLIVER – '

13

Mitchell in London: Glittering prizes

Harry the barman caught Mitchell's eye at once, and signalled above the throng simply by raising his arm vertically above his head and pointing horizontally with his forefinger towards the furthest corner of the bar.

'Ah! News from the Führerbunker!' Audley waved some signal of his own from the corner.

'And not a moment too soon.' Colonel Morris more than ever reminded Mitchell of Professor Gwatkin's description of James I – *never drunk, but seldom quite sober*. 'David here was just about to regale me with one of his military anecdotes – "These wounds I had on Crispin's day", God help us!'

'That is not strictly true.' Audley adjusted his spectacles, and Mitchell thought of Professor Gwatkin again. 'I was about to adorn a tale, if not point a moral . . . I was merely reminded of an episode in Normandy in '44, that's all. I will not waste it on you if you don't want to hear it, damned Yankee!'

'Southern trash, *if* you please!' Howard Morris leered at Mitchell. 'Not *your* old war, Captain . . . but you can choose.'

Harry danced in front of them. 'One pint of draught Guinness – one pint of best bitter – one large Founder's Port . . . and eight minutes to "Time" gentlemen. Same again?'

'Same again,' agreed Howard Morris. Then he frowned at Mitchell. 'Are we celebrating or drowning our sorrows?'

'Is Oliver St John Latimer alive and well? Or dead? Or in durance vile?' Audley's spectacles had slipped again. 'What tidings, Paul?'

'David, I *told* you – ' The CIA man was hushed by Audley's gesture.

So the Americans had got the news as well, thought Mitchell. And Morris had presumably been deputed to pass on some of it, and to find out how the British were reacting.

'He's all right, David.'

Audley nodded. 'So we are celebrating our sorrows. Oliver has been lucky – and it is always better to be lucky than beautiful.' He raised his glass. 'I drink to our deputy-leader!'

Mitchell drank. 'Jack wants you back, David.' Then he thought: we might as well hear what Morris chose to reveal. 'But I could use a couple of pints first. So tell us about the *bocage*.'

Audley's eyes narrowed slightly. 'If you insist – '

'I don't insist,' said Howard Morris.

'But you are now irrelevant, Colonel Morris . . . It was in '44, as I say . . . And it befell this armoured regiment – '

'As it might be . . . the West Sussex Dragoons, for instance?' interrupted the American.

'As it might be any poor devils – the Northamptonshire Yeomanry, or the Bombay-Irish Lancers – ' Audley waved him away ' – taking a breather before next morning's massacre . . . And they damn well knew there was a German 88 somewhere on the ridge ahead, waiting to take the first poor sod . . . *But they didn't know exactly where he was, you see*?' He spoke to Mitchell only.

It was the same with all old wars – Troy and Waterloo and Normandy, thought Mitchell. Only those who could remember the minor details still cared about them.

'So . . . there was this road block, with a warning notice, to stop the unwary from going too far.' Audley took another sip. 'And – would you believe it? – some careless fellow took it down, and forgot to put it back . . . so some other poor unsuspecting fellow from another unit swanned down the road in his armoured car and was brewed up . . . It was really quite scandalous.' He shook his head. 'Quite scandalous.'

'Yeah,' agreed Howard Morris. 'But you did find out where the Kraut gun was, I take it?'

'Right. We – the Bombay-Irish Lancers – *they* mortared the day-lights out of *that* one next morning . . . Unfortunately, they had a couple more on the reverse slope, only that's another story – which I shall not tell you.' Audley looked at Mitchell. 'But I do think that Bill Macallan did plan to send me in where angels feared to tread, to . . . to find out if there was an 88-millimetre anti-tank gun in Sion Crossing – would that be about right?' He paused. 'Who was he?'

Mitchell glanced at Howard Morris. But, if Audley was popping the question so openly, that must be the way he wanted it. 'His name was Robinson, apparently, David.'

'Robinson?' Audley frowned. 'Do we know him?'

'Not from Adam. He was on Macallan's American Debreczen list from long ago, but nobody sussed him out after Macallan was sacked.'

'What did he do? This Robinson?'

Mitchell shrugged. 'Nothing very much. He was a successful industrialist. Mostly chemicals, with some hightech later on . . . and some political clout – he had a finger in a lot of pies in the south . . . They're checking up like mad now, apparently.'

'And how did he come to Sion Crossing?'

'He simply retired there.' Mitchell took another drink. 'He was . . . he was a sort of recluse, with a private army hired to keep his property private. But also lots of money for local charities – he was very patriotic, and all that.'

'Yeah!' Howard Morris grimaced. 'Like – the *Star-Spangled Banner* and the *Bonnie Blue Flag*, and not a whiff of the *Red Flag*, is what you mean.'

Audley cocked an eye. 'What was it – an ultra-safe house? To co-ordinate the KGB coverage of the Atlantic coast?' The eye cocked at Morris as well as Mitchell. 'Or maybe a communications centre?'

Mitchell tried Morris too. 'We don't know yet – ?'

'Nor do we.' The CIA man's shoulders lifted. 'They had a lot of sophisticated equipment scattered around . . . Sensors in the woods near the house. And Mulholland tripped a warning net in the river . . . In fact some of the stuff self-destructed before we could get to it, so we won't know for sure till we've picked up the pieces . . . It all happened rather quickly – your Wing-Commander Roskill became somewhat insistent on the subject of Oliver Latimer's survival, David. So the Sheriff and the Feds went in hard and fast.'

'Ah . . . but you were all ready to do it.' Audley looked down his nose at his friend. 'You knew something was up – you were all set to go in, with that FBI-CIA liaison group, you tricky sod!'

'Not me, David – not me!' Morris shook his head. 'I was just as much taken for a ride as you were . . . I only met the Cookridge woman – I never saw the false Cookridge . . . She got him into the embassy, into her step-father's ante-room. I got the call from there, so I thought it was kosher – it was a con job, and I was conned . . . Remember *The Sting*?'

'Who was he?'

'The false Cookridge? We don't know that yet, either. Probably a bit-part player off Broadway. Or a pro con-man . . . We're still checking.' Another shrug. 'The fact that *she* was genuine was good enough for me, anyway. And I guess I was good enough for Oliver.'

Now they were at one of Colonel Butler's question marks. 'What had she got to gain? Why did she do it?'

'She loved her father – her real father . . . And as he was dying he made a plan, to vindicate himself. All she did was to carry it out.'

Audley swayed forward. 'And Winston Mulholland?'

'Macallan briefed Mulholland himself – and paid him.

324

He knew Lucy couldn't handle a job like this by herself.'
Morris drank. 'Not that she didn't have the balls for it
. . . I figured her for one tough lady when I met her, and
by all accounts she's her father's daughter right enough.'
He wiped his moustache. 'But it seems she had second
thoughts about your Mr Latimer, and paid Mulholland
danger money to pull him out. Which I somehow don't
think she'd have done for you, old buddy, with what her
daddy told her; you were scheduled for full payment,
with accumulated interest.' The white teeth showed. 'I
guess you could call that "capital punishment". You were
lucky, man!'

Audley's face hardened. 'She's talking then?'

'Singing like a bird.' In spite of friendship, Morris
didn't seem too unhappy. 'Unlike your esteemed colleague, who is maintaining a somewhat battered stiff
upper lip, as you might put it. Which is perhaps just as
well, because it seems there are a lot of dead bodies lying
around out there – and floating in rivers – they're all over
the goddam' place . . . And the local sheriff and the
Feds, plus our liaison group and the State Troopers –
they had a shoot-out on some bridge . . .' Morris rolled
an eye at Mitchell. 'I tell you, Captain, it sounds like a
re-run of the War between the States. But old Hugh,
your gimpy Wing-Commander – he's blaming it all on
Mulholland. He says that Mr Latimer wouldn't hurt a
fly.'

'And what does Latimer say?'

'He maintains their joint innocence.' The eye rolled
back to Audley. 'It's rather odd – he's insisting that
Mulholland acted under his orders . . . In fact, he refused to leave without a written undertaking that no
charges will be made. He's really been rather difficult.'

Mitchell gave Audley a quick look. 'And what does
Mulholland say?'

'He doesn't say anything. He's in intensive care, full of
bullets.'

That was an odd sequence, thought Mitchell. 'Oliver doesn't know one end of a gun from the other, Colonel.'

Morris raised the hand which didn't hold his glass. '*I* believe you, having met the gentleman in question. But the Sheriff thinks differently . . . Still, I'm sure we'll go along with whatever Colonel Butler decides, in the circumstances. We don't want any Anglo-American disagreements – okay?'

Morris was doing his duty, decided Mitchell. There was so much dirty linen here that all those still alive would be given a fresh set – and an airline ticket – even including Winston Spencer Mulholland, if he survived intensive care.

'What's going to happen to the woman?' Audley was still hard-faced, almost vengeful.

Morris regarded him quizzically. 'You tell me what she's done, and I'll tell you what's going to happen to her.' He scratched his head. 'She's made fools of us – and you . . . But we're not rushing to throw the book at her for that.' He finished scratching. 'Even if we can find the right words in the book . . . which I doubt we can do . . . I think we'll leave her well alone, David.'

Audley said nothing.

Morris nodded. 'You ask me . . . I think Bill Macallan worked that out too. That's why he hired Mulholland – to do the dirty work *and* to protect her, from us as well as the other side.'

Audley considered that reply for a long five seconds. Then he smiled his own peculiar Audley-smile, coldly disarming. 'Yes . . . you're probably right: *The less said, the better*, as my old Latin master used to say . . . yes.' Then he sat back, nursing his glass. 'Yes. But then, perhaps you could answer one small question?'

'Fire away.' Morris composed himself seriously.

'I will.' Half a lifetime before, as a callow youth, Audley had commanded a tank in Normandy, Mitchell remembered. 'Just when did you tumble to Miss Lucy Cookridge and Winston Mulholland, Howard?'

'When?' Morris's frontal armour was thick enough, but only just.

'Yes.' Audley was flanking him now, looking for the fuel tank. 'I know how Hugh Roskill got to Sion Crossing, because we sent him there. But how did the entire Union army get there so quickly?'

'Ah . . .' Morris nodded, as though a great truth hitherto hidden from him had been revealed.

'Amazing efficiency, would that be?' Audley was hull-down behind Morris now, with his gun-layer's finger on the button. 'Or miraculous quick-reaction? It does you credit, either way.'

Morris retreated into his almost-empty glass. 'A bit of both.' He put the glass down empty, wiped his moustache, and signalled again to Harry. 'But they did get a tip-off.'

'A tip-off?'

'Uh-huh. About *you*, old buddy.' Morris signalled again. 'Not *me*, of course – I was as far up the creek as you were – out in the cold, and frozen in . . . I was conned, like you.' Morris nodded to Harry. 'Same again, please.'

'And just in time, sir,' said Harry, unsurprised.

'Yes.' Morris came back to Audley. 'The first word was that you were up to something on our patch, David – that you'd hired Mulholland to clear the way for you . . . And they thought your budget might just about run to him.'

'*I* hired Mulholland?'

'That was the tip. Meeting in London first. Then a rendezvous at Atlanta airport.' Morris nodded. 'And we – *they* . . . do take you seriously . . . so they staked Atlanta to receive you.' With no glass, Morris was able to spread both hands. 'You should be complimented. They wouldn't do it for just anybody!'

A word formed on Audley's lips, but Harry arrived with the drinks to forestall him.

'TIME, GENTLEMEN, PLEASE!' Harry winked at the American. 'The clock's five minutes fast, of course, sir. Take your time.'

'We are all drinking too much,' said Audley. 'It may be good for the Chancellor of the Exchequer, but it's bad for us. As of now – after this one – I shall go on the wagon for a week – or until next Friday, anyway . . . *But Latimer turned up – right?*'

The extra minutes had perked up Morris. 'Same old firm – trusted colleague . . . *senior* colleague – it fitted, you see.'

That was nasty, thought Mitchell.

'And Mulholland turned up, too.' Morris nodded. 'Having left a trail from London a mile wide, for any fool to follow. And that was enough for our man, with a Fed breathing down his neck . . . Because we're not supposed to trespass on *their* patch – it was already getting sweaty under the armpits by then – '

The FBI and the CIA treading on each other's feet: Mitchell translated that into British English, and took the point, having on occasion experienced his own problems with the Special Branch.

'So Mulholland met Latimer – ' Audley had no time for union demarcation disputes, typically.

'With the Iron Lady Lucy in attendance.' Morris lowered his face and raised his glass. 'And that really screwed them up – Miss Lucy *Cookridge* – she made it *political* – huh?'

'Your people identified her?'

'Jesus Christ – what do you think, David!' Morris slammed the glass down. 'Mulholland and Senator Cookridge's daughter! That really slowed our people up – the same way it slowed you.'

That was exactly right, thought Mitchell: the Senator's respectability and their fear of offending him had inhibited their reactions. And that, presumably, had been the intention of the plotters.

Morris weakened. 'And by then they'd had another tip-off anyway.'

'Oh yes?' Audley pretended to drink. 'And where were all these useful intelligences coming from?'

He wasn't even asking what the tip-off was – because he knew that was coming; the truth was, drunk or sober, or midway between those extremes, they both knew their business and each other, these two.

'From a pay-phone – a call-box – ' Morris corrected himself ' – to the right number. Mulholland knew the form. That was what he was paid for.'

Audley waited.

'The word was that you were interested in Debreczen again, David. They couldn't ignore that – not after they spotted Latimer in Atlanta.'

'So what did they do?'

'They started moving men in – by agreement with the Feds and the locals . . .' Morris pursed his lips. 'It was getting kind of delicate, what with Mulholland and the Cookridge girl . . . and Latimer.'

'And Mr Robinson,' supplemented Audley mildly.

'And him, yeah.' Morris showed his teeth. 'There was this Civil War parade going on in town. No one was quite sure what was happening, I guess.'

'Until Jack Butler told Hugh Roskill to start making waves?' Audley's voice was still mild. 'May one inquire further about Mr Robinson? Or are your lips sealed?'

Morris made a face. 'Do you need me to put Robinson together?'

'I suppose not. He must have been a long-time traitor. Debreczen and before, even?'

'All the way back to the war, they reckon.' Morris nodded soberly. 'He was OSS. Left the service and went into industry. Never touched politics until near the end of his career – a real deep-cover man . . . No one suspected a thing.'

'Except Bill Macallan,' murmured Audley.

'Except old Bill. But who was going to listen to him? In his day old Bill wasn't even sure about the President of the United States – remember?'

'How could I forget?' A muscle twitched in Audley's

cheek. 'Robinson's going to be awkward for you – ' He stopped suddenly. 'Or is he?'

'Well . . .' Morris's expression became bland. 'It all depends on how things are at Sion Crossing right now. But there was this explosion in one of the out-buildings, like I told you . . . Sounds to me like that could have the makings of a tragic accident.' He shook his head. 'When people get careless with explosives – say, when they're experimenting . . . Lots of guys can get killed that way, David.'

For a moment Audley was silent again. 'Yes . . . yes, I can see how that might happen, Howard.'

'Uh-huh. Seems there was a senior Russian official from the UN visiting him at the time, too. But he was lucky – like your Mr Latimer . . . They were probably walking in the grounds, admiring the magnolias or something.'

'Or something.' Audley nodded.

'Or something,' agreed Morris. 'So they'll both be going home very soon, I'd guess.'

'Like Coleridge's wedding guest – sadder and wiser.' Audley looked round the empty bar suddenly. 'I think it's time for us to go – Jack will be worrying about us.'

Harry appeared magically, wiping a glass. 'Will that be all, gentlemen?'

'Almost all, Harry.' Audley smiled at Morris. 'We are going, but Colonel Morris will have one for the road on my slate – if that okay?'

'For you, sir – ' Harry moved back towards the beer pumps.

'Just tell me one other thing, Howard.'

'If I can, old buddy.' Morris smiled back.

'Two things, actually . . . Bill Macallan must have kept up a lot of contacts – to suss out Robinson, and to know how to put his hand on Mulholland . . . It even looks as though he might have known about my little Debreczen tickle last year . . . He certainly knew a lot about *me*, it would seem – eh?'

Morris thought about the question seriously. 'Certainly looks that way, I agree . . . He did have *friends*. Because there was always a school of thought said he'd been railroaded . . . And when he got really sick . . . people visited him. I guess maybe they talked too much.'

'Yes.' Audley nodded. 'So just what is the official thinking – did he really get on to Robinson by chance, because of his Civil War studies? Or did he use his Civil War studies to cover his investigation? Which came first – the snake or the egg?'

Morris frowned. 'Hell, David – that's a hard one . . . And I'm not privy to official thinking – I'm pretty much in the doghouse.' He looked at Audley intently. 'All I know is that he was a helluva smart guy. And he was bedridden. And he was dying.'

'Yes. And they do say that concentrates the mind wonderfully.' Audley nodded at Harry as the final pint appeared.

'It does, sir?' Harry cocked his head. 'Would that be an income tax demand?'

'It would in your case, Harry.' Audley passed a twenty pound note across the bar. 'Because you're part of the black economy.'

'I'm not prejudiced, Dr Audley.' The note vanished. 'It's the colour of their money that counts, that's all.'

'Very proper!' Audley turned back to Morris. 'It was nicely done, anyway – however it was done.' He turned to Mitchell. 'Let's go to where glory waits, Paul – '

But outside he ignored the waiting car.

'Let's walk. I need a little fresh air.'

The sound of the city was mixed with its smell: eternal traffic far and near, brick-dust and drains and carbon monoxide and the river, all accentuated by the warm darkness.

'It *was* nicely done,' said Audley. 'Whoever did it.'

The river predominated. Not so filthy now, much of it

331

re-cycled *via* the Thames Water Board from unmention-able sources, but mixed with an untainted fraction from the springs and water-meadows of Gloucestershire and Oxfordshire, far away.

'Whoever?' Mitchell realized that Audley was thinking aloud, buying time before he faced Butler.

'Yes.'

They were heading towards the nearest bridge.

'Yes. Because I can't help trying to hope that *he* wasn't as smart as that . . . That maybe we've been conned twice over . . .'

'He? *Macallan* –

'Macallan? David?'

'Twice . . .' It was almost as though Audley wasn't listening to him. 'Say . . . if the CIA had known about Robinson for a long time, but now they'd decided they had to close him down . . . But they didn't want the Russians to know how long they'd been on to him . . . So *they* sent us up the road towards the 88 – maybe?'

He? *Robinson* –

'I don't know, though – ' Audley crossed the road towards the bridge without looking either way ' – I just can't see Howard Morris sending me up the road . . . It isn't his *style* – '

Mitchell had to run to keep up with him. 'But he didn't David – he sent Oliver.'

'So he did.' The name made Audley miss a step as he reached the safety of the riverside pavement. 'He sent *Oliver* – but he couldn't have known Oliver would go, could he?' He shook his head. 'No . . . on balance, I think Howard's in the clear: he just smelt a rat, and did his best to scupper the plan . . . but without offending Cookridge. Only he didn't quite scupper it, that's all.'

They were close to the bridge now.

'So that just leaves Macallan, David.'

'Yes.' Audley paused to look over the parapet at the dark water below. 'Just Macallan.'

Mitchell waited. Audley's face was invisible in the light of the nearest lamp, and his expression was distorted by unnatural shadow.

'Just Macallan . . . He must have followed my career, such as it has been . . . And when they knew he was dying his friends would have talked more frankly, I suppose. He nodded at the water. 'And then he got word from that researcher of his, about the mysterious Mr Robinson of Sion Crossing.'

The river smell came up strongly. 'And the researcher was killed, David.'

'Yes . . .' Audley shivered suddenly. 'I'm getting old.' Then he squared his shoulders. '"The baked meats of revenge are best eaten cold", they say . . . It certainly would have been a beautiful revenge – sending me to my death to prove that he'd been right . . . He knew he was making his own crossing to Sion – he'd be there on the other side, waiting for me, when I made by own crossing – on his instructions . . . I *like* that . . . that's a damn good revenge, it really is!'

There was no understanding David Audley in this mood: all his thoughts were on Macallan and they were admiring thoughts. Poor old Oliver didn't come into the reckoning at all.

'I'd like to believe that,' said Audley. 'It would be nice and neat – *Sion*-bloody-*Crossing*!' He started walking again. 'I wonder whether there really *is* any treasure there –' He threw the thought over his shoulder at Mitchell ' – if there is, it was perfect . . . and if there isn't I'll bet he'd salted the evidence nicely, to lead me on . . . But even if that didn't work, he knew I'd be hooked by his name – and hooked by the memory of Debreczen . . . He'd have got me one way or another – whatever I found out would have merely led me on.' He chuckled suddenly. 'That's cunning for you – in a good con trick your victim always helps you . . . In fact, it's so good . . . it's almost a pity it failed, by God!'

That was too much. 'It didn't altogether fail, Daivd. He got Robinson. And it sounds as though he nearly got Oliver.'

'So he did – so he did!' There was no hint of sympathy, let alone gratitude in Audley's agreement. 'In a way we have all benefitted, in fact – we all have our glittering prizes.'

'What?'

'My dear fellow . . . Jack Butler thinks the better of you – and of James Cable . . . And he thinks no worse of me that he did before.' Audley nodded to himself. 'And I have made the acquaintance of Lady Alice Marshall-Pugh, through whom I shall in due course make friends with Senator Thomas Cookridge. And that will prove very useful, I have no doubt.'

God almighty! thought Mitchell. 'And Oliver?'

'Oliver?' Audley lengthened his stride. 'Oliver St John Latimer has derived the greatest benefit of all, my lad. He has what he needs most, I suspect.'

'Oh yes?' The irony would be lost, but he must attempt it. 'You mean . . . he's still alive?'

Audley thought for a moment. 'That is a benefit, certainly . . . For him, if not for us.' Then he shook his head. 'But . . . no . . .'

'What then?'

'Experience.' Audley patted the parapet. 'Experience at the sharp end – which he has never had . . . The next time Oliver St John Latimer reads a report, or writes an order, he will know that there's flesh and blood at the other end of it.' He patted the parapet again. 'Being frightened is an experience you can't buy. I'd guess that he has discovered that in Sion Crossing.'

They were almost across the bridge. Up-river the lights twinkled on the Thames like jewels, all the way to Westminster.